A Fine Looking Soldier

Secret Soldier Vol. 1

Jane Hadley

To the women who refused to settle for the status quo.

Author's Note

A Fine Looking Soldier takes place in Minnesota in 1861, at the start of the US Civil War. The next year, the US-Dakota War breaks out in New Ulm. The systemic dispossession of the Dakota and Ojibwe in Minnesota is not at the center of this story, but it is part of the characters' context. Trouble is, the characters aren't aware of the extent of it. As European settler colonists, both of the main characters take for granted the land they stand on and they haven't the faintest clue the extent to which it was stolen.

The US-Dakota War is a wound that still hasn't healed in Minnesota. Many Dakota people are still exiled to reservations in Nebraska and South Dakota to this day. It's a violent and horrific event and the way we tell its story still hurts. Bloody battles were fought at New Ulm and Birch Coulee. Fort Snelling, where this book is set, was where Dakota people were rounded up and kept in a concentration camp at the fort's base. Many Dakota men, women, children, and elders died there, as well as on the journey to exile in Nebraska, South Dakota, and elsewhere. The largest mass execution in the history of the United States was committed in Mankato, hanging 38 Dakota men who'd been convicted in sham trials some of which weren't longer than five minutes. It's far past time the US-Dakota War narrative centered on Dakota voices, and therefore, it's not a part of this Euro-centric story. However, I want to ensure readers understand that this story takes place on stolen Dakota land and I encourage you to watch the Dakota 38 documentary to learn more.

Furthermore, slavery plays a dominant role in the war our main characters will participate in as soldiers. Abolition and a great deal of political rhetoric drives our main characters. However, they are both white and free and the perspectives of the enslaved are not directly shown in this narrative. The literary world doesn't need anymore privileged white ladies imagining what it might be like being enslaved and making tragic romances out of it. There are some excellent Black historical romance authors who have done spectacular work in this area, including Beverly Jenkins and Alyssa Cole. If you haven't read their work, get ye to the bookstore. Post haste.

Your obt. srvt,
Mrs. Jane Hadley

Krueger
Robinson
Hower
Schaefer
Smith
Osborn
Williamson
Webster

PROLOGUE

St. Anthony, Minnesota
Tuesday, August 21, 1860

LIGHT FROM THE LANTERNS outside licked against the windowpane, casting the dark attic room in long shadows. Cate held her little half-sister tight as she strained to hear what the mob outside was shouting. She couldn't make out many words, but the volume, the guttural rage echoing against the glass, made clear how "peaceable" the group was. Indistinct shapes moved amorphously through the heavy rain that streamed down the windowpane. Cate's heart flipped in her chest as thunder clapped and a bolt of lightning illuminated the scene below for a split second in sharp relief.

A throng of men, brandishing muskets, were stomping in the mud outside the neighboring house. The free Black family who lived there—Mrs. Grey in particular—had been directly involved in the liberation of an enslaved woman from her vacationing Mississippi master earlier that afternoon. Judge Vandenburgh had sat the case and declared Eliza Winston free, as the new Minnesota state constitution clearly stated that no person would be permitted to enslave another. When Cate first read about the case earlier in the week, she'd given it relatively little consideration. Of course, she'd thought, the woman's freedom was a foregone conclusion.

She was embarrassed to admit it, but she was shocked at the lengths her neighbors were willing to go to appease the wealthy Southern tourists coming to take the air at the head of the Mississippi River. Apparently, the affront was enough to drive men to take up arms and a—was that a fence post? It was—a fence post cum battering ram intended to break down the door of her neighbors. Cate squeezed Etta's little hand and prayed that the Greys hadn't been foolish enough to harbor Eliza Winston herself in their own home. Surely they'd had enough sense to spirit her away someplace safer?

"We want that slave!" The shout was muffled, but the message was clear. Cate felt sick. How could she be so naive as to think that the verdict of the case was cut and dry. She clearly had no notion as to the true character of her fellow St. Anthonians.

Cate's heart hammered in her chest and her little sister, scarcely four years old, looked up from the yoke of Cate's nightgown to determine how to react. If the mob opened fire, Cate would have to find a way to get Etta and her mother out. Father was downstairs with his rifle, but he was only one man. If she opened the sash, they could perhaps shimmy down to the rain barrel and take cover behind the chicken coop. Filled with a sudden surge of urgency, she pried Etta's fists from her nightgown.

"Etta," she whispered urgently as she looked the little girl squarely in the eye. "Everything is gonna be just fine. You just listen to Sissy and stay quiet. Can you do that for me?"

Etta's big brown eyes blinked and she nodded.

"You're a brave girl," Cate said assuringly.

"Grey, open up!" came another muted shout from next door.

Cate craned to see out the window at the sound of splintering wood. The mob had slammed the fence post into the door again and this time, it crashed in. She could just make out the men through the window swarming into the dimly lit house. Cate felt her gorge rise in her throat, but she choked it down as she rose and flung open her trunk.

"Here, put on your dress," Cate ordered as she tossed the homespun plaid at her sister.

"Cate!" Margaret's Irish lilt sounded tight as a piano string calling from down the stairs.

"We're getting dressed," Cate called back, stealing her expression for Etta's sake. She flung her corset over her nightgown and struggled for a moment with the busk as she made sure Etta pulled her arms through the sleeves of her dress.

Margaret's auburn head appeared at the top of the stairs. Her eyes were wide, but her face was trained into fragile resolve. Cate's stepmother hauled herself up the rest of the stairs and sat on the edge of the bed that Cate and Etta shared, holding her belly heavy with child. Etta hurried to wrap herself in her mother's skirt.

The shouts outside dulled. Cate craned over the bed to see out the window.

Lanterns were held by a few of the men, but the bulk of the mob had moved inside the Grey's house. Mr. and Mrs. Grey had been ejected and stood outside in the downpour, Mrs. Grey holding baby Toussaint while her husband, Ralph, held William. The small boy was of an age with Etta, and Cate looked quickly back at her half sister and positioned her body to ensure Etta could not see her friend, nor any of what transpired outside the door to the Grey's house. The bulk of the mob was inside, ransacking from the sound of it.

"Are they looking for that woman who got her freedom?" Margaret whispered, her eyes round and her jaw tight. She was twenty-five, of an age with Cate, and perhaps this experience would teach her to take an interest in the news of the day, instead of preferring to take everything in through her husband's dinner table grumblings.

Cate nodded and approached the sill, peering out to discern the situation. The only reason Margaret even knew about the Eliza Winston case at all was because Cate had made the mistake of bringing it up at dinner, earning her a swift rebuke from her father.

"They're searching the house now."

One of the men standing outside with the Greys teetered on his feet, laughing and swinging his lantern around jovially. The brittle nausea that had seized the center of her chest lurched.

"I think they're drunk," Cate reported.

Margaret's expression darkened.

Cate felt her face heat and her heart continued to pound. She'd read about mobs like this, all sorts of horrific stories between Jane Grey Swisshelm's newspaper and the reports coming out of Kansas. She felt the same roll of righteous anger boiling in her chest that she usually felt when she read those papers. Or when she argued with her father. Cate frowned.

"Where is Father?" she asked, turning to look at Margaret. Her stepmother flickered a glance at her before she turned to Etta and said, "There there, now, darling. Everything will be just fine."

Cate's jaw worked, and she set her lips into a thin line. "Margaret," she said, sharpening her voice like a filet knife. "Where is my father?"

Margaret met her eyes. Then her gaze darted to the window and back. Cate clenched her fists so tight her fingernails dug painfully into her skin to keep herself from swearing. Miraculously, she didn't say anything. She just pulled the front of her wrapper tight, buttoned it down the front, and strode resolutely to the stairs.

"Cate, wait!" Margaret called out. "He's not participating! He's trying to talk some sense into them!"

"Like hell he is," Cate muttered, her bare feet stomping down the stairs. When she reached the bottom, she saw that Father's rifle wasn't hanging in its place over the hearth. Her lips curled as she flung open the front door.

"Cate, tis dangerous! Come back!"

Cate ignored her stepmother as she strode into the pouring rain. The mud squishing between her toes reminded her too late that shoes would have been prudent. Her braid was soaked within a minute and her wool wrapper didn't fare much longer, but she didn't care. She had no thoughts—only waves of anger, frustration, disgust crashing in one after the other, suppressing her fearful nausea and filling her with righteous purpose.

"Stowell!" she barked as she approached the fellows who stood at the entrance of the Grey's home, their eyes trained on the sodden family they'd ejected into the storm as though they were hostile prisoners. Mrs. Grey's face was like stone, but her eyes widened when they alighted upon Cate, as if to implore her to get away. Cate hesitated. She'd never known an expression like that on Mrs. Grey's usually earnest countenance. The pause was enough to bring her slamming pulse into her awareness and Cate grasped at her anger like a lifeline.

"Is that Miss Stowell?" It was Jackson, the grocer. Cate absorbed another blow to her vapid intuition and swore she'd never frequent his business again.

"Where is my father?" Cate crossed her arms over her chest and willed the force of her voice to overpower the indignity of her drenched state.

Jackson blinked at her. "Better get back inside, Miss. It's no kind of weather for a lady."

"It's no kind of weather for young children, either, *Mister* Jackson,*" Cate retorted, pointing accusingly at the two small boys held by their parents. "Where. Is. My. Father."

"Cate, get back inside."

Her father emerged from the house, his boots squelching in the mud and his craggy face unmoved as ever. Cate didn't squirm under his hard regard; he delivered it too often at this point for it to have any of its intended effect.

"Not without you," Cate replied.

"This doesn't concern you. Get back inside."

"'Whoever despises his neighbor is a sinner,'" Cate spat the Bible verse at him like it were a weapon. Her father glanced at the Greys and frowned more deeply. Then, he stalked forward, seizing Cate's arm in his hand as he passed and yanked her across the yard towards their house.

For as much as the pulpit liked to remind women how innately moral they were, it sure didn't seem to get Cate anywhere when calling out bullheaded men. Every time she had tried to assert her so-called moral authority, she was chastised for sticking her head into unwomanly topics. Such things were not her concern, lest they ignite her "sensitive womanly emotions". But Cate knew better. She was a laundress. For as much as the sanctimonious men of this town liked to think they were of superior intellect, she had seen their underclothes. It didn't matter how important the man was—none of them seemed terribly capable of wiping their own ass.

"Stop meddling in matters you don't understand," her father gritted out. Cate scowled as she twisted her arm painfully in his grip.

"I should say the same to you," Cate replied. "I've never known you to be a thief."

"By your own logic, the slave cannot be property, so how can I be a thief?" her father snapped as he led her towards the front door of their house. "It is our sacred duty to protect the prosperity of the two cities by restoring the slave girl to her rightful owners. It's *them* that's thieves!" He brandished an accusing look at the Greys, still standing outside their house, waiting for the bastards to finish ransacking their house.

Cate shook her head. "I don't know why I expected anything different from you."

She stepped into the house after him, her bare feet tracking mud across the wood planks. Father stomped in behind her, released her arm, and slammed the front door shut.

"If you come out here again, I swear on your mother's grave, Cate, I will put you out on the street!" Mr. Stowell shouted, taking the liberty his own home afforded him to disregard his volume.

Cate lifted her chin and made a point not to flinch. Then, gripping his fists tightly, her Father took a deep breath, making a show of getting a hold over himself. He shook his head and muttered, "When will you learn your goddamn place?" Growling in exasperation, he went back out into the rain and slammed the door again behind him.

Cate's chest heaved and her heart raced. She was of a mind to charge right back out again. She didn't need him. She could take in laundry, she could find a place, she could find a way. And no matter how difficult it was, it would be far better than being trapped with this ignorant bastard and his replacement family.

"Cate?" It was Margaret. Hovering apprehensively in the sitting room. With Richard Ellis. Cate nearly choked in mortification.

"Oh no, look at you. You're soaked through." Margaret crossed to her, draping a swath of concern over the awkward tension that permeated Mr. Ellis' regard.

Cate's chin quivered. She clenched her fists in her sodden skirts. Her anger petered out, and the desperate shame of impotence, of not being able to do one good thing despite her best efforts, overtook her. Of appearing the petulant child, the filial failure, in front of Mr. Ellis. She slumped against the door and stared resolutely at her muddy feet. *Hell* if she was going to let him see her cry.

Margaret turned to direct an apologetic look at Mr. Ellis, then crossed the room quietly. She leaned over Cate. "Cate, love, come on. Let's get you into some dry clothes."

Cate flinched her arm away from Margaret's soft touch. Why must she be forced to be seen like this? Why couldn't Margaret just be distant and uninterested, like her father? It was almost worse to be cared for by this relative stranger, who was scarcely older than her, when her father could literally not care less.

"Leave me *alone*," Cate hissed.

"Mrs. Stowell," intoned Mr. Ellis' smooth tenor. "If you will permit me a moment alone with my betrothed?"

Margaret straightened and frowned, searching Cate's face. For her part, Cate carried on staring at the floor. It was her father who had encouraged Mr. Ellis. She would have said he selected him, but it wasn't much of a selection when there was only the one suitor. Mr. Ellis was, as far as she was concerned, an extension of her father, an instrument to both dispose of her and regulate her in one fell swoop.

Margaret nodded—just as Cate knew she would—and stooped to deliver a brief, awkward embrace about Cate's shoulders.

"Be civil," she whispered, "You catch more flies with honey than with vinegar."

She regarded Cate with an imploring expression, one that struck Cate as both pleading and preemptively disappointed, then headed up the stairs to the attic room.

Silence settled like thick, gloaming dust in a long-disused room, filling every crevice.

Mr. Ellis regarded her with forced nonchalance, as if he hadn't just inadvertently witnessed her father reaming into her. As if she wasn't in a soaked-through dressing gown with bare, muddied feet. As if it weren't the middle of the night, as if the town weren't falling apart trying to renounce a scrap of justice being done for a woman held like chattel. Cate hardened her expression and braced herself.

"It's been quite the night, hasn't it?" Mr. Ellis said conversationally, running his fingers over his mustache. He wasn't a bad-looking sort, she knew that intellectually.

"Indeed," Cate deadpanned, pushing herself off the wall to her feet.

"If I didn't know better, I might think you were becoming quite the politician," Mr. Ellis said wryly, his eyes twinkling as he went to her, taking her hand as if to remind her that she was his.

Cate swallowed thickly and slipped away. She crossed to the nearest chair and studied the threadbare upholstery. Richard Ellis had laid his intentions bare not a week ago, proposing in her kitchen, while her hair was wrapped up in a kerchief and her hands chapped with chilblains from the cold laundry basin. Her father hadn't hesitated to point out that in her twenty-five years, she hadn't received any better offer so she was in no position to be picky. And though he plainly favored Richard's suit, Mr. Ellis wasn't her father. True, Ellis had free-soiler tendencies, but his interest in her was genuine. And that was a novelty. She supposed she hadn't lied when she said yes, she would like to marry him. No point in admitting it had more to do with wanting to leave her father's house than it did any returned affection.

Cate sighed. *Catch more flies with honey…*

"Nonsense, I wouldn't give a fig for politics generally," she hedged, her voice pathetically thin and reedy in her own ears. "But …"

She turned around and looked up at him. The years spent reading Douglass and Garrison and Weld and Swisshelm, all the rehearsed debates she'd conducted with herself in the washroom, percolated in her mind. She *knew* how to defend her position. She thought of the women abolitionists she'd read, their virtue and moral superiority lacing their words, and she met his eyes squarely and earnestly. "But I do know my Bible. And I know God did not create men to be treated as animals by other men. He made us in his image, yes, but we all vary. Some are tall, some are small, some with blue eyes, some with brown. Why should the color of our skin be so divisive when these other variances are arbitrary?"

Mr. Ellis's brows flickered in confusion. She sighed, half impressed he hadn't interrupted her yet. She searched her mind for words that would capture her feelings, but also would appease his notion of how she should behave. While she wanted to shake him with rage, she instead tried to appeal to his conscience.

"I know women are supposed to shun politics, but politics have invaded every aspect of our lives," she pleaded. "Men fought and died in Kansas territory for less. We are naive to imagine that these men toting guns through the city tonight are only interested in the peaceable restoration of property. If there were no threat, why bring a gun? We are a hair-trigger away from another bleeding Kansas. Meanwhile, Congress is in shambles and Southerners are threatening rebellion if Lincoln wins the presidency. What am I supposed to do? If you think a woman should silently lose her husband to ideological wars and not even wonder why—it's just too cruel."

Mr. Ellis regarded her with furrowed brows.

"I admire your fervor," he said.

Cate's lips parted as she felt the tension ebb from her face. It shouldn't affect her so, but she couldn't remember the last time anyone had said anything so affirming to her.

Then he sighed with a wry smile. "It is passing sad to see such keen intelligence wasted on a woman, but you will be such an incredible teacher of thoughtful and tenacious sons. And surely, under your guidance, they will become the discerning and intelligent citizens this democracy so desperately needs."

His words fell on her like a ton of bricks. Cate's jaw set tightly and she inhaled deep through her nose as she fought a swell of despair rising in her chest. Yet, he stood unabashed, as though he'd been perfectly complementary. The prickling of frustrated tears behind her eyes drove the cycle of shame home. She hated nothing more than the helpless and utterly useless waste of energy that was crying.

"Oh, darling," Mr. Ellis cooed as a traitorous tear slipped down her cheek, closing the space between them and resting his hands on her shoulders. "Please dry your eyes. I assure you, I will do nothing so foolish as to abandon my work and my wife for some political war."

He tipped her chin to force her to look at him. It took all her focus to keep her lip from trembling.

"You can depend on me," he pledged, his mustache stretched across his smile. Then, he gently kissed her and she thought she felt another piece of her soul crack and break under the weight of his expectations. He reached out and tentatively squeezed her hand. "I, um ... I love you."

Cate squeezed her eyes shut and snatched her hand away, covering her face with her hands. How? *How?* How could he hear her words, see her distress, and think this was the right time for such a sentiment? Did he even understand what love meant? Did he just feel the ghost of tenderness, spurred by his own fantasies of her bearing him successful sons, and misconstrue it for love? She didn't know much about love, but she knew one thing for damn certain. Love did not condescend.

"I'll be right back," she lied and pushed past him toward the door.

"Wait, where are you going?" he asked, ruffled perhaps that she hadn't returned his sentiment.

"I'm going to bring my father back."

———

I

New Ulm Township, Minnesota
Saturday, December 22, 1860

SNOW WAS FALLING SOFTLY from a low, gray sky as Henry's father pulled the sleigh up short.

"Something's happened," his brother Peter said, hovering above his seat. Franklin, the bolder of Henry's twin brothers, stood and, having made his swift assessment, vaulted from the sleigh.

"Franklin, Warten Sie," Henry's mother protested, reaching for Peter's sleeve, but the remaining twin was also already taking his leave of the sleigh to bound through the snow toward Turner Hall.

Relegated to the rear-facing seat by his older brothers, Henry craned his neck to see the hall. The building was the largest in town, forty by seventy feet built with rough-hewn logs felled in the area, with a small tower at each end. A group of men milled in front, bundled tightly in wool coats, scarves, and hats, conferring seriously with one another. Henry made to leap out as well, but his mother held him back, a hand on his knee.

"Won't you stay and escort your mother?" Mutter chided in German as Henry's father pulled the horses up. Henry looked longingly at the group assembled and set his jaw. He was inarguably a man now at twenty-one years old. He should be with the other men, taking his place in the community, not left behind to wait with the women.

He resisted the urge to roll his eyes and nodded curtly to his mother, stepping begrudgingly out of the sleigh and offering his mittened hand to her. She arranged her crinoline to its best advantage before alighting from the sleigh. Even though they were bundled tightly against the cold, traveling by wagon box mounted on runners, Anna Schaefer's gentle upbringing in Stuttgart demanded the maintenance of dignified appearances. And that meant ladies required an escort, even if they were alighting from their transport at a humble rough-hewn hall in the middle of a snowy prairie.

In a distant way, it was amusing to see his mother try to navigate the snow drifts while maintaining an air of dignity as they made their way from the sleigh to the cleared walkway. Henry did his best to provide her with stability, his own legs knee-deep in snow as he tried to hurry them along so he could hear what the men near the entrance were saying. Henry looked across the yard for his father, but he was still tying up the horses. Henry would have to escort his mother inside before he could beg off and join the group.

Henry was unable to catch much as they passed the group of men and proceeded into the gymnasium, hanging their coats and hats on the pegs at the entrance. With chairs set around the edge of the room, the usual equipment of parallel bars and pommel horses had been stowed away to make space for dancing. His mother pulled him by the elbow towards two other matrons—Frau Müller and Frau Leonhäuser—who were exchanging pleasantries near the dias where the band was warming up.

"Guten Aben," Mutter said, inclining her head. The other matrons responded in kind.

"What has become of your husband?" Frau Müller inquired in formal German.

"He is merely securing the sleigh before joining us," Mutter replied, matching her aggressive formality. "My Heinrich was good enough to escort me."

Henry averted his eyes to hide his incredulous expression. The accordion heaved as his mother and her friends competed for who could be the most demure and socially correct. Henry shifted his weight from one foot to the other and looked over his shoulder. Where was his father?

Henry spotted his brothers entering the hall. They were deep in conversation, gesticulating excitedly with their hands as they were joined by several of the other young Turners, huddling together across the gymnasium. Henry watched them with yearning. None of his mother's friends were forcing their sons to escort them. Why was it just him that was being infantilized in this way?

Just then, Vater entered with Herr Bauer. Henry breathed a sigh of relief and dropped his arm out from under his mother's hand. She glared at him but said nothing. She did, however, wrap a firm hand around his forearm, pulling it back up into the proper position.

Henry glanced back again. His father lingered at the door, in conversation with Herr Bauer.

"Mutter," Henry hummed. "If you'll excuse me, I'm going to find out what the fuss is all about."

Mutter looked sharply up at him and glared. "Heinrich, did I understand you correctly? Are you proposing to abandon me here?"

Henry sighed. Now Frau Müller and Frau Leonhäuser were looking at him with gleeful schadenfreude. He'd just dig himself deeper if he managed to embarrass her in front of her friends. He turned and stooped to murmur into his mother's ear, hopefully too low to be overheard.

"Mutter, matrons are at full liberty to chaperone each other—"

"—That is entirely not the point, Heinrich," Her voice was louder, inviting Frau Müller and Frau Leonhäuser to tacitly participate. "My dear friends, I apologize for my son's ungentlemanly behavior. He's been too long on the prairie."

Henry pressed his lips into a thin line and tried not to roll his eyes. If they were all going to disapprove of him anyway, he might as well give them something to disapprove of.

"Bitte entschuldigen Sie mich!" Henry excused himself with a bow of his head and turned, making a beeline across the gymnasium to his father and Herr Bauer.

"Surely Lincoln won't let them go," Herr Bauer was saying, rubbing his fingers through his whiskers gravely.

"Let who go?" Henry put in as he joined them.

"It will be war for certain," his father replied as though Henry hadn't said a thing.

"War?" Henry's eyes went wide. "What's happened?"

Herr Bauer awkwardly acknowledged him with a glance, then looked back at Vater. "I can't see another way out of it. If their legislature is going to put them in such a treasonous position, what else is to be done? It isn't as though there were an article of the constitution outlining the procedure for peaceful secession."

"Vater, Herr Bauer, please, what has happened?"

Vater looked up at Henry then and frowned. "Heinrich, what are you doing here? Your mother asked you to chaperone her."

Henry gritted his teeth against the heave of his frustration and forced a smile that looked more like a grimace. "She is enjoying the company of Frau Müller and Frau Leonhäuser, sir. Neither of those ladies need to be chaperoned."

His father's frown deepened. "You know your mother is loath to move through these functions without a proper chaperone."

Henry knew better than to argue, but he couldn't let this stand. He turned his head and spoke low, though, to minimize the risk of forcing his father to save face. "None of the ladies here require a chaperone, except perhaps the unmarried ones. Why does Mutter need a chaperone?"

Vater blinked slowly. Henry braced. "You're right. Go and chaperone your cousin Christina. I'll send the twins to tend to your mother."

"Vater!" Henry exclaimed exasperatedly, then winced. While it was excusable that Peter and Franklin would not think to include him in their affairs, his father knew better. His father didn't even try to shepherd him into the community, to provide him with means to step into manhood and become an independent member of the community. He had two grown sons already; what did he need a third one for? It exasperated him to no end, but being petulant about it would do him no good.

"Herr Schaefer, come now, put the boy out of his misery," Herr Bauer said with a chuckle. Henry's father did not reply with similar amusement, but continued to frown at his son. Herr Bauer regarded Henry with pity and said, "It seems that South Carolina's legislature has made a formal declaration of secession."

"Secession?"

"Indeed. They have declared their independence from these United States with the intention of forming their own confederation."

Henry gaped.

"It seems they believe the northern states have conspired to elect a man to the presidency whose opinions and purposes are hostile to slavery. Therefore, they feel they must declare independence to protect their so-called property." Herr Bauer's tone was light, wry, and steeped in sarcasm. Vater shook his head, his lip curled in disgust.

"They make a mockery of democracy," Vater hissed. "They do not put their lives on the line for freedom. What an outrageous and backwards lie. They only rebel to protect their own power and wealth."

Vater sighed, rubbing his brows exasperatedly with his fingers. Henry forgot his impatience for a moment at the drawn, despondent expression on his father's face. It was a reminder that his father had fought in his own futile rebellion back in Germany, before Henry had ever been born. He'd paid dearly for the loss too. It was how they'd ended up here, in the middle of the snowy American prairie, pursuing the Utopia they lost to the tyranny of the German Confederation.

"Do you think Buchanan will declare war?" Henry whispered.

"He can't declare war," Bauer replied. "That would be acknowledging that there is a country to declare war upon. Besides, Buchanan is too much of a Southern gudgeon to do anything. Lincoln will surely inherit the whole sordid mess."

But there would be war. Henry knew it deep in his bones. He wished desperately that his father had spent even a fragment of the amount of time describing his battle experience as he had expounding upon the philosophical imperatives of the 1848

German Revolution. Perhaps if he had, Henry would feel a bit more prepared for the prospect.

Vater glowered at Bauer for a moment, then turned his glare upon Henry. "Heinrich, that's enough. Go to your mother. She will be devastated when she hears this news. Be a good boy and make sure she has an enjoyable evening."

Henry gritted his teeth. "I thought you were going to ask Franklin and Peter to do it?"

"But they are not right here in front of me being churlish. Get on, now, go."

"Now, Herr Schaefer, surely the boy must have his own designs for an enjoyable evening—"

"Thank you for your insight, Herr Bauer, but I know how to father my son. You heard me, Heinrich."

Henry's chin worked for a moment and he glared at his father before turning on his heel and marching back across the gymnasium. It wasn't fair that he had to bear all the familial burden when his brothers were free to conduct themselves however they chose. How was it that the duties somehow all fell to the third son? Were not the second and first sons to bear the brunt of the responsibility?

He was only halfway back to his mother when Christina bounded up, her wool skirt dusted with snow, and effused, "Did you hear the news?"

Even his flighty little cousin knew before he did. Henry turned his glare on her.

"Not for want of trying," he ground out.

Christina's blue eyes were wide as saucers and she grinned with excitement. "South Carolina is gone!" She paused for effect. "They said they're their own country now and a whole assembly of other states are going to join them!"

"Wait, other states?" Henry whirled to face her. "Which ones?"

"They're saying Mississippi, I think? Or was it Missouri?" Christina frowned. "They really should give them some more distinctive names, I think. Oh, Henry, it's war for certain!"

She seemed gleeful about it. Albeit, she was somewhat of a glutton for drama, but even so. Henry frowned at her. She didn't notice, but instead whirled on him with wide eyes.

"Henry! You don't think you'll enlist, will you?"

Henry looked back at his father, conferring with Herr Bauer, and his brothers at the center of another group of younger men. He wondered if they were making plans to enlist without him.

"Perhaps," he replied at length, his eyes still on his brothers.

"Oh Henry, you can't! Your mother would be devastated—don't you remember Cincinnati? She's been so delicate since then."

"Oh, come now, Christina, this is different. If Lincoln resolves to defend the Union, it will be a real war. Not some scrape with Know-Nothings in the streets."

The band began playing the Grand March just then. Henry found himself sourly paired with his cousin for the dance. As they passed and nodded to other couples, he could hear snatches of conversations, hushed whispers speculating about the implications of South Carolina's affront to democracy. Henry could not focus on the dance steps. As the couples paraded across the gymnasium floor, he felt his resolve build. It felt wrong, but he hoped for war. He hoped that Buchanan would act to reign in the rebels quickly. He hoped that Lincoln would take action if Buchanan did not.

He hoped that the war would last long enough for boys from Minnesota to see battle. He felt terribly guilty for desiring deathly violence, but what other way could there be? Not only did there seem no course left for the country to find compromise, but for Henry himself, how else could he escape his mother's coddling and prove himself? If he stayed here, he would rot in the shadows of his brothers like an over-watered seed.

———

II

Faribault, Minnesota
Saturday, April 20, 1861

Henry stood with Peter and Franklin outside the court-house among a huge throng of young men eagerly awaiting the recruiting captain. News had spread like wildfire of the attack on Fort Sumter over the past week and Governor Ramsey had promised a regiment to bring the southerners to heel to the newly-inaugurated President Lincoln. It was here. It was war. And Henry was ready.

His body hummed with excitement as he craned his neck to look over the men gathered outside the courthouse. His mother had been in tears as they set off yesterday from New Ulm. Henry knew he should have felt guilty for causing her such distress, but this was what he'd been dreaming of for months now. A chance to get out of the remote frontier and do something of consequence. Show the world what he was made of.

"Look at these Grünschnabel," Peter said in German, hands on his hips as he surveyed the crowd. "I'd bet not one of them has ever picked up anything more dangerous than a hoe."

Franklin snorted. "We'll show them all how we do it in the Turnverein, right Heinie?"

Henry crossed his arms and rolled his eyes. There were a lot of fellows here. He'd had no idea there were this many men in Rice County, much less this many who fancied themselves soldiers.

The crowd hushed as a man in a crisp, navy blue paletot stepped out of the courthouse, flanked by two others similarly smartened up. Casting a superior eye over the crowd, the officer raised his eyebrows in surprise.

"Gentlemen of Faribault, the Governor will be pleased to hear how many of you are in support of the Government, and in favor of the maintenance of the Union. We've been instructed to recruit seventy-six able-bodied men and after our officers, we can use about sixty of you. Will the men with their own guns please identify themselves?"

Men across the crowd held rifles aloft. Henry looked around wide-eyed as he realized there were well more than sixty men gathered here. He and his brothers had no rifles amongst them—it hadn't even occurred to him that it might be a criteria for selective service. The only rifle in their home belonged to their father and he was certainly not sacrificing it for the cause, not when there were Indians roaming the area looking for food. If the three Schaefer brothers wanted to enlist, they'd need to be chosen. Peter and Franklin seemed to be coming to the same realization because they began twisting and squeezing their way toward the front of the crowd.

Henry followed his brothers' lead, doing his best to slip between the other young men. But while his brothers were tall and slim, Henry was shorter and broader. Where they were able to slide past, he found his way blocked. Not to mention that other men were seeing the writing on the wall as well and trying to jockey their own way toward the captain and his officers. In an instant, Franklin and Peter were nothing more than two sheaves of wheat-colored hair floating through the crowd and Henry was trapped behind a throng of mill men eager to make their mark on the field of battle.

The captain peered out at the crowd, attempting to count the riflemen and separate them from the others. Henry continued to try and shoulder his way forward, but the other men were now actively barring his means of catching up with his brothers.

"Gentlemen, attention!" one of the lieutenants bellowed authoritatively. The jockeying and hum of anxious murmurs ceased as every man tried to model his suitability for the service. "Captain Dike and myself shall select sixty men for our company and then the rest of you may register your names with Lieutenant Thomas. If those rebels aren't licked after the three months service currently called for, we may fall back on you for aid."

With that, the three commanding officers set off into the crowd. All those with rifles were accepted (except for one boy whose voice hadn't yet dropped) and then the lieutenants began selecting men, seemingly at random.

"Sir, I have a rifle at home!" one man shouted. It earned him a point and a nod from Captain Dike.

"I also have a rifle at home!" Peter shouted, reaching his hand into the air and taking full advantage of his height. The Captain pointed and nodded at Henry's brother and Peter shouted in triumph, then proceeded across the road to the field in which the lieutenant was organizing the selected men into ranks. Franklin inexplicably followed Peter and to Henry's horror, the captain did not seem to notice. Henry redoubled his efforts to squeeze his way to the front of the throng, but at this point, the other men gathered were wise to his scheme and blocked him back.

"Get back, greenhorn," one man spat. "Let the real Americans do the fighting."

Henry gritted his teeth and pressed down on the urge to show the bastard what it meant to fight. He'd done enough wrestling at Turner Hall that he was confident he could take the other fellow. He clenched his fist at his side.

The crowd was just beginning to get rowdy when the captain climbed back up the steps of the courthouse and shouted, "Gentlemen of Faribault! Attention!"

The crowd simmered down. Henry cast a glance over at the men selected for service. They stood straight with self-satisfied smiles on their faces, listening to the lieutenant give instructions unintelligible from this distance. He spotted Peter and Franklin among their ranks, grinning and casting each other congratulatory glances. God *damn* them. He shouldn't have been surprised that they left him behind, but *hell*, it still provoked him.

"We have reached our allotment," the captain announced and the crowd that remained immediately expressed their frustration. "If there is a need, we will certainly call on you for your service. Please form an orderly line if you would like to register your name with Lieutenant Thomas."

Henry felt his chest tighten and his stomach fall as he set his mouth in a straight line. This had been his chance. He'd boggled it. If he'd just been more assertive, stuck closer to his brothers ... if he had taken his father's gun. His fists clenched tight as his sides and he glanced back again at Peter and Franklin as he reluctantly began to make his way into the registration line. Now they'd come back with all the glory, with medals and stories of gallantry, and he'd be the same old Heinrich, stuck in a limbo between boyhood and manhood, planting wheat and potatoes for the rest of his days.

Later, the twins approached Henry as he sat glumly on the curb of the boardwalk edging Main Street.

"What happened to you, Heinie?" Peter asked exasperatedly, throwing his hands up. "I thought you were right behind us."

Henry glared. Franklin set a heavy hand on his shoulder. "Don't worry. I'm sure it'll only be a month or two before they put out another call for soldiers. I hear the Southerners are drawing most of the officers from West Point, so it won't be so easy to tamp them down."

"I can't go back home," Henry croaked and buried his face in his hands.

Franklin and Peter exchanged uncertain looks.

"Well, maybe you shouldn't," said one.

"Maybe you should stay here," said the other.

"After all, if you went back to New Ulm, you might miss it when they call for reinforcements."

Henry looked up at them, his head tilted skeptically. "Mutter won't stand for it."

Peter shrugged. "She doesn't need to know."

"We'll just ... imply you're with us." Franklin offered. Was it possible that flicker of his eyes was guilt?

Henry looked up at his brothers under his brows. "You'd do that?"

"Just until you can enlist and get to Fort Snelling. Then you can write Mutter and Pater and tell them you got transferred to a different company."

Henry frowned. "And what do you propose I do in the meantime?"

Franklin deferred to Peter, who shrugged and replied easily, "Get a job."

———

III

St. Anthony, Minnesota
Saturday, April 20, 1861

"Your heart will grow to love him."

Cate gripped her hands tightly together on her knees. Her shoulders, jaw, her chest—everything was tight with the effort to hold in her frustration. It was the night before her wedding. Tomorrow she'd have to vow to love, cherish, and obey Richard Ellis until death parted them. And the entire thought of it made her stomach churn.

"Just wait until there's children," Margaret continued, her fingers tucking a few stray hairs behind her ear. "When someone has made it possible for you to bring something so small and miraculous into this world, there is no way to deny him your heart."

Cate hadn't intended to actually be present at her own wedding tomorrow morning. After the mob had descended upon the Grey's home and she'd seen Mr. Ellis' true character, she'd taken in piles of laundry, working her fingers to the bone in hopes of growing her pile of pennies into something of use. Her plan had been to book a steamer ticket out of town, maybe cart herself out farther west. But then her father had taken ill and had been laid up for nearly the entire winter. Cate had been obliged to invest both her money in support of meeting her father's accounts and her time to focus on caring for him rather than take in more laundry. With Margaret beholden to her new infant, she and Cate had made certain to keep her father as isolated as possible, lest baby Joseph fall ill too. So with her funds cleaned out and Mr. Ellis eager to be married come the first signs of spring, she found herself in her attic room, penniless and out of choices with a wedding first thing in the morning.

"Get some sleep," Margaret said, standing and giving Cate's hand one final squeeze. "All will be brighter in the morning."

The stairs creaked as Margaret made her way back downstairs. Cate's candle was burning low, casting more shadows than light across the small attic room. Etta was breathing soft and slow in the bed already. Cate refused to allow herself to think about how different her new bedfellow would be come tomorrow. Her best calico dress was laid out on top of her trunk, packed with the trousseau her grandmother had started for her and that she and Margaret had finished. A lifetime of preparation for what? Serving a husband and rearing children? Was that all there was? Cate swallowed hard and reminded herself to take a deep breath.

There had been a time, not so long ago, back in Pennsylvania, when she thought she might like to be married. When she saw George Jacobs and his wife together at the Philadelphia Society of Friends meetings, she thought she would like the same happiness. A man whose eyes followed her with such tenderness. Someone whose quiet jokes were meant only for her ears. The serialized novels Cate had read in her youth had filled her imagination with romance and love matches and honorable men with titles and fortunes. She had been content with her lot then, daydreaming about a handsome fellow while sewing handkerchiefs for her trousseau.

But then she had read *Uncle Tom's Cabin*. And then Frederick Douglass, William Lloyd Garrison, Solomon Northrup. Pamphlets by Angelina Grimke and speeches by Sojourner Truth. Catherine Beecher and Elizabeth Cady Stanton. And it became abundantly clear that those novels were just fiction. A fantasy to placate women to waste their lives tending to men. If women did indeed possess a stronger moral connection to God, then wasn't it her duty to use it? Cate had thrown herself into abolitionist texts in spite of her father's condemnation of them as radical. He still never missed an opportunity to grumble about how it had spoiled her for marriage. As loath as she was to admit it, perhaps he was right. After all, she was about to become the ward of a pedantic (and penniless) law student who had traveled west because he couldn't secure a position in more civilized lands. Now that she'd turned twenty-six, he was the last option she had left.

Cate sighed. There was no way she was going to be able to sleep, so she rose, pulled on her wrapper and padded downstairs in stocking feet. Slipping into the kitchen, she hovered her hand over the stove and stoked it, taking the heavy iron from the shelf and letting it heat on top. A pile of trousers were draped across the kitchen chair, waiting to be pressed. If she wasn't going to sleep, she might as well finish the Pioneer lumber mill's laundry. They didn't much care when her wedding was, as long as their lumbermen had trousers to wear while dancing logs on the Mississippi.

She reached for the oil lamp and set the glass shade aside. She hesitated with her sputtering candle in hand. She felt momentarily guilty for wasting the oil, but then lit the wick anyway. Surely after pressing a few pairs, she'd begin to get drowsy. She just had to get out of her own head. Placing the shade back onto the lamp, Cate reached down and swung the table leaf out, draping her ironing-cloth across it. She took up the first pair of trousers and snapped them in the air to shake out what wrinkles she could.

As she held the pair of trousers by the waistband, a heady thought crystallized in her mind. They looked about her size.

Cate held the trousers out in front of her. The waistband seemed right and they were a good length for her height too. She stared at the brown cotton twill for a moment, tracing the seams with her eyes as she chewed her lip. Perhaps.

She looked up at the kitchen door, listening for anyone in the household stirring. Ensuring that the drapes were closed, she shrugged off her wrapper and draped the cotton oak leaf print over her ironing-cloth. She held the trousers out and pulled them over one leg then the other. She tucked her nightgown in between her thighs and pulled the waistband up over it, fastening the buttons down the front with bold fingers.

She was tall enough. The cuffs just grazed the top of her foot. She flexed her knees. She felt strangely naked without any heavy skirts.

What if…

What if she were to just disappear? What if there was no Cate Stowell come dawn for Richard Ellis to wed? What if she became James or Frank? Charles had a sort of dignified ring to it…

A log in the stove cracked as it burned and crumbled, startling Cate out of her thoughts. Right, she was ironing. Snatching up her thick rag, she picked up the heavy iron and held it up near her cheek, close enough to tell that she had left it too long and it would scorch the clothes.

She shook her head. This was foolish. If anyone caught her trying on the trousers of her customers, she would be laughed right out of town. She set the iron on the edge of the stove, balanced on its back end so it could cool. She should just go to bed. Every girl got married at some point in her life. Even Angelina Grimke and Elizabeth Cady Stanton had married. Marriage was not, she chided herself, the end of the world.

She removed the trousers and restored them to the pile on the kitchen chair. She pulled her wrapper back on, flipping her dark braid out of the collar before fastening it. Margaret was right. What she needed was some sleep. She turned the wick down on the lamp to extinguish the flame and took up her stub of a candle. Every woman felt such anxiety the night before her wedding. This was just normal prenuptial jitters. It was time for her to tuck away childish fancies and take up her place in society. She would do well to focus on what marriage might afford her, rather than lament the freedoms she was losing. For one thing, she wasn't going to be stuck under her father's thumb anymore. That was a marked relief. (Although she wasn't optimistic about what Richard Ellis' thumb might be like.)

Her candle held to light her way, Cate tip-toed quietly out of the kitchen and down the hall. As she pivoted around the newel post, her eyes snagged on her father's cap and jacket hanging on a peg next to the front door. She stilled, taking them in for a long moment.

The notion that you could somehow pass for a man is truly ridiculous, she chided herself. *Go upstairs and go to sleep already.*

But she didn't. She just stood in the hall, holding her candle, staring at her father's hat. Just next to the peg hung a small, scratched looking glass. She shook her head and rolled her eyes. *Come now,* she thought, *You would never pass for a boy. I'll prove it to you.*

Setting her candle on top of the newel post, she stepped over to the cap and pulled it squarely onto her head. Taking up her candle again, she peered at her reflection in the small mirror.

She scoffed, murmuring, "Nothing more than a poor excuse for fancy dress."

Even so, she tucked her hair into the cap with her fingers. If she squinted, her tall stature could assist the illusion. She pulled on her father's jacket as well. She shrugged to settle the wool around her neck, pressing her lips into a firm, masculine line. Her shoulders were broad enough, her jaw sharp enough. Her round eyes and soft, smooth cheeks made her seem significantly more youthful than her actual age, but ... who knew? If she really committed to the act, perhaps folks would be fooled. Especially folks who had never seen her before.

Men across the city had been clamoring for a chance to fight the rebels after what had happened at Fort Sumter. What if she disguised herself and enlisted? She felt a squeeze of longing in her chest. Cate met her own eyes in the mirror and imagined herself in uniform, facing down the enemy.

She shook her head and snorted derisively. Now that would be a desperate endeavor indeed.

She gave herself a flippant salute in the mirror, then turned to the side, hunching her shoulders a bit to reduce her bosom. Her breasts were small to begin with and without the assistance of her corset, it was surprisingly easy for the swell of her breasts to disappear beneath the heavy drape of the jacket. If she was strong enough to wring laundry all day, surely she was strong enough to build earthworks or load a cannon ball. She raised her dark eyebrows at herself in the mirror.

She was fairly certain servicemen were required to have a medical examination upon enlistment. There was no way to keep a doctor from noticing she was the wrong sex. Shaking her head, she pulled off her father's cap and shrugged out of his jacket, hanging both carefully back on the hook. It was a flight of fancy, really. A ridiculous notion.

Regarding herself in the mirror once more, her wispy dark curls doing their best to twist free out of her braid, the image of her belly large and round burst into her mind's eye unbidden. She swallowed hard over the lump that appeared in her throat.

"If God intended me to be a man," she whispered to her reflection, "I'd have been born one." She knew how to care for children. Perhaps she would find her purpose in a few of her own. Surely they would look like her too. Not just like Richard Ellis. Her chest felt tight and wrong.

Cate wrinkled her nose and turned toward the steps.

Everyone gets married, it's not the end of the world.
Everyone gets married, it's not the end of the world.
Everyone gets married, it's not the end of the world.

———

The next day, Mrs. Richard Ellis was quiet the entire wagon ride from the church. Margaret held her hand, plucking a stray thread from her calico dress, and said, "Well, that was a very nice service."

Cate didn't answer.

Instead, she looked out over the ridge at the glutted Mississippi River, flooded from a week of rain and snowmelt. She could have simply disappeared, trekking over to St. Paul, maybe taking work as a lumberman somewhere, but she'd been too afraid. Having never been a man, she feared they would have ferreted her out right away. While the idea of fighting in a regiment filled her with excitement—imagine *finally* doing her bit for emancipation—reinventing herself as a laborer did not hold the same appeal. Was there really a difference between the hard labor of housekeeping and the hard labor of lumber milling?

So here she was, riding with her stepmother in her father's wagon, on her way to the reception Mr. Ellis was hosting at the defunct university hall. He had acquired modest lodgings at his boarding house for the two of them and Cate was staring down the prospect of her wedding night taking place above the bedroom of a stranger. She could not have designed a much more mortifying scenario if she'd tried.

When their wagon pulled up outside of the towering edifice of the main university building, Cate felt a sense of displacement that made her profoundly lonely. Mr. Ellis—she supposed she should probably think of him as Richard now that they were married—bounded down the steps to offer her his hand as she descended the wagon box.

"Hello, Mrs. Ellis," he said, his mustache stretched over his beaming smile. He was thin and angular, cutting a sharp figure in his wool jacket and trousers. He wasn't a cruel man. None of his irritating behaviors were harmful or brutish. He seemed to like her well enough. And he wasn't bad-looking either—perhaps a little skinny, but he was of a height with her, which was more than a good many men could claim. Dark hair slicked down, that infernal mustache crawling over somewhat crooked teeth. Large brown eyes, a little sunken but certainly not unfeeling. She felt guilty that she could not be happy with the arrangement, but no matter how much she calculated his individually inoffensive attributes, she could not come up with a sum that satisfied her. Cate searched his eyes and wished she could feel as carefree as he seemed to be. But she could not shake the feeling that while he only stood to gain a wife, she had lost her self-determination in the exchange.

Accepting his proffered hand, she arranged her hoops and stepped gingerly from the wagon box. Despite the chill in the air, and their fingers both swathed in gloves, she could feel the warmth of his hand in hers. This would be alright. It had to be. Even as a mediocre lawyer, he walked a charmed life, but he would still bleed were he cut, same as her. *Don't let perfect be the enemy of enough*, she reminded herself and tried to return his smile.

The reception was objectively very fun. Margaret and some of the other ladies from her church had prepared a wonderful spread of venison and a variety of pies and preserves. The cake was incomparable. Margaret's brother brought his fiddle so they were able to do a few reels and country dances, which lifted Cate's spirits more than she would like to admit, especially given her clumsy dance skills. But this was her wedding, which meant there were few people whose company she did not already enjoy and perhaps it was the tipple of raspberry spirits, but by the end of the evening, she felt much more at ease and optimistic about her future.

Which was good, because she still had to go to Richard's lodgings and consummate their union in a cramped boarding house bed. The thought of this led her to sneak another glass or two of raspberry spirits, so that by the time she was seated on the driver's seat of Richard's borrowed buggy, she didn't much care what the rest of the night held.

Mrs. Greenleaf, the widow proprietress of the boarding house, greeted the newlyweds and showed them upstairs and into a small, cozy room containing a lovely oak bed with a crochet lace coverlet. Richard set Cate's suitcase on the dresser as Mrs. Greenleaf shut the door firmly behind her. When he turned to face Cate, she could see he was nervous too.

"I apologize for the accommodations," Richard said with a helpless shrug. "I have a meeting at the mayor's office on Monday with good prospects for a position, but it will be some time before I'll have the means to build you a proper house..."

Cate mirrored his shrug and said, "Don't worry, it's fine."

Richard strode across the room on his spindly legs and took her shoulders in his hands. "You are a saint for being so forgiving, but it is not acceptable. You deserve a place to call your own."

Cate met his eyes. She liked to see him this way—nervous, unsure. It was a side of him she had not seen before. Perhaps it was the wine or perhaps it was his eagerness to please, but she grasped him by the cheeks and gave him a chaste kiss.

Their union was awkward, fumbling, vulnerable. It was not explosive nor passionate, but it did feel safe. And that was more than Cate could have hoped for, given the circumstances. He was responsive to her and ensured he did not hurt her. Cate found she rather liked it. It felt nice to be filled that way.

When he became enthralled in his own passions, Cate watched him curiously, observing his wet panting and his attenuated thighs working diligently. He had a narrow patch of dark hair on his chest, not more than a few dozen hairs really, and she wondered what made it grow particularly right there.

She was startled when he strained against her suddenly, letting out a yelp and collapsing on top of her. She had understood of course how it all was supposed to go but she hadn't anticipated quite such a startling climax.

"...Richard?" she asked, tucking her chin to try and get a look at his face nestled against her neck. She could feel his moist breath on her shoulder. "Are you alright?"

He let out a contented sigh and turned towards her. His mustache tickled her cheek as he murmured, "You're lovely."

It was the first time he'd ever said anything like that to her. Given what had just gone on, it didn't feel particularly poignant. More of an afterthought, really. And it wasn't evident whether he thought she looked lovely or felt lovely or was just lovely in manner. Did it matter?

After a moment, he rolled off of her and curled up under the coverlet, a contented smile across his lips. Cate shifted uncomfortably as she noticed a distinct wetness between her thighs. Yanking her chemise down, she tucked herself under the covers as well and turned to one side to face him. Though she could sense that he'd decided the consummation had concluded, she still couldn't help but feel that there should be ... more to it than that. She'd had longer encounters with herself before her younger sister was born and she'd had her own bed to sleep in.

"...Richard?"

"Hmm?" he mumbled, not opening his eyes.

Cate couldn't bring herself to name what was missing, much less ask for it. That wasn't the kind of thing a virginal bride would say on her wedding night and despite her usual penchant for bluntness, she was trying hard to be a proper wife. So she settled on, "What are you thinking?"

"Oh, nothing," he said, nuzzling his face into the pillow.

She believed him.

———

IV

Fort Snelling, Minnesota
Monday, July 22, 1861

HENRY HEARD THE BUGLE sound *reveille* for the first time curled up in the prairie grass outside the walls of Fort Snelling and the tune swelled in his heart like a homecoming. Though he'd slept deeply, Henry was stiff and sore from the unyielding ground, and his muscles bemoaned the ache of endurance walking over varied terrain for two days straight. Stretching, he did his best to hide his discomfort from his friends, Elias and Jacob. He'd met them working farm labor in Faribault and when the call for a Second Regiment had finally come, all three of them had jovially signed their names over to Lincoln.

"Wake up, lazy bones," Elias Hower said, nudging a foot at Jacob's shoulder. "I know it's not a rooster crow, but it's our new call to meet the day. We'd best get used to it."

"I'm awake, I'm awake," Jacob Robinson grumbled, swatting Elias' boot.

They would have been at the fort as soon as the call for more troops was printed in the newspaper nearly a month ago, but between their employer's resistance to letting them go and the disorganization of the Rice County volunteers, they'd only just arrived yesterday. While they were all similarly exhausted, Henry wasn't about to seem ill-equipped for the miles of marching that would likely be required of them once activated for service as he got to his feet. Jacob, for his part, did not seem to harbor similar concerns and complained loudly about his knees as he rose.

Sitting up, Henry inhaled the dewy summer air and grinned. Yes, he was tired and sore, but he was tired and sore and happy. He couldn't shake the feeling that something important lay straight ahead of him and that, by association, he too was important.

Fort Snelling was positioned at the top of a tall bluff, overlooking the confluence of the Mississippi and Minnesota Rivers to the northeast. Its limestone walls were two stories high, holding within the barracks, commissary, and other buildings.

"We'd better hurry up," Elias said, brushing grass off his coat. "Company A's been on post duty for a month now—we don't want to fall behind."

"Eh, I'm sure we'll do just fine," Jacob Robinson shrugged. He'd only fastened the very top button of his coat.

"Well, if you aim to be promoted, you should turn yourself out a bit better than that," Elias chided with a sidelong glower at Jacob's coat.

Henry looked down at his own wrinkled coat and trousers and his hat that was all but crushed after being used as a pillow. It didn't matter. Soon enough, he'd be uniformed and equipped. A proper soldier, straight-backed and swathed in Union blue.

"I don't aim to do nothing except kill Rebs," Jacob grinned, snatching up a long blade of prairie grass to chew.

The threat of violence felt distant on this fine, sunny morning, with birds singing and the breeze rustling through the trees in the river valley. Henry didn't know about killing Rebs, but he'd learned wrestling and sparring at the Turner Hall. He couldn't imagine how a civilian could more ready.

"Hurry up, the others have already gone to breakfast," Elias fussed as Jacob bundled his things up inside his blanket and slung the whole makeshift haversack over his shoulder. Henry similarly stowed his own belongings and followed Jacob and Elias towards the fort gate. Inside, the enticing smells of fresh-baked bread rode on the wind and the parade grounds teemed with fresh recruits drawn out by their stomachs. Not having their own barracks assignment, Henry and the others lined up outside the commissary for tin cups of coffee and heels of fresh baked bread.

"Is this it?" Jacob complained, regarding the bread in his hand. "I could have sworn I smelled bacon."

"That's just wishful thinking," Elias pointed out, ruffling the younger boy's chestnut hair then shoving his head. "Beggars can't be choosers."

Jacob glowered as he smoothed his hair with his hand. "I'm about to sign my life away for three years—"

"—I can't imagine them Secesh will last that long," Elias put in.

"Regardless, I should think we're entitled to some real food."

Walking into the busy parade ground, they found a spot to sit on the edge of the boardwalk lining the officer's quarters. They settled in to eat their breakfast side by side, surveying the new soldiers moseying around waiting for drills to start.

Henry took a big bite of the bread and washed it down with some coffee. It wasn't particularly a revelation, but it was fresh and soft.

"A pat of butter wouldn't hurt," he conceded.

"A rasher of bacon," Jacob insisted, holding his tin cup aloft, "and nothing less!"

A young man—more a boy really—sitting on the boardwalk on the other side of the post from Henry gave a soft snort. Just audibly, he muttered under his breath, "What are you, some sort of breakfast evangelist?"

Henry leaned around the post to look at the fellow with a chuckle. "If that were only a real job, he'd be well-suited," Henry murmured in reply.

The boy, apparently startled he'd been overheard, looked up at Henry with round, dark eyes like a deer poised to run. Henry gave as ingratiating a smile as he could manage. Just then, he noticed over the boy's shoulder a group of men nearby straighten up and remove their hats. Standing, Henry spotted a group of well-dressed people making their way down the boardwalk toward them.

"Who is that?" he inquired quietly. Jacob and Elias craned to get a good look.

"Oh! That's our Colonel, Horatio Van Cleve," Elias said. "Governor Ramsey gave him his commission. He was an enlisted man in the '30's—that's how he came to meet his wife, you know, as her father was a commander at several forts including this one—and I imagine he'll have much to teach us."

Jacob jabbed his elbow into Elias' ribs. "What are you, his biographer?"

Henry peered at the older man nodding genially to the enlisted men who had recognized him, for they were among the minority in the droves of fellows joking loudly amongst themselves. Their colonel was tall and reedy, with a calm, quiet face and round spectacles on his nose. As he approached them, Elias sprang to his feet and saluted to the man, a perfect vision of a soldier to Henry's eyes.

"Sir," Elias greeted and the Colonel regarded him, his eyes lifted in some amusement.

"At ease, soldier," the old man said genially, his beard twitching with a smile. Elias nodded and dropped his hand, but did not sit again until the Colonel quitted the boardwalk and proceeded to the offices in the hospital building.

"How did you know that?" Jacob complained, regarding Elias from the corner of his eye.

Elias shrugged. "While you were snoring, I was playing euchre and getting the lay of the land."

Jacob rolled his eyes.

Henry nudged him with an elbow and said, "Well, you can at least count yourself lucky to be well-rested. I imagine that's more important for a good soldier."

"And not running around acting the insufferable know-it-all," Jacob added, crossing his arms.

Elias scoffed. "Absurd. You delight in the fact that I know everything. After all, if I didn't perform this important service for you, who would? You'd be lost without me."

"Oh poor me, whatever will I do without a heavy burden of useless gossip?" Jacob bemoaned.

Elias glowered. "You asked."

"Fellas," said an older fellow, rather short of stature with a thin mustache. It was Ned Osborn, one of the other Rice County Volunteers. "The Lieutenant wants us to meet near the Round Bastion for instructions." After scarfing down what was left of their bread and coffee, Henry hurried across the parade ground with Jacob and Elias, following Osborn and the others who had marched up with them from Faribault. The boy from the boardwalk and a number of other fellows tagged along until there was a decent mob of thirty or so men descending upon the Round Bastion.

The Round Bastion was a tall, stone tower at the west end of the fort near the entrance. Slots were cut into the thick stone for musket muzzles to peek out before Minnesota had ever become a territory. As Henry and the rest of the men gathered between the base of this structure and the guard house, Lieutenant Thomas stood tall, his eyes flickering to account for every man. Seemingly satisfied, he nodded and shouted, "Attention Rice County Volunteers! We've been directed to join our men up with a few other groups to form Company K."

Lieutenant Thomas had delayed their departure from Faribault for several weeks trying to recruit enough men for their own company. He'd finally given it up as a bad job and headed north with about twenty-five men. The call for three years instead of three months had changed a good number of fellows' minds. Henry leaned over to Elias. "Does it matter what company we're in?"

Elias shrugged and kept his eyes forward. His lack of response indicated that now was not the time for questions. Henry turned his eyes back on Thomas, a little abashedly.

"We will join the rest of the company outside, just south of the gates, and Captain Noah will take roll. Follow me."

Henry did exactly that. Gravel crunched under his feet as he did his best to look like he belonged in the army. Elias' insights about the Colonel had shaken him a little bit. Elias clearly had dedicated himself to the task of distinguishing himself and his knowledge served him well, helping him deliver due respect to his commanding officer. How had Elias known how to stand and salute so well? Henry wanted to convey the same level of discipline, but he simply didn't know where to begin. He'd never fought before. He'd scarcely ever shot a rifle before. And he suspected that shooting a deer was decidedly different than shooting a man, especially in the context of a strategic battle.

Outside of the two massive wood gates, the dirt road proceeded down a steep incline along the Minnesota River bluff to
the boat landing below. About fifty men gathered with Henry
in a grassy spot on the high ground opposite the road. The
men themselves were of every variety, the youngest appearing
about sixteen to the oldest perhaps forty. While many of them
largely sported the same cut of sack coat and trousers in varying
sober colors, there seemed no shortage of fashionable facial hair
among them.

At the head of the group stood a man on the stump of a tree
who could only be none other than Captain Noah. He stood
with his arms crossed over his chest as he looked down a long
nose at the men gathered around him. His hair was thinning
in spite of not appearing any older than thirty and he wore
a neatly trimmed beard that made his long face appear even
longer. His eyebrows were arched and his eyes looked lazy, but
Henry suspected this denoted less about how the Captain felt
and rather more about how his face generally rested.

"Soldiers," the Captain began. The group of men continued
to hum with conversation. The Captain lifted an eyebrow and
then turned his head, looking down at another officer standing
next to the stump. This man bellowed, "ATTENTION!"

That did the trick. The men quieted immediately, some with
wide eyes, others with defiant grins, and still others with straight
posture as though trying to prove their worthiness. Henry was
among this latter group.

"Welcome to Fort Snelling," the Captain said once he had
the attention of the group. "I am Captain Noah and I am your
commanding officer. There are groups of you from all across the
state, from here in St. Paul, to Minneapolis, Faribault, and even
as far afield as St. Cloud. Allow me to be the first to thank you
for your service.

"Now, the first step to mustering you in is to call roll. When
you hear your name, please respond as present." The Captain
looked down at a list in his hand and proceeded to call roll.

As Henry waited for his name to be called, he wondered
how his brothers were faring. The First Regiment had marched
out a month before, loaded on steamers and sent downriver to

Chicago, then on to Washington DC. In spite of all his anger with them for leaving him behind, he hoped that they would be safe on their mission. Though admittedly, hearing Franklin and Peter bragging about their heroic roles among the first men in the whole country to volunteer to defend the Union were not among the top experiences Henry wished to endure anytime soon. He absently cracked his knuckles as he waited to hear his name called.

"Wilbur Little."

"Present."

Henry wondered again if it mattered what company a man enlisted under. Some of the companies were organized before the call to enlist went out, or they had formed under the call for the First Regiment and been passed up. Those men knew each other, had drilled together already. They were farther along in creating a camaraderie among their unit. Henry worried that since this company was combining with men from various towns, that they wouldn't have the same rapport, the same level of cohesion, which would then undermine their ability to fight effectively. Perhaps that was why they were Company K and not Company A or B.

"Heen-ritch Chafer," Captain Noah called.

Henry paused, looking around. But then after a moment, he realized that the Captain was mispronouncing his name.

"Present! Sorry, sir, it's Heinrich Schaefer."

The Captain blinked at him. "Bless you."

Jacob snorted. Elias covered his mouth and raised his eyebrows, trying not to grin. Henry glowered at them, feeling his cheeks heat with embarrassment. The Captain had already moved on to calling the next name.

"Charles Smith."

"Present, sir." The boy from the boardwalk claimed this name. He stood a little ways away, his posture stiff and serious. There was something about his face that Henry found fascinating. His cheeks were smooth, belying his youth, and his delicately sharp features paired with his deep-set eyes made him look like the romantic hero from a gothic serial illustrated plate. Seeming to sense that he was being observed, he glanced up and caught Henry's gaze. Henry cracked his friendliest half smile, the one he saved for his brother's friends and his gymnasticks instructor. The boy raised a thick, angular brow and his eyes darted quickly away.

"And that, gentlemen, concludes roll. At this time, the Lieutenants will form you into squads of eight men and once assembled, assign one among you the sergeant. Sergeants may then in the coming weeks of training promote a corporal under the advisement of Lieutenant Thomas."

Elias exchanged wide-eyed looks with Henry and Jacob and immediately they clustered themselves together. They weren't the only ones. Other men quickly arranged themselves among their friends to suit the apportioned number.

"Hey, Hower, get over here," Ned Osborn beckoned to Elias, and he dragged Jacob and Henry along with him to stand near Osborn and three others. The seven of them stood in a group and craned about looking for an eighth member before all the other groups filled. As Henry's eyes traveled across the company, he noticed the boy—Charles Smith—again. His hat, a little too large, had slipped over his brows and he adjusted his collar awkwardly as he stood alone. Henry's eyes narrowed.

"Hey, you!" he called. The boy looked up with those large eyes as he hesitated. "Come here. We need one more."

The boy glanced around as if unsure Henry was speaking to him. Then, perhaps seeing how the other men had congregated into groups, he shuffled over to Henry's side. So gathered, they waited for Lieutenant Thomas to arrive and formally assign them as a squad. When he did so, his eyes flickered over them, confirming their number, and said, "Alright, you're Squad Seven. Osborn, you'll be Sergeant."

The older man grinned and his friend, Thomas Webster, elbowed him in a congratulatory sort of way. They were both over thirty and carried themselves with the kind of natural confidence that got one promoted to sergeant as a matter of course.

Leveling his gaze at Osborn, the Lieutenant said, "Get me a roster of your men and meet at the office after dinner for training." Then he walked off.

Elias looked at Osborn sidelong and frowned after the Lieutenant.

"Oh, don't be jealous, Hower," Osborn chided him. "You'll make a fine corporal."

After the lieutenants finished formally acknowledging the squads the men had by and large formed on their own, the Captain mounted the stump once again.

"Sergeants, report to the Lieutenants to receive bunk assignments and a time for your squad to undergo the surgeon's exam. Exams will proceed this afternoon. Once you're done with that, recruits may have recreation. Sergeants report to the office for drill training. Your first company drill will be with Lieutenant Webster tomorrow morning. Reveille will play at sunrise. You are to report to the parade ground by 6 o'clock tomorrow morning for roll and further instructions."

Henry's head spun a bit. It had come so fast, he wasn't sure he'd gotten all of it. He glanced around at his fellow recruits; he couldn't have been the only one. Charles Smith stood just to his left and Henry was startled to find he'd gone white as a sheet, his eyes wide and his jaw tight. Puzzled, Henry tried to run through what he'd heard again. Had there been an instruction couched in there somewhere that should cause Henry to be concerned?

He glanced over at the boy again. Smooth-cheeked as he was, he wasn't precisely baby-faced—he had finely-carved, sharp features, a stormy brow, and the kind of petulant pout that would make his cousin Christina swoon. But Henry'd bet a dollar that fellow was too young to enlist.

Henry leaned over and nudged the boy with his shoulder. The boy startled.

"Don't worry," Henry assured under his breath. The boy looked up at him from under furrowed brows and glared.

"Why would I be worried?" he snarled in a voice just husky enough to suggest it had already dropped. Henry shut his mouth and frowned. He hadn't meant to be condescending, but he realized too late that he had been, perhaps even more so than his brothers ever had. He knew what it was like to be patronized and he refused to do it, to this boy or anyone else. He was going to do better.

V

Cate adjusted her second-hand hat again as she followed her new squad inside the fort, where Sergeant Osborn led them to their assigned lodgings. She'd been walking the world as a man for two days now, but it didn't diminish the constant fear that she'd be seen for what she really was every time she met someone new. The threat of the imminent surgeon inspection was not helping this anxiety.

The barracks inside the fort were under the north wall and consisted of two long buildings, each one story in height. The larger of these, intended to accommodate two companies, Osborn explained, was divided into sets, each set having an orderly-room and three squad-rooms on the main floor, while below in the basement were a mess-room and a kitchen. The other barrack was intended to be occupied by one company only; and the orderly-room, squad-rooms, mess-rooms, and a kitchen were on the same floor. Company K was to be quartered in the latter, while Company G and I occupied the former.

Sergeant Osborn led them along the covered boardwalk and turned into one of the doors along the wall that faced out onto the parade ground. When Cate entered, her stomach sank. The room couldn't be larger than fifteen feet square. It was fitted with three bunks, built of scantling posts that supported three tiers of berths, standing endwise with narrow passages in between and the foot of the beds towards the door. The mattresses were nothing more than muslin slips stuffed with straw. Opposite the bunks was a large, outdated stone fireplace and in the small space remaining between stood a pine table with six chairs. The entire room smelled musty and old, and a bit like it hadn't been entered, much less cleaned, since the First Minnesota mustered out a month ago.

They were going to make all eight of them share this tiny space? The scant privacy she'd presumed she'd have camping outside of the walls of the fort were dashed upon the decaying wood floors of this tiny room.

"While there's room enough for you all to have your own bunk at present," Sergeant Osborn intoned, "as they muster new recruits to fill our company, you'll eventually have to share."

Cate swallowed thickly. As if the physical exam weren't terrifying enough, now she had to figure out how to maintain her entire existence out of this room without being discovered, and share a bed with one of these louts? How was she going to get dressed? Or clean herself? She wasn't even sure where the privy was yet. And of course, just the mere prospect of that made her feel like she was in need of it.

While she'd only donned her disguise for a few days, she'd been planning in earnest ever since the call went out for the Second Minnesota Regiment. She'd given domesticity her level best, but... Well. Richard was a fine husband in terms of his standing. He'd gotten his position at the mayor's office, acquired more suitable lodgings, and even hired a maid to help Cate with the household chores. She'd had it better than most wives in St. Anthony. But no matter how she counted her blessings, there was still a gaping hole in her chest that grew wider every time Richard treated her like a child or reprimanded her for digging her nose into issues not "fit" for ladies. Which was daily. Cate had a short temper and fervent beliefs. If she could stop, she would have done it long ago. She thought Richard might get used to her political interests, but instead, he'd doubled down. He'd even taken the liberty of canceling her newspaper subscriptions. It wasn't enough. It wasn't even close to enough. So she'd made a plan to disappear from under Richard's nose and get out of the state undetected, while also setting herself on the front lines of a cause she'd been desperate to fight for since she was fifteen. To have sacrificed so much only to be found out and sent back before even getting mustered in—it was intolerable. She refused to allow it.

The rest of the squad eagerly lurched forward to claim their bunks. There were nine beds across the three scaffolds, so there were two beds to spare, given the Sergeant bunked in the orderly-room. One man claimed the bottom bunk nearest to the door and as Cate recovered from her initial shock, she realized she was about to miss her chance. Before she could decide whether a top or bottom bunk would be best, the German with the unpronounceable name approached her, presumably to give her more condescending platitudes.

"Are you alright?" he asked, his warm voice showing only the slightest hint of the accent with which he'd pronounced his name during roll.

No. She was not alright. She was two breaths from swooning in a ripe panic, the thought of which was completely mortifying. She never swooned. That was for silly, idiotic women whose understanding of hardship revolved around what their cook had the audacity to serve with tea.

"I just didn't expect..." Cate began, then caught herself. She had been about to say *I just didn't expect such a lack of privacy*, but that would have been suspicious. Wouldn't it?

The German laughed. "Yeah, I had expected to be sleeping on the ground, too! Lucky us, huh?" He elbowed her in the ribs and grinned an easy, floppy smile revealing a row of straight, white teeth. Cate couldn't help but stare. Then she forced herself to smile too, although it probably came out as more of a begrudging grimace.

"Lucky us," she murmured as he pulled her into the room by the arm. Christ, but he was handsy. Did men usually touch each other this much?

The bunks had all been claimed except for the final scaffold in the far corner, and the middle bunk on the center scaffold. Cate was surprised the men seemed more keen to sleep aloft than to claim the bunks nearest to the floor, just from a point of convenience, but as they began climbing up the scaffolds, she saw how flimsy they were. Were they to collapse, the soldier on bottom would take the brunt of the damage.

"Which side do you want to be on?" the German asked her, yanking her attention away from the scene of clambering comrades, more monkeys than men. Wait—they weren't expected to share yet, were they?

"Excuse me?"

"Top or bottom? Which bunk do you want?"

"...You're asking me?"

"Yes...?"

"Don't you have a preference?"

The German shrugged. "Sure, but one must be gracious to one's comrades if we are to fight together." That grin again. She reminded herself to breathe.

Cate tore her eyes away from his face and assessed the scaffold, then him, with a raised eyebrow. The German was only a few inches taller than her, but he was broad-shouldered and well-muscled. If the upper bunk were to give way from underneath him, she would invariably be crushed by his ... well. The thought of being under him didn't wholly upset her, to be honest, as he was a fairly well-formed man. Regardless, though, from a practical standpoint...

"Top," she asserted firmly and gave him a curt nod of thanks. He shrugged affably and tossed himself back on the bottom bunk, crossing his legs at the ankles and bringing his arms up behind his head with a sigh.

Cate lingered. Yes. A very well-formed man indeed.

————

The sun was beginning to set, casting long shadows across the parade ground as Henry and the rest of Squad Seven wandered around the fort, waiting for their squad's turn to be examined. He was grateful that it was easy to follow the others to their next destination, because all the limestone buildings looked much the same. The examinations had been implemented in the order the squads were formed that morning, so being Squad Seven, they ended up dead last. Their company wasn't full yet, at only fifty odd men thus far, and Captain Noah had suggested they pass the time by writing to their friends back home and encouraging them to join up. Of course, with the title of corporal dangling like a carrot over his head, Elias took this very seriously and went hunting for paper and a pencil. Henry assumed Charles Smith had similarly struck out to write correspondence, because he had disappeared shortly after.

Those that remained took a stroll up to the Half Moon Battery, which overlooked the bluffs at the confluence of the two rivers. They stood along the rail, speculating about the inspection and the drills expected in the morning, but the view was so tremendous, it commanded their singular attention. To the left lay the deep, blue valley of the Mississippi and to the right, the broad stream of the Minnesota River. It flowed through a comparatively open vale, with swelling hills and intermingling forest and prairie visible for what must have been miles upriver. A triangular island was formed between the rivers that lay immediately under the fort. Its level surface was partially cultivated, but towards the farther shore, it was thickly covered with wood. Beyond their junction, the united streams glided at the base of high cliffs into the narrowing valley below. Forests buffered the river from the prairie that sprawled to the horizon.

While the river valley had already been cast into twilight, when he turned and looked opposite toward the Round Bastion, the US flag flying just east of its base was still kissed in sunlight as it flapped in the evening breeze. Henry had never really thought much of the flag before, but now that he was laying his life on the line for his country, its symbol suddenly felt more personal.

Many of the men from the other squads and from Companies I and G were laughing, singing songs, and playing raucous games of euchre. Other squads filtered through the parade ground below, undergoing their exams and then being dismissed. It was frustrating to still be waiting when everyone else was already celebrating.

Finally, Sergeant Osborn returned and led their squad to line up on the parade ground.

Bathed in the pink shadows of the setting sun, Lieutenant Thomas called men to line up by their surnames, repeating roll as the eight of them arranged themselves in alphabetical order. Henry was pleased to see Charles Smith again, even though his hands were deep in his pockets and his shoulders up near his ears. Henry reminded himself that this fellow was probably terrified he'd be discovered underage for enlistment. His smooth chin was set forward as he carefully followed the officers with his eyes.

Giving the boy a nudge with his elbow, Henry muttered, "I don't know about you, but I'm getting pretty sick of waiting."

Smith looked up at him, his brown eyes round and hard under dark brows. Henry delivered his most ingratiating smile in response and offered a hand. "I don't think we've been formally introduced. I'm Henry Schaefer."

The boy glanced down at his hand and then back up. He didn't respond and he didn't take Henry's hand either. Henry faltered; he hadn't expected such a cold greeting after making such an effort to be gracious.

"And you are Smith, right?" he prompted, his smile wavering.

The boy blinked. "Charles Smith." His voice was small, a further sign that this boy was likely not of an age to enlist. Henry could see why he might be put off at the moment. It probably had nothing to do with Henry and everything to do with nerves in the face of a physical exam which could very well reveal him as underage. The weight of those nerves had likely been weighing him down all day.

Henry smiled, letting his hand drop, and said, "Well, Smith, I'm happy to know you."

Smith gave a curt nod, training his eyes back on the ground. Henry looked down the line and noticed that the surgeon had begun his inspection, a recruiting officer accompanying him and taking notes in the roster. Turning back to Smith, Henry gripped his shoulder and leaned in to whisper, "We were watching the inspections of the other squads from the battery and I don't think you have anything to worry about."

Smith's brows knitted together and somehow, his eyes managed to grow wider and more guarded. "What's that supposed to mean?"

"Oh, sorry, I don't mean to presume, but you look young is all," Henry said, pulling his hand back as Smith shrugged him off. "For service. But I heard the surgeon is wore out from all the exams he's done today and is just asking basic questions."

Smith blinked at him, arms crossed across his chest.

"So I don't think you have anything to worry about," Henry concluded. "I'm sure by now the man's so cross-eyed he couldn't tell a soldier from a settee."

Henry grinned but found himself the only one amused. The boy gave him that stare again, like he was speaking a different language.

"You sure like to talk," Smith observed.

"Do I?" Henry frowned. "I guess I've never had the chance to find out before."

Smith deliberately set his inscrutable stare back on the surgeon. Undeterred, Henry tilted his head and continued to study his new comrade-in-arms. As rude as this kid was, he felt like he understood how he felt. After all, he had been the young one out in his own family for far too long. He kind of liked being on the other side of that, feeling like the elder for once. And underneath the boy's veneer of irritation was thick and palpable anxiety, an anxiety Henry recognized.

"I have two older brothers," Henry continued by way of explanation. "Between the two of them, I could never get a word in edgewise. I suppose I do like to talk, but I've never had the chance to find out until now. It's kind of nice not being interrupted all the time."

Smith looked over at him and raised a brow. He opened his mouth as if to say something but right then, Sergeant Osborn approached, watching the two of them with a warning look and allowing his proximity to quiet them rather than barking at them for silence.

———

Cate's heart pounded like her ribs were the drummer boy's snare. She leaned forward to look down the line at the surgeon making his way toward her, the orderly sergeant taking careful note at his side. It didn't look like he was inspecting the men too closely, and he certainly wasn't asking anyone to remove their clothes, which was in itself a great relief. All afternoon, she'd been terrified that she was going to be strip-searched in front of the whole company, and her fear had been so palpable that she could barely choke down any food or drink.

"Don't worry, it's all going to go fine."

The overly familiar whispers of Henry Schaefer were the last thing she needed right now. Poor fool could go play big brother with someone else. At any other time, his tedious attempts at conversation would be more tolerable—perhaps even enjoyable to get to know someone in her unit—but none of that could happen until she got this physical exam over with. For there was a non-zero chance that her service would end right here. Her fate depended on the surgeon. She could only hope that this well-intentioned blockhead was right.

She looked up a few inches at Henry Schaefer. He had a wild thatch of straw-colored hair atop a square face set with kind, open eyes. Most certainly German, as if the name hadn't already been a dead give-away. His skin was tanned, probably from working a farm somewhere. And he had remarkably good teeth...

She inwardly shook herself. What was wrong with her? She had much more important things to worry about than the relative dental hygiene of her comrades right now. Such as mentally preparing to subvert the surgeon's assessment of her fitness for service. It went without saying that lacking a male member was likely high on the list of disqualifying physical defects.

"I know," she hissed at him, glaring and then looking pointedly toward Sergeant Osborn standing near them. "Shut. Up."

Henry put his hands up in surrender and pressed his lips together in a pledge to silence. He still had a stupid smile pinching into his cheeks, like he thought her irritation was amusing. It sparked her temper, though she couldn't be certain whether she was more irritated with him for his condescension or herself for finding it utterly charming. Nothing about a man making light of her distress, regardless of the reason, was charming, no matter how good-looking he was. She'd do well to remember that.

The surgeon was nearly upon them and Cate hoped he couldn't hear her heart beating out of her chest. He had a truly enormous beard, perhaps compensating for the thinning tuft at the top of his head, and a mustache so long it seemed to curl completely around his upper lip and into his mouth. His blue eyes were drawn and lined with fatigue as they danced over each man in turn. As he neared, she focused on the questions he was asking the men ahead of her. Name? Age? Occupation? These were all questions they'd already been asked upon enlisting so she inferred that he was checking their roster for accuracy.

It seemed like both an eternity and a half second when he began to address Henry Schaefer.

"Name?"

"Heinrich Schaefer." Definitely German. He didn't even anglicize the pronunciation.

The orderly sergeant's brows flew together at the foreign sound of the name. "...Can you spell that?"

The surgeon looked supremely put-upon as Schaefer took the time to spell his full name for the orderly sergeant.

"Age?"

"I turned twenty-two in May," Schaefer replied.

"Occupation?"

"Farmhand."

Cate glanced at him sidelong, feeling a little smug with herself for guessing his work correctly. Although in Minnesota, even in St. Anthony, guessing a man's occupation was farming was like guessing a flipped coin would come up heads.

"Do you have any defects that would prevent you from serving your country on the field of battle?"

"No, sir."

"Show hands please," the surgeon said. His beard was so large, his mouth was completely obscured, and the whiskers seemed to flap about of their own volition.

Schaefer held out his hands and the surgeon studied them. Cate couldn't imagine what he was looking for—a missing trigger finger, perhaps? She glanced down at her own hands and wondered if her fingernails were too effeminate or her wrists too fine-boned. Though she had calmed considerably already having watched the previous examinations with scarcely anything that could be construed as invasive or potentially revealing for the concealment of her sex, her heart pounded nonetheless. She had no idea if there was some medical way of telling a woman by her hands. Certainly if she had been a lady, her hands would have been soft and delicate, but her time as a laundress had worn her hands rougher than Richard's.

The surgeon nodded at Schaefer after inspecting his perfect teeth and then leveled his gaze on Cate. She squared her face and met his gaze as evenly as she could, bearing down on her nerves with the force of her determination. If she did not entertain the possibility of being discovered, surely it couldn't do anything but work to her benefit.

"Name?" he asked perfunctorily.

"Charles Smith, sir," she confirmed. She thought the orderly sergeant looked relieved as he easily checked her off.

"Age?" the surgeon droned. Here came her first hurdle. When she had enlisted, she had been informed of the age limitations and the need for parental permission if one was under twenty-one. So she had listed twenty-one, even though in her man's guise, she knew she didn't look a day over eighteen.[9] But she had written it at the time, thinking it would be best to ensure she didn't have to jump through any such foolish hoops as acquiring her parents' permission to enlist.

"Twenty-one, sir," she stated clearly, covering her nerves with as thick a layer of confidence as she could muster.

The surgeon eyed her for a long moment, and she could see Henry Schaefer out of the corner of her eye watching her with far too much earnestness to appear anything less than suspicious. She held the gaze of the surgeon evenly, almost daring him to challenge her. He opened his whiskers as if to say something, but then glanced at the rapidly accumulating twilight and gave a shrug to the sergeant. The orderly eyed her, but marked her off in his ledger nonetheless.

"Occupation?"

"Lumberman, sir."

"Do you have any defects, physical or mental, that would prevent you from serving your country on the field of battle?"

Cate compelled herself to maintain eye contact. "No, sir." Her fists curled tightly at her sides.

"Show hands," the surgeon repeated. Cate swallowed hard and held out her hands. Her fingers were long and slender, with what would have been elegantly rounded fingernails if they weren't swollen at the cuticles with chilblains. She'd been taking in laundry on the sly while Richard was clerking for the mayor to save up for this particular adventure.

"Are these chilblains caused by working the logs on the river?" the surgeon asked. Cate would have to thank this man for making things so easy for her.

"Yes, sir," she affirmed almost too eagerly.

The surgeon nodded knowingly. "Open and close your hands."

Cate did so.

"Teeth," he demanded. As she opened her mouth, he took only a cursory glance before nodding at the sergeant and moving on to the next man. Cate stared after him for a moment.

Was that all? She could scarcely believe her good luck. She had been so fearful that she'd face a full physical examination, where every inch of their bodies would be inspected for defect. She understood the regulation was to do a full stripped physical exam. She was abundantly grateful that this particular outfit was not deigning to take the time such an endeavor would entail. To be honest, if she had been a commanding officer, she supposed she would have prioritized training too.

When she looked up, Henry Schaefer cracked that crooked smile. His eyebrows lifted as if to say, See, I told you. Cate firmly rejected the urge to look up at him coyly—some feminine habits were hard to break in the presence of a man with shoulders like that—but she couldn't help her lips curving into a small, relieved smile. Lifting her fist, she shook it briefly at Henry. He grinned, shaking his fist in return.

After inspecting each man individually, the surgeon ordered the new recruits to march across the parade ground and back. Then, he nodded to Sergeant Osborn, who read them the Articles of War and dismissed them for the evening.

And that was that. Once the company was full, they'd have a formal muster ceremony, but for all intents and purposes, she was officially a member of the Second Regiment of Minnesota, Company K. As she stood in the twilight, surrounded by her squad-mates who were whooping and giving each other those half man-hugs, she felt a sense of clear purpose for what felt like the first time in recent memory. She was going to fight for something that mattered.

———

VI

Monday, August 5, 1861

WHEN *REVEILLE* SOUNDED, CATE WAS already awake. Which would not have been a problem in the slightest, if she hadn't been trying to sneak quietly out of the officer's latrines. The sun hadn't even peaked over the horizon, but it was already hot and had been for some days now. Cate slipped out of the latrine as quietly as she could and softly replaced the door in its frame, her eyes darting up and down the pathway that ran between the fort wall and the kitchens of the officers quarters.

"Soldier."

Cate winced, her shoulders shooting up near her ears, before she turned and regarded whomever it was with as placid an expression as she could muster.

"Sir?"

The officer was a lieutenant, by his stripes, pale and lean with side locks whose fullness was emphasized by his clean-shaven chin. Cate didn't recognize him, so he must have been a Company G or I officer.

"If you are in need of a privy, I think you will find the soldier sinks perfectly serviceable." His eyes narrowed as they pointed at her hand, still on the latrine door. Cate pressed her lips together to keep herself from pointing out that there was absolutely nothing serviceable about a flimsy scaffold jutting out from the steep north bluff with a series of holes cut in, allowing the user's waste to free-fall a hundred feet into the river. Instead, she forced her eyes downward and gave a stilted nod.

"Yes, sir. It won't happen again, sir."

The lieutenant stood silently for a moment before she realized he was waiting for her to leave.

"Am I dismissed, sir?" she prompted. The lieutenant blinked. He must have been one of those green officers who'd never been in the army before and was still getting accustomed to its hierarchical protocol.

"Yes, dismissed," he said, fumbling his awkwardness away with a straighter spine and a sterner expression. Cate nodded and tried to keep her stride dignified as she hustled back to her barrack. The rest of the squad would already be waking and she didn't want them to get too curious about where she'd been.

Cate had only two weeks of army experience, but in that time she'd learned a great deal about relieving herself in secret. Not only were the officer latrines were much more sanitary than the soldier sinks by virtue of the fact that they were built over a naturally occurring chasm along the southeast wall, but they were private, with six individual stalls. Using them meant timing her bowels a lot more than was strictly convenient, but she was beginning to get into a routine.

Although, now that she had been caught out, she would need to think again about when to acquire her morning relief. Unless she could secure a series of rapid promotions, she'd just have to hold it until the officers were busy with their breakfasts and prepping for their morning drills.

As she crossed the dusty parade ground, she overshot her bunk room and climbed the far end of the boardwalk to ensure that if anyone saw her approach, she was coming from the direction of the soldier sinks. The windows of the barracks were all flung wide open day and night to circulate the air, but when temperatures were pushing one hundred degrees, there was little to be done to improve the poor ventilation of the rooms.

Which was in evidence when a wall of thick, stifling air greeted her in the bunk room, reeking with the malodor of perspiring men. Though *reveille* had concluded, most of the fellows were slow to rise in the swampy heat and there was a lot of snorting and grumbling as they stirred in their beds. She padded to her bunk quietly, slipped off her coat, and began scaling the scaffold when Henry Schaefer rolled over and grumbled on the lower pallet.

Most of the other boys had taken to sleeping in various states of increasing undress during the heatwave, and Schaefer was no exception, opting to rest in naught but his shirt. As he rolled languorously toward the edge, his eyes not yet open, he flipped his leg over the side of his bunk. His lack of blanket or drawers left her with quite a lot of pale thigh to consider.

She swallowed, hanging halfway up the scaffold for a few seconds, unable to shake her gaze from the stretch of flesh. It wasn't just a bit of thigh. It was his whole leg and a fair amount of buttock.

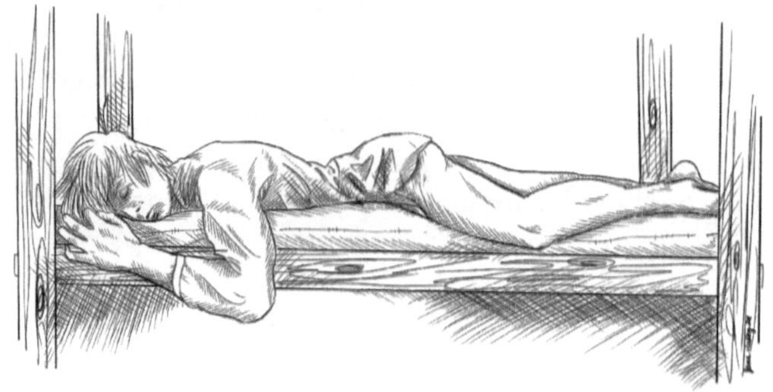

Schaefer looked up at her bleary eyed, and Cate bit the inside of her cheek hard, if for no other reason than to punish herself for leering. She frowned disapprovingly at him to distract from the fact that her cheeks were burning. Lord, she was lucky she was not actually a man, because the unbidden arousal that sight had inspired most certainly would not have gone unnoticed.

"Where were you off to this early?" he asked, squinting up at her through one eye as though keeping the other closed could somehow prolong his rest. "Nature called," she shrugged, looking over at the wall so she didn't have to try and meet his eyes when his flank was on such obscene display. She had never seen legs like that on a man before. Most men wore trousers so loose the shape of their legs were a mystery. Any legs she'd had the opportunity to see unshrouded had bore the lean, sinewy signs of hard work, or, as in Richard's case, the thin underdevelopment of a man confined to study. A man's legs had never struck her as an object of desire. But these ... *Jesus*. Schaefer's thighs were thick, well more than she could wrap two hands around. Milky white and lightly fuzzed with blonde hair. Powerful. Endurable.

Cate flung herself into her bunk and buried her flaming face in her pillow. What in hell's name was she doing? Sure, there was no privacy to speak of in the barracks, so it was a matter of course that they'd all see one another in a state of undress. And lechery seemed to be a currency of fraternity in this all-male environment, but not by any means applied to one another. Cate had to get to the war front, not just to get out of the state and the legal obligations of her marriage, but to fight to make a goddamn difference. If she were caught out now for unmanly behavior, she'd be delivered right back into her former life and that would be unbearable. She needed to get a hold of herself, stop attracting untoward attention, and maybe earn corporal while she was at it. A challenge to be certain, because Sergeant Osborn had already mentioned favoring Elias Hower and the conceited fellow was doing his level best to appear as though he deserved it.

Hearing the scaffold creak, she glanced over with one eye. Henry Schaefer regarded her with a raised brow, his full height bringing him eye level with her.

"Time to get up, Sleeping Beauty," he teased. His smile, unlike his teeth, was crooked, and it was not at all fair that the morning light filtering through the window lit up his chaotic hair like some sort of halo.

"Smith, you got the day and the night mixed up again?" Robinson piled on. Cate rolled her eyes. If she'd learned anything in her first few weeks in the army, it was that the boys loved to rib each other. Truly, every other thing out of their mouths was some sort of jibe. It was exhausting.

"Or did you get double guard duty again?" Schaefer teased. Cate fought the urge to hit him and failed, smacking her pillow out at his face. He ducked and laughed. "Jesus, still sore about that, are you?"

She was still sore. Literally. She'd had a hell of a time with the fellows in Squad Six trying to steal her rations last week and she'd finally had enough of it, so she'd popped the nearest bastard in the nose and earned a sore jaw and double guard duty as reward. It'd been somewhat liberating to finally let loose her frustration, but it also hurt enough that she was loath to repeat the performance. At least the sonsofbitches had moved on to fresher prey.

The dynamic in her own squad wasn't much different. They all seemed to know each other and ragged on one another incessantly. Half the time, she didn't understand that they were joking, and it made her look like an ignoramus. She hated it.

Realizing that waiting for her embarrassment to fade was a futile task, she peeled herself off her sweat-damp bed, scrubbed her hands through her short curls, and waited until Schaefer had occupied himself with his trousers before slipping off the edge to the floor. Keeping her eyes carefully averted from the entirely too provocative enrobing display Schaefer unwittingly performed, she snatched up her hat and pushed her oily hair back underneath it.

While the rest of the boys had a great deal more dressing to do, Cate had no choice but to sleep nearly fully clothed. She even wore her waistcoat to bed, fearful that her stays would be visible through her shirt if she didn't have an additional layer on, especially when she was perspiring. Which was all the time now.

As she plucked her trousers away from her sticky legs, she grimaced. She'd been in the same clothes for the past two weeks and it was untenable. She'd performed her escape in somewhat of a rush, dashing on a set of clothes she'd nicked from the Pioneer lumber mill laundry over her chemise and corded stays. It hadn't occurred to her that another set of clothes would be necessary because surely, the army outfitted soldiers with uniforms. But the Federal government hadn't shown up with the goods yet, which meant that even if she could find a private place to change her clothes, she didn't have anything else to put on. It didn't matter how much she washed with a cup of water and cloth in the officer latrine; if she didn't have clean clothes to change into, she was condemned to perpetual malodor. Outside of the immediate horror of being conspicuously filthy, her monthly courses were drawing near and this was becoming more and more of an immediately pressing problem.

Cate wrinkled her nose as she shrugged her coat back on, catching a whiff of her own foul stench. As a laundress and a human person, this state of filth was disgusting, humiliating, and completely unacceptable. She needed to find a way to get her clothes to the laundresses. Last week, Schaefer had offered her one of his shirts and she'd been so humiliated to realize he'd noticed her smell and so terrified of how much she might enjoy wearing Schaefer's shirt, she'd practically bitten his head off.

She was surviving. She had to keep reminding herself of that. She was sharing a room with seven other men and somehow managing to keep her sex a secret without raising suspicion. Despite being sleep-deprived and a bit thirsty from her efforts to limit the number of trips she had to take to the latrine, she was doing well in drills. And while she certainly didn't fit in with the other boys (Lord, how could she—she'd never in her life been in such close confines with so many men), she wasn't a pariah by any means. Her altercation with the fellows from Squad Six last week, though setting her back considerably in Sergeant Osborn's regard, had earned a sort of incredulous respect from her own squad, which, in spite of the ache in her jaw, was surprisingly satisfying.

"Smith!"

Cate startled. Schaefer was looking at her funny. What had she done now?

"Elias asked you a question," he said by way of explanation.

Cate looked over at the doorway where Elias Hower stood. For a second, her heart thumped, just as it did any time she was paid undivided attention. The fear of being discovered was always present, keeping her shoulders tense and her nerves jumpy.

"Smith, have you seen my hat?" Hower repeated somewhat more impatiently. Cate's eyes flickered over the other men in the room. They were all staring at her in a way that made her arch a brow.

"Of course not, what would I want with your hat?" she said. "As you can clearly see, I have one of my own." She doffed it for emphasis.

Elias Hower leveled her with a grim stare, suspicious but lacking in evidence to convict. He looked from one man to the other. Fatherly Thomas Webster shrugged. John Williamson, a gangly fellow with big ears, looked at Jacob Robinson who looked back at Williamson and they both had the dumbest grins on their faces. If Cate was a betting man, she'd put her money on the two of them as the culprits. Wilbur Krüger, a stout German swathed in hair both front and back, scratched his head.

After an overly long silence, Hower threw his hands up and stormed out into the early dawn. As soon as he was well away, Williamson and Robinson began snickering. Williamson pulled a hat out from under his pillow and dropped it on his head.

"Fellas, be quiet. Tattoo means lights out!" he mocked in what was apparently his best Elias Hower voice. Robinson snatched the hat from his head and put it on his own.

"Here comes the lieutenant! Hurry and look smart while I lick his boots!"

All the boys were cracking up now. Schaefer kneeled on Robinson's bed to reach across and his friend tossed it to him. He pulled the floppy felt over his own head and said, "You boys better believe that when I'm corporal, I'll have you all court-martialed for that!"

Cate was fairly certain she'd actually heard Hower say as much. Something like a smile was teasing her lips when Schaefer pulled the hat off his head and tumbled it down his arm towards her. She stared at it for a moment, and realized the rest of the squad was watching her expectantly.

"Keep it," she said, affronted. "I don't want his lice."

The squad broke into a gale of laughter. Cate tried to keep her mouth firmly serious but failed quite miserably.

————

At present, their drills were being conducted with sticks rather than actual rifles. Henry had a sizable one he'd found near the mouth of Minnehaha Creek with the perfect knot to serve as a trigger guard. As Lieutenant Thomas led their company through the different forms of the School of the Soldier, Henry noticed with satisfaction that he was beginning to have space for thought as he executed the positions.

"Shoulder ARMS!" shouted Lieutenant Thomas.

Henry positioned his stick on his right shoulder, feeling his finger curl gratifyingly around the knot of his pretend trigger guard, and his eyes sought out the top of the Round Bastion, where civilians gathered to observe their drills. While it was pleasant to be admired by the unenlisted, the primary object of Henry's wandering gaze were the ladies. And lo, there they were, waving fans in the oppressive heat, carrying parasols and whispering to one another in their bell-shaped summer dresses. Henry stood a little taller, wishing fervently that their company had uniforms and rifles while being thus displayed to the public.

"Support ARMS!"

Henry switched his stick into the crook of his left arm and held his hand flat over his stomach. While Elias was single-mindedly pursuing his new dream of being promoted, Jacob was pursuing the visiting ladies with the same doggedness. He'd managed to get one girl writing to him from St. Paul and was hoping to get a pass to take her on a stroll Sunday afternoon. Henry was still annoyed that he'd got stuck with guard duty the day Jacob had been flirting with ladies on their usual leisure. Jacob was confident that Henry would have had a similar opportunity to attract a doting pen pal, if he'd only been there.

"Rest!"

Henry brought his right hand up to support what would have been the stock of his stick. He looked up again at the edge of the Round Bastion. They were too far away to discern the age or beauty of the visitors but that didn't stop him from squinting his eyes in order to try.

"Eyes RIGHT!"

Henry turned his head slightly to the right and found himself looking into the eyes of Lieutenant Thomas. The lieutenant gave him a flat stare and that was more than enough of a reprimand for Henry.

"Eyes FRONT!"

Henry adjusted his gaze forward and resolved to focus on the drill. Charles Smith was ahead of him in ranks. His dark brown curls were slicked to his neck with sweat. He was a tough nut. He insisted on sleeping in his clothes and never changed his garments; he didn't seem to have as much as a spare shirt. He stank to high heaven and never fetched any water to give himself a cursory wash in the mornings. His face constantly looked like he was facing down a herd of stampeding horses, but any attempt to help him was greeted with the prickliest defenses. Henry supposed there were greater sins than pride, but it was increasingly difficult to feel bad for him when he regarded Henry's offer of one of his spare shirts with such unbridled offense as to border on disgust.

The orderly appeared just then and tapped Lieutenant Thomas on the shoulder. The lieutenant listened, then nodded.

"At ease, soldiers," Lieutenant Thomas commanded. "We are issuing you boys uniforms this afternoon."

Henry's heart leapt. Wish a thing enough and it appears!

"They are not federal issue—those still haven't come through. But you will be expected to wear these uniforms for daily duties and keep them clean and presentable for dress parade."

Jacob turned to Henry and shrugged. "Better than nothing, I guess."

Henry supposed he agreed. But he really wanted that navy blue coat with the brass buttons. The forage cap with the Union badge on it. Without the uniform, it felt more like they were playing at soldier than actually training to be one.

Lieutenant Thomas closed their drill and directed their company to march to the Quartermaster's Office. There, he called roll and each man of their squad was measured for a hat and trousers before being issued plain, dark pantaloons, a blue wool overshirt, two cotton shirts, drawers, and black hat.

Jacob frowned at the overshirt. "Don't they know it's hot as hellfire out here? Tell me they don't mean for us to wear this in this weather."

Henry shrugged but didn't wholly disagree. The wool of the shirt was light, but it was coarse and wanted for an undershirt to protect the skin from chafing.

With their new makeshift uniforms in hand, they all hoofed it back to their barracks to try it all on. As the rest of the boys dropped their trousers in exchange for their new ones, Henry couldn't help but notice Charles Smith wasn't among them. This wasn't the first time this happened. The boy was often missing only to materialize again right when he was needed, pretending like he'd never been unaccounted for. No one would blame him if he was bashful—although they'd certainly tease him for it. Henry thought it was a bit endearing, but of course, if he said anything about it, he'd get rowed up. Henry tried not to be too annoyed about it as he undressed and pulled on his new clothes.

———

Cate stripped down to nothing but her boots and stockings inside the officer's latrine stall and scrubbed her skin with a handkerchief wetted from her tin cup. It was futile. She needed to buy a bar of soap from the sutler and ... and somehow find privacy and space and a small wash basin. Her hair needed scrubbing and her skin needed to *breathe*.

On the day Cate had left St. Anthony, she'd worn her own chemise and corded stays underneath the men's clothing. She'd just felt so naked already in the trousers that to waltz around town with her breasts flying free felt like a tempting of fate. She still felt terrified by the prospect of leaving off the stays and moving about the fort unbound, even though it was horribly hot and she was fairly small-chested and the stays were stained yellow with sweat. Besides, she couldn't very well hand the stays and chemise to the laundresses and ask to have them washed. Yet another thing she'd need space and water and privacy to clean.

There was nothing for it. She had to find a way. No matter how she looked at it, the biggest problem was that she needed to find a sustainable way to keep herself clean. All the other fellows did standing baths in the barracks, some scrubbing themselves under the cover of their shirts while others threw modesty to the wind. (It was entirely unfair and also probably very good that Henry Schaefer was the former sort, and Wilbur Krüger was the latter.) Cate imagined she would work her way up to washing with modesty as the others did, but she couldn't get herself to do it yet. She was trapped in a horrible cycle of filth, and it was drawing more attention to her than it would have if she just bathed like the rest of them did.

None of this ruminating was a productive use of her tenuous time in the officer's latrine, though. Once Cate managed to scrub her skin raw enough to resemble feeling clean, she pulled the first of her two standard issue shirts on over her bare chest. She pulled on the drawers and trousers next. Then, with the same sense of shame and comfort as a child who clung to a security blanket, she put her stays back on. They would prevent her from doing any sort of standing bath in the barracks, but she couldn't stomach the idea anyway, let alone execute it, so it didn't matter. Over the stays went her second shirt, and over that, the new wool overshirt. She was already sweating.

———

John Williamson laughed, donning his hat and haphazard uniform. "Attention Squad!"

Henry played along, standing tall and steady next to his bunk, his heels in line and his thumbs touching the side seams of his trousers.

Jacob shrugged the overshirt on and looked Henry up and down. "Hey, where'd you get the same shirt as me?"

"Oh, you know, here and there," Henry replied.

"Oh, doggone! I got the same one too." Elias put in, his own uniform shoved on over his shirt. "Maybe I'll trade this one in for one with some officer's stripes."

"You know what they say about wishful thinking." Smith had materialized near the doorway, dressed in his new uniform and acting like he'd been there the whole time. His overshirt and trousers sagged adorably, like a boy trying on his older brother's clothes. Henry tried to ignore him.

"How do I look?" Henry asked the room with no small amount of swagger.

Smith raised discerning eyebrow and looked down his nose at Henry. "Looks a little small."

"Well, maybe you and Schaefer should trade?" Thomas Webster suggested, and if Henry didn't know better, he would have thought he was serious.

Smith clearly did think he was serious, as he cringed and fervently exclaimed, "I think not!"

Henry frowned. Lots of the boys liked to rag on each other, but when Charles Smith did it, it didn't feel like a joke. Whatever tentative comradery they'd had that first day must have been some sort of aberration, brought on by the boy's fear of the physical exam, because all of their interactions since then had been utterly off-putting. Henry made a point of being friendly—he'd gone out of his way on several occasions to try and include the boy. But Charles Smith was stubborn as a mule and twice as disagreeable, and for whatever reason, the kinder Henry tried to be, the more he got verbally kicked in the teeth.

"Where've you been?" Henry asked pointedly. He wondered if Smith would squirm knowing his disappearance had been noticed, but he didn't. He just shrugged and said, "Nature called."

Henry rolled his eyes. "And you decided to get dressed in there too?" What a harrowing notion. The soldier sinks were nothing more than a ramshackle hut perched on the edge of the bluff. Every time Henry used it, he had visions of himself plummeting 200 feet to his death with his trousers around his knees.

Smith's lip curled. "No point in wasting time, is there?" And then he turned on his heel and started to leave again.

Henry reached out and grabbed his arm. "Now where are you going?"

Smith jerked away. "What are you, my mother?"

"I'd hate to see you miss another roll call."

"Good thing I have someone like you to look out for me," Smith retorted, just as sarcastic. "I'm just taking my things to the laundry. Don't get your dander up."

He stalked off down the covered walkway. Henry couldn't help but glare out the window, watching his progress.

"Why do you let him get under your skin so easy?" Elias said with a passing glance. "Just let him reap what he sows."

Henry crossed his arms. "I guess. I just—I'd hate to be in a life or death situation with him. I don't trust him to choose duty over pride." Also, Smith seemed to detest him and it was killing Henry that he couldn't figure out why.

Elias hissed in a breath between his teeth. "Well, we almost certainly will."

———

VII

Cate twisted her neck under the raw wool of her new shirt collar as she strode down the boardwalk with her laundry. The laundresses of the fort set themselves up near the well, which was dug in the middle of the gravel walkway at the southern end of the parade grounds. The sutler and the munitions house were both nearby, the shadow of the Round Tower stretching over them as the sun set. She knew the wife of Robert Nelson, corporal to Squad Six, was amongst those employed to handle the laundry for their company.

Cate wondered for a moment how her fate might have been different if she had joined up as a woman in that role instead. After all, it would have been significantly easier than mitigating the constant threat of being discovered and discharged. But if she had enlisted as herself, she would increase the chance that Richard would find her. Besides, while it was a constant concern that her comrades would figure out that she was one cock short of a man, the work was far and away both easier and more purposeful than laundry. Cate refused to accept that the only way women could support the war effort was by washing soldiers' sweaty shirts. She was strong enough and fast enough to keep up with whatever the officers threw at them. The fact that she wasn't allowed to enlist based on some misfortune of birth was ridiculous.

Cate had another purpose in visiting the laundresses. Her monthly courses were imminent and she needed more than a flimsy handkerchief to keep the whole situation in check. She needed guard-napkins—baby diapers would do in a pinch—but she had no idea how to ferret out where to find them without compromising her secret. It didn't bear thinking of that it was possible they might not arrive. Richard hadn't been a particularly demanding husband, but he hadn't been celibate either. She'd taken precautions, using the wash discreetly obtained at the pharmacist, but the fear that she could be in a delicate way far outweighed the pressure of finding a solution to manage getting her courses in secret. She firmly set herself in preparation for the latter and entirely avoided considering the former. She'd survey the laundry—perhaps an inspired solution would present itself.

The laundresses were chatting and laughing as they each worked a different role in the laundering process. One woman, stout and loud, scrubbed shirts against a washboard held between her knees as she sat on a stool before a wide wash basin. A second, with a tangle of red hair coiled at the back of her neck, was boiling the shirts like a witch's brew in a massive kettle over a fire, while a third woman was wringing out cleaned shirts with intimidating strength. A fourth woman, older than the rest with graying brown hair escaping a cotton sun bonnet, snapped the shirts out in the breeze and placed them in a heaping basket, which Cate presumed they would then take out to dry on lines, or perhaps shrubs and bushes, outside of the fort walls. It was this laundress that Cate approached.

"Good afternoon," she said politely, dipping her voice down for Charles Smith's husky tenor. "How much to have a few pieces laundered?"

The woman looked up at Cate—or rather, Charles—and regarded him for a long moment.

"How many pieces have you got?" she finally replied, her sharp, blue gaze making Cate feel a little wrong-footed.

"Just a few—socks, trousers, shirt, waistcoat," Cate replied, unfastening her bundle to show the laundress. The chemise, pointedly not included in her laundry, was tucked in a tight bundle in her trousers pocket, awaiting yet another strike of innovative problem-solving.

"Is that all?" she replied and then wrinkled her nose as she took a closer look at what Cate had brought. "Oh, little lamb, when was the last time you had these washed?"

Cate pressed her lips together sheepishly. The woman pursed her lips in response and held out a hand. "Oh, hand it here. We'll get these done for you by tomorrow, most like. It's ten cents per piece and an extra three if you want 'em ironed."

Cate's brows couldn't help but shoot up at the price. It paid to have a corner on the market, apparently. Struggling to train her expression to polite neutrality, she nodded and dug in her pocket for her coin purse.

"No need to pay until they're all done," the woman replied, gathering up Cate's bundle.

"Oh, thank you," Cate said. As expensive as it was, she didn't mind paying these ladies. It was a hard job, made harder by her own neglect, and she didn't envy them the task.

———

When Henry came out of the sutler, a letter held gingerly in his hands, he saw Smith talking bashfully with the laundresses. His big doe eyes were round and his lips twitched up in a cordial smile, all deference and boyish manners. This should not have bothered Henry. This should not have tracked with him at all. Maybe it was the letter addressed to him in his brother's hand, or the hot weather, but whatever it was, just the sight of Smith set Henry's teeth on edge. Nice to know the sonofabitch had every capacity to be cordial. He just didn't deign to treat his comrades with that same sort of regard.

Henry skirted the laundresses and stepped up onto the boardwalk as he unfolded the letter from Peter. Skimming the lines dashed out in German, he almost didn't see Jacob and Elias, sitting in the shade on the edge of the boardwalk.

"Whatcha got there, Schaef?" Elias asked as he snatched the letter from Henry's hands. He looked at it for a moment and frowned at the German words. Henry glowered at him and snatched it back.

"Letter from my brother."

"One of the ones in the First Minnesota? Oh bully! Were they in the battle at Bull Run?" Jacob asked eagerly, turning round.

"Um, yes." Henry shifted uncomfortably. It was difficult to not remind himself that he could have been there with them.

"Did they kill any Rebs?" Elias grinned. "Or did they run away with the other cowards like they said in the paper."

"That was unconscionable," Jacob commented. "If I'd been there, I would have stood the line and fought. Wish they'd hurry up and send us out to the front."

"I don't know about any of that," Henry said slowly. "Peter didn't say."

"Well, what did he say?"

Henry looked back down at the letter and felt a flock of unnameable feelings surge in his chest. He cleared his throat. "He says they saw heavy fighting. He said it was hard to tell who was friend or foe. They were commended, I guess, for their bearing, though, as the two other regiments in their battalion returned in confusion."

Jacob scoffed. "At least our Minnesota boys were brave enough to stand their ground."

Henry opened his mouth to reply, but Elias said, "Small consolation for that embarrassment. Dear God, this was our first chance to show those Rebs that they can't just change the rules whenever they don't like what the rest of us voted for. And we ran away. It's disgraceful."

"I think what Henry's brother was trying to say is that they didn't run away," Jacob pointed out. "The papers—at least the national ones—ain't telling that story."

"Should they?" Elias countered, and the two of them devolved into debate about whether one regiment acting with honor constituted newsworthiness when the whole of the battle had ended in an embarrassing and disorganized retreat. Henry stood awkwardly with his letter for a moment, trying to determine whether he should wait for a chance to get a word in or cut his losses and go. It didn't seem to matter to his friends that his brothers were alive and safe, thanks for asking. Or that Henry was not sure how he felt being trapped here, unsure if he'd ever see action, while his brothers came home heroes. Or didn't. He swallowed that down and stuffed the letter in his pocket as he turned away from Elias and Jacob and stalked back down the boardwalk from whence he'd come.

———

Cate turned back towards the boardwalk, leaving her laundry in capable hands. She reached under her collar again to scratch. This overshirt must have been made from the itchiest wool on earth. She wished they'd issued a clean spare to wear while she got it washed as well. Perhaps several times. Vigorously.

She found herself face to face with Henry Schaefer, who looked entirely unlike his usual affable self as he stalked off the boardwalk. His face was hard and pinched, his head down, and his fists were clenched at his sides.

"You look fit to be tied," Cate drawled as he approached.

Henry glanced up at her from under his brow, his chin set tight. He opened his mouth as if to tell her off, but then he shut it again and brushed by her instead. Cate looked over her shoulder at him and rolled her eyes. What a bore. Elias Hower and Jacob Robinson were seated on the edge of the boardwalk engaged in a heated debate, so Cate ambled over.

"What's got Schaefer's goat?" she asked, thumbing after him.

Hower looked up suddenly. "Huh? Oh, Henry? I dunno."

"He's German. He's always moody," Robinson shrugged. Then the two of them carried on debating whether the Battle of Bull Run had been a complete disaster or just a mitigated one. Cate leaned against a pole, relishing the novelty of chiming in on a political debate without being told to know her place. But in spite of herself, her eyes followed Schaefer's retreat. He nearly collided with one of the laundresses—the pretty red-haired one—and the heavy basket full of wet shirts she'd hitched up on her hip slipped from her grip and thudded to the gravel with a precarious teeter. The laundresses all exclaimed in warning as Schaefer and the red-haired laundress scrambled to right the basket before its clean contents cascaded all over the gravel. Cate had to check her own impulse to spring in action. That was half a day's work in that basket.

The laundress stooped to pick up the basket and almost clocked heads with Schaefer as he did the same. He leveled those perfectly straight teeth on the laundress and Cate felt her lip curl.

"Criminy, Schaefer, save the knight-in-shining-armor rou-tine," she muttered and pushed herself off the wall. Schaefer was tugging on the basket as Cate neared and she could hear him insisting, "No, please. Allow me to be of assistance. A pretty girl like you shouldn't have to be carrying such a heavy load."

It wasn't a strange thing to say. Cate had heard plenty of similar things leveraged at girls throughout her life. Never at her, of course, because she was plain and homely and she couldn't remember anyone ever describing her as pretty, even on her wedding day. But it was the kind of patronizing nonsense that incensed her, because of course a pretty girl like that laundress could carry such a heavy load. She carried loads like that every day. It was her *job*.

"She doesn't need some blowhard to save her from her work."

Cate had blurted her thoughts out loud again. Rather loudly this time, given she was still halfway between the boardwalk and the blowhard in question. The laundress regarded her with ex-asperation, and Cate realized, now that she presented as a man, that she sounded just as patronizing as Schaefer had. But she also really didn't want to help Schaefer flirt with this laundress, so she barreled on without bothering to interrogate why. "These laundresses are doing good work day in and day out. If the load was too heavy for her to carry, she wouldn't have laden it with as many pieces. Besides, if you want to help, why not help them all, not just the 'pretty one'?"

Cate was now insulting everyone. Christ. She crossed her arms and watched Schaefer's reaction carefully as she prepared to double down.

"Are you serious right now, Smith?" Schaefer hissed. "I'm just trying to help."

"I'm not going to say no to a little help," the laundress put in with a shrug.

Cate looked from Schaefer to the laundress and back. "Won-derful." Cate shouldered past Schaefer and grabbed the laundry basket. It was heavy and larger than she was used to, but she lifted it just fine, bracing it awkwardly on her chest after she flinched it away from her own hip (lest she risk accentuating her body's shape). The basket in hand, she glared fiercely at Schaefer. His blue eyes met hers and they might have been stirring if they weren't quite so dilated with anger. Cate set her jaw and punctuated her words towards Schaefer, even as she addressed the laundress. "I'd be happy to assist without any prerequisites or expectation of favors."

"I didn't have any expectations or prerequisites," Schaefer fired back, reaching out to pull the laundry basket from her arms. "I'm just trying to help, same as you."

"Fellows," the laundress said with a bemused smile. "There's really no need to fight over carrying the laundry."

There wasn't. It was supremely stupid. Cate distantly understood that. Regardless, she turned her glare upon the laundress just as Schaefer did the same.

"I'm not fighting," Schaefer insisted.

"I'm just trying to teach this dunderhead a lesson," Cate retorted at the same time.

"Who're you calling a dunderhead?" Schaefer gave a sharp yank on the laundry basket and she wasn't sure what happened next, but he must have slipped on the gravel or something because he went careening backwards. Nothing else tracked for Cate for the next moment—not the laundresses or the curious soldiers gathering around them on the parade ground—because her attention was completely focused on making sure the clean laundry did not go careening to the dirt as Schaefer fell. This was the reason why she didn't let go and instead pitched forward, landing in a heap on top of Schaefer.

Voices from the soldiers gathering around them began to hum in excitement.

"Jumpin' Jiminy, Smith took him down!"

"You gonna take that from that little runt?"

Cate could sense they were attracting a crowd, but she couldn't care about anything except the pile of wet shirts that Schaefer was trying to wrestle his way out from under.

"Stop that!" Cate shouted in her most commanding voice. "You're gonna ruin everything!"

"Goddammit, Smith, get off me!"

"Just stay still, you ignoramus!" She'd managed to keep the basket from toppling over, but a significant portion of the load had fallen out and heaped between them. Shoving the basket aside, Cate scrambled to her knees over Schaefer to gather up the shirts and save them from skimming the dirt. There were several that had been sacrificed already, and she'd heard the laundress shout her dismay, but Cate was determined to minimize the remaining potential damage as much as she could. She didn't do it for the laundress or saving face. She was simply driven by an instinct honed from years of experience with how much goddamn work laundry was.

"What the hell are you doing?" Schaefer yelped and squirmed, kicking the ground and rocking Cate to and fro.

"Stop moving, for God's sake, Schaefer, you're going to ruin the whole load!" She shoved forward with her armful of laundry and her knuckles collided with something soft and wet.

"Sonuva—!" Schaefer yowled. Cate's thighs squeezed together around his sides as she startled. Had she just hit him? Whoops. His knee wedged up and jabbed into her rear-end and she pitched forward, wet shirts and her own weight collapsing onto his face.

The soldiers went up in a cacophony of belligerent mayhem. Before Cate could regain her balance, she was sent careening on her back. Shirts flew all over the place and she tried to catch as many as she could, but Schaefer took firm hold of her shoulders and pinned her down on the ground.

"Okay, come on Henry, that's enough." It was Robinson, pulling on Schaefer's shoulders. Schaefer tried to jerk away from him, and Robinson pitched forward and stumbled. His foot caught under Cate's knee, and he hurtled on top of Schaefer, which sent his weight forward and effectively caught Cate at the bottom of a two-man pile.

"Stop!" Cate gasped and seized Schaefer by the shoulders, shoving against his superior weight quite futilely. He had a good forty pounds on her, all in muscle. She could tell because her ribs felt like they were liable to buckle. Schaefer pushed up and glared at her as Robinson rolled off his back to his feet.

Hell, when Cate had idly thought it wouldn't be so bad to be under him, this was *not* what she'd had in mind. His nose was bleeding and his hair was wild and she should have been worried about whether or not he was about to hit her, but all she could think about was how she could feel his breath on her mouth. Something of her thoughts must have shown in her face, because he hesitated, his shadowed expression some mixture of anger and confusion.

"Soldiers, STAND DOWN!"

Schaefer looked up, and Cate saw Lieutenant Thomas, upside down from her vantage, glaring at the two of them with dismay. Schaefer scrambled off of her and stood in the position of the soldier, his nostrils flaring and blood running down his lip. Robinson straightened as well. Cate hauled herself off the ground and assumed the same position. She was dazed, dirty, and fighting hard against the strong urge to sink into the ground and disappear.

"What is the meaning of this?" Lieutenant Thomas demanded, his severe gaze flickering back and forth between the three of them.

"Schaefer was disrespecting these ladies," Cate reported, but her voice was drowned out by Schaefer.

"He punched me, sir!"

"Sir," Jacob Robinson exclaimed, doing a poor job of hiding how entertained he'd been. "The two of them were fighting over who would help the laundresses carry their basket."

Cate felt her cheeks burn in shame. When put into so many words, it sounded childish bordering on the absurd. The lieutenant's brows crawled across his forehead as he took in the accusations.

"Who is your sergeant?" he demanded.

Robinson fielded this one as well. "Sergeant Osborn, sir."

The lieutenant zeroed in on him. "Were you involved in this disorder?"

"No, sir," Robinson replied, scrambling to stand in the position of the soldier. Dust puffed from his trousers as he smacked his hands to his sides. "I was just trying to break them up."

Lieutenant Thomas shifted his gaze over Robinson, then the rest of the bystanders. "And you didn't run to tell your superior officer immediately? Tell Sergeant Osborn that you three boys just earned yourselves a week of guard duty."

———

VIII

Thursday, August 8, 1861

CATE WAS JOLLY AS she made her way down the dark road to the ferry landing for guard duty in the lunging shadows of midnight. Finally, after three nights and days of guard duty, with only four hours of sleep at a time, she'd landed the post she needed to get herself a proper bath. When she'd been down there at 6 o'clock, she scoped out the area to ensure the security necessary for a dip in the river. She'd brought her thin wool blanket slung over her shoulders under the cover of keeping warm in the night air, but she had every intention of using it to dry herself. The bar of soap she'd acquired from the sutler bounced merrily in her pocket along with her soiled chemise as she picked her way down the steep hill in the dark.

At the foot of the bluffs, she could make out the dim shadow of Jacob Robinson, sitting on the sand next to the ferry. She was to relieve his two hour duty after four hours off. They had been in that cycle day and night since the incident Monday. She imagined he was as petulant as ever, but she tried to put her disdain away. During the last few days of duty, she'd had plenty of time to reflect on her method of setting the boys at a distance with her prickly temper. She had determined it was drawing far more attention to her than it deflected. She suspected a quiet comradery might serve as better cover.

Admittedly, she was irritated that, once again, she was putting herself in a position where she could not speak her mind, where she had to navigate the feelings of others before her own, but she took comfort in the understanding that this time, it was in the pursuit of peaceful discourse and was not a required as a prerequisite of her femaleness. She could certainly afford to be kinder while still standing by her own opinions.

"How's it been?" she asked as she approached, her jolly mood conveying her sentiment with remarkable sincerity.

Robinson turned. The waxing moon revealed his fatigued eyes and tight jaw. "Fine."

Still mad, then. Cate steeled herself.

"Hey, I, uh … I'm sorry you got looped into this," she ground out. "It's not fair that you're being punished the same as Schaefer and I when you didn't do anything."

"Damn right," Robinson replied. "It's not like I'm trying to get promoted or nothing, but that don't mean I want to get into trouble." He paused and gave her a flat look.

"I said I'm sorry," she said through her teeth. It was a hard sentiment to admit to. After a brief pause, she gave into the temptation to offer an excuse.

"You see, my sister is a laundress," she said, inventing the closest thing to the truth she could offer. "If anyone were to treat her like a public woman, I'd … well, I'd kill him."

"Fine," Robinson shrugged. "I think that's a gross exaggeration of the actual circumstances, but fine. Maybe don't hit anyone in the face next time?"

Cate set her mouth in a thin line and tried desperately not to argue. For once, it worked. "Fine."

Robinson smirked and handed the musket on his shoulder over to Cate. She decided the gesture was a tacit mark of truce.

"'S been pretty quiet. There's bats up there in the bluff," he said, "so watch out."

She was not entirely sure what she was meant to watch out for—bats weren't liable to stage a siege on the fort—but she nodded anyway. His boots crunched up the gravel road, ascending to the barracks for a few hours of sleep.

Cate assumed the "support arms" position. Her eyes only took in the dark, churning waters of the Minnesota and Mississippi combining for a brief moment before she began to ruminate. Was she grossly exaggerating the situation? She didn't understand what the point of calling the laundress pretty was if not to highlight her desirability in Schaefer's estimation. It was not an empty compliment, devoid of meaning. It was a statement of value, in the currency that ruled the lives of women since the day they were born. Beauty was the most coveted blessing and greatest curse, a mark of marriageability and also of physical risk.

Cate chewed on a hangnail. Girls regardless of their beauty had to guard their bodies with constant vigilance, living in fear of the insatiable appetites of men. But they were afforded no power with which to do it! Given a dark room and a guarantee of secrecy, what man would respect a lovely young woman's wishes in the face of temptation? Cate wished she could say that of course most men would not succumb to barbarity, but she'd known too many people who failed to meet her expectations and she couldn't muster the confidence to believe it. Regardless of whether some would not fall, the fact remained that there were many men who *would* seize upon such an opportunity and therefore, any man could present potential danger. Perhaps this was why men had to declare ownership over their women—as fathers and brothers and husbands—to protect their honor with the power only men were permitted to yield. And once a woman had "fallen," no matter how pretty, she lost that protection because she ceased to offer the purity men and society desired. There was a dichotomy, in fact, between the women they fucked and the women they married. Were women even people, or were they just vessels? For pleasure, or for progeny. Cate swallowed hard against the lurking knowledge that her courses had not yet arrived. She wasn't late yet, but that didn't really inspire unassailable confidence.

"The power to create life, most likely," she muttered to herself, shaking the inconvenient thought away with the weightiness of philosophy. "Adam was jealous of Eve's ability to create children. So he took control of her with his superior strength."

If she were stronger, if she were heavier, she could have taken Schaefer. She was strong for a woman, but that feeling of helplessness when he'd had her pinned to the ground, it was something she would never forget. It had taken her breath away and the thing that scared her the most was that in the moment, she'd both feared and desired it.

She sighed in frustration. She could go in circles like this all night.

Shaking her head, she pulled out the soap bar from her pocket, shifting the musket aside and breaking position. She tilted her head to look up the bluff. Lights had been out since 9, but even at midnight, she couldn't quell the fear of being discovered with her clothes off. Perhaps she'd take a turn around the shoreline to check for anyone lurking, just to make sure.

When she returned, she was even more worked up about the endless abuses men inflicted upon women. Whenever she started composing her own Declaration of Sentiments, it was a sure sign that she was spinning and she needed to snap herself out of it. Otherwise her resolution to try and mend her relationships with her squad would be nothing but good intentions as she continued to take out her existential anger on her ignorant comrades. It wasn't their fault, per say. After all, who would doubt that a power one was granted since birth was undeserved?

Cate leaned the musket against the ferry on its landward edge. Then she crouched on the first plank and began unlacing her boots, steeling herself.

"Just take a bath," she murmured to herself. No one was going to come near here at night. It was dark, the moon was scarcely waxing, and the clouds were intermittently obscuring it as well. Being fearful was not giving her any kind of succor.

Even though it was dark and there was no one around, she still carried her boots into the tall prairie grass and undressed in a crouch under the cover of the waving sheafs. She folded her issued clothing carefully, then carefully tucked her yellowed working stays underneath. She made a false start toward the river before she doubled back to pull her soiled chemise out of the pocket of her trousers. Once she was clean, she could wash the chemise too and have it as a spare undergarment. She set it atop her other things in an effort to remind herself should she become flustered or distracted by further philosophical ponderings. That done, she waded naked on the far side of the ferry, soap grasped in one hand.

Her skin prickled with goose flesh as it hit the water and she forced herself to step into St. Peter's stream, her toes squishing into mud and sand and rocks. When she reached waist-high water, she steeled her resolve and crouched, dunking herself up to her neck.

As she got used to the cold water, she dipped her head back, letting the river's current comb through her short curls. She let out a deep sigh and took what felt like the deepest breath she had taken since she'd first nicked those trousers from the lumbermen's laundry and found they fit. Gripping the slippery soap bar carefully, she ran it along her arms, neck, face, and head, working a lather into her hair. Her nails scraped grease and dirt from her scalp.

After a few minutes, she experienced great satisfaction running her fingers through her clean hair, feeling only smooth scalp and fine strands dancing in the water like seaweed. Next, she set to work scrubbing down her body, the soap slicking over her skin beneath the persistent current. Sloughing off layers of dirt and sweat, she felt like she was going through some sort of metamorphosis. It was not a lofty, literary change, but rather a physical one, her body breaking free from a chrysalis of filth. Despite the cold water and the dark night and the ever-present fear of being discovered, she felt a deep sense of contentment come over her. Of rightness. She was going to need to get ferry landing guard duty more often.

Her previous frustrations seemed to ebb away with the current and her heart felt lighter than it had in at least a year. Certainly there were still many challenges ahead of her (her impending menses chief among them), but she was free. She had grabbed her life by the horns and was making it her own, in spite of the risks. She let her arms float wide around her, tipping her head back and breathing deeply.

Her fingers were brushed by something cold and hard. Startled from her reverie, she stood up in the water and saw the musket swirling down the river, its wooden stock trying to float as the steel barrel sank slowly in the rapidly accelerating current. Shortly before the confluence, the steel won out and it disappeared below the surface.

"No!" she squeaked, staring after it. It must have fallen from where it was leaning against the ferry and gotten swept away in the current. Rifle muskets were in high demand. There was a shortage and the Federals were having a hard time finding enough to equip the troops as it was. She was going to be in so much trouble.

Slogging through the water, she tried to get to the spot where the musket had gone down. Just off the end of the ferry, she dove under, grappling blindly at the sand with her hands again and again. She grasped nothing but a few weeds and river muck. She tried to open her eyes underwater but she could see nothing in the dark, murky water. When she surfaced a third time, she was so far afield she was almost swept into the Mississippi's current. She splashed back to the end of the ferry.

It was futile. There was no way she was going to find it in the dark. With one hand on the end of the wood ferry, she stared helplessly at the swirling water for a moment.

"Smith?"

Cate just about choked as the voice snapped her right back into the world where her sex was her greatest liability. She immediately spun herself under the ferry, submerging until just her nose and eyes peeked out, hoping the cover of darkness would disguise her wet head bobbing amidst the rippling water. What time was it? She still had time before she was supposed to be relieved, didn't she?

A shadowed figure walked out onto the ferry. The boards creaked above her head. Through the cracks, she could see his shadow obscure the night sky. Her heart hammered against her ribs.

"Smith? Where are you?" Goddamn it all to hell, she knew that stupid voice. It was Henry Schaefer.

———

Henry's eyes strained against the darkness, searching for any signs of life in or out of the water. That little recalcitrant was supposed to be on guard duty, not loafing around. When Osborn found out about this, Smith was going to be doing extra duty for the rest of his life.

There was no sign of anyone. The night was quiet, except for the croaking of frogs and crickets chirping. The water bur-bled in St. Peter's stream. Henry reached behind his head and scratched his neck. No soldier was so arrogant he'd shirk penalty guard duty. That was a sure-fire ticket to a confinement cell. Smith was a horse's ass, for certain, but he wasn't stupid.

Henry walked back up the ferry and onto the sandy beach.

"Smith!" he called, louder this time. "Don't think for a minute I'm gonna cover for you."

Nothing.

What was he supposed to do now? He was supposed to be on duty, but there was no guard to relieve, no report to gather, no musket to exchange. He supposed he could go back to the fort and wake up a superior officer, but then he would leave the post unmanned and he wasn't sure what was more important—reporting Smith's desertion of his post or making sure the checkpoint was protected. He dithered on the beach for a good minute before calling out again.

"Ha ha, Smith, real funny," he said. "You got me, now come out."

Still nothing. A cool breeze rustled the leaves and the hair at the back of his neck. He felt unsettled.

Goddamn that son of a bitch. Everywhere he turned, it seemed, Charles Smith was there to make his life hell. He scuffed his boot in the sand and started walking around the general area, listening hard for any signs of life. River babbling. Toads croaking. Crickets chirping.

A strong wind picked up and threatened to whip his hat off his head and he held it on for a minute as he stepped into the grass. Out of the corner of his eye, he saw a flash of white and his heart jumped in his chest as his first thought was that it was some sort of spirit. Which was, of course, ridiculous—his family were all Freethinkers, they didn't believe in spiritualism—but that knowledge didn't make him feel better. Snapping his head toward the movement, he saw a white shirt of some kind caught on a shrub, billowing in the breeze.

He stepped toward it and plucked it from the twigs.

"What the..." he muttered as he held the garment out in front of him. It was some sort of undershirt or shift and it smelled horrible. The laundresses must have missed some pieces when they put the washing out to dry. But ... this shirt was not clean. No way it came from anywhere except the rankest of men. Why would they put it out to dry on the shrubs when it was dirty?

Eyebrows knit in confusion, he scanned the trees. What in the Sam Hill was going on here? The garment was short-sleeved, which made Henry wonder if it was a woman's. Was Smith having some sort of stinky-boy liaison with one of the laundresses or something? The notion made him scoff aloud—the boy was too soft and young to attract a woman's baser instincts, surely. Unless it wasn't a woman. That thought left a strange taste in his mouth.

"Hello, is anyone down here?" he called again. He felt anxiety percolate in his chest. He couldn't even pin down what he was afraid of. No rebels were anywhere near Minnesota. Although, he supposed the Democratic sympathizers could certainly pull something as they had done last summer after Eliza Winston was freed. The most likely hostile would be the Indians but as far as he knew, they were too busy trying to save a failing crop back on their reservation near New Ulm to furnish an attack all the way up here at Fort Snelling. It had never even occurred to him that when he served guard duty, he was actually guarding against something or someone specific.

It occurred to him now. Confused and unsettled, Henry resolved to wake up Sergeant Osborn for further instructions. The idea of standing guard alone during the witching hour of the night with no weapon, with nothing to do but wonder what happened to Smith, put him on edge. Gripping the fetid garment in his hand—whatever it was, it felt like evidence—he started back up the gravel road, trudging the steep incline in the dark, his ears sensitive to the tiniest rustle of leaves.

He was halfway up when he heard a quiet splash and he whirled around, eyes straining against the dim night. What he would give for the Great Comet to still be around, illuminating the night sky with its immortal tail. It had waned in the past few weeks now, fading to nothing but a fantastical memory, a cosmic marker of a singular, broken year that would never be forgotten.

Nothing could be seen in the grass below and the ferry landing itself (being positioned round the point of the bluff) was not in view from his current vantage halfway up the road. This whole thing was giving him the willies. Henry wrinkled his nose and walked up the incline, faster this time.

He was just approaching the large, wooden door to the fort when he heard footfalls pounding behind him. His heart leapt into his throat and he spun on his heel, fists clenched and knees bent, ready to defend himself.

Charles Smith was running after him, full tilt, looking disheveled and out of breath, holding his hat with one hand as he sprinted the rest of the way up the incline. Henry's fear turned to anger and he charged toward him, meeting him halfway.

"Where the hell have you been?" Henry demanded, not bothering to disguise his temper.

Smith winced. "Sorry ... nature called."

Henry furrowed his brows and curled his lip in exasperation. "Nature called? For that long? In the middle of the night? Why didn't you answer me when I called for you, then?"

Smith pressed his lips together in a thin line and shrugged. He looked like he was actively trying not to say something snide. His overshirt was partly tucked into his trousers and he had his blanket slung haphazardly over his shoulders.

"Is your hair wet?" Henry asked, his eyes peering at the boy as he took a step closer.

Smith's hand flew to his hair. He winced and countered backwards as he said, "No. Yes. Just greasy."

Henry didn't say anything, but held his gaze for a long moment. Smith squirmed under his scrutiny. The normally inscrutable bastard was hiding something. Henry had never seen him act this nervous, except for maybe on muster day. And even then, he'd covered a mite better than this.

"Hey, what are you boys doing down there?"

The voice called from up above, from the guard platform above the fort entrance. A man from one of the other companies was on duty up there, peering down at them through one of the narrow slits in the limestone wall.

Henry turned. "Sorry, there was some confusion about relieving the landing post."

"We've got it figured out," Smith chimed in.

Henry turned back with one brow lifted. "We do?"

Smith blinked defiantly. "Why wouldn't we?"

Henry's eyes narrowed. "Because you're acting ... peculiar."

"I don't know what you're talking about," Smith laughed, his voice a little too high for it to be real.

"Fine," Henry sighed. "What's the report?"

Smith shrugged. "Quiet. Bats were flying about. So watch out for that, I guess."

Henry's eyebrow raised again. "Huh. I didn't see any bats, but I did see this flying about," he held up the filthy shift. "Care to explain?"

Smith's eyes widened for a moment, then his nose wrinkled as he blinked at the garment. "What the hell is that?"

"I haven't the faintest. I found it caught on a bush down by the landing."

Smith raised his eyebrows and pressed his lips together suggestively. "Well, I guess you better keep your eyes peeled for naked ladies down there while you're at it."

Henry's eyes widened in surprise. "What? Why?"

Smith shifted awkwardly, his eyes darting from the garment to Henry and back. "Well ... isn't that a lady's chemise...?"

Henry looked at the yellowed cotton with no small measure of disgust for whatever "lady" might have caused it to get so filthy. "Is it? I suppose it is..."

"I dunno, maybe," Smith shrugged, his eyes avoiding Henry's. What was that boy up to? Henry had never seen him look so guilty, so agitated, so ... suspicious. He studied the boy more closely.

"Smith, where's the musket?"

Smith looked up at him with those round, doe eyes, lips parted innocently. "What musket?"

Henry had to shake himself from the urge to question whether there had indeed been a musket after all. No. He refused to be pulled in by a charming face. "The musket. We had a musket we were trading off earlier in the day. Where did you leave it?"

Smith frowned and shrugged. "I never got a musket."

There was a long pause.

"I just figured they'd asked for it for a different position," he added nonchalantly.

Henry gave Smith a sidelong glance. He couldn't find a chink in the explanation to reveal it, but he just knew that Smith was lying.

Another long, pregnant pause passed between them.

"Well, I'm, uh, I'm gonna go get some sleep," Smith said, throwing his thumb toward the fort. "I'll see you at reveille."

Henry watched him trot off like the boy had just grown three heads. What was he up to, talking to him like he was looking forward to seeing him in the morning? Henry narrowed his eyes. He had toyed with the idea of dozing off during duty, but now he was going to make sure to scour the area for ... well, he wasn't quite sure. But if Smith was that nervous, surely there was something down there to explain why.

———

IX

Friday, August 9th, 1861

REVEILLE SOUNDED AT DAWN as usual. Henry shifted groggily in his bed, groaning. He'd only just gotten to sleep a few hours ago, after finishing his completely uneventful duty down on the ferry landing at 4 am. He hadn't found anything amiss—in fact, the utter lack of anything suspicious frustrated him to the point that he'd become exhausted by the effort. He'd been ready to flop into bed unconscious by the time Jacob came to relieve him, but when it became evident that the musket they were generally equipped with for guard duty had gone missing somewhere between Jacob handing it off to Smith and Henry relieving him from duty at 2 am, Henry had ceased to feel so drowsy.

He'd tossed and turned for quite some time, unable to put the pieces together. The missing musket, the strange underclothes, and Smith's being away from the post didn't make sense. He couldn't put his finger on what it was, but Charley Smith was up to something. Something that being a petulant teenager newly enlisted in the army couldn't explain.

Henry wasn't sure how much sleep he managed to get, but he did get some because reveille woke him out of an unpleasant dream. He scrubbed his hands over his face and looked up at the creaking scaffolds that usually held Charley Smith above him. His eyes narrowed. The lady's underclothes made him think that the little jackanape was having some sort of liaison under the cover of night, but the missing musket complicated things. Did he sell it to someone? If he'd lost it somehow, to a foe or to some foolishness, then why act like it was never there?

Henry dragged himself off his straw tick and sat at the edge of the lowest bunk for a moment, trying to convince his eyes to stay open. Jacob wanted to report the musket missing right away, but Henry had convinced him to hold off a few days. He was sure Smith was up to something bigger than a stolen musket. And if they reported him, he'd know they were on to him. Smith made a big mistake last night and Henry wanted him to think he'd gotten away with it. An officer would be obliged to dispense consequences, but Henry had the luxury of waiting, watching, and gathering more information. It was only a matter of time before he misstepped again.

Speak of the devil, there was the little snipe now, appearing in the doorway already dressed and alert, his round eyes smudged with dark circles. He peered in quietly from under his dark brows, observing the men dressing for roll call. It took Henry a moment to figure out how Smith had gotten out of bed without nearly jostling him out as well, but then he remembered Smith would have been at his duty post when reveille sounded. He was to report for roll and then return to his post for the duration, until Henry had to be down there at 8 to relieve him. That's right—Henry had heard him leave to relieve Jacob. That was how he knew how little sleep he'd gotten.

Henry stood in his shirt and drawers and shucked off the soiled shirt. Reaching into his haversack, he pulled a freshly laundered one out and over his head, buttoning the placket up the front. He could feel Smith's eyes on him, but he made a point to ignore him and participate in whatever mundane banter the other boys were getting up to. He didn't want Smith to know he was on to him.

"This guard duty is going to wreck me," Jacob whined as he rolled out of bed. "I just got to sleep and that damn bugle goes off."

Henry shook his head. "You should have just stayed up."

"I know," Jacob huffed, "but Mary is coming round today and I want to look my best."

"Gotta get that beauty sleep," John Williamson teased.

"Just tell me I don't look like I got two fists in the eyes," Jacob said, looking resignedly at Elias. For his part, Elias just grimaced, inhaling sharply and shrugging. Jacob groaned pitifully, his face in his hands.

Dressed in their makeshift uniforms, the squad lined up on the parade ground outside of their barracks, assuming the position of the soldier as Sergeant Osborn approached them from the orderly room.

"Good morning, fellows," the Sergeant said and launched right into roll call. After all the boys had reported present, Osborn closed his book on one finger.

"Before I hand out assignments, I want to take a moment to make an important announcement. I have decided to promote one among you to Corporal."

Henry looked left and right among his comrades, trying to discern who might be the lucky soldier (or unlucky, depending on how much time one wanted to spend learning tactics). Elias straightened with wide, eager eyes. Jacob's head was bouncing back and forth looking for a clue too. Tom Webster and Krüger exchanged glances. Smith's eyes squeezed shut, his mouth twisted up like he was bracing for a blow. Henry raised a brow.

"Now that I've received approval from command, I am happy to announce that Elias Hower will be our corporal."

"Well done!" Tom Webster exclaimed, slapping Elias on one shoulder. Henry cracked a smile; as much as they had made fun of him for it, Elias had been working very hard for this promotion.

"Fellas, order," Osborn warned, but he was smiling too. "Save your congratulations until after I give you your assignments."

The murmurs quieted, though Elias couldn't manage to stop grinning. In fact, the only one of their squad who was not smiling was Charley goddamn Smith. The brat was sulking on the end of the line, shoulders dropped and lips curled. Not only did he look disappointed, but he actually almost seemed angry.

The assignments doled out by Sergeant Osborn were of no surprise to anyone. Jacob, Henry, and Charley were all on guard duty again. The rest of their squad was living in luxury while the three of them worked off their sentence for disorder, because while they were all on guard duty, none of the other squad-members were needed for it until their punishment was over.

After Osborn released them for breakfast, the boys gathered around Elias to congratulate him and give him some friendly guff about his accomplishment. Henry turned to join them, but Sergeant Osborn was at his side.

"Schaefer, I need to see you, Robinson, and Smith for a moment," he said, addressing both Henry and Jacob, who stood next to him. "Wait here a moment."

The Sergeant rounded up Smith, who'd already been making for the gates. Once all assembled, Osborn leveled a serious expression on the three of them.

"It has come to my attention that the musket you were issued last night has gone missing," he stated. Henry tensed. He couldn't help but look at Smith. Surely he would confess now that he had been caught. He hoped Jacob wouldn't throw him over for not reporting it sooner. He'd been determined to dig deeper into Smith's mischief before he notified the brass. Ah well, muskets were in such high demand that he supposed he shouldn't be surprised that command noticed.

A long pause passed as they all waited to see who would talk first. The Sergeant didn't let up his gaze as he waited. Henry kept his eyes pointedly on Smith, watching and waiting for him to own up. Surely he wouldn't reveal all that he was up to—there was certainly more to this than a missing musket.

Jacob was the first to cave. "I gave the musket to Smith at midnight when he relieved me of the post. Henry said he didn't get it when he relieved Smith at 2."

Henry was glad he hadn't told Jacob about Smith not being at his post either. He certainly hoped Jacob would not be taken as a prisoner of war because it clearly didn't take much to get him to give up a comrade under pressure.

Smith's jaw worked as he stared at the ground under Sergeant Osborn's scrutiny.

"Smith, what do you have to say to that?" Osborn prompted.

Smith let out a long sigh and looked up wistfully. "I'm sorry, sir. I ... uh, it fell into the river."

Henry's eyebrow rose incredulously. Sergeant Osborn blinked, clearly not expecting such a confession and Jacob let out a hiccup of nervous laughter.

"I tried to retrieve it, sir, but it sank faster than a shot off a shovel and it was too dark to see where it had gone," Smith added, scrubbing his face with one hand.

"Bunkum," Henry accused without thinking.

Smith looked up at him with alarm, apparently shocked that he had the audacity to say such a thing to his face.

"I don't need your help, Schaefer," Osborn directed.

Henry's brow furrowed. "Yes, sir," he muttered.

Osborn studied the three of them for another long moment and then said, "Very well. That was foolish of you, Smith. You'll be doing dish duty next week, once your guard duty is done. And suffice to say, you'll be assigned to a different post tomorrow. I won't have a repeat of the incident by allowing you near the water."

Henry looked up at Osborn slack jawed. Did he actually buy that poor excuse for an explanation?

"But sir—" Henry began, but the Sergeant cut him off.

"None of that, Schaefer. You're all dismissed."

Henry stood for a minute with his mouth flapping as Jacob made for the mess hall and Smith sulked off toward the fort gates. His chest swelled with anger. How dare that little snipe act so entitled when all he ever did was cause trouble? Maybe Osborn was fooled by his bogus excuse, but Henry certainly wasn't. Something else was going on, and that musket was a part of it.

Henry turned and quietly stalked after Smith. The gates were open and officers were making their way in and out. There were stables to the west of the fort walls, as well as a larger parade ground so that all the companies could have a space to drill at the same time. Smith started east, down the road to the ferry landing, which unlike inside the fort wasn't nearly as busy this early in the morning. Henry quietly followed, boiling.

He had just started down the incline after him when Smith turned abruptly on one heel and glared at him.

"What do you want?" he demanded. Henry felt his blood swell through his body as his heart pumped harder. He wanted to lay bare that he knew what the brat was up to, but the fact was, he didn't. He couldn't quite talk himself down from a confrontation, though—he was itching to give Smith what he deserved. So he settled on, "What's your problem?"

Smith rolled his eyes. "Other than you?"

"You didn't drop that musket in the river. That's bogus. If you had, you would've told me about it when I asked last night."

"Maybe I was embarrassed and I didn't want you to know," Smith shot back, sounding not the least embarrassed.

"Maybe you're hiding something and you're bad at lying."

Smith's eyes widened with disdain and shouted, "Maybe I'm just trying my best like everyone else, but since you've decided you hate me, I just keep getting treated like a pile of horseshit."

Henry pulled a sharp breath in through his nose. It was still sore from when Smith had punched him. How dare he insinuate that he was doing to Smith just what his brothers always did to him. Henry urgently sorted through all the ways the bastard had him fit to be tied this morning, looking for a way to prove it was all Smith's own fault. "I find that hard to believe when you can barely muster a singular commendation to Hower this morning. Elias has worked hard for that promotion and rather than congratulate him with the rest of the squad, you stalk off like some petulant spoiled brat."

Smith set his jaw. "And you mean to tell me that Hower was entitled to it? Why? Because Osborn promised it to him the day he was made Sergeant? Tell me how that is more fair." Smith closed in on Henry a few steps, shoulders squared.

Henry faltered. He'd forgotten about that. But he wasn't about to back down so easily.

"Be that as it may, but who has worked harder than Elias since then? Certainly not you," he spat. "All you do is look down your nose like you're better than the rest of us. You wanna know something, Smith? I'll let you in on a little secret—just because you're from the city doesn't mean you're smarter than everyone else."

"Just because I look young doesn't mean I'm stupid, either," Smith retorted. "So what if Hower has spent the last month kissing up to Osborn? That doesn't make him better at tactics or drilling or leading." He took a shuddering breath and held up a hand. "You know what? I'm not mad the Sarg didn't pick me. I've been in more of my fair share of trouble and I know that. But let's not pretend that it's not just goddamn favoritism."

Smith turned on his heel and strode off. This was quite possibly the most infuriating thing he could have done, given that Henry was itching to grab him by both shoulders and shake that arrogant sneer off his face. It was an unfamiliar sensation, given that he'd never much liked sparring in the Turnverein. He hated competition, perhaps because he often ended up losing because he wasn't good enough or big enough to win. But there was something about Smith that just got under his skin and triggered his temper. Maybe it was just that Smith saved up all his disdain for Henry for no apparent reason and didn't deliver the same acidity to anyone else, in spite of the fact that Henry had tried very consciously to include him. He didn't need to be friends with him, but a little gratitude, some kindness, some comradery would be nice. Hell—sooner rather than later, they'd be on a battlefield together and they'd have no choice but to work together. To say he was beginning to regret inviting Smith to join their squad would be a massive understatement.

"You gotta be joking if you think you're gonna be anyone's favorite with an attitude like that!" Henry shot back, a little too late, a half-hearted dig that smacked more of a schoolyard than a barracks.

Smith just raised one hand in a rude gesture without breaking his stride. Henry glowered and watched him go for a moment, trying to decide to pursue him or not. Henry wanted to make sure that he knew everything Smith was up to, but it was hard since as soon as Smith was relieved from his post, Henry had to assume it, and by the time he got back, Smith was usually catching a few hours of sleep in the barracks. He couldn't follow him from here—Smith would know he was lurking around down there with him.

"Verdammt," he swore, throwing his fists at his side. He turned and started back up the hill. Toward the top, he glanced over his shoulder, trying to see if he could spot Smith settling into his post from his vantage at the top of the bluff.

But Smith wasn't there. Henry's stomach turned as he tried to peer through the tall prairie grasses down on the road that snaked between the bluff and the river's edge. After a moment, he spotted movement heading south, away from the Mississippi and the fort. That had to be him. Forgetting all about breakfast, Henry kept his eyes glued to the movement as he dogged after him on the bluff above. He would need to stay out of sight if he was going to figure out what the little weasel was up to.

————

Was she mad that Hower had been promoted? Yes. It was the worst kind of favoritism. Did she really think Charles Smith should have been promoted instead? Of course not, not after all the mistakes she'd made. It was stupid that as Cate Stowell, she spent so much time longing to be noticed, to be a part of something bigger, to be a person of consequence, and now that she was operating as Charles Smith, she struggled with the opposite. She needed to fade into the background, go unnoticed, but her inclinations from years of trying to hammer her way into important conversations barred to her sex were hard to break. And Henry Schaefer seemed to know just how to set her off.

Cate picked her way along the edge of St. Peter's stream below the bluffs, where trees and grass had been razed to make way for constructing the incline road up to the fort. Beyond that, where the sharp, gray rocks of the bluff gave way to sloping, green hillside, was the relatively lavish farmhouse of Franklin Steele. And waving behind the house from laundry lines like so many tiny white flags were what Cate could only hope were diapers.

She didn't have any more time to waste on being angry at Henry Schaefer. She had reached a particularly low point today and it wasn't because she'd been caught losing the musket in such a supremely stupid way. No, the low point was that she was going to steal from a baby in order to maintain her masculine artifice. She'd felt the familiar curl of pain deep in her belly this morning. In spite of the considerable relief the sensation had brought her, there was no more putting it off. She was out of options.

As she approached the hillside, she stepped off the road into high prairie grass waving in the breeze. The sun was shining today, but the temperatures were mild, as they had been for much of the summer, excepting that heatwave at the beginning of August. And last summer too, now that she thought about it. It was passing strange, this cool weather, but it wasn't any stranger than any of the other mad things that had happened this year. The Great Comet. The inauguration of Lincoln. The splintering of the country and the outbreak of civil war. Cate's seizing of her own fate and transformation into a soldier. Nothing about this time felt normal and that seemed in some way very appropriate.

The Steele farmhouse was large, with two full stories plus a third half-story attic, and a kitchen built off the back. Franklin Steele was the sutler at Fort Snelling and had managed to acquire ownership of the fort and the surrounding land when it was decommissioned in 1858, although rumor had it that he was not paid up and the military now possessed the property in fact. Regardless, Steele found himself in a very profitable position, claiming he was leasing the fort back to the government and running the ferry service and sutlery. It was a wonder his house wasn't bigger.

A fence rounded the laundry lines behind the house, white underclothes of all kinds flapping in the wind at the peak of the bluff. The hill was steep but not any steeper than the incline road that she'd been climbing up and down the past few days. Her eyes darted back and forth, grateful the prairie grass provided a measure of cover.

No one seemed to be in the enclosure as she approached. The laundry itself provided ample cover from the house's windows, since Cate advanced from the bluff. The diapers were hung on the third line, so she was additionally lucky in that regard. Glancing around once more, Cate sprang over the fence in one smooth leap, landing on the markedly shorter grass inside the enclosure. Keeping her body low, she crept toward the line with the diapers and looked up at them, steeling herself.

She was not a thief. She abhorred thieves. But at this point, she had no choice. The only other option she could think of was to place herself at the mercy of Mrs. Nelson and hope she would be willing to help and not report her. Which could really go either way, if she was being honest, and she couldn't place herself in such jeopardy. Even if Mrs. Nelson was willing to help her, the expectation that she keep the secret from her husband, from the other laundresses ... Cate just couldn't trust anyone enough. Which left her to figure this out for herself.

She reached up and snapped a white rectangular diaper from the line. Then another. Then another. The weight of shame settled in over her shoulders. Because her ability to wash these was so variable, she thought she might take a few more, just to be safe. But there were only six on the line. She couldn't bear the thought of putting a frontier mother out of the supplies she needed to keep her baby dry and healthy, even if her husband was Franklin Steele. She pocketed the three diapers, their fates to become sanitary napkins thus sealed, and crept back to the fence.

As Cate vaulted back over the fence, she thought she caught sight of something—or someone—ducking under the grass in the distance between the farm and the fort. She blinked twice, her heart thumping hard up in her throat as she froze like a deer, glancing this way and that. There was no further sign of any activity, at least not this far out from the fort. Taking a deep, quavery breath, Cate hurried through the prairie grass toward the steep hill back down to St. Peter's stream.

When Cate rounded the bend in the river and the Mississippi ferry landing came back into sight, bathed in the first rays of early morning sunlight, she saw her post occupied. Thick, straight yellow hair glinting in the sun, shoulders that had no right being on such an insufferable man—Henry Schaefer was at least a half hour early to relieve her from her post. Cate swore colorfully to herself as she approached.

"I would have thought you'd still be stuffing yourself on griddle cakes and bacon," she said glibly when she was within earshot. Schaefer turned his clear, blue eyes on her and smirked.

"Not this time," he replied, his gaze pointed and even with hers. His unbridled anger from earlier seemed to have been sharpened to a deadly point. "I came down here early and lucky too, because I found the post once again mysteriously unmanned. I wonder why that might be."

His eyes rested on her significantly and she could see his temples tense as he set his jaw. She recalled the movement she had seen in the grass up on the bluff. Had he followed her? At that distance, it was unlikely he would have seen just what she had done. Cate peered at him for a long moment, her heart racing as her mind churned through sarcastic retorts minimizing enough to put him off her tracks. "Your commitment to tracking the timing of my bowels is admirable."

Henry's eyebrow lifted. "Given how often nature seems to call you, I should be concerned for the state of your health."

She couldn't help it. One side of her mouth twitched up in amusement and she pinched her lips together to try and disguise it. This infuriating man was going to be the end of her military career, she just knew it. He was far too nosy—and far too appealing for her to behave sensibly around him. Even after he had tackled her the other day, she still couldn't help but be distracted by his physicality. Who wouldn't after seeing him change his shirt this morning, his wide shoulders wrapped in sinew, tapering down over a hard chest and flat, narrow waist? Farmer's tan or no, she could not get the image out of her mind. It was utterly unfair that such a tempting form had to house such an unpleasant personality. Not to mention threaten her entire burgeoning military career with his overly-active pursuit of petty retaliation. Perhaps she just needed to let him punch her back and he would leave her alone.

"Thanks for your concern, Schaefer, but I am fit as can be," she assured flippantly. "Except for—I keep getting these headaches, right here at the back of my head, as if I had been dashed against the ground or something..."

"That sounds most concerning. Perhaps if you learned how to fight, you wouldn't find yourself in such pressing circumstances."

Cate's nose wrinkled. That one smarted.

"Learn how to fight ..." she repeated, feigning confusion. "Oh, if you're referring to what happened the other day as 'fighting,' then yes, I suppose I might be wanting an education in tackling those smaller than me like a rabid dog."

Henry rolled his eyes and shook his head. "Yeah, play the victim like you didn't start it."

"I didn't!" she exclaimed, her voice cracking into her upper register and making her sound like a pubescent little boy. She cleared her throat before continuing. "I wasn't the one who was strutting around flirting with women working hard at a job you couldn't even do if you tried. I'd be willing to bet if your mother were the judge of the issue, she would not find me guilty of the first strike."

Now it was his turn to be rankled. "Regardless, you struck the first blow."

Cate rolled her eyes and shrugged. "You reap what you sow."

"And you fight like a coward," he accused, stepping forward and putting his body in her space.

She met his gaze evenly even as her pulse quickened.

"Your play for dominance is charming, but I shall have to politely decline your invitation to make a demonstration of physical superiority for the moment." She bit the inside of her cheek to prevent herself from adding 'as much as I'd like another chance at being under you.' She always got a bit brazen right before her courses—it was most inopportune. "I presume that since you're here now, I am no longer needed, so I'll just be off back to the barracks for a bite to eat. Thanks ever so."

She turned on her heel and made a point not to look back at him, even though she was dying to see the look on his face. She had more pressing problems to tackle than trying not to flirt with Henry Schaefer when he was about to throttle her.

———

X

Friday, August 9th, 1861

THE BUGLES SOUNDED OUT, calling the men to their after-noon meal. Henry was just making his way to the mess for dinner when Jacob entered the parade ground, accompanied by a group of ladies he'd escorted from the ferry landing at the end of his guard duty.

There were three young women and a matron as chaperone. One of the young ladies walked on Jacob's arm, smiling delight-edly at the squads marching through the parade ground as she floated across the lawn in a pink gingham dress draped over a full crinoline, small puffs at the top of each sleeve. She must have been Jacob's paramour, Mary. Her light brown hair was parted starkly through the middle and topped with a bonnet carefully adorned with silk flowers and ribbon. Her cotton gloves grazed Jacob's sleeve as she let him lead her around the parade ground like a puffed up rooster, smiling as he explained where every-thing was and to what purpose.

Henry doubled back from his intended path to the mess in an effort to effortlessly run into Jacob and his little entourage. The two other young ladies, he presumed, were Mary's friends, and the matron her mother. Jacob had casually pointed out that Mary would easily be able to connect Henry with a charming lady pen pal, and he had every intention of making her acquain-tance as soon as possible, dinner and Smith be damned.

He managed to cross paths with them outside Colonel Van Cleve's house at the head of the parade grounds.

"Robinson, I see you've brought some guests up with you from the ferry landing," Henry said, grinning as he approached.

It took Jacob a moment to notice him, as he was mid-sentence describing how he wished to show Mary the view from the Half Moon Battery. For a moment, Henry felt awkwardly obtrusive and simultaneously invisible as he stood waiting to be acknowledged.

"Oh, Henry! There you are!" Jacob exclaimed belatedly, stepping forward as the group of women opened their posture to include Henry. "I've been hoping to run into some of the fellows from our squad. Miss Coleman, this is Mr. Schaefer. He's up from New Ulm. We worked the farm together in Faribault before enlisting."

Jacob's girl offered a gloved hand in greeting. "A pleasure to make your acquaintance, Mr. Schaefer."

"Henry, this is Miss Coleman, my pen pal I've been telling you about," Jacob said, grinning like his pig had won the blue ribbon prize at the fair. "And this is her honorable mother, Mrs. Coleman."

The matron, whose gray-streaked brown hair mirrored that of her daughter's in both style and sleek texture, inclined her head demurely and said, "Charmed."

"And this is Miss Anna, my pen pal's younger sister, and her cousin, Miss Walsh."

Miss Anna couldn't be older than fifteen and smiled in the gawky way of a teenager who had grown taller much faster than she had grown wide. Given her youthful face, Henry was surprised she was wearing a dress that reached the ground and didn't fasten in the back.

Miss Walsh was shorter, perhaps around twenty, with an ample bosom and slim, corseted waist. She was a bit long in the chin and her eyes were a little close together, but they alighted upon him from under two flat eyebrows as if *he* were the prize pig. Though she appeared of an age with him, she giggled like a much younger girl. Henry tried to give her his winningest smile.

"Thank you for your service, Mr. Schaefer," Miss Walsh said when she had recovered from her fit. Her cheeks flushed pink, and Henry simultaneously enjoyed and felt discomfited by her obvious attention.

"New Ulm, is it?" Mrs. Coleman asked. "Are your people Turners then?"

Henry blinked in surprise. It was a very pointed question and one that made him wonder whether there was a correct answer in her estimation. "Why, uh, yes. My father is a member of the Turnverein from Cincinnati that came by way of Chicago to found the township."

"A fascinating group, indeed," Mrs. Coleman sniffed. Henry shifted from foot to foot as she continued. "We had a group of Turners in our ward in St. Paul, that is until Lincoln's call for men went out this spring. They have veritably fallen apart since then, with nearly all of their members off with the First Minnesota to fight."

"That's a shame," Henry replied, watching the matron carefully for further signs of her opinion. "I'm sure they will resume their activities once the war is won." He didn't want to offend her, as many outsiders stood opposed to the anticlerical convictions of the Turnverein, but it would also be a betrayal to the honor of his family (not to mention a lie) if he were to display disdain for the group. He didn't know the St. Paul Turners specifically, but his childhood in the Cincinnati Turnverein had shown him in no uncertain terms that folks generally perceived a democratically-run secular group as radical, even in America. And while Miss Walsh wasn't exactly Princess Alice, she had a fine figure and he certainly wasn't so shallow as to reject the attentions of a woman just because she wasn't the absolute prettiest girl in the room. He'd come of age in such a small town, with so few eligible girls, he was used to dancing with other boys, so he wasn't picky.

Mrs. Coleman agreed politely, but her eyebrows were skeptically raised.

"What's a Turner?" Miss Anna chirped. Her face was round and delicate like her sister's, but a little over-large for her narrow shoulders to carry off just yet. She was going to be a lovely young lady—in a few years. Henry smiled cordially at her with no more than a distant glance.

"Indeed, Henry, I don't recall ever hearing about this society of yours before," Jacob agreed, looking at him with amused interest. Shameless liar. He and Elias had spent countless hours ribbing him about his gymnasticks routine back in Faribault. Henry shifted on his feet.

"Uh, how to explain…" he stalled, clasping his hands in front of him for want of something to do with them. "The Turnverein is a community dedicated to cultivating the two principal components of man—the moral and the physical. A sound mind in a sound body, as it were."

The girls blinked in confusion as Mrs. Coleman scratched her forehead and avoided his gaze.

He shrugged. "It's just a community organization focused on self-improvement. We have community lectures and concerts and the like. Just a well-rounded education, really." Perhaps if he made it sound normal enough, they'd lose interest and change the subject.

Jacob grinned at Mary and her sister by proxy. "Don't forget the *gymnasticks*, Schaef."

Miss Walsh raised her thin, flat eyebrows at him. "*Gymnasticks*? What's that?"

Henry's smile became tight. "Uh, the physical part. There is an emphasis on physical exercise and improvement among the Turners."

Jacob continued grinning. "He can do handstands."

All four ladies looked at Henry sideways. Each seemed to have a very different response to this, from dubious to fascinated and perhaps even a bit titillated.

Encouraged, Jacob added, "And flips."

"Well, that sounds like something I would have to see to believe," Miss Coleman quipped playfully. Henry grimaced, a flush threatening to light up his cheeks. While Jacob and Elias had begrudgingly appreciated his routines, they had also given him *endless* torment for it. They made it abundantly clear that most people had much better things to do than to perfect handstands and single leg swings around a pommel horse.

"Speaking of seeing to believe," Jacob interjected blessedly, "let's take these ladies up to see the view from the Half Moon Battery."

Henry followed after him and Miss Coleman, offering his arm to Miss Walsh. She giggled again as she took it and squeezed his forearm in what seemed to be a thinly veiled attempt to determine his relative strength.

As Jacob led them around the commander's house, Henry scrambled to find something to say to Miss Walsh.

"Have you been having an enjoyable summer?" he ventured.

She smiled and it quite improved her looks. "Very fine indeed, except for all this horrid war business. Our church coordinated a wonderful fundraiser for the troops last weekend and I nearly knitted my fingers to the bone making socks to contribute. So I'm quite glad that is done, at least for now."

Henry studied her as she spoke. She didn't attempt to conceal or control her visage like some vain women did. Her dress was practical, just simple coat sleeves and a few pintucks on the bodice for adornment. Despite her high giggling, she didn't carry herself with trepidation. He quite liked a confident step in a woman.

"So what kind of *'gymnasticks'* do you do?" Cousin Coleman asked rather ham-fistedly, her mouth stumbling over the word even as she attempted to wield it like she knew what it was. Her blue eyes danced on his face before looking down again, trying to hold in a smile.

Henry held back a sigh. Demonstrating routines at the Turner Fest in New Ulm was one thing, but being a novelty outside of the Turner community made him feel like a circus side-show. Besides, he wasn't all that good anyway, and he was very out of practice since leaving home.

"It's really nothing terribly interesting. Just tumbling, really. Those who get very good might be termed acrobats, but it's not so much about spectacle, but rather honing skill and physical function."

Her eyes were large when she said, "What kind of function?"

Henry swallowed hard. She was looking at him with a small secret smile, and it made him feel like he was on display, like he was some sort of amusement for her to consume. "Um, like strength and endurance and precision."

Their group made their way up the wooden staircase to the top of the Half Moon Battery.

"Hmmm," Miss Walsh murmured, eyes alight. "I can't imagine. I do hope you'll do a demonstration for us."

Henry blanched. He'd thought maybe his routines would be of interest to ladies, but after Elias and Jacob gave hims such a hard time, he wasn't sure whether it was more impressive or embarrassing. Even if he were to demonstrate his best routines, he'd need parallel bars or at least some rings and that would require a production much larger than he wanted to pursue in front of all the men. He supposed he could do a handspring or a front tuck, maybe a handstand, but at this point he was much too self-conscious to pursue it.

Luckily, the view from the Half Moon Battery was incredible enough to draw everyone's attention on this fine summer day, with the two rivers meeting at the tip of Pike Island, reflecting the bright blue sky and the path of the river valley cutting through the serene green prairie. The ladies gathered at the edge of the wall and gazed down with a chorus of sighs. Henry stepped up to join them. Such a spectacular view was hard to resist, no matter how many times he'd seen it.

He supposed he didn't really deserve to worry about defending the Turners or his family. He still hadn't sent even one letter to his mother. His brothers were still covering for him, so as far as she knew, he was with them at the front. It was probably kinder to let her believe that, because then she could imagine they were all together. If she knew he was all on his own, she'd worry herself half to death. Maybe show up at the Fort and try to command him to come home. Just the thought of it made his stomach curl with potential humiliation. He really wouldn't put it past her.

He set his hands upon the stone, warmed by the summer sun, and looked down at the landing immediately below. The ferry was on the shore, a horse and wagon driving off of it and towards the steep incline road. Smith manned the post down there, standing alert and quiet as the ferryman and his passengers passed through.

As if he could feel Henry's gaze on him, Smith looked up, his shadowed eyes as sharp as ever. After following him earlier, Henry's suspicions had only amplified. He half expected to look down and find the post vacant *again*—that was how little confidence he had left in the boy. He hadn't been able to get close enough to see what Smith was doing at the Steele farmhouse, but any fool could see he was taking measures to not be caught out by the way he'd moved through the grass and over the fence. Whatever he was up to, it implicated the landlord of the whole fort. The more he thought about it, the more Henry became certain that this was no series of coincidences, no mere tryst gone awry.

He held Smith's gaze for a moment with his own steely glare, hoping that the weasel would perceive that his days of secrecy were numbered. The superior little bastard quirked a brow and smirked. Henry's fingers dug into the stone wall. Shameless. He could at least have the decency to look furtive or abashed about whatever sinister endeavor he was pursuing. Henry found himself unaccountably flustered and redoubled his glare in compensation.

"Hey, Elias! Over here! I want you to meet someone!"

Jacob was hanging over the other edge of the Half Moon Battery opposite Henry, flagging Elias down presumably at the ground level.

Elias made his way up the whitewashed stairs in short order, and Jacob conducted the array of introductions once more.

"Mrs. and Miss Coleman, Miss Anna, Miss Walsh, please meet my friend and newly promoted comrade, Corporal Hower," Jacob said with a flourish. Miss Walsh perked up and smiled fully, with her teeth, extending her hand to Elias.

"Corporal, my, what a pleasure to meet you," she gushed. "Thank you for your service."

Now that Henry had heard her say it twice, he realized what it sounded like when she meant it.

"Elias worked with Henry and I on the farm in Faribault, too. But now he's become too important for the likes of us!"

Elias laughed. "Nonsense. I've always been too important for you."

Miss Walsh giggled again. *She sure does have a way of making a man feel special*, Henry thought cynically. Perhaps he should have done a handstand after all.

"Well, this is just wonderful," Jacob said. His grin was wide, but he swallowed hard. Henry peered at him. "I can't imagine a better time than now to deliver our news, with all of my favorite people and yours, Mary."

Jacob turned to Mary and took her hands in his. "Well, my dear, when is the happy day?"

"Pardon, but what day can you mean?" she replied, though a pink flush rushed into her cheeks and her breast visibly fluttered with her breath. Miss Walsh began giggling again and Miss Anna grasped her cousin's hand tightly in anticipation. Mrs. Coleman stood knowingly, her lips pursed in satisfaction.

"Why, everybody knows we are going to get married, and it might as well be one time or another; so, when shall it be?" Jacob quipped, shrugging his shoulders with a grin.

Mary's eyes were a veritable well of happy tears as she threw her arms around his neck and exclaimed, "I can't see why it can't be this Sunday, you magnificent joker!"

Mrs. Coleman's smile wavered as she said, "Now, Mary—"

But Jacob cut her off. "Yes, we must make haste because I'll be called to the front before you know it. I can't leave here without making my vows to you first."

Mary's happy tears may have been infiltrated by tears of sadness. As much as this was an exciting prospect for Jacob, it was terrifying to imagine that the little time left to them before the Second Regiment mustered out might very well be the only days they ever have together.

"The magistrate will be here on Sunday," Elias contributed. Mrs. Coleman paled as Mary wiped away a tear and turned her wide, hopeful eyes on him. "We expect a new batch of recruits to take the oath. Perhaps he could arrange for some happy nuptials as well."

"Well, we shall certainly have to speak with our priest," Mrs. Coleman put in, perhaps a little more strongly than necessary, placing her hand possessively on Mary's forearm. But Mary only had eyes for Jacob and gazed at him with such ardent fervor that Henry felt the absence of that emotion like a hole in his own chest.

"A wedding at the fort! Can you imagine?" Miss Anna gushed, clapping her gloved hands together. Jacob and Mary just stared at each other like two love-struck cows, hands clutched together. Mrs. Coleman made a show of pulling a dainty watch out of her pocket and gasped in shock at the time.

"My gracious, girls, but it's almost 3 o'clock! We must be getting back home," she exclaimed.

"But Mother, Bridget has supper well in hand, can't we stay a little longer?" Miss Anna protested.

"My sincere apologies, gentlemen, but we really must be going," Mrs. Coleman insisted, glaring at her younger daughter. "Corporal Hower, would you be so kind as to escort us to the ferry?"

Elias looked from Jacob and Miss Coleman to Mrs. Coleman. The happy couple was veritably nuzzling each other's hands. Soon it would be faces if they were to leave them much longer.

"Of course, it would be my pleasure," he murmured, raising his eyebrows significantly at Henry.

Mrs. Coleman gestured for Miss Walsh to take Elias' proffered arm, which she did without as much as a second glance, much less a farewell, to Henry before being led down the steps.

"Mary," Mrs. Coleman chided with a warning tone. "Mary, you will have the rest of your lives for this, come now."

Miss Coleman gazed soulfully at Jacob as she bid him farewell, but even their abrupt departure was not enough to chip away at the happy grins they both wore, their eyes only for each other.

"'Parting is such sweet sorrow,'" Mary quoted as she felt her way down the stairs, her eyes locked on her new fiancé.

"What?" Jacob replied, staring back at her just as moonily.

"It's Shakespeare, my darling!" she called back as she ducked out of sight. "'That I shall say goodnight till it be morrow!'"

Jacob leaned in towards Henry with a bemused expression. "What in the Sam Hill is she talking about?"

"It's a play," Henry supplied. "*Romeo and Juliet*. I think it's supposed to be romantic but I never really understood why, because the lovers kill themselves in the end."

Jacob just stared at him, his brow furrowed in confusion. "That's horrid."

"One of them pretends to be dead so they can run away together, but the other one doesn't know she's not actually dead, so he kills himself, and then she wakes up and sees he's dead and kills herself. It's a tragedy."

Jacob's expression grew incredulous, and then he busted out laughing.

"Women are a mystery, to be sure," he chuckled. "I can't wait to spend my whole life figuring her out."

Henry's chest tightened. They were headed to the front soon. He could very well die on the battlefield before ever getting the chance to figure out a woman's mysteries. As soon as the thought surfaced, he stuffed it down deep. There was no use in mourning until—unless—that actually came to pass.

———

XI

Cate was exhausted. Sleeping no more than four hours at a time for four days was getting to her. Not to mention the distress over her courses. In the afternoon, her stomach had curled in a familiar dull ache that signaled her blood was imminent. With a few tacks from her needle, she'd fastened one of the diapers she'd stolen from the Steeles to the inside of her trousers. It wasn't long enough so she had folded it on a diagonal and the extra padding between her legs brought her at least some comfort in the face of her ever more daunting charade.

After she was relieved from duty at 8 o'clock that evening by a sullen-looking Henry Schaefer, she reported to her barracks for a late supper to find out that Jacob Robinson had made a proposal of marriage to his little pen pal and been accepted. The boys were all gathered around where Jacob was sitting at the small table, leaning toward him or even standing behind to hear the gossip. Cate sat on the edge of Schaefer's lower bunk, close enough to hear but not in the middle of the conversation.

"Well done, Robinson, well done!" Someone from Squad Six said, popping into their room to smack Jacob on the shoulder. "And not a moment too soon, as well."

Cate tried to concentrate on eating her tin of cold beef stew and bread and not roll her eyes. If she succumbed to the temptation, she was liable to give herself a headache.

John Williamson, standing opposite Jacob and behind where Krüger sat shuffling playing cards, laughed. "No kidding! By the time we get back from the front, you'll likely be greeted by a brood of little brats."

The temptation to roll her eyes was too strong. Cate couldn't resist. She wrinkled her nose with effort but ultimately gave in.

Tom Webster guffawed. He'd left a wife and two children back in Hastings. "If you come back to more than one baby, let's hope they're twins, because otherwise there will be some questions that need answering."

Jacob shifted in his seat, visibly uncomfortable as he tried to laugh with the rest of the men around the table.

"But seriously, Jacob," Webster continued after wiping a mirthful tear from his eye. "There is nothing more wonderful and terrible than joining together only to have to part again."

"To know divine pleasure only to sacrifice it at the feet of the Union!" Elias Hower declared, a laugh hiding below the surface of his bravado.

Jacob glowered. "I know, but why would I wait only to lose her to some other man while I'm at the front? There is no better time than now."

Webster's smile waned and he placed a hand on Jacob's shoulder. "Fellows, come now, this is serious. We're all facing down the field of battle in a few months. Let the boy have his happiness."

The other men ducked their heads, sufficiently chastised, but not enough to stop snickering.

"Well, my friend," Hower said, slinging his arm around Jacob's shoulder. "As your corporal, I will certainly support your petition for a furlough. And if you remember all that I told you about making a woman smile, I am sure your brief honeymoon will be nothing but happy."

He waggled his eyebrows significantly at Jacob. The other boys leaned in eagerly. It amused Cate how they clambered to show their great knowledge of women, yet when each spoke, the others hung on his every word as though they were collecting valuable secrets. It didn't seem to matter if the men were young or old—they seemed desperate to compare notes through this manly pretense of expertise.

"How to make a woman smile, huh?" John Williamson repeated, grinning. "Robinson looks like he could use a refresher."

Jacob looked suddenly very interested in his hands. Hower preened and lowered his voice conspiratorially.

"Well, gentlemen, the secret to a happy wife is of course maintaining a happy marriage bed."

"Quoth the bachelor," Webster quipped, rolling his eyes.

"One need not be a married man to know his way around a woman," Hower chided, his eyebrows raised in innuendo. Cate pressed her lips together to stifle a snort of laughter threatening to bubble up.

"No, he just needs to pay," Wilbur Krüger interjected in his heavy German accent, his big chest squeezing out a loud, deep laugh. Cate couldn't resist laughing along with the rest of the boys.

Hower shook his head and carried on, undeterred. "It might surprise some of you to learn, but a woman can experience the same pleasure a man does in the marriage act."

Several of the men's eyes grew wider. All of them leaned in with interest. Even as she let out a long-suffering sigh, Cate couldn't help but tilt her head to improve her ability to hear. Of course a woman could reach a pleasurable release; this she knew well enough from experience. But the proposition that a woman might experience the racking, shuddering finish the way Richard had admittedly peaked her interest. She begrudgingly acknowledged that she, too, was getting roped into Hower's pretense, but she was too curious to care.

Smug with the rapt attention paid to him, Hower continued in a hushed tone. "Imagine, if you will, a woman's body. Between her legs, she is indeed the inverse of a man. So one must conclude that if you are to bring a woman pleasure as a man might experience, one must bring her to her climax through the equal but opposite force that oneself might enjoy."

More than one brow furrowed in confusion. Cate's eyes narrowed incredulously as she turned this notion over in her mind. This did not align with her own experience, but she had no frame of reference to corroborate it with.

"What's that supposed to mean?" Williamson complained loudly, throwing his hands up and leaning back against the scaffolds of Cate and Schaefer's bunk.

"Perhaps," Webster conceded thoughtfully. The other men deferred their attention to him fully, much to Hower's chagrin, but surely even he had to admit Webster had the most verifiable experience at the table (well, unless one counted Cate). "I think that is a logical way of thinking about it. I would add that one might take more time in one's effort, too, as a woman's heart needs time to acclimate to the situation, both physically and emotionally, most especially the first time."

Cate's knee jiggled. She wondered if Richard had had this same conversation with his chums before their wedding. He had been tender, he'd been attentive, but he'd never once asked what would please her. Perhaps if he had, she could have instructed him towards where his efforts might have had the greatest effect. Perhaps then, it might have been more than nice. Perhaps it could have been as revelatory for her as it had seemed for him.

Jacob nodded at Webster earnestly. "Yes, of course. I want to do right by her as well as I can before I have to leave."

"Surely you will!" Hower exclaimed. "While I certainly wouldn't repeat it here in such an open forum—being an officer, it wouldn't be decorous—but I'm happy to share with you the tricks I've learned."

"Wonder where he learned those tricks," Williamson muttered snidely to Cate, nudging her with an elbow. She wrinkled her nose. She'd promised herself to keep a low profile, but she just couldn't hold her tongue any longer. The nudge from Williamson was just the tacit encouragement her argumentative streak needed to barge into the conversation.

"Perhaps you might do better to ask her what she likes."

All of the men swiveled their heads to look at Charles Smith. Cate shrugged nonchalantly under the scrutiny. "I mean, what better authority on a woman's pleasure than the woman herself?"

Hower's brow furrowed incredulously. "Perhaps if she were a public woman, but Jacob is marrying a genteel girl. She will not have known pleasure, so how is she to know what to tell him?" Hower put a patrician hand on Jacob's shoulder and added in a low voice, "Not to mention she shouldn't have to. If he asked, it would make him look completely green."

Cate blinked. "But he is."

The men stared. Jacob blanched.

"...Aren't you?"

This might have been one of those Man Things that was anathema for no apparent reason. This was exactly why she needed to shut her mouth and keep a low profile.

Webster came to her rescue, his brow furrowed as he tapped his chin with one forefinger. "No, the boy has some sense of it. It is good to listen carefully to the woman. Her sighs or grumbles will let you know when you have the right of it."

"But what if she doesn't say anything at all?" Jacob implored, his shoulders beginning to tense with anxiety.

"Then ask her," Cate cut in again impatiently, in spite of her better judgment. "A girl doesn't need to be a public woman to know what she likes."

Incredulity met her once again, but it only spurred her on. She was dangerously close to full debate form now.

"Surely you all, regardless of your experience with women, have conducted some exploration by your own hand?" This was perhaps a shocking notion, akin to accusing the room of self-abuse. Cate probably should have softened the blow, but she was too deep in now. "What makes you think women don't explore themselves similarly?"

A perfect row of slack-jawed mouths formed soft Os of shock. Even Webster, it seemed, hadn't entertained this possibility as he frowned thoughtfully. Cate was distantly surprised none of them flew into a moral rage, but perhaps that simply indicated none of them were Quakers.

"What makes you think they do?" Williamson squawked, his expression caught between scandalized and titillated.

Cate's brain caught up with her mouth and found she had scandalized herself. So she boldly lied. "Growing up the only boy in a two-room cabin of seven older sisters gives one a harsh reminder that men and women are a lot more similar than they are different."

Jacob grimaced. "Ugh, God, Smith! No!"

"You broke Robinson!" Williamson squealed gleefully.

Cate tried not to grimace and nodded sagely at the others. God, her and her big mouth. "It is a terrible burden of knowledge. I also know way more than any man should about a woman's monthlies."

They all groaned in disgust, as if she'd just tossed a dead animal on the table as a prank. Hopefully that would get them to back off.

Williamson gagged theatrically. "How can you talk about that while you're eating?"

Cate widened her eyes dolefully. "Most days, I can scarcely sleep for the horror of what I know."

Jacob's eyes were round and haunted. "...What else do you know?"

"Can we play euchre now?" Krüger complained, shuffling the cards together for the umpteenth time. "*Der Bubi* will figure it out by and by and lights out is soon."

Webster heartily agreed, and the others followed as Hower coordinated teams and Krüger began dealing cards. Cate reminded herself to thank him as she sopped up the last of her stew with the crust of her bread. She was so exhausted, she set her tin aside to wash later before climbing up into her own bunk. She just needed to get in some shut-eye before her next guard duty. Hopefully the boys would keep their card game somewhat quietish. Not that she was holding her breath.

———

The room was dark when she was jostled awake. It was Schaefer, returned from guard duty and climbed into the bottom bunk. Cate groaned and rolled over, batting at her pillow to find a more comfortable position on her right side. The waxing moon cast a wan glow through the open window, and she could hear the frogs and crickets performing their midnight opera outside. Krüger was snoring lightly and blessedly the rest of the men were, at least for the moment, sleeping soundly without significant racket. (Sometimes, they played their own symphony of guttural snorts for her late night listening pleasure.)

The bunk swayed again as Schaefer clambered around down there. She imagined him circling the bed like a dog trying to find the most comfortable position. There was a whisper of fabric being pulled about and she craned her neck slightly over the side, peering through the shadows to find out if he was removing his shirt again.

The pretty picture of his bare chest had dogged her all day, invading her thoughts whenever she was otherwise unoccupied. It was like having a tune stuck in one's head, only this was a mental image of a very well-formed man with a dusting of light blonde hair on his chest. Having spent much of her waking hours standing guard duty, she'd spent more time than she would care to admit revisiting the memory from every angle. The way he'd pulled the neck of his shirt over his head, how his strength swelled under pale skin that sharply contrasted with his sun-browned forearms. The way his wide shoulders sloped down to the hard planes of his chest, flowing in sharp definition to his narrow waist. She now viscerally understood what folks meant by "strapping lad". The man was honed like a fine knife. The other boys were fit from farm work, but Henry Schaefer was on another level. He must have chopped one hundred years worth of firewood to build that kind of muscle. Next time she saw him, perhaps she could make a point to get his shirt dirty so that she might be treated to seeing him change it again.

Chiding herself for her lecherous thoughts, Cate realized she was now fully awake, hyper aware of the rhythmic snores of Krüger and the rapidly waning minutes until her next guard duty. She rubbed her face into her pillow, which still smelled like unwashed hair, and muffled a frustrated grumble. She tried to clear her mind and imagine her body heavy with fatigue—not a terribly tall order, given it was true.

She heard Schaefer exhale as he settled into his pillow, the whole scaffold creaking again as he turned over in his bed. He usually slept in his shirt, his trousers hanging on the hook at the foot of his bed, which reminded her how his thighs had that same strapping quality as his shoulders. Richard spent so much time sitting and pontificating that his legs had been thin and underdeveloped. But Schaefer? His thighs were powerful, like they could endure a great deal of ... repetitive activity without fatigue... Cate's teeth worried her lower lip as she felt a flush rush into her cheeks and in between her own thighs.

She imagined what it might be like to have Schaefer above her, working away as Richard had on their wedding night, his breath huffing, his voice catching in his throat as a flush spread across his taut chest. She wanted to dig her fingers into those shoulders, feel that hard muscle straining against her. The weight of him on top of her. She realized she was holding her breath and carefully let it out as quietly as she could, giving her thighs a gentle squeeze that sent a current of pleasure through her low belly.

And that was when she heard it. A soft, rhythmic pat of skin on skin. She thought for a moment she had conjured it in her own lurid imagination, but as she tuned her ear, there was no mistaking it. Her brow knitted together as she strained to isolate the sound above the ambient noise of the night. Then she heard a huff of heavy breath below her and she realized all at once that Schaefer must be pleasuring himself.

Cate's blood burst into flame. She had to bite her lip to stop herself from letting out a soft whimper. Dear God. There was an enormous amount of effort spent in Abolitionist and Quaker circles on the virtues of restraint, quiet innuendo suggesting that the waste of a man's seed on something as indulgent as self-pleasure could rot a man's mind if he was too weak-willed to stop. Cate was dying to know what would push Schaefer to give in to such a shameful indulgence.

She breathed shallow, frozen in the effort to listen, to pick up every minute sound. She should be embarrassed by association. Ashamed of what she was hearing and how she could feel her pulse throb between her thighs as she squeezed them tight together in time with the rhythm Schaefer was setting. The shame should have been a deterrent. It wasn't. With her moral conscience locked out, she ran a loop of fragmented fantasies through her mind's eye. She couldn't focus on anything aside from the sharp urge to wedge her own hand down her trousers, mixed with what she imagined he might look like while fucking her. God, but she'd enjoyed being stretched and filled when she'd been married. More than she'd ever expected. Richard was a pedantic bore, but he hadn't displayed any aversion to her enjoyment of their marriage bed. How much better would it feel if she was pinioned under a body she was actually attracted to? She swallowed hard.

Dammit to hell.

Somewhat helplessly, she let her right hand snake in between her thighs, her fingertips pulling out an unintentional sigh from her lips. Cate hadn't done this since she'd left Richard, but if she wasn't going to abstain from squeezing her thighs to the obscene sounds of her comrade below, she might as well do it quick.

She feared he might hear her and strained to detect any variation to his heavy breaths, any sound that would indicate that he knew what she was about. But the fear of him realizing she was listening, playing along, did nothing but feed her desire. She buried two fingers inside herself, marveling at how slick and yielding she'd become, and slid her thumb hard against the apex of her quim. The bunk began to tremble gently with Schaefer's effort—or perhaps it was hers—and her conscious thought gave way to brief flashes of ways she might have him, imagery of his bare body, and what she imagined he might look like in this very moment, working himself over with his hand just below her. Her hand was crushed between the pulsing force of her thighs, but she did not stop. That dark, primal pleasure was blossoming in the pit of her stomach, and it drove her already reckless streak to a fever pitch.

She wondered what would happen if she climbed down below, unabashedly watching him and letting him know that she knew what he was doing, what they both were doing. She imagined his cheeks flushed, his lips soft and open with want, his eyes unwaveringly meeting hers. She imagined him gasping, shuddering, spending between his fingers, her gaze on him all it took to send him over the edge and into a state of heedless surrender. It was precisely this thought that hitched a grunt in her throat as her cunt pulsed, and she felt the pleasure she'd been building turn over in waves. There was no way he didn't hear her, but the knowledge of this was so distant, so muted by more blissful sensation, that she couldn't manage to care.

As the feeling subsided, she took in a shaky breath and grinned. She had never quite managed such a delectable finish with Richard (or to be more precise, by herself, after Richard had fallen asleep). The scaffold trembled, and she heard Schaefer's echoing grunt below her. The sound made her want more. Cate pressed her head back into her pillow and planted her hands at her sides. She could feel the aftershocks blossoming into sweet potential. God, she desperately wanted another go. She held herself still and listened. Surely, Schaefer would say something now. Acknowledge that she was awake, that she knew he was awake, that something had occurred between them. Kind of.

What would she do when he said something? Brush it off? Deliver some snide comment? Dare him to climb up the scaffold and join her? God, what if she said nothing and just climbed in with him? Scaled his body like a tree and shoved his hand into her trousers? What would his reaction be to discover she was a woman? Even as her breath hitched with a rise of arousal, the sound of Schaefer's breath quieted.

She waited. She didn't dare say anything. The more time that went by, the less fogged her mind became and the more apprehension she felt. Soon she heard nothing but the crickets and the frogs and damnable Krüger sawing logs. Did Schaefer fall asleep? Was this yet another thing that men did that they never talked about? They'd just pull themselves off together and pretend like nothing ever happened?

It was about this time that she noticed a new warmth between her thighs. Her courses had arrived.

Hooray. She was mixed with a feeling of bone-deep relief and horrific apprehension. The reality of her ruse and its constant companion, the fear of being found out, settled around her again. It cut off anything that even remotely felt like connection.

Suffice to say, she didn't fall back asleep before it was time for her to rise and relieve Jacob from guard duty. By morning, she looked a wreck, her eyes blotched with dark circles, the lack of rest making her snap like a dog at whoever was so unfortunate as to cross her.

———

XII

Sunday, August 11, 1861

"Article i: Every officer now in the army of the United States shall, in six months from the passing of this act, and every officer who shall hereafter be appointed shall, before he enters on the duties of his office, subscribe these rules and regulations."

Henry stood at attention with the rest of Company K as the Captain read off the Articles of War again for the benefit of fifty new recruits who mustered in that day. The rest of the troops had heard these before, when their squad underwent the inspection, but it was pertinent to read it again as the magistrate was on the premises and ready to administer their oaths. A collection of civilians, including Jacob's betrothed, were gathered on the Round Bastion to observe.

"Article 2: It is earnestly recommended to all officers and soldiers diligently to attend divine service..."

It was very difficult to track Captain Noah's droning recitation of the articles among so many contingencies and addendums. Especially when it had to do with religious practices Henry had no use for. His eyes lingered over his comrades in ranks in front of him. Charley Smith stood directly before him. Henry briefly entertained the idea of flicking him in the neck, just to torture him. He'd been absolutely unbearable the last few days. Henry liked to think it was because he knew his days of lurking about were numbered, but he conceded it was more likely because Smith was upset that they'd brought themselves off together the other night.

Smith struck Henry as one of those uptight Grahamites, who never drank and only ate certain foods and thought going off like that as a form of self-abuse. It certainly would explain why he was such an asshole. And while the Turners were in some ways equally as obsessed with physical health as the Grahamites, they approached the body with more curiosity than control. Men had desires that needed, from time to time, to be dealt with. It certainly didn't threaten their health, that was for certain. (Henry would know by now if it did…)

A niggling part of his mind reminded him that while it was certainly not unusual to overhear a man bring himself off in a barracks, it was perhaps a bit indecorous to work at it at the same time … but he'd be damned if he was going to defer to Smith at the expense of his own release. He'd been fairly far along by the time he'd noticed the little muted huffs above him, and he wasn't ashamed to admit it gave him a certain amount of gratification, knowing Smith was not deterred but perhaps even driven on by the whole thing. It was satisfying to imagine the arrogant bastard prostrate and vulnerable for once.

"Article 5: Any officer or soldier who shall use contemptuous or disrespectful words against the President of the United States, against the Vice-President thereof, against the Congress of the United States, or against the Chief Magistrate or Legislature of any of the United States, in which he may be quartered, if a commissioned officer, shall be cashiered, or otherwise punished, as a court-martial shall direct; if a non-commissioned officer or soldier, he shall suffer such punishment as shall be inflicted on him by the sentence of a court-martial."

Henry blinked. Whoever had written these articles had very much liked the sound of his own words. Henry gave up trying and allowed his mind to spin the puzzle of Smith's treachery from every angle instead. In addition to Smith's horrific attitude in the past week, he'd been sneaking off even more often, sometimes with scarcely an attempt at an excuse. Yesterday, Sergeant Osborn had tried to order the boy off to the hospital, assuming he was sick if he had to beg off for personal privilege so often, but Smith had deferentially refused, insisting he was fine.

Henry rolled his eyes. If he was so fine, he wouldn't need a privy every few hours. Were there such a thing as divine justice, dysentery would be the perfect punishment for the little turd. Except that Henry didn't believe it was a call of nature at all. That couldn't explain why Smith was sneaking around the Steele farm or why he had stolen that musket. Henry was certain he was up to something more sinister. He couldn't understand why Sergeant Osborn wasn't similarly suspicious.

"Article 6: Any officer or soldier who shall behave himself with contempt or disrespect toward his commanding officer, shall be punished..."

He wondered if there was anything in the oath about behaving with contempt or disrespect toward fellow soldiers. Because if that was the case, Smith was going to need a year's worth of guard duty for all the vitriol he spewed.

"Article 7: Any officer or soldier who shall begin, excite, cause, or join in, any mutiny or sedition, in any troop or company in the service of the United States, or in any party, post, detachment, or guard, shall suffer death, or such other punishment as by a court-martial shall be inflicted."

Henry's eyes narrowed. That word again. Sedition.

The other day, he'd picked up a copy of the *Chatfield Democrat* in the mess hall, and having nowhere to be until his next guard duty, he'd taken to browsing. Generally, he abhorred American Democrats, though not as much as the Know Nothing party that had terrorized Cincinnati's German neighborhood six years ago and sent his mother halfway to a nervous collapse. But there was something to be said for knowing the mind of one's opposition—even if one found it contained nothing.

There had been an article about the Alien and Sedition Acts, and the federal government shutting down several papers in New York as seditious. He'd noticed it in particular because he hadn't been familiar with the word. The author, in true journalist form, bristled at the proposition of the papers being suppressed, touting free speech and free press as he simultaneously threatened insurrection against "Uncle Abe" for making his will law. Henry had asked Tom Webster in passing what it meant and he'd said treason or rebellion. Wilbur Krüger had been in the barracks at the time too and together the three of them collected a number of expressions in both English and German that sufficiently addressed Henry's confusion.

Sedition was why they were at war. The Confederate states had chosen rebellion over recognizing Lincoln's presidential victory. Henry's eyes bored into the back of Smith's head as he turned over a suspicion he had not previously considered before. The theft of a gun, the sneaking around, the inexplicable anger after being passed over for the corporal promotion ... was it possible that Smith was some sort of Southern Democrat spy? That he was doing some sort of work to undermine the military and defense of the union?

"Article 8: Any officer, non-commissioned officer, or soldier, who, being present at any mutiny or sedition, does not use his utmost endeavor to suppress the same, or coming to the knowledge of any intended mutiny, does not, without delay, give information thereof to his commanding officer, shall be punished by the sentence of a court-martial with death, or otherwise, according to the nature of his offense."

Henry was listening now. He'd decided to keep quiet, to wait until he had more evidence before going to Command with an accusation. He was certain Smith was up to no good, but he wasn't entirely sure what that "no good" was. But if he kept quiet and something happened, apparently he could be held culpable for knowing something was amiss and not reporting it. Henry grimaced. His accusations were tenuous at best—that was why he wanted to wait for something more conclusive. But if even tacit knowledge was an offense worthy of a court-martial, that put a real damper on his timeline.

He screwed his eyes shut and tried again to think over all the evidence he had collected. He was unabashedly tuned out from the Articles reading now, but his realization struck him with a tangible sense of urgency. Based on what he had heard about the man, Franklin Steele was an opportunistic Democrat who had acquired the fort through some sort of cronyism with the former Governor and Senator Rice. Senator Rice... wasn't he the one who had all but said that the South was perfectly within their rights to secede from the Union? Was Smith somehow in league with Rice and other Southern sympathizers through Steele?

He wracked his brain for all the things he'd caught Smith doing thus far. Sneaking around when he should be on guard duty—that he'd caught him at several times. Rendezvousing at Steele's farm. Stealing the musket, of course. That lady's chemise was always an outlier. The most logical conclusion was that Smith was having some sort of liaison with a woman when he was supposed to be on guard duty, but there was something off about that explanation. For one thing, the shift was so filthy, he couldn't imagine any woman wearing such a thing willingly. No level of destitution could account for a garment being so in want of a wash. Unless...

———

Cate listened attentively to the Articles of War, trying to ignore how the sun beat down on the dusty parade ground. It was hot enough to be uncomfortable, but not quite hot enough to sweat. It was consistent with how this week had been going.

To her great distress, she had been reassigned to guard duty at the post barn this week, which was nice in its quiet seclusion outside the gates of the fort, but not nearly as convenient as the ferry landings for washing and drying guard-napkins. She'd ended up pilfering water from the horses to wash with. It was less than ideal, but she'd managed. Now that the heaviest of her blood was done, as well as that awful slog of guard duty, she was feeling awash in relief and decidedly more optimistic than ever before. Their platoon was drilling quite well, and new recruits had arrived. Soon, their regiment would be full, and they'd be off to the front to do some real fighting. After the cowardice of the volunteers at the Battle of Bull Run, she was eager to prove her own courage and provide yet another example as to why men weren't nearly as hard nor strong, nor women as weak and emotional, as everyone seemed to believe.

The Articles of War thus read in their entirety, in as dreary a fashion as Captain Noah could muster, the Magistrate approached and smiled upon the men of Company K.

"Greetings, soldiers!" he called, his voice booming. "I am most honored to administer to you this day Sunday, August 11 in the year of our Lord eighteen hundred and sixty one, the oath of allegiance as soldiers defending the United States of America. Rather than pontificate as to the glory of your position and the bravery you are about to display, I shall leave those words to more able men and perform my duty under the law. Please, honorable gentlemen, repeat after me..."

Cate felt her heart in her throat, her eyes wide and eager as her tongue formed the words quietly. Under the hum of the voices of her company, she was quite sure that her honor-bound use of her birth name would go undetected.

"I, Catherine Stowell, do solemnly swear that I will bear true allegiance to the United States of America, and that I will serve them honestly and faithfully against all their enemies or opposers whatsoever; and observe and obey the orders of the President of the United States, and the orders of the officers appointed over me, according to the Rules and Articles for the government of the armies of the United States."

When the recitation was complete, Cate felt a sense of immense satisfaction blossom in her breast as the civilian onlookers cheered for them. She straightened in her makeshift uniform and enjoyed the way her body fell into the soldier's position so naturally.

The captain ordered the sergeants to break ranks for the afternoon meal, and Cate strode happily towards the mess hall when Sergeant Osborn's voice called her to attention.

"Squad Seven, front and center!" the Sergeant called. She joined the other boys and noticed Henry Schaefer once again staring her down like some sort of cat stalking his prey. She refused to dignify his nonsense with a glance and was pleased with how easily she was able to let it roll off her back. After letting herself indulge in his quiet show of self-pleasure a few nights ago, she'd been certain something would change between them, but he'd been colder toward her, if that was even possible. The unspoken whatever-it-was that had affected them both stayed silent, and it made her angrier than ever that his stupid defective personality had to be housed inside such an alluring package. So it was to her great relief that she could honestly say she didn't care what he thought at present, so high was her mood.

"Gentlemen, the time has come for us to accommodate our lodgings for the new recruits," Sergeant Osborn said once they had all gathered to hear him. "As we were told when we first formed our squad, the barracks you occupy will now be needed to house three squads."

Cate's high spirits sank quicker than that damn musket had sunk to the bottom of the river. Three squads in that tiny room? That could only mean sharing bunks. She had completely forgotten about that. She pressed firmly down on the panic that tightened her chest.

"In order to prevent in-fighting," Osborn gave a pointed glare to Henry and Charles, "I have taken the liberty of assigning you bunk-mates."

The men all grumbled. Cate stood still and quiet, not trusting herself to make any other response. Goddammit Schaefer—he was still glaring at her. It was unnerving.

"Our squad will occupy the first berth. Hower will join me in the orderly room while the rest of you will share in the following formation."

"Permission to speak, sir?" Jacob piped up, his face tight with anticipation.

"I'm not taking requests," Osborn replied preemptively. Jacob scowled but did not continue.

"The bottom-most bunk will be occupied by Krüger and Williamson."

Krüger shrugged and Williamson deflated. The skinny younger boy was the only logical choice since Krüger was large and would leave no additional space on the 6 foot by 3 foot pallet.

"The middle will be Webster and Robinson."

They looked sullen but given they could have been assigned to Krüger, not terribly disappointed. Cate felt like she was going to choke as she deduced her own bed-partner.

"And up top, we'll have Schaefer and Smith," Osborn concluded, a severe warning look on his face. Cate didn't heed it.

"But sir," she interjected. "Certainly it would not be wise to—"

Osborn cut her off with a stern glare. "I'll brook no argument. I have taken careful consideration of this plan, and it is my fervent hope that you will all stop with this ridiculous in-fighting and learn to work together. We'll see the front in a matter of months. There is no room for feuds when lives are on the line."

"But sir—"

"No. Now, you are dismissed to your meal. Move your effects to your assigned areas, and clean the remaining beds in preparation for the new squads to join you before drills."

And that was that. The rest of the squad walked away. Cate wasn't terribly aware of how poorly she was hiding her displeasure until Robinson passed by and patted her on the shoulder. She couldn't quite find a way to make her legs work. Not only was she going to have to share with one of the other men, bringing the ever present threat of being found out literally into her bed, but it just had to be the one who simultaneously made her want to fondle and strangle him.

Schaefer sauntered over to her with a smarmy smirk on his lips. "You won't see any trouble from me as long as you're playing by the rules."

Cate watched him incredulously as he strolled off to the mess on those *damnable* thighs. What was that supposed to mean? He'd caught her in a couple of unfortunate situations, of course, but she hadn't done anything that she hadn't paid her due for. She was on dish duty every day this week for the musket. Surely he'd accept the simplest explanation was the most logical; she was just a dumb kid with a big ego who kept sticking his foot in it.

She couldn't shake the twitchy feeling of imminent dread, though. He'd found her chemise—and hid it somewhere, she wasn't sure where. He had one piece of solid evidence to reveal her. She was pretty certain he'd seen her at the Steele's farm, too. Perhaps he'd realized what she was doing. Could he have put it together?

Cate scarcely tasted the food she was served in the mess. Afterwards, she wandered listlessly into the barracks, where the rest of the squad was already working to move their effects and clean the space (if what they did could constitute cleaning; Cate would scarcely dignify it as tidying).

She paused in the doorway. The top-most bunk was a good five feet up. She would be well and truly trapped up there, especially if Schaefer slept on the outside. She stared at the bunk, her hands limp at her sides. What if he tried to bring himself off again, but this time right next to her? She wasn't sure anyone had the self control to look the other way and feign sleep in that tight of quarters. The thought, which would have excited her a few days ago, now made her feel sick to her stomach.

The boys were gathering up their things, stowing extra shirts and hats into satchels that would hang off the end of the scaffolds on old hooks. Letters, cards, *carte de visites* of loved ones, all of it got transferred over.

"At least we'll have two blankets when it gets colder," Robinson said encouragingly. Williamson glared at him before regarding Krüger's hulking form.

"This is humbug," Williamson muttered as he came to stand next to Cate. "We're grown men, we can choose for ourselves who to bunk with."

Cate crossed her arms. "Agreed."

Williamson groaned. "I might as well sleep on a matchbook for how much room I'm gonna have."

Cate sighed in solidarity. Schaefer crossed the room with a bundle of his things in his arms, watching her with unveiled contempt and suspicion. She was up shit creek without a paddle. She needed to come up with a plan quickly, because if he was as close to suspecting her secret as she thought he was, he could collect the proof quite easily as she slept. Once reported, it would be a quick strip search with the surgeon before she was tossed out the door and back into the arms of her more-than-likely outraged husband. If it was between exposure or throwing Schaefer on the rails first, she was more than willing to sacrifice him. She'd sworn to protect the Union with her life. She had no intention of breaking that oath—not without a fight.

———

XIII

Low clouds had rolled in over the fort, teasing the dry prairie with the threat of rain. The barometric pressure fell tantalizingly slow as the swath of gray hovered over the large drill ground. They were in company dress parade that afternoon, modeling formations for the new recruits who stood observing atop the Round Bastion with their sergeants. Other new fellows were serving on marker detail for the more experienced troops to use as landmarks as the company marched through the formations. The adjutant rode around the mass of men, barking instructions that were becoming increasingly more difficult to make out as the wind picked up.

Henry had an unloaded musket rifle to practice with this time. He wielded it with some conceit, as Smith was the only one in their squad still relegated to practicing with a stick. Served him right. But they were new at the company formations and that, mixed with the inability to hear the captain's directives for the wind, led to more than one drill ending in chaotic confusion. He could understand why the Battle of Bull Run had gone so poorly if the troops were as green as this.

The bugle for supper came not a moment too soon, and the men piled into the mess to inhale an army's worth of boiled potatoes and cold beef as the clouds began to release their rain. Henry listened to the conversation only halfway. It wasn't that Elias' gossip about the new squads they were bunking with was uninteresting. It was that he could not stop turning over his theory about Smith in his mind, checking it from all angles. It seemed outrageous, but it also made perfect sense. It was the only way he could come up with to explain all of Smith's unusual behavior. When it came down to it, he would rather speak up and be wrong than be silent and court-martialed.

So when Smith excused himself to begin another round of dish duty, Henry leaned in close to Elias and Jacob and hissed, "Fellas—I think Smith is up to no good."

Elias and Jacob exchanged weary glances.

"Why Henry, I could never have guessed you felt that way," Elias deadpanned.

Henry rolled his eyes and carried on. "Obviously we can all see that he's a sonofabitch, but I mean something more nefarious, possibly even ... sedition."

As quiet as he was trying to be, that got the attention of Webster and Krüger.

Elias regarded him with high eyebrows. "That's a serious accusation, Henry."

"Are you sure you aren't just trying to find reasons to hate him?" Jacob said patronizingly. "I mean, he apologized for landing us in guard duty. He's terse, sure, but I'm not sure I would even qualify him as a 'sonofabitch' anymore, much less a traitor."

Williamson slid down the bench to join the conversation and shrugged. "At least not this week, in any case."

Henry gritted his teeth. "No, I'm very certain that it's more than personal dislike. I have been tracking his movements since he lost that musket, and he's up to something. I've got a pretty good hunch on what it is too."

The boys leaned in to listen. Elias pressed his lips together. "Right, but before you begin, just know that because I'm an officer now, I'll have to kick these accusations up the chain. At least, I will if there's any merit to them."

Henry glowered at Elias' sardonic expression.

"This is serious, Elias," Henry intoned. "You see, the night that Smith supposedly dropped the musket in the river, he wasn't there when I came to the post to relieve him. This is a 2 am guard duty, mind you. I looked all around, called for him. Nothing. Nothing, that is, except a *lady's chemise*."

The boys all exchanged glances, and Williamson laughed in the way only a teenage boy with lady's underwear on the mind can.

"Smith? I didn't know he had it in him," Webster remarked, crossing his arms and nodding appreciatively.

Henry frowned. "I know what you're thinking, but I don't think that's what was going on. As I was going back up to the fort to wake Sergeant Osborn, Smith showed up. He was nervous, clearly trying to convince me that nothing was amiss."

Jacob shrugged. "That sounds pretty consistent with what Webster implied. It's not anything to write home about."

"I thought that at first, too, but I didn't even realize it was a lady's chemise right away, because it was *filthy*." The boys waggled their eyebrows at each other. Henry huffed in frustration. "I mean, it was rank. It stank ... like a man."

Elias' eyebrows furrowed together. The rest of the boys mirrored him. Jacob looked more confused than anything.

"Are you trying to imply that Smith was wearing a lady's unmentionables?" he asked. Webster snorted and Krüger veritably guffawed.

"Oh, Heinrich," Krüger snickered in German. "I knew the Turnverein hold the Greeks in high regard, but this is taking *Phaedrus* a little too literally."

Henry's eyes snapped on him and he scowled.

"What did he say?" Williamson asked.

Jacob shrugged, and Elias' nose scrunched as he ventured, "Not sure, but I think it was something about the Turners."

"What's a Turner?" Williamson pressed.

Jacob's face alighted like some sort of devil, and Henry glowered firmly at Krüger before he said, "Enough, that's all beside the point. What I'm trying to say is that I think Smith is using lady's clothes to disguise himself and gather information to pass on to the Democrats, maybe even the Confederacy."

The boys laughed even more heartily. Webster regarded him like he might one of his children. "A Confederate spy? This far northwest? That doesn't make any sense. Besides, even the Democrats in the state house have conceded their skepticism to support the war effort."

"Why shouldn't it?" Henry retorted. "We were the first state to offer up men to President Lincoln after Fort Sumter. Even in the Bull Run disaster, the First Minnesota performed well. Our men pose just as much of a threat to the Southern cause as soldiers from New York or Pennsylvania. Certainly distance alone can't protect us—not when the Rebs are so eager to capitalize on their advantage and the Mississippi provides an easy path straight to our doorstep."

"But a woman?" Jacob asked, stuck on the previous point. "When would he be performing this charade?"

"I think that's what he's up to when he's disappearing," Henry asserted. "He's young enough to pull off the illusion, and he can move undetected. Civilians come in and out of the fort with impunity. He could don a disguise, lurk around and listen for secrets from command to pass on to the Rebs."

"And who is he passing this information to, then?" Elias asked, his fingers steepled as he looked down his nose at Henry.

"Franklin Steele," Henry retorted.

His friends exchanged dubious looks. Williamson looked utterly confused. "You mean the sutler?"

Henry nodded. "Hear me out. Steele is the sutler, but he also owns the land the fort is on. When the army occupied it, he lost out on his investment."

"I dunno, I heard he's charging the army rent," Webster chuckled.

"He's *also* a friend of Senator Rice and Henry Sibley, both of whom are prominent Democrats and have voiced sympathy to the Confederate cause."

Elias rolled his eyes. "Rhetorical posturing after Fort Sumter does not a Confederate sympathizer make. Those men must find opposition to the Republicans in order to set themselves up for reelection. They're anti-Lincoln, not anti-Union."

Henry let out a frustrated growl. "Just because they've recanted doesn't mean they have changed their sentiments. Steele is at the very least war-profiteering. Whatever he's up to, Smith is in league with him."

"And how do you know that?" Elias retorted, crossing his arms.

"I saw Smith sneaking into the Steele's farm-yard when he was supposed to be on guard duty," Henry shot back, his ability to provide conclusive evidence in response catching Elias off-guard.

Webster gasped. "What if Smith is having an affair with one of Steele's daughters?"

The jaws of both Jacob and Williamson dropped in salacious delight.

"Or his *wife*!" Williamson escalated, grinning. The boys laughed, and Henry rubbed his forehead in exasperation. Why couldn't they see what he saw? Smith wasn't just a hard case. He was *hiding* something. And Henry was almost positive, despite his friends' skepticism, that he was right.

"Trust me," Henry assured, "Smith is *not* having an affair. I was right behind him during the oath today. I did not hear him say it. He was just moving his lips."

"Sneaking off during guard duty? Leaving lady's unmentionables lying around? Climbing fences of the lady in question's house? Sounds a lot like an affair to me," Webster said, smiling knowingly. "I once climbed the trellis of my wife's parents house to steal a kiss in the middle of the night. It's a lot more likely than masquerading as a woman to spy for the Confederates, is all."

Henry had to concede that it probably was, but he *knew* better. It couldn't be an affair. If Smith was slaking his lust with a woman, why would he bring himself off in the middle of the night? But he couldn't tell them that. "Then how do you explain the missing musket?"

Krüger snickered, tucking his heavy head to his chest.

"Oh, Schaefer, don't be jealous," he simpered, this time in English. "No matter who Smith is fooling around with, it's your bed he'll be coming back to each night."

The boys exploded in laughter. Henry felt his face turn red as he gripped his fists tight. Not only were they refusing to take his accusations seriously, but they were actively mocking him. He thought these fellows were his friends, but clearly he was nothing more than the butt of a joke, just like he'd always been.

Little Heinie, always good for a laugh. Henry swallowed around his frustration and glared them all down.

"Fine, don't believe me," he said, gathering up his fork and tin plate as he stood. "That's just fine. I'm going to prove this is more than just some affair. Smith is hiding something big, and I'm going to find out what it is. When I prove it, you're all going to eat your words."

He made a point to glare at them all in turn, even as he distantly understood he was coming off more crazed than intimidating. They all smirked and exchanged glances. Henry heard one of them whistle as he stalked off.

When he looked over his shoulder as he exited the hall, they were all talking merrily again. It was as if he didn't even exist.

————

Cate cast a furtive glance over her shoulder as she sloshed her guard-napkins in the river, scrubbing them with her new bar of soap as quickly as she could. The river valley was bathed in shadows as dusk fell, the rain from earlier scudding towards the edge of the rapidly darkening sky. The last ferries had departed back to Mendota and St. Paul for the night, but even so, Cate stayed well away from the landings, manned as they were with a twenty-four-hour guard. She walked alongside St. Peter's stream to the Minnesota River, where she washed and rinsed her rags in the low, silty water. If she was going to share a bed with Schaefer, she was going to need to take as many precautions as she could manage.

After some consideration, she decided not to try to wash her corded stays again. She'd tried when she was stationed in the post barn, washing in a bucket of horse water, but it had been difficult. And now that she knew she'd be sharing a bed with another man, she wanted to make sure she had as much armor as possible to obscure her softer parts. If Schaefer were to reach around her, she didn't want anything to appear amiss. The thought of it made her swallow hard.

Once she'd scrubbed the rags as well as she could, she decided to make her way along St. Peter's stream for a cleaner rinse than the Minnesota could provide. She made her way down the path, soapy rags bundled in her hands, until she came to a clearing with access to the riverbank, about halfway back to the fort's incline road.

As she turned into the clearing, she stopped dead in her tracks. Someone was already there. And he looked like he was ... dancing?

Cate stepped back behind a tree and peeked out. Maybe it wasn't dancing. It looked a bit more like calisthenics, perhaps. Fast, vigorous calisthenics.

The man was bent with his back to her, reaching down and easily grasping his right foot, bringing himself upright, and then bending for his left foot. Back and forth, rhythmically. It was mesmerizing.

It took a moment for Cate to realize she knew the shape of that backside. The color of the hair. The curve of those shoulders and thighs. God damn it to hell, it was Henry Schaefer. Of course it was. Of course.

All of a sudden, he dropped down into a crouch, his knees splayed wide, and he set his hands squarely on the ground. Then, in a fluid motion, he turned himself upside down, pushing his legs up with unexpected grace to stand on his hands. Cate's mouth dropped open.

In this position, he faced her. She flinched, trying to conceal herself behind the tree, but she had seen the flash of recognition in his eyes before she ducked back.

"Smith!" he shouted. "Stop sneaking around!"

She stepped out from behind the tree, her hands with the rags behind her back, and tried to lift a sardonic brow, but she really couldn't manage it. Schaefer was on his feet again, dusting off his hands and glaring hard at her.

"Uh ... sorry," she muttered, her eyes flickering up and down his form against her better judgement. She was too surprised to reign herself in.

Schaefer stalked a few steps toward her, and it took her a long moment to stop staring at him and realize that he was looking for a fight.

"I'm not anymore pleased with the new bunk arrangement than you are, but maybe try to give a man a little privacy before he loses all of it completely," he snarled, marginally more aggressive than the situation really warranted.

"I beg your pardon, good *sir*," she said sarcastically, making a little bow. Schaefer's eyes flashed. His hands shot out and seized her tight by the shirt and her heart slammed in her throat. She looked up at him with irrepressible alarm. His brow was angry, but his eyes widened a bit and his lips softened slightly. Holy God, what was happening?

Cate's hands were waylaid holding the rags and she didn't want to bring his attention to them, so she merely glanced down at his hands gripping her overshirt. She looked up at him again and opened her mouth to say something, but nothing came out. Schaefer's lip curled in a way that should have read as angry, but she thought she saw threads of something else in his blue eyes, something indulgent, eager, maybe even hungry. Her knees wobbled.

"So, uh," she said, then licked her lips because her mouth had suddenly gone quite dry. "Is this how you keep yourself so hulking?"

Sarcasm was a tricky thing. She didn't mean it to be sarcastic or biting—truly, it was an honest question—but it was immediately evident that he heard it as some sort of insult. His nostrils flared, and he shoved her away as he shouted, "Leave me the HELL alone!"

Cate stumbled backwards and then, not to be outdone, shouted back, "HAVE IT YOUR WAY!"

She turned on her heel and stalked off, the stupid wet rags in her hands for all to see, goddamn the consequences. She glanced over her shoulder, half-convinced she'd see him charging at her with fists raised, but he didn't. He glared at her, pulling one arm across his body in another calisthenics-style stretch as he paced around the edge of the clearing. He disappeared behind the trees as Cate hastened away, presumably to resume whatever ridiculous fitness regime he'd been doing.

By the time she reached the incline road, she was swallowing hard against a strange amalgamation of anger and arousal. She'd nearly forgotten about the guard napkins in her hands that she still needed to rinse in the stream. Doubling back, she picked her way to the shore between the two ferry landings, somewhat out of the view of both guards, and rinsed her rags in the gently flowing water.

"What in the world have I done to deserve this," she muttered to herself as the soap made small bubbles dance on the surface of the water. "First bunk-mates, now this? God," she looked up at the darkening sky shot with pink, "are you trying to punish me?"

This was what she got for breaking her marriage vows. For lying. For being such a shameless lecher in the barracks. For being endlessly contrary. She was full of vice. She wouldn't put it past the heavens to punish her for it. If society knew, they certainly would.

She wrung her napkins out as well as she could, then stuck them in her pockets. She would hang them under her overshirt on her hook. Hopefully they would dry out and nothing would cause them to fall out into the view of everyone. If God were indeed out to punish her, they probably would.

After washing her hands in the stream, she splashed water on her face. She was going to share Schaefer's bed tonight. She needed to keep her wits about her. As enticing as he was, he was also smarter than she'd given him credit for. And he had it in for Charles Smith.

———

XIV

Sunday, August 11, 1861

THREE FEET BY SIX feet was really not enough space for two men. Additionally, a fifteen foot square room was not enough space for eighteen men to bed down in. The two new squads were full of eager recruits, one group from Hastings and another down from St. Cloud. They were loud, boisterous, and loved euchre; Krüger was in hog heaven.

Henry avoided the barracks for as long as he could before it got too dark, stalking around the grounds outside the fort walls and then down the bluffs in the watershed to try and shake off his anger and frustration about how stupid the squad had made him feel about his suspicions. It didn't seem to matter what he thought or felt. In the eyes of everyone else, he was a fool. He wasn't much of a Turner, he wasn't much of a soldier, and he wasn't even much of a sleuth. Not to mention, he was a downright shit excuse for a son. Even though it had been months and months, he still hadn't mustered up the courage to write to his parents. He wasn't trying to avoid them either—somehow it seemed like he'd be less rotten if he'd at least made the conscious decision to sever ties. He just couldn't face them. Not until he had some sort of accomplishment to write home about.

Doing his old warm-up routine had helped him calm down, though Smith had almost thrown a wrench in that as well. He couldn't tell if the boy had been impressed or cruelly delighted by Henry's gymnasticks. The boy's eyes and his mouth told entirely different stories ... just further evidence that he was a scoundrel. Ultimately, Henry'd been too angry to get to the bottom of it.

He made his way back to the barracks after dark, sweating in his shirt-sleeves from his exertions. He made the slightest sniff towards uniform when he reached the gates by throwing his overshirt over his shoulders and buttoning the top button. His routine had helped him clear away the darkest of his thoughts, at least for now. It was difficult to feel sorry for oneself when one was trying to balance on one's hands. Sure, the boys didn't believe him about Smith. But they generally regarded him well and he fit in a lot better than Smith did. He wasn't a complete outcast. And surely, once he revealed Smith for the scoundrel he was, they would concede how dismissive they'd been. All he had to do was to show them.

When he arrived back at the barracks, the room was raucous and full of men laughing, singing, and playing euchre. One of the boys from Hastings had sneaked a flask of whiskey in and was passing it around. When Henry arrived, Jacob was smiling in a slow, lop-sided way and exuberantly encouraged Henry to join them. He had a sip or two and was not at all surprised that Smith was bundled up on the top bunk, pretending to sleep. He felt his initial theory about Grahamitism might hold true, though he wasn't sure what a Grahamite would be doing spying for the Confederacy. He supposed insufferable prudery didn't necessarily discriminate against politics.

It took nearly a full hour after lights out was called for the room to actually go quiet. Circumstances being so crowded and the weather continuing to be mild, Henry opted to sleep in his clothes, just as many of the other men did. He climbed up and perched on the edge of the top bunk, his back against Smith's back. He tried to arrange himself so they didn't touch at all, but it proved too precarious, so he conceded and let his back rest against Smith's. He wasn't sure if the boy was sleeping at that point, but it seemed for all intents and purposes that he was. Regardless, he didn't bite Henry's head off as anticipated, which was good because Henry had been fully prepared to retort that he wasn't about to fall five feet to the floor in his sleep just because Smith couldn't abide the thought of touching his bunkmate. Besides, after what happened a few nights ago, sleeping back to back should be of no consequence whatsoever.

As Henry closed his eyes to sleep, he replayed the encounter he'd had with Smith by the river. He hadn't seen him approach so he couldn't be sure, but he seemed to have been coming from the Minnesota River side. There was hardly anything over there. It didn't make sense. Another detail to add to his list of suspicious behaviors.

The boy had been slack-jawed when Henry turned his headstand. He'd been so mad at the time, but upon reflection, it was actually pretty funny. Sometimes he wondered if the reason Jacob and Elias mocked his gymnasticks was because they were jealous. It gave him deep satisfaction to imagine arrogant Charley Smith taken aback by his superior skill.

The more he thought about it, the more he was convinced that Smith had been impressed, shaken from his usual condescending attitude to watch Henry in some measure of awe. His usual contemptuous expression had dropped, and he'd led with an apology, which was decidedly out of character. And his eyes when Henry had taken him by the collar ... he'd thrown out that sarcastic remark, but his eyes had been round and unguarded. Given the evidence at hand, one might even conclude that Smith was somewhat moony for Henry, in spite of himself. Henry couldn't help but smile at the irony of that notion.

He must have dozed off at some point, because he woke to the scaffold creaking quietly. Next to him, he could feel Smith sliding down the bed, pushing himself to the end with his hands before slipping silently down. His heart racing, Henry pretended to be asleep. Dammit, he couldn't afford to entertain any sympathetic notions about this villain. He had to stay on his guard at all times until he figured out exactly what Smith was up to. He heard soft footfalls on the floor, then the quiet creak of the door as Smith slipped out.

Henry sat up in their bunk. This was it. This was his chance to see what Smith was up to.

He slipped off the side of the bunk and followed Smith out the door on bare feet, his eyes straining in the chill darkness that bathed the parade ground.

A brief look around showed Smith slinking through the shadows toward the fort entrance. Henry pursued, padding silently over the boardwalk and then the gravel damp from the earlier rain as he wove between the sutlery and the munitions.

Just as he wondered how Smith planned to get out of the gate with guards on duty, Smith carried on in the shadow of the hospital on the far side of the gate, following the wall round the fort and down to the lower level of the officer quarters.

Unlike the soldier barrack basements, which were scarcely more than dank cellars and accessible only from the inside, the officer quarters had their lower level kitchens open to a narrow passage that ran between the fort wall and the officer barracks. Some of the officers paid a cook, while others let their wives have run of the kitchen. Now that the regiment was nearly full, the three companies had veritably filled the fort to the brim. It was a treacherous risk indeed for Smith to sneak off now, with so many more people around to catch him.

Henry kept a distance between himself and Smith, doing his best to stay quiet and ensure Smith didn't know he was being followed. As Smith picked his way behind the officer's quarters, he furtively glanced behind him as he reached a door across from one of the officer latrines. Henry quickly pressed himself up against the wall, doing his very best to stay out of sight. He waited a good, long moment and then a few seconds more before peering around the curve of the building toward where Smith had been.

The passage was empty. There was no sign of Smith.

Henry swore under his breath and padded up the passage, towards where he'd last seen Smith. From that vantage, he could see down the rest of the passage to where the Half Moon Battery emerged at the northwest corner of the fort. Scanning the boardwalk above and the passage below, Henry spotted a kitchen door ajar just a few feet from where he'd last seen Smith. Henry took stock of the location, determined to find out whose quarters these were. The boy must have snuck inside.

He couldn't say for certain the kinds of things Smith might acquire by sneaking around the officers' quarters in the middle of the night, but he could certainly speculate. Maneuvers, tactics, battle plans—surely there was information of that kind with their Lieutenants. The officers studied all the time, referring back to their tactics manual regularly, sometimes even reading the drills aloud as they trained their squads. Perhaps Smith had wanted to become corporal in order to gain access to a manual. Perhaps now that he'd mucked that up for himself, he was looking for another way to acquire one.

As Henry's mind turned, he realized that Smith was likely to retreat back the way he'd come. And if he arrived back before Henry did, he would know he had been followed. A sense of urgency pumped through Henry's veins and he hurried back down the passage. He had to get back to their bunk before Smith did. He had to be lying down, curled up under his blanket, snoring lightly in feigned sleep, lest he be discovered tailing Smith.

Henry hurried back through the shadows of the two-story limestone hospital, across the gate, and down the boardwalk back to their barracks. He fought to regulate his shallow breath as he scrambled back up the scaffold to the top bunk.

"Henry, is that you?" Jacob murmured from the middle bunk. "What're you doing?"

Henry shushed him harshly.

"Quiet," he hissed, "Smith snuck out so I tailed him. He could be back any minute."

"Where did he go?"

"Shhh, I'll tell you later."

"You expect me to be able to sleep until then?"

"Shut. Up."

Jacob grumbled, and Henry could hear the rustling of his blanket as he tried to settle back in. Webster snorted in his sleep. Henry flung his blanket over his legs and turned toward the edge of the bunk, trying to resume the position he'd been in when Smith snuck out. His heart still hammered in his chest as he tried to calm himself, anticipating the moment when Smith would slip back through the door. He wanted Smith to think his movements had gone undetected. As much as he felt sure that his hunch was right, he still hadn't seen anything that would serve as solid evidence to accuse him. This realization raised his ire and made it harder for him to smooth his breathing. At this close proximity, he didn't want his body to give him away, no matter how well he could lay still and keep his eyes closed.

The door creaked. There was soft rustling. Smith must have been digging around for something in his satchel. Henry resolved to find a way to investigate later, perhaps when Smith had dish duty.

Fabric rustled on the hooks as Smith climbed up the scaffold. Henry prayed that Jacob would have some sense for once and keep quiet. Carefully, Smith crawled up the bed and settled himself on his side between the wall and Henry. His back was cool against Henry's. He could feel his lungs expand and contract.

And there was a coarseness, a subtle series of ridges down his back. Henry hadn't noticed it before. He tried to tune into the feeling without moving. It couldn't be his spine, could it? The boy wasn't that skinny. Henry wanted to shift, to straighten himself out some so that his back would have more contact with Smith's, but he didn't dare move. The sensation puzzled him, beckoned him, rooted suspicion deep in his bones. It was another piece, a clue—he was sure of it. It taunted him because he knew he couldn't do anything to find out more.

He told himself he would wait until Smith fell asleep, then try to feel out what it was. Even as he told himself this, he yawned. In the end, he fell asleep before he could be sure Smith was and the chance was lost.

———

XV

Monday, August 12, 1861

WHEN REVEILLE SOUNDED, IT was still dark inside the barracks. Cate blinked her eyes open, but all she could see was the dimly lit, whitewashed walls. The air was chilly, but she felt uncommonly warm. It wasn't until she tried to roll onto her back that she was rudely reminded of her bunk-mate, whose shoulder made a firm obstacle to her attempt to shift.

The rest of the men were groaning as they stirred in the relative darkness of early dawn.

"Webster, get off," she heard Robinson complain. "I'm not your wife."

Webster snorted awake and said in a groggy, disappointed tone, "Unfortunately."

Cate sat up and ran her fingers through her tousled curls. Schaefer rolled onto his stomach to look down over the edge of the bunk. He smelled like rain and earth and sweat and she had no business cataloging his scent right now, for heaven's sake.

"Aagh, my shoulder is all kinked up," Williamson moaned from below.

"Did you sleep in the same position all night, then?" said one of the boys from St. Cloud.

"Have you seen my bunkie? I didn't have a choice."

"*Guten morgan*," Krüger rumbled.

"You gotta master the simultaneous turn," the St. Cloud boy replied. "When you turn together, you can get off the offending limb and still have space."

"Maybe we should do some drilling on that point," one of the other St. Cloud boys replied with a laugh.

Cate slipped down off the foot of the bunk, her bare feet waving for purchase on the lower bunk rail. As she lowered herself down, Schaefer's feet filled her vision, hanging off the edge of the bunk, and her nose wrinkled at the sight. His feet were black with dirt, like he'd done the previous day's drilling barefoot.

"Schaefer, your feet are filthy," she accused as she hopped to the floor. "If you know you're sharing a bunk with someone, the least you could do is wash up before bunking down."

"I hate to break it to you, but you don't smell like a bed of roses yourself, Smith," he retorted even as he pulled his feet up and under his blanket. She rolled her eyes as she tried to determine which pair of boots were hers in the dim morning light. He wasn't wrong; she'd managed standing baths in the officer's latrines, but was overdue for another scrub-down. Thing was, she couldn't find the privacy to do it now that guard duty had ended. Besides, she was fairly loath to risk it again considering how close she was to being caught the last time. She'd just have to find a way to do a more thorough standing bath somewhere private. Somehow.

Looking around the room filled with men bumping around each other trying to get dressed and ready for roll call, she shifted uncomfortably. She was a veritable sheep in a lion's den. It was far past time for her to buckle down and get serious. No more mistakes. No more false alarms. This was war. She had to admit that Sergeant Osborn was right. She couldn't continue to jeopardize her chance to fight the Rebs for some stupid feud.

Last night, Cate had woken up certain that she was bleeding through her trousers. She had taken great pains to sneak out of the barracks, right under Schaefer's nose, to go to the officer's latrines and check. Turned out, she'd just been paranoid. She still had a light emission, but nothing that'd needed immediate tending. The courses would peter out and finish within the next few days. And she'd almost blown her cover just to check. It was humbug like this that she could not afford anymore. She had to get herself in line, tamp down her argumentative streak, and focus on the task at hand. Train for war. Fight like hell. Be a force for justice in the world. Any ignoramus with half a brain could argue; it took real courage to stand up and put oneself on the line to fight for what was right. She pulled her overshirt on and carefully pocketed her dry guard-napkins as she buckled her belt.

Corporal Hower poked his head into the room.

"Anyone seen a journal?" he asked tightly. The din was such that only his own squad members, at the bunk nearest the door, could hear him. The boys looked at each other and shrugged.

"Nope, sorry," Webster said.

"What kind of journal?" Robinson asked.

Hower gave a brusque sigh and said, "You know the one, Jacob. My leather field journal. I was keeping my notes in it for drills and now I can't find it."

Robinson shrugged with his hands up. "Search me."

"Don't you even," Hower snapped, shaking an accusing finger at him. "If I find out this is just another farce like with my hat, I'm gonna tan your hide."

Robinson snickered as Hower swung out of the room and stalked down the boardwalk. Once he was out of earshot, Schaefer spoke.

"But really, Jake, do you have it?"

Robinson gave a sigh and said, "I wish. That would have been a good one."

Cate took extra care to look sharp that morning, even smoothing down her hair with a wet comb. She stood extra tall at roll call, focused on accepting her dish duties with a crisp "Yes, sir!" She made a point not to look at Schaefer, whose eyes could be felt on every step she took to mess, his suspicion bearing down on her. She ate her breakfast with prim efficiency and focused on ignoring the banter bouncing around her. Quiet and observant. No mistakes. Schaefer could watch her as closely as he wanted. He'd tire of it before long.

As soon as she was done, she went down to the washroom to scrub an army's worth of dishes (well, at least a companies' worth). The two other lads assigned from the other squads were content to goof off. Cate tamped down the frustration that threatened to bubble up. She did her work (and a fair bit of theirs) quietly and efficiently. Her head was nearly all the way inside a massive soup kettle, scrubbing bits of grease and crusty potato with a stiff brush when she was interrupted from her task.

"Smith."

She looked up, eyes wide and guarded, as she turned slowly and saw Schaefer standing in the doorway. His eyes were accusatory and his mouth grim as he beckoned her over. She felt her stomach drop. The dozen or so steps to the door took an eternity to traverse. She didn't even dare let herself articulate her fears inside her own head. Asking "what if" would only shake her composure more. If a reckoning was imminent, she'd need her wits about her.

Silently, Cate glanced at the other two fellows as she approached. They were playing at drying dishes while laughing over some comrade's unfortunate showing at baseball the night before. She looked Schaefer up and down for a moment, trying to gauge her risk, before ultimately following him out of the washroom into the cramped landing at the foot of the stairs.

Cate crossed her arms over her chest and looked up at Schaefer like he was a supreme inconvenience, covering for her trembling hands. "What's this then?"

Schaefer's eyes were dark, his brow burying them. The corners of his mouth twitched up in satisfaction.

"I know your secret."

Cate's breath flew out of her chest. It felt like the floor had dropped out from beneath her. It was all she could do to train her face to a neutral expression.

His eyes narrowed. He opened his mouth as if to say something more, then closed it again. He smirked. And with that, he turned and climbed up the stairs to the ground level, leaving Cate slack-jawed and choking on her own fear.

"Fuck," she whispered, her tongue thick and sour in her mouth. Her hands were shaking and she couldn't manage to move from where she stood as her mind raced. It was too late. No amount of focus was going to save her now.

He was probably on his way to reveal her to Osborn right now. He was going to tell him her true identity and she would be taken to the surgeon for a confirmation. After being thoroughly humiliated, she'd be thrown out. Or worse, they'd send for Richard.

She looked up the stairs, then into the washroom, where her kettle sat waiting for her. She couldn't take this lying down. She'd sworn an oath. She was here to fight. No blockhead farm boy was going to send her back to Richard Ellis before she ever got to see battle.

Gritting her teeth, Cate gave in to her instincts and raced up the stairs, taking the steps two at a time. She rounded the barracks, skidding on the gravel. Bursting out onto the parade ground, she searched the groups of men walking around, taking full advantage of their leisure until 9 o'clock called them to drill practice. It took her a moment, but she found the shock of straw-colored hair moving toward the officer's barracks. Heart in her throat, she raced across the parade ground, dodging a group of laughing fellows from Company I and nearly crashing into the orderly sergeant carrying reports.

She caught up to Schaefer as he was mounting the step onto the boardwalk in front of the officer's barracks. She had no plan, no strategy. She just had to stop him. She was shaking with energy as she leapt up, launching herself off the step to tackle him from behind.

He swore as he staggered with surprise, but he didn't go down. Instead, she found herself clinging onto his back, her hands gripping his shoulders, scrabbling for purchase around his neck, and her feet wrapped around his waist. She squeezed his throat and he reached overhead and grappled with her shirt, yanking her as he dipped forward and threw her to the ground. Soldiers nearby eagerly gathered around to watch as he stood over her.

"You son of a bitch," he growled. However, what he was about to do next was unclear, because she threw a resolute punch to his crotch. He dropped to one knee with a groan and she scrambled to make the most of his momentary incapacitation.

She turned to all fours and launched herself on top of him, throwing him back and knocking him against the stone wall of the barracks.

He gripped her by her shirt and she elbowed him in the eye, not entirely on purpose, as he pulled her off kilter. Catching herself on one hand, she squeezed her thighs around his hips and steadied herself as he tried to throw her off. He was stronger and heavier than her, but she had the superior position. She used it to her advantage and delivered a forceful punch to his left cheek. His head snapped to the side and he shouted, his grimace contorted in rage and pain. His blue eyes slid onto her and she got the sense that she had made another mistake.

He grabbed her by her shirt collar and yanked her close, then pushed off the ground with one bent knee and toppled her over.

He laid full out on top of her and wrapped his legs around her knees, disabling her ability for leverage. She found herself struck by her own helplessness and fear bloomed cold in her chest. Schaefer's hand was still in her shirt and Cate held her arms up to protect her face as he raised a fist. She squeezed her eyes shut and braced for the blow. But the blow never came.

"Soldiers! Order, I'll have order this minute!"

Peeking out one eye, through her fingers, she saw Elias Hower holding Schaefer's arm with both hands, his stance wide as he and Sergeant Osborn yanked him off of her.

Schaefer stumbled to his feet and spat blood on the boardwalk. Wiping a hand over his face, he snarled at Cate and shouted, "Damn rascal son of a bitch!"

"That's ENOUGH!" Sergeant Osborn commanded, looking up at Schaefer while Hower held him back. He turned and glared down at Cate. "The both of you."

"Sergeant, what is the meaning of this?" Lieutenant Thomas approached, slightly out of breath. His eyes darted between Schaefer, who was straining against Hower, and Cate, who propped herself up dazedly on her elbows. Her blood was buzzing with fear and fight so much it made her dizzy. "To the guardhouse now until I can figure out what to do with you."

The soldiers gathered all went quiet.

"But, sir—" Cate tried.

"Get them out of my sight," the Lieutenant ordered. His cheeks were red with anger ... and embarrassment? Cate blinked again as Robinson pulled her to her feet. Captain Noah stood to one side among the observers, his hands behind his back and his expression severe. His eyes met hers and she immediately cast her gaze down.

So much for lying low.

———

XVI

Henry was gonna kill Smith. He could feel his left cheek swelling where the little duffer had hit him. Elias led Henry across the parade ground, holding him firmly by one arm, and he squirmed under the stares of the regiment watching as he and Smith were led to the guardhouse. Jacob had Smith, shuffling along ahead of them, and Henry glared so hard he must have felt it, because Smith looked back over his shoulder at him.

Smith's eyes were round as saucers and smudged with shadows from too little sleep. He didn't look as angry as he did desperate, which just confirmed in Henry's mind that his theory was right. He was a scoundrel and a spy. He'd be willing to bet Elias' journal would turn up somewhere among Smith's effects.

"That's the last straw," Henry muttered so only Elias could hear. "That little piss pot is finished."

"Please don't make wild accusations," Elias sighed, tipping his head back. "You're already in enough trouble as it is."

"He started it, Elias," Henry hissed defensively. "He tackled me out of nowhere. I can't think of anything more incriminating."

"Some tangible proof, perhaps?" Elias suggested with an eyebrow raised. "Seriously, Henry, this kid is not worth it. He's not some espionage mastermind. He's a smarmy little brat who's too big for his britches. Don't let him bring you down to his level."

Henry let out a growl and carried on swearing, but in German, as Lieutenant Thomas led them into the guardhouse. The narrow, one-story stone structure was nestled along the fort wall between the front gate and the Quartermaster's warehouse, opposite of which was the Round Bastion. Entering the guard room behind them, the lieutenant ushered them into the prison room. This Henry expected, but when Lieutenant Thomas crossed the room and opened the door to one of the cells, he became markedly less steady.

The cells could not have been much more than six feet by eight feet. Despite there being two available cells, Lieutenant Thomas made a show of throwing them both into one cell for Captain Noah. The small, dark space had a sobering effect on Henry's outrage, as the reality of the punishment set in. They could be court-martialed. Elias was right. This was serious and he was being treated on the same level as Smith, even though all he had done was defend himself.

In New Ulm, boys who tried to get out of trouble by throwing another over the rails were punished just as harshly as the guilty party. Now was not the time to lay out his case. It would just make him look like a child trying to avoid responsibility. Henry pinched his lips tight to keep himself silent.

"If you're going to fight, do it in here," Lieutenant Thomas snarled at the two of them. Henry had never seen him so mad. "Let me know when you've worked it all out and maybe you won't be docked a month's pay."

"Thomas," Captain Noah intoned. He didn't say anything, but his eyes fell onto the heavy wood door of the cell. Then, the captain picked up a lantern and placed it wordlessly inside the cell. Lieutenant Thomas glanced at his superior officer with irritation, then proceeded to slam the prison room door shut behind them. The lock clunked into place with stark finality.

Henry felt like the wind had been taken out of him. He drew in a steadying breath, waiting for his eyes to adjust in darkness so he could take stock of the room around him, but they never did. The cell was barren, with no windows to speak of and very well-pointed stone walls. It was pitch dark. Though it was broad daylight outside, the only indication of the hour within the cell was what scant light made its way through small cracks in the roof beams. None of the cracks were big enough to allow light enough to see by.

Henry spun on his heel and groped blindly for the lantern, pulling his flint out of his pocket and striking it on the steel to cast sparks. The scant light from the sparks did little to help him arrange the wick of the candle in the proper place to catch.

"Just to your left."

Henry felt blood rush in his ears at the small directive coming from Smith's corner of the chamber.

"Shut your filthy trap," he snapped. It took him a good long while to get the candle lit, but once it was, he was able to hang the lantern on a hook in the wall and see Smith standing against the far side in stark, flickering shadow like a cornered racoon.

"What in the actual hell was that all about?" Henry snapped.

Smith looked him squarely in the eye and crossed his arms.

"Self defense," he replied curtly.

"Excuse me?!"

Smith leveled a glare at him. "Don't act like you weren't trying to find the Sergeant to report me."

Henry's lip curled defensively. "So what if I was? If you aren't hiding anything, what do you care if the officers come poking around?"

Smith sighed and shook his head. He said nothing. Henry waited for a moment, but the silence only thickened. He sighed as well and leaned against the cell door.

"If anyone was practicing self-defense, it was me," Henry continued, sliding down the wall to sit on the floor, gingerly exploring his tender jaw with his fingertips. He glared hard up at Smith, whose features were largely cast in shadow. His posture was turned in, clasping his biceps tightly with his hands as he bowed his head. Henry hadn't expected him to be cowed like this, to be so resigned to his discovery. He had imagined he'd try to throw him off his trail, to defend, to misdirect, to engage at all whatsoever. This passive silence was unnerving.

Henry spun a snagged thread on his trousers in between his fingers.

"I wouldn't sit down there if I were you," Smith intoned.

Henry sneered at him. "Where else am I supposed to sit?"

"There's rats."

Henry scrambled back to his feet, even as he retorted, "How would you know?"

"Didn't you see them when we were posted here last week? They'll steal the food right off your plate if you let them, little varmints."

Henry peered at Smith. He could not get a read on him, and it wasn't just the dark room and the guttering tallow candle. He could see the planes of Smith's face, the trained neutral expression, the dark, deep-set eyes under a set of brows that belonged on a much older, grumpier man. Even as he stood in a vague imitation of informality, casually leaning against the back wall of the cell, he watched Henry's every move under guarded lids. Either he was resigned to the fact that Henry had caught him out, or he was calculating his next move and Henry was in way over his head.

"So I assume that by attacking me from behind, you admit your guilt," Henry taunted, looking down at his hands as he cracked his knuckles. He looked up out of the corner of his eye to track Smith's response.

"I don't recall admitting to anything," Smith replied, his deadpan tone making a mockery of his professed innocence. "I can't even imagine what the charges might be."

Henry's eyes turned steely. "Bunkum. You know."

Smith's eyebrow lifted. "Well, if you know, and I know, then who in this cell are we keeping it a secret from? The rats?"

Henry's fists curled. "Just admit it! You're stealing military tactics to undermine the Union."

Smith jerked back, stunned.

"You're a spy," Henry spat, the word sour in his mouth. "And I for one am not going to sit silently while you put all of our lives in danger."

Smith pressed his lips together and made a suppressed, guttural sound. And then he burst out laughing.

Whatever Henry had expected from him in response to his accusation, it was not that.

"A spy? Me?" Smith managed to say between guffaws. "Why on earth would you think that?"

Henry's eyes narrowed. "Nice try, but I'm not going to be put off so easily. The gun, the rendezvous with Southern sympathizers, the disguise—"

"—The disguise? What disguise?"

"That filthy excuse for a lady's unmentionables I found by the river. You were acting so strange, but I know what you were about now. You were using it as part of your disguise so you could gather tactical secrets undetected."

Smith pressed both hands together against his mouth and closed his eyes. "Let me get this straight. You think I was disguising myself as a woman to steal tactical secrets?"

Henry glowered. He got the feeling he was being mocked. "Yes."

Smith's lips pressed tightly together, his eyebrows high. "The tactical secrets in the Hardee's drill manual?"

Henry shrugged, looking away to disguise the fact that he did not know what that was. "Among them."

Smith dissolved into laughter again. It took him two tries to compose himself enough to say, "Hardee is a Confederate! I don't think he needs me to help him discover tactics he wrote himself."

Smith doubled over to laugh some more. Henry worked hard to suppress the urge to hit him. There was nothing he hated more than to be treated like he was stupid.

"Fine, I didn't know that about Hardee's manual, but the manual isn't the only source of tactical information being bandied about our regiment's command. Colonel Van Cleve went to the US Military Academy."

Smith snorted. "Yeah, thirty years ago!" He held his stomach as he carried on laughing, leaning one shoulder against the stone wall.

"Oh my God," Smith sighed, wiping moisture from his eyes. "And, uh, the Southern sympathizers? Who might they be?"

Henry scowled and clenched his fists. *This is his defense,* he reminded himself. *He's trying to put you off.* "You were sneaking around Franklin Steele's farm. He's a known Democrat—"

"Democrat? A Democrat is not a Southern sympathizer as a matter of course."

"Steele is in with Sibley and Rice, and Rice said he thought the Southern states had the right to secede!" Henry shouted. "I read the newspaper, don't treat me like I'm an idiot."

Smith snorted again. "Wow, that is quite the series of assumptions based on, what, one newspaper quote? They should make you the prosecutor on my court-martial. I'd be sure to get off."

"Verpiss dich," Henry hissed in German as he took one step forward and snatched Smith up by the collar, pinning him up against the far wall. It was satisfying to see the snide grin fall off Smith's face as Henry's superior strength startled the derision out of him. In New Ulm, they had been sharply discouraged from using anger and physical strength as a force for influence in the Turner Hall's training. That was reserved for times of war and the defense of their community. While they might spar or wrestle to hone their strength, any interaction that devolved into an actual fight was immediately stopped. He'd never had the opportunity to realize the power his strength could garner against a smaller foe, the power to influence, to silence, to coerce. That power was both intoxicating and terrifying. His grip on Smith's collar faltered.

"You might consider taking this seriously," he sneered, "because regardless of whether you get off or not, the accusation of sedition is enough to destroy your entire military career before it ever starts. They don't need you—there are plenty of men out there willing and able to fight for their country. And I'm not taking any chances of being brought up on charges with you because I knew something was wrong and didn't say anything."

Smith studied him, his defiantly raised eyebrow lowering as he came to understand that what Henry said was true.

"I don't even care if I'm right or not," Henry continued, seizing upon his advantage. "By making the accusation, I will ensure that everyone is watching you, that they're looking into what you're doing. Maybe you're not a spy, maybe you're not conspiring sedition, but I know for damn sure you're up to something. No matter what it is, once I lay out what I know, they're not going to rest until they put the pieces together."

Smith delivered a flinty stare as he deliberately plucked his collar from Henry's fist, smoothing it back over his neck with all the dignity he could muster. His nostrils flared with heightened breath, and Henry could swear he detected beads of sweat forming on his brow in the flickering candlelight.

"What if..." Smith's jaw tensed as he swallowed hard. He tilted his chin up and tried again. "What if I could prove my patriotism?" His eyes darted to the cell door and back to Henry. "What if I could prove to you that I've not broken any of the Articles of War? That my behavior is easily explained by a relatively innocuous reason?"

Henry's jaw worked as he took a step back. "Fine. I'd love to see you prove me wrong. Despite what you might think, I'm not just out to make your life miserable."

Smith gave him a withering look.

"What? I'm not," he insisted, crossing his arms. "Though I can't imagine how you expect to explain stealing that gun..."

Smith smiled humorlessly and shook his head at the floor. "And despite what you may think, that is actually the one thing I've been completely truthful about."

"Bull. Shit," Henry spat, pushing his weight forward again so that Smith flinched, and his hands involuntarily rose in his own defense, pushing back against Henry's shoulders. Henry forced himself to step back again. Despite how satisfying it was to see Smith flinch, he was not going to be the kind of man who took advantage of his power. He was not like his brothers.

"I'll prove to you I'm innocent," Smith repeated, more warily this time. "I'll explain everything. I'll even answer your questions. All I ask in exchange is that once I prove you wrong, you must swear not to tell anyone the truth."

Henry's brow furrowed. "If you're innocent, why the secrecy? If it's not treasonous, why are you so worried someone will find out? Be a man and take some responsibility for God's sake."

Smith screwed up his face painfully. "It's not so simple. I ... I guess I'm not sure it's technically legal, but I can certainly prove I'm not hurting the Union's cause. And I know for a fact I'm not breaking the Articles of War or our oath."

Henry stared at him in the dim light. He would be lying if he said he wasn't sorely tempted by Smith's offer. He had been completely focused on getting to the bottom of Smith's motives for weeks now, and he desperately wanted to know what was really going on. And Smith was offering it up to him, willingly. It had to be some sort of trap.

"How will I know you're telling the truth?"

Smith scrubbed his face with his hands and sighed. Looking away, he said resignedly, "I have incontrovertible proof."

"Right now? In this cell?"

"Yes."

"How convenient." Henry peered at him sidelong. "What if you tell me, and I disagree with your interpretation of the Articles?"

Smith's brow furrowed. "What do you mean?"

"What if I think you *have* violated military law even though you think you haven't?"

Smith pursed his lips. "You have accused me of sedition. You are culpable to report sedition or mutiny. You are not responsible for other offenses. If you agree, you forfeit your right to tell. No matter how you feel about it."

Smith's jaw flexed. Henry wrinkled his nose. He was trying to find the trap. This was Smith, after all. There had to be a catch. He supposed he could swear but then decide to break his oath later depending on what he confessed. But breaking his word … it would have to be really awful to get him to break his word.

Smith shook his head and sighed impatiently. "If you're not going to take it seriously, then you can just forget I said anything."

"No, wait, wait," Henry waved his hands in the air, as if Smith had anywhere else to go at present. "Why? Why now?"

Smith leveled him with a patronizing glare. "You're blackmailing me. I rather thought I didn't have a choice."

Henry winced and nodded. The power of intimidation was intoxicating indeed. It didn't sit well with him to be reminded of how it made him behave.

"It's not like you're my trusted friend, Schaefer. We hate each other," Smith pointed out matter-of-factly. Henry couldn't tell why, but the bluntness of that word stung. "If I could think of literally any other way to get you off my case, mark my words, I would do it. But they didn't let us bring weapons in here, did they?"

It took Henry a moment. "Are you threatening to kill me?"

"It's a joke, you blockhead."

Henry let out a frustrated growl. "Fine, alright, I won't tell. I promise."

"Swear it."

"I swear it."

Smith was not having it. "Swear on something you actually care about. Like you mean it."

"Fine, fine," he flung up his hands and took a steadying breath to tamp down his frustration. "I swear on the Union, auf das Vaterland, on my mother's life. I swear on my honor and my own life that I will not speak of anything you tell me here in this cell, providing you can prove you haven't been disloyal or betrayed the Union."

Smith stared up at him under his thick brows. He took a deep breath and closed his eyes. Then, pressing his lips together and wincing slightly, he spoke in a low tone.

"I'm a woman."

———

XVII

CATE HELD HER BREATH and watched Schaefer carefully. Her throat felt like it was going to close as she waited for him to react.

His eyebrows knit together in confusion. Then, he laughed.

"Nice one, but really—"

"I'm serious," Cate said firmly. "I am a woman."

"But..." he scrambled, "you run faster than Jacob. You can lift just as much, drill just as long ... No, no, you're putting one over on me."

Cate glowered at him and crossed her arms over her chest to hold back her heart's hammering. There were a thousand retorts boiling to her lips, but she suspected none of them would be particularly helpful. Instead, she stayed quiet, waiting. She could see the wheels turn in his head. A part of her feared he wouldn't add it all up, that his prejudices would refuse to allow him to put it together. That she would have to prove it to him. The thought of doing that—it made her stomach turn flips.

Schaefer's chin worked. He swallowed hard, his jaw flexing, his Adam's apple catching—it was ridiculous that something so small, so subtle, should transfix her when she had so many more important things to focus on right now. Then, as if in slow motion, she saw a blush rise in his neck, travel through his cheeks, and go right up to his hairline.

"The shift..." he mumbled.

"Mine," she confirmed.

"But the visit to Steele's farm...?"

Now it was Cate's turn to flush. "Things got ... complicated. I wasn't ready for the barracks to be such tight quarters."

"What has that got to do with Franklin Steele?"

Cate winced. She rubbed a hand over the back of her neck. "I didn't visit Franklin Steele. I just ... borrowed some things from his laundry line."

"I don't understand."

"Uuugggh, I ... my monthly ... courses ... came. And I needed ... supplies."

If it were even possible, Schaefer flushed brighter. If the room had been any dimmer, he might have lit it up.

"Right. Got it," he confirmed, his lip curling uncomfortably.

A long, awkward pause thickened the air. The walls of the small cell suddenly felt very close.

"And the sneaking around the officer's quarters?"

Cate's eyebrow quirked. "Following me, then, too?"

"Of course I did! I thought you were spying for Chrissakes!"

"Well, that explains why your feet are so filthy."

"Just answer the question."

"The officers have private latrines." She shrugged. "The risk of trying to use them outweighs the risk of being caught with my pants down in the soldier sinks."

Schaefer nodded slowly. "And that's why you wanted to be corporal?"

"Yes."

"So you could use a private privy?"

"When you say it like that, it sounds ridiculous."

"That's because it is ridiculous." Schaefer took off his cap and rubbed his hand through his hair, making it stand up like prairie grass before he replaced it. "So when you disappeared for a call of nature, you weren't technically lying."

"Not usually. Nothing particularly unnatural was going on, if that's what you mean."

Schaefer leveled a pointed look at her. "I wouldn't exactly call anything about this 'natural'."

Cate met his eyes defiantly, unprepared for how deep that comment struck. She had a thousand things to say on that matter, but they all came at once and her tongue got stuck. She exhaled slowly and looked away. "People see what they expect to see."

Schaefer's eyes skimmed over her body unabashedly, his eyebrows knit in confusion. Her skin tingled under his assessment.

"You're too tall for a girl," he said at length.

"Indeed."

He crossed his arms, looking at her like some sort of confusing piece of artwork. "But why?"

Cate blinked. "I should think it's quite obvious."

He stared at her blankly. She sighed. It looked like she was going to have to spell it out for him. "If I want to fight for the Union, I have to be a man. So I became one."

It was perhaps an oversimplified version of what happened, but she really had no interest in his opinion on Richard and her failed marriage.

"What could be so important in this war to make you give up your entire life just to fight?"

"I could ask the same of you."

He tilted his head to the side as he looked away, nodding. "Fair enough. You said you had proof?"

"What?"

"What do you have, some sort of papers or something?"

She stared at him. He stared back.

"Papers," she said slowly. "Like, some sort of woman papers?"

He frowned. "When you say it like that it sounds stupid."

"It is stupid. Schaefer, I don't need papers. I have this." She swept her hands down the sides of her body. "What more proof do I need?"

He blushed again and Christ, if she didn't revel in causing it. The idea of having to reveal her body as proof was both mortifying and the slightest bit tantalizing. The part that was tantalized also served to further mortify her. Her eyes swept up to the cell door and back. The only thing worse than being caught fighting again would be getting caught in a more compromising position. She wasn't so ruled by her senses to fall victim to such a foolish temptation. Besides, just because she was a woman didn't mean that Schaefer would automatically have interest in her anyway. If men were that simple, surely she'd have been married years ago.

Schaefer looked at the floor and grimaced embarrassedly. "Oh, I ... I don't need that kind of proof. I really don't."

There, as she thought. Cate swallowed against any potential feelings of self-consciousness. He glanced up at her again and his expression, so confused and embarrassed, was an image that she might keep for later, just to remember how soft and vulnerable he could be. "But, I ... I just really don't see it. I don't understand. You don't look like a woman."

The words stung. Perhaps if she hadn't been so attracted to him, it wouldn't have felt so cruel. He certainly didn't mean it to be (for once). And it wasn't anything she didn't already know—she was too tall, too broad of shoulder, too foul-tempered. Her face was too angular, her brows too thick, her expression too critical and off-putting. These were the things that ensured she was unattached until twenty-six. These were the things her father leveraged towards her when she'd wanted to reject Richard's attention. They were the same things that had dogged her for years.

Certainly, she was still a veritable outcast, but at least during this past month at Fort Snelling, she could say what she wanted. Even if all the attention she'd received since enlisting had been negative, at least they had known she was there. In a dress, she became completely invisible. Silenced. No more interesting than a sideboard.

So yes, it did sting to hear him point out how unfeminine she was. But it was also vindicating. The attraction she'd been harboring aside, she'd been working hard to ensure she kept up, performed, and maintained her facade. Here was proof it had worked. Even as she was telling him that she was a woman, he still couldn't see it. This proved that she was better suited to the male sphere to begin with. If she could get out of this situation, maybe she could find a way to belong here. Only Schaefer stood in her way.

"Thank you, that was the point," she drawled.

"What did you ... That is, how ...?" He gestured vaguely around his chest.

She rolled her eyes. "I have stays on."

"Like a ... corset?" The way he hesitated to say it was adorable, like he'd never even seen one before. It suddenly struck Cate that he probably hadn't. Coming from a small, newly-founded town, the youngest of three brothers—was it possible Henry Schaefer had never seen a disrobed woman?

He seemed so much older than Williamson, but now that she thought about it, he was closer in age to him than he was to her. He just looked older.

Cate pressed her lips together to keep a cat-like grin from creeping across her face. "Mmhmm."

His eyes widened as something came together for him. "Last night, I felt like there was something strange about your back. Was it laces?"

It had not even occurred to her that he might feel her laces through her shirt while they shared a bunk. She realized her mouth was open and she closed it. "Most likely."

He had not realized his mouth was open yet. He looked at her now with unfiltered curiosity, but he didn't seem to share the tension she was experiencing. He looked more fascinated; his embarrassment had faded and he now regarded her like a novelty. She shook her head. If she got through this, she'd be sharing this cell with him, using the same chamber pot, sharing the same bunk once they got out. Better to rip all the mystery out of the situation in one fell swoop. The more he knew, the less he would want to find out. Then maybe he'd leave her the hell alone.

Cate lifted her overshirt up and over her head, then shrugged off her suspenders. Schaefer made a choking sound. She'd already set upon her shirt buttons before he managed to get any actual words out.

"Wait, uh, what are you doing? That's not necessary," he insisted, flapping a hand at her as he glanced toward the cell door. "Seriously, stop," he hissed. "I believe you."

Her shirt had a buttoned placket that went down to her sternum. She pulled the two sides of her shirt apart and revealed the top of her working stays, stained yellow with sweat and compressing her bosom such that only a small, vague mound appeared across her chest when she pulled the shirt taught.

"Alright, I get it, I get it," he rambled, averting his eyes to the rough-hewn wood floor. He was leaning against the far wall, as far as he could get from her.

"Good," she said, buttoning her shirt back up matter-of-factly. "Now, will you keep your mouth shut?"

Schaefer rubbed his forehead with his fingers, eyes still steadfastly on the floor. "Yes. Alright. Yes, yes, you have my word."

Cate felt like she was exhaling fully for the first time since he'd confronted her in the scullery this morning. "I had better."

———

Henry sat on the hard floor of the cell, rats be damned, worrying the splintering wood planks with his fingers and trying his damndest not to picture Smith naked.

He—she—sat on the other side of the room, but with the cell so small, they both had to curl their legs under themselves to keep from touching.

It all made a sinister sort of sense, but even after Smith had shown her stays to him, he was having a hard time reconciling the snide boy he'd come to loathe with the woman she'd revealed herself to be. He knew intellectually, but his eyes could not perceive it, even as her baby-smooth cheeks and arch neck unmarred by an Adam's apple confirmed her story.

The entire revelation had additionally served to ruthlessly castrate his anger towards Smith. While he still resented him for being such an insufferable little jackanape, he couldn't blame him either. Of course she wanted to keep people at a distance. Of course she pushed him away. Of course she punched him in the jaw. She did it all in defense of her secret.

He made a half-hearted attempt at reviving his resentment, but all he could muster was a sort of desperate embarrassment. He'd tried to pummel her. He would have too, if the others hadn't intervened. Regardless of whether she was a woman or a man, he'd known he had the superior strength, and he'd fought her anyway. Even after all the training in sparring and self-control, even after his brothers had beat on him for sport, he'd still done it. It shamed him deeply.

The only thing he could muster that even remotely resembled the energy of his previous sentiments was a sort of mild irritation that he'd become her unwitting accomplice. It was a completely inappropriate and unsustainable charade, one he was now complicit in. Not even complicit—he was her bunkie, he could be implicated for colluding with her and his moral character could be called into question.

He should have been furious with her. But he wasn't. In fact, the more time that passed in the cell, the more he found curiosity to be his dominant sentiment. His shame, embarrassment, irritation, and dislike couldn't compete with the growing fascination, the multiplying need to know her story.

"Smith?" Henry startled himself that he'd spoken the name aloud. "But ... uh ... how?" The dam of polite interest had been breached.

Smith leveled a flat glare at him. "Could you be a little more specific?"

"And ... why?"

"That's an entirely different question than 'how,' which I must point out, is also not a complete sentence, much less a complete question. Besides, haven't we already covered that?"

"Were you a schoolteacher?"

The efficiency of the withering look Smith set on him made him more confident in his guess.

"No." She crossed her arms and looked at the wall.

Henry peered at her, trying to imagine her in a dress. He still could not do it. He tried to think about everything he knew about Smith, all the clues he'd gathered. None of them—not the frequent privy visits, the sneaking off, the shift (which, now that he was no longer in need of it as evidence, he had every intention of throwing down the latrine)—offered any threads that he could form an inference from.

"Are you actually from St. Anthony?"

Smith's glower deepened. "Yes," she replied, almost indignantly.

"Are you actually a lumber... man...?" Henry shook his head. What a stupid question.

"No. They don't tend to let ladies dance the logs." Her eyebrow quirked. He thought it might have been amusement.

"How long have you been dressing this way?"

"Not long. Just since June."

Henry's mouth dropped astonishedly. "That's not long at all. That's ... quite impressive, actually."

"Thanks." Deadpan.

"What made you do it?"

Smith opened her mouth, then shut it again. She regarded him under the shadow of her thick brows, the masculine of the brow and the feminine of her round eyes battling for dominance in the composition of her face. It took a long moment of her searching his face, her eyes becoming markedly more narrowed, before she said, "That's not any of your business."

"I've been unwittingly made your accomplice, so I should think I'm entitled to something," he replied more defensively than he expected. "Besides, you said you'd answer my questions."

"You are not an accomplice. If anything, you're a blackmailer. You backed me into a corner. I could either tell you the truth or accept the consequences of your more baseless accusations, which, as outrageously unfounded as they were, would have certainly led to more scrutiny than I am willing to bear."

"Blackmailer?" he squawked indignantly. "I was trying to protect—"

" —Military secrets?" she mocked. "Yes, of course, very noble. How dare I suggest otherwise."

Henry glowered. "I already know the most explosive secret. What's the harm in telling me the story?"

"No."

He threw his hands up. "Ugh, you're impossible."

"Good."

They fell into silence. Though she had made clear how she felt about answering his questions, every moment he was left to think, he felt like he concocted a thousand more.

"Salutations, fellas!"

A voice greeted them from outside the cell. The sound nearly made Henry jump out of his skin. He scrambled to his feet and turned toward the door. "Is that you, Elias?"

"The very same. Are you all done fighting, yet?"

Henry and Smith exchanged significant glances.

"Yes, sir," Smith said firmly.

"Oh good," Elias said quickly as the lock turned in the door. "Because there's been a munitions shipment, and our barracks was chosen to do the heavy lifting. We could use the extra hands."

"Is Lieutenant Thomas amenable?" Henry asked as Elias opened the cell door, light from the guardhouse window making him squint.

"If it were up to him, you'd sleep here for a week, but speaking for the squad, your arms are needed more than your spirit needs crushing. He's begrudging, but he's given leave for us to let you out. Just give him a wide berth." Elias leaned in, leveling a serious stare at the two of them. "And if you ask me, I would make sure that you never, ever use your fists to solve problems again, unless it's a Reb you're pummeling."

Henry nodded earnestly. All that nervous suspicion, the sleeplessness, the anger, felt like it had been swept out from under him, and now he just felt exhausted. Exhausted and completely confused. He could hear Smith's footsteps follow behind him as he squinted against the light flooding through the windows of the guard room.

Jacob was outside to greet them.

"Oh, thank God," he exclaimed. "I was getting nervous you'd be in lock-up for my wedding!" He grinned at Henry but also afforded a friendly glance at Smith. Henry looked quizzically between the two. Were they friends? Since when? Had he been so wrapped up in his own bunk theories the past week or two that he'd become completely oblivious to anything else happening?

"Catch up!" cried Williamson from the gate. The four of them jogged to join him. The young man grinned ear to ear.

"We're getting guns!"

———

XVIII

Henry spent the entire time lugging crates up the steep incline road watching Smith. He still could not believe he was a woman. (She. Dammit, he could not keep that straight.) Smith kept up with the rest of the squad. He lifted, strained, and juggled his end of the crates without complaint. He staggered, but no more than the average youth of similar height and build. Physically, he fit in. It was an anomaly Henry could not reconcile. He tried to imagine the boy in a dress, and while he had previously understood that his smooth cheeks would allow for the illusion, he could not reconcile a gown as Smith's normal state of dress, not even the most plain farmwife frock.

When the guns were secured in the armory and the squad was finally dismissed for some leisure before supper, Henry trailed behind the others, his eyes still following Smith absently like he'd entered some kind of trance. He didn't notice when Jacob doubled back and fell into stride next to him.

"Well," Jacob said, "how was jail?"

"Terrible," Henry replied, his eyes still following Smith. She didn't walk like a woman at all. No sway of the hips or anything. She veritably swaggered, as if there were anything to speak of between her legs. Dear God, what was wrong with him? Henry scrambled to think of something—anything—else as he felt his cheeks heat.

"So Smith's not a spy after all, then?"

Henry let out a sigh and scrubbed his face with both hands quite miserably. "No. He's not."

"I'll admit, I thought you were as mad as a March hare talking all that nonsense in the mess yesterday, but then he snuck out in the middle of the night and I couldn't help but wonder if maybe you might be on to something. Did you find out what he was up to?"

Henry felt discomfort slither over his shoulders as his eyes fell away from Smith and regarded Jacob sidelong. He was going to have to tread carefully to keep his word. He wished he could think straight right now. He felt all higgledy-piggledy, still reeling at the ever-expanding implications of Smith's revelation. He hadn't had any time to figure out what he was going to say to the other boys, who apparently still wanted to know what had become of Henry's wild spy theory despite finding it whole-heartedly ridiculous.

"Let's just say that when I confronted him about it in confinement, he laughed at me about as hard as the rest of you did."

"So he denied it?"

"Of course," Henry shrugged. "He had a reasonable explanation for everything."

"Did he?" Jacob pounced, an eager smile on his face. "Do tell!"

Henry held back a grimace. He'd never been particularly good at lying, but this was too big to fumble for lack of skill. Not only was his word of honor on the line, but Smith's very livelihood as well. Who knew what kind of miserable life she'd have to return to if she was found out. Women didn't just throw their whole lives away to fight in a war—not when they were expressly prohibited from doing so. A young woman with a loving family and good prospects wouldn't do that. Besides, the amount of teasing he would earn after Smith was gone would be nothing in comparison to the inevitable inquiry into Henry's own moral fitness. Regardless of what Smith said, he would be culpable for sharing a bed with her. There were only so many salacious implications that could be borne; the command couldn't just turn a blind eye to it.

"He made me swear I wouldn't tell," Henry hedged, but as soon as he said it, he knew it was too enticing to put Jacob off.

"Oh, sure, and now you're putting Smith's confidence over mine?" Jacob said. "Come on, tell me. I promise I won't let it get back to him."

Henry shook his head.

"It was a woman, wasn't it?" Jacob guessed.

Scheisse. Henry's heart hammered and he tried very hard to keep his face straight as he shrugged. This was terrible. He'd lose every last shred of honor if even his word was worth nothing. He felt sweat bead at his temple.

"One of the laundresses, maybe?" Jacob added, watching Henry's face carefully for confirmation.

Henry slowly exhaled the breath he'd been holding. His friend meant that Smith had been liaising with a woman, same as they'd surmised when he'd made his accusation in the mess yesterday. He hadn't guessed the truth. Henry pressed his lips together and shrugged again, perhaps a little bit too hard.

"Or was it actually Franklin Steele's daughter after all?" Jacob laughed.

"That's ridiculous," Henry said, but he was so tense that his tone struck more squawky than flippant.

"Wait, are you serious?"

"I'm not telling you, Jacob."

"Yeah yeah, I know, you're not telling me. But seriously—Steele's daughter?"

Henry winced, because he was a terrible liar and he was out of his depth and he just wanted Jacob to leave him alone.

"Oh my God." Jacob's eyes were like saucers. He looked ahead of them at Smith striding across the parade ground towards the mess. "You're kidding."

It didn't matter whether Jacob was barking up the wrong tree or not. People trying to pry into Smith's business presented the same level of threat regardless of the reason, and now, whether he wanted to or not, Henry was in the business of protecting Smith's secret. Though, if Henry cared to admit it, he had no desire to tell at all. The entire thing was too mortifying to consider. If suspicion of Smith's sex was leveraged, what would they do to confirm it? Strip search her? He had no affection for Smith, but he couldn't bear the idea of any woman enduring such indignities. Besides, he couldn't deny that he was somewhat thrilled to be the only one in on the secret.

"I'm not telling you anything, Jacob. Leave. It. Alone."

"Absolutely, mum's the word," Jacob pledged giddily.

Henry grabbed Jacob's shoulder and stopped him near the well. "Jacob, I mean it. It's none of our business, and if rumors start going around about Smith's personal business, it's going to wreck whatever tentative truce we have, so please *please* keep your big mouth shut."

"Criminy..." Jacob rolled his shoulder out of Henry's grip. "I didn't know you'd become such fast and loyal friends. I won't say anything."

Jacob looked away, and Henry felt him go distant. God, this was so frustrating. He couldn't throw off his actual friends over this, but he had no idea how to walk that line when the inquiry was so direct.

"It was just a call of nature," Henry grasped. "Last night. It was nothing. I guess I read one too many dime novels or something."

Jacob gave him a wry look. "Or we're just so bored, cooped up in here drilling every day, we gotta come up with something interesting to talk about."

Henry chuckled. "Yeah. You're not wrong there."

"If I have to play one more game of euchre, I think I'm gonna scream."

———

That evening, the boys played a raucous game of poker—not euchre—with the squad from Hastings in the barracks. The tiny room was hot and muggy and smelled of sweat. Instead of icily refusing to play and pretending to sleep, Smith allowed Williamson to cajole him to join. He seemed more relaxed than he had in weeks. He drank from the flask when it was passed and swore mightily when he lost. And he actually smiled, laughed, and told a couple jokes, although most of them were still at someone else's expense. It seemed a weight had been lifted from his shoulders. Perhaps because that weight had been transferred directly onto Henry's.

As Henry glanced up at Smith from across the poker table, he had to keep reminding himself that Smith was a girl. He kept stumbling over pronouns in his own mind, struggling to remember to think "she" instead of "he". He'd seen Smith's corset, for God's sake. He'd seen the curve of her waist, the swell of breasts laced down. He had no doubts on that count. But once that was concealed again under baggy, government-issued clothes, he started to wonder if he'd imagined it all. He sighed. He'd just spent too many days obsessing over Smith, too much time worrying about the girls Jacob had brought to the fort, and now, with this behemoth secret weighing him down, he was bound to feel confused.

Henry was just about to ante up when he froze in horror.

The night he'd met Jacob's fiancé, after returning from guard duty. He'd been tired and frustrated and had spent too much idle time agonizing over Miss Walsh and his endless parade of romantic failures. And he'd brought himself off in his bunk. And he'd heard Smith do the same.

And Smith was a woman.

Henry choked and stood suddenly, hitting his knees against the table and knocking his chair over. The boys around the table all looked up at him, startled. Smith glared at him.

"I, uh," Henry stammered, all too aware that his cheeks were burning red. "C-call of nature."

And he dashed out the door, outside into the twilight of the parade ground, where a few men from Company H were stubbornly finishing up a game of baseball despite the waning light.

He rubbed his hands over his face and groaned helplessly. He squatted down on his haunches and tried to just breathe. Could women even do that? Bring themselves off? He tried to imagine how it would even work, based on what he'd heard from Elias and others, based on dirty CDVs he'd seen, but his brain kind of short-circuited at the mental image, mostly because he just could not imagine Smith with the soft body of a woman. He'd thought nothing much of Smith doing that when he thought he was a boy, but now? Knowing the truth? He was completely and utterly mortified.

"You're not going to just shit right there, are you?"

Henry looked up and over his shoulder at Smith, standing there with his hands on his hip—*her* hands on *her* hips—like some sort of disapproving lieutenant. He stood quickly, dusting his hands on his trousers, and resisted the impulse to assume the position of the soldier.

"What's got you all skittish?" she asked pointedly, lifting a dark eyebrow. "Not having second thoughts about our arrangement, are you?"

Henry shook his head. "No, no, it's not that." His cheeks burned and he twisted his mouth up painfully.

"If you're worried about being bunk-mates, don't be," Smith said firmly. "I don't want you to treat me any different."

Henry blinked, grateful for the excuse to not discuss that wayward evening a few nights past. There was no way—none—that Smith hadn't heard him. He'd actually restrained himself less in an effort to make Smith uncomfortable. He lurked around the fringe of the memory, reluctantly noticing the traces of elevated pleasure he'd experienced, something he'd thought was just due to competitiveness or pique when he'd believed Smith to be a man. He shook his head and forced himself to just forget about that. He was nervous about bunking up with Smith. That was it. No need to mention something as mortifying as the other night.

"Yeah," he agreed vaguely. "Should I ... just sleep with my back to you?"

He could not stop blushing. He'd be lying if he said that there was no part of this realization that was arousing, though he would rather jump off the ledge of the Half Moon Battery than let Smith know that. Instead, in a matter of an hour, he'd have to crawl into bed with her. *Sheisse.*

Smith crossed his—*her*—arms. "At the very least. I don't want anything to do with being bedfellows. This is a forced arrangement. The sooner we muster out and I can get a space of my own, the better."

Henry swallowed hard.

"But I guess," Smith added, shrugging, "better you than anyone else."

"...What does that mean?"

"Well, you already know," she murmured in a conspiratorial tone. "So I don't have to worry about you finding out."

She flashed her eyebrows at him significantly and headed back into the barracks. Henry's mouth felt strangely dry. At the doorway, she turned around and leveled a dark brow at him.

"Weren't you going to the privy?"

Henry stared back at her blankly. "Huh? Oh, yes." He turned and stalked unsteadily toward the soldier sinks, his ears burning.

———

Lights out found Henry reluctantly climbing up the scaffold to find a way to wedge himself between the edge of the bunk and Smith, who'd already retired and curled up in the corner where the bunk met the wall. For all intents and purposes, she appeared to be sleeping, but there was a stubborn set of her chin that made Henry think it was more of a willful approximation than actual sleep. Now, to slip into the scant space left for him with the bare minimum amount of contact. (He didn't care to admit that this was likely the greatest challenge he had faced in the army thus far.)

He crawled forward, the straw mattress sinking noisily under his knees. When he was ready to set himself down on his side, he sort of listed away from Smith to turn and nearly lost his balance, looking five feet down over the edge with some trepidation. Across the way, one of the Hastings fellows sniggered at him.

Henry glowered and tried to remind himself that in the dark, he was nothing more than a shadow. No one could see how embarrassed he was, or that he was sort of half aroused by this entire humiliating experience. He tried to squeeze himself alongside her with careful control, but he ended up awkwardly flopping down, his rear-end nearly on top of hers.

"Watch it," Smith snapped and shouldered him off. Henry's face was already screwed up into an agonized grimace, so he couldn't very well grimace further, but he sure did blush harder as he scooted himself away from her. Nervous about sharing a bunk indeed—how could any man be stoic in a situation like this? If Smith expected him to calmly forget that she ever told him her secret while he was sharing a bed with a woman for the first time in his adult life, well ... she could go jump in a lake.

There was nothing for it. In order to create the proper distance between his body and hers, he had to perch precariously on the edge of the bunk. He could do it, but as soon as he fell asleep, he'd either relax back into her or fall off the edge. It was untenable. Slowly, in minute increments, he let his body sink back into hers. Perhaps if he did it slow enough, she wouldn't notice.

This was ridiculous. None of the men in this room were able to find their own space in their bunks. Everyone was smashed together; there was nothing for it. If Smith didn't like it, he—she—could keep it to her damn self.

He let himself relax, his spine unfurling against hers. She didn't respond; she merely shifted slightly, though he couldn't say whether it was towards or away, per say. She was warm and firm and her hair tickled at the back of his neck. He could detect the ridges of lacing along her back, just as he had the night before. Only this time, he knew what it was and that knowledge made his skin buzz. Oh hell, if he was going to be her co-conspirator, he was going to need to get over whatever embarrassing response all this was.

He had to keep his eyes open because when he closed them, he kept imagining Smith's face on the nude *carte de visite* Elias had kept under a loose floorboard in their lodgings on the farm in Faribault. He banished the image resolutely. He was not going to let himself get worked up over that. Smith was nothing like the soft, curvy image from that CDV. From head to toe, she was hard, angular, and unwelcoming. The farthest anyone could possibly be from the velvety embrace of the woman in the CDV.

It was just because they were in such tight quarters, facing down three years of guard duties and battles and death. It was the kind of environment that stoked the fires of passion, that made a man search for the nearest warm comfort, lest he be marching off to his death. The idea of Henry's own death felt abstract and slippery, but the vague feeling that he was running out of chances was high. It was high with everyone.

A chorus of snores bounced around the room. He was exhausted from carrying munitions up the bluff, his face ached where Smith had punched him, and for all intents and purposes, he should have fallen asleep as soon as his head hit the pillow. But his tiny world, encapsulated in and around the walls of the fort, had been turned upside down today. It might have been the longest day he could remember. He had so many questions, and in the absence of answers, he couldn't resist the temptation to speculate.

He imagined Smith's father and brother had enlisted in the First Minnesota and she couldn't bear to be left behind, so she enlisted too. Maybe she had no family and no means of survival, so she disguised herself as a man to earn a better wage. Or perhaps, she was running away from a cruel, pro-secession family who found her Union loyalty extreme.

Henry could speculate all he wanted, but he was still no closer to the answer. He didn't even know her real name. The fact that she lay beside him, her breaths deep and even in sleep, her back warm on his... Her mystery enticed him in a way that he'd never felt when he thought he was ferreting out a spy.

———

XIX

St. Paul, Minnesota
Sunday, August 25, 1861

IF SOMEONE HAD TOLD Cate two weeks ago that she would be attending a friend's wedding in St. Paul, she would have laughed in their face. Friends were a liability for someone like her, yet here she was, tromping down Fort Road with her squad, heading for the church with the rest of the boys. In a way, telling Schaefer her secret had been the best thing that had happened to her since joining up. Now that he wasn't relentlessly trying to figure out the anomaly that was her, she was free to smooth over some of the conflict she had stirred up, quietly participate in the activities in the barracks, and try to earn the trust of her squad-mates.

Since official Union uniforms still hadn't come through, the squad turned out in their Sunday best. Cate wore the jacket and trousers she'd nicked from the lumber yard laundry months ago (had it already been that long?), freshly laundered and pressed. Her hair was smoothed under her hat with some hair grease the boys had been passing around this morning. They'd all had a shave too, so she was glad not to be the only smooth-cheeked one of the bunch. Even Robinson had given up on his scraggly beard for his wedding, which was a relief, because it only grew on his jaw and made him look like he had a strap holding his hat on. Mary Coleman seemed, for all intents and purposes, a fine prize and Cate admittedly didn't understand how she'd come to choose Robinson out of all the soldiers at the Fort, but one could not account for taste.

The Fort road ran east along the bluffs, affording an excellent view into the river valley as they made their way past the occasional farm and woods. As they neared the city, the houses became more dense. After a little more than an hour of walking, Sergeant Osborn led them left up Bay Street, away from the bluff, and onto Seventh Street proper, which would lead them more or less straight into the heart of the city. The road was a veritable straight shot and they could see a steeple or two, as well as buildings as tall as four stories ahead.

The conversation by the second hour had gone dry and they all walked together in a somewhat companionable silence. Cate enjoyed the cool breeze on her face, the sun dappled through the leaves of trees, and the dust kicked up by her feet. It reminded her of walks on the river she'd taken in her previous lift, and found that the experience in free-moving trousers was far superior. She internally commended herself for her audacity and fortitude. The threat of being discovered was worth the freedom dressing as a man lent her.

"Shall we sing a song?" Tom Webster suggested after the silence among them had stretched for some ten minutes. The younger fellows groaned as Webster shrugged in a most fatherly way.

"Oh no, Tom, not again," complained Osborn. "None of your songs are any fun."

"They're all church songs," added Schaefer, "And we're headed there already."

"What have you all got against hymns?" Webster replied, a little ruffled. "They're a mite better than those ribald little ditties those boys from Hastings were singing."

The boys all broke out in laughter.

"Oh wait, how did that one about Jeff Davis go again?" Hower laughed. "One night as Jeff lay fast asleep; With his wife hugged to his heart—"

"Corporal," Sergeant Osborn said with a warning tone. Hower pressed his lips together and tried not to smile. The other fellows, including Cate, bent double laughing.

"Wait—if we are to entertain, surely the man of the hour would have a preference," Cate cut in, gesturing at Robinson.

"Yes!" agreed Hower. "Jacob, how might you like to spend your last hour as a bachelor?"

Robinson's eyes sparkled with amusement, darting among the faces of his comrades. "I'm not sure I have much of a choice at this point. I'll need every minute that remains just to walk to the church."

Hower nodded impatiently and said, "Yes, yes, of course, but there are plenty of entertainments that can be pursued while walking. If you want to hear Webster's hymns, for example, so be it. Who are we to object to anything our bridegroom wishes?"

The rest of the fellows looked to Robinson expectantly. He preened under the attention, peering at his squad-mates with an impish spark. At length, his eyes alighted on Schaefer and he grinned.

"Ah, I know just the thing!" he exclaimed. Schaefer returned his gaze with guarded incredulity. "Schaef, show us your routine."

Hower lit up as the other men murmured in confusion. "Yes, your routine!"

Schaefer glowered and crossed his arms. Cate peered at him. Was this the calisthenics thing he'd been doing when she'd run into him on the riverbank last week?

"No, no, I'll just slow us down," Schaefer demurred.

"Come on! It's my wedding day!" Robinson protested.

"That's precisely it," he said. "I would hate to make you late to your own wedding."

"Henry, come on," Elias cut in. "We all agreed to entertain him."

"I didn't agree to anything."

Robinson booed and the rest of the squad followed. Cate grinned as she joined in. Schaefer looked at her with an expression of betrayal.

"Fine," Schaefer said, glaring daggers at each of them in turn. "But keep the ribbing down, would you?"

Robinson eagerly nodded and Hower declared, "You hear that, fellows? Only words of elaborate praise!"

The boys laughed and Schaefer shook his head in annoyance. He started swinging his arms around him, stretching his shoulders in turn before bending at the waist to stretch his legs. Cate pressed her lips together to suppress a grin. He hopped lightly on his toes and stared down the worn dirt road before them. John Williamson exchanged a look with Cate that hovered in between skeptical and amused. If Schaefer's routine was anything like his little dance down by the river, she could see why he was reluctant to show it to the rest of the boys. Cate had done calisthenics once in Pennsylvania and it had a sort of flavor unique to morally superior teetotaller women.

Schaefer bounced up and down, stalling.

"Get on with it, Schaef," Hower called, grinning somewhat superiorly.

Schaefer shook his head, took a deep breath, and then took off at a run in the grass along the center of the road. After a few paces, he threw himself foot over hand in circles, turning like he were tied to the wheel of a cart. After three rotations, he bounced back onto his feet and then launched himself into another turn, only this time he faced forward and launched himself off both hands at once, springing back to his feet. Cate's eyebrows lifted in surprise. Certainly not the fancy dance routine she'd seen by the river. This was entirely different, and wholly remarkable.

The boys murmured collectively as they quickened their pace to catch up. Schaefer turned briefly and looked back at them. He dusted his hands and lined himself up again with the road. Then, he leaned forward and balanced himself up on his hands, his arms fully extended, just as he'd done down by the river. Color flushed his cheeks and he puffed slightly with effort as he began to walk rather shakily forward on his hands, his legs straight, toes pointed to the sky.

Williamson let out something between a laugh and a shriek and Webster clapped his hands.

"Bravo, Schaefer!" he cried enthusiastically. "Why didn't you tell us you had all these unique talents?"

Robinson grinned. "Just you wait, Webster! He's not done yet."

Cate's left brow arched higher as she turned back to Schaefer's increasingly more intriguing antics. Where on God's green earth did he learn all this? The entire routine had structure; this wasn't the sort of thing a bored country boy picked up while herding goats or something. It was very intentional. If nothing else, it explained why he was so much bigger than the other boys.

Schaefer went back onto his feet and was rotating his wrists absently as he took a deep breath. Pausing, he turned and looked back at the rest of the squad. "Sorry, I'm a bit out of practice."

Webster blinked, flummoxed.

Schaefer gave an apologetic half-smile and turned. His shoulders shrugged with a deep breath and then he leapt into a sprint again. A few paces off, he dove forward onto his hands, flipping over once, twice, three times and then—

Cate's breath caught in her chest for a moment as Schaefer tucked himself into a ball and his hands did not touch the ground at all as he spun midair for a split second. Turning his body a full 360 degrees, he drove his feet forcefully back into the earth. He bent his knees and put his arms out wide as he stumbled a step forward, but then quickly regained control. Cate's mouth went a little dry as she noticed how his trousers stretched tightly across his thick thighs.

Webster let out a whoop and Williamson, Robinson, Hower, and the Sarg all applauded loudly. Cate reminded herself to close her mouth and slowly clapped her hands together. Krüger, looking largely unimpressed, or at the very least, unsurprised, provided polite applause as well. Schaefer regarded them with a bewildered expression, still somewhat guarded as he waited for them to catch up to him. He dusted his hands off on his trousers, leaving a smeared handprint on his thigh that mocked Cate. *Look where a hand might touch*, it seemed to say. Cate screwed her face into a scowl as she tried to stuff that useless thought away.

"More!" Robinson shouted delightedly, clapping.

Schaefer frowned at him. "I don't think my wrists can manage much more. I reckon I've done my fair share of the entertaining."

"Where on earth did you learn all that?" Webster asked, grab-bing Schaefer's hand and shaking it exuberantly.

"Why do you think they call them Turners?" Krüger replied, his German accent thick with amusement.

"Wait, who are the Turners?" Williamson asked.

Robinson laughed. "Oh, I get it! Because they *turn*."

Krüger gave him a wink and carried on walking past Schaefer. The other men followed but at a slower pace, patting Schaefer on the back and giving commendations. After a few minutes, Schaefer got his shoulders out of his ears and relaxed some-what, awkwardly accepting praise and relentless questions from Webster in particular. Cate didn't trust herself to say anything without licking her chops like a hungry cat, but inside, she was eavesdropping and hanging off every last word as Schaefer explained his upbringing with the *Turnverein*, the *gymnasticks*, and the arena his organization had built in Ohio. While on the surface it seemed a very strange upbringing, in a way it reminded her of the Quakers she'd grown up with in Pennsylvania.

"I heard they've got an arena in St. Paul," Hower mentioned. "We should pass by it in a bit."

Schaefer regarded him with interest. "Really? I wonder if they'll have rings or a pommel horse, or if non-members of the local chapter are allowed."

"A what kind of horse?" Cate couldn't help but ask.

Schaefer flushed adorably. Some men might toss out termi-nology they know is unfamiliar to sound superior—Cate could think of one ex-husband in particular—but Henry not only hadn't meant to confuse anyone, but he was actually embar-rassed he'd inadvertently done so.

"It's a false horse, or rather, part of a false horse..."

"That sounds positively morbid," Cate observed.

"Well, it's just leather and sawdust, it's not as if it were a real horse."

"Which part?" Robinson asked, his eyes twinkling with mis-chief.

"Well, the legs and the body, I suppose."

"But no head then?"

"Right."

Williamson blinked at him incredulously. "What the devil do you want with a headless false horse?"

Henry wrinkled his nose and shrugged. His self-consciousness seemed to swell again. "Do handstands and leg circles. Leg crosses..."

The boys stared at him blankly. Cate wondered if the arena did indeed allow non-members use of its facilities, because her baser instincts dearly wanted to know what this leg circle business was about.

"My God, what kind of man had the time to dream all of this up?" Hower laughed.

Henry glowered at him but Hower didn't seem to notice.

"Truly, while the rest of us are doubled over breaking sod and building a civilization out of this wilderness, some German dandy has the time to dream up a thousand ways of building his body without actually doing anything useful."

Henry sighed, quickening his pace to move ahead of the group. Cate glared at Hower but Webster cut in first.

"You must admit, though, it was quite impressive. I've never seen anything like that before!"

Hower nodded dismissively. "Of course, it's very novel. I just can't see what the point of it is," he shrugged, then laughed, "other than to show off, of course."

"If anyone here is a show-off, it's you," Cate snapped without thinking. The boys all turned and looked at her wide-eyed. Glaring back defiantly, she realized too late that Hower was an officer and she wasn't supposed to speak disrespectfully to her superiors. Oops. "What? You could break a hundred acres of sod, but you could still never do that." Of course, instead of excusing herself or apologizing, her first instinct was to double down. She tried to soften her words without backing down, turning to look at Henry's retreating back. "The only way would be to practice. A lot."

Henry didn't turn, but he wasn't so far ahead that he couldn't hear the entire exchange. He scratched the back of his neck with dusty fingers, like he could feel her eyes on him.

"Oh ho, do my ears deceive me?" Hower replied, his voice still playful and unfazed. "Did I just hear Smith coming to Schaefer's *defense*?!"

"Commendations to Lieutenant Thomas," Webster added. "Looks like the time spent in the guard house made fast friends of these two."

Cate regarded Webster with some disgust. "Don't be ridiculous. I'm not defending Schaefer; I'm upbraiding Corporal Hower."

Robinson and Williamson exchanged trepidatious glances. Hower's mouth dropped open at the brazen insubordination. Then, the awkward silence was shattered by Sergeant Osborn's hearty laugh.

"Very well, Smith, I see now why you might have made a decent corporal yourself," he chuckled, clapping a hand on her shoulder. "You certainly have no trouble doling out reprimands."

Hower looked bewilderedly between the Sarg and Cate, but the rest of the men laughed along. Schaefer hung back a bit to rejoin the group, sniggering. Cate gave him a castigating look. Then, turning her attention back to the Sergeant, she said hyperbolically, "Thank you, sir. Someone in this outfit must strive for decorum."

The boys howled at that. Cate did well keeping a straight face as she stalked ahead of the group, gaining on Krüger at the front. She very much hoped that Sergeant Osborn's humor extended to himself somewhat. It was hard to break the habit of prickliness, especially since it worked well to keep them all at a safe distance. Well, most of them, anyway.

Krüger gave a deep chuckle as she stalked past him.

"You keep that Turner at arms-length," he rumbled at a conspiratorial volume. "They have no scruples."

Cate peered at him sidelong. "What's that supposed to mean?"

Krüger smiled placidly and shrugged. He said something in German, but she had no idea what it meant and wasn't terribly inclined to inquire further. She stalked ahead so that she was at the front of the group and looked on toward the city. She scratched at her forehead, prodding at her discomfort carefully, trying to untangle its cause but also rather fearful of it. Was Krüger somehow aware of how Schaefer caught her attention? Was she looking too much, too long? Why would he think she was worth warning off? Did he know something about Schaefer that she didn't? Did he suspect her?

Cate shook her head and sighed. She wondered if it was possible to join a different squad. One that didn't make her existence even more complicated. One that didn't have Henry Schaefer in it.

———

XX

Jacob Robinson's wedding was a lot of things. Dry was not one of them. While the ceremony was held during the morning service at the large Catholic church on St. Peter's Street and 6th, the reception was at the public market house just north on 7th Street, where the clergy's scrutiny did not reach. And not only was the second-floor hall filled to the brim with what seemed to be every friend, neighbor, and distant relation of the bride, but each and every one of them appeared to be both Irish Catholic and abundantly thirsty.

Henry had wondered if he might encounter some Germans here as well, since Jacob had confirmed his suspicion some weeks ago that Mary and her family lived on the edge of the German *Turnverein* neighborhood on the west side of the city. However, it seemed Mr. and Mrs. Coleman's hospitality only extended to those who shared their mother country (or more specifically, their religion), with Squad Seven being the only exception.

Wine, whiskey, and beer flowed through the afternoon as fiddlers played lively reels for the younger set to dance to. The bride's sister Miss Anna was scarcely more than a blur and hardly missed a dance the entire party. As for Henry, he worked up quite a sweat dancing his way through a gaggle of distant cousins and neighborhood ladies. He'd engaged Miss Walsh for one dance and though it had been enjoyable, neither he nor she had been too keen on pursuing a second. She'd been engaged for several dances with some Irish fellow and Henry was proud of how content he was with that.

Krüger wasn't much for dancing, unsurprisingly, but made quick work of befriending the men hanging around the beer barrel, his deep laugh making it easy to track where he was. Elias tried to start a wager on who could dance with the most girls, but no one took him up on it. That didn't seem to deter him from competing regardless. Williamson disappeared part-way through the night, only to return an hour later looking *very* pleased with himself. Webster and Sergeant Osborn acted as Jacob's surrogate parents, his own having passed away some years ago, working around the room and making friendly small talk with the bride's father and uncles. Only Smith was able to attend such an enormously lively party and spend it sitting at a table with a Byronic scowl on his face, a glass of whiskey in his hand. Though he'd been his usual level of prickly since the walk into town, he'd been positively mean since the ceremony.

When his calves could hardly stand it any longer, Henry sat out a particularly lively schottische and leaned over to Smith, whispering, "You know, it is incredibly rude for an eligible young man to refuse to dance when there are girls without partners."

Smith only glowered in response, sipping defiantly from her glass and flat-out refusing to have a good time. A Grahamite in spirit, though without any apparent aversion to spirits.

So while it was no surprise that come sunset, they were all three sheets in the wind, it was worth remarking upon that Smith was all sails set. As they made their merry way back toward Fort Road, he lagged somewhat behind, walking like he had a brick in his hat and refusing any attempt to assist him.

Henry was feeling rather sauced himself. He'd tried to help Smith along, but she'd elbowed Henry hard in the side and hissed, "Don't treat me any different."

So Henry kept pace with the rest of the boys, checking over his shoulder from time to time to make sure Smith was still there, staggering along behind them. Elias was running down a play-by-play of all the girls he'd danced with, reading off his dance card to prove he'd won the wager with himself, while Krüger sang a German drinking song loudly. Henry tried to join in, but he only knew the Swabian words. Since Krüger was singing a Bavarian version, he glowered every time Henry mucked it up, so Henry quickly gave up.

"After that, I danced a reel with Miss O'Gara. She was real light on her feet but not much of a conversationalist if I'm honest—"

"Maggie was an excellent conversationist—converseator? ... Talker. Anyway!" Williamson broke in. He'd only danced with one girl, then disappeared for some time, and now he couldn't stop singing the praises of this Maggie (whom, by the way, no one in the squad had met, and whom Henry was not entirely sure was real).

Webster and Osborn led the group, chatting amiably among themselves as old friends deep in their cups were wont to do. Both of them had had their fair share of drink but showed it less than the younger boys. Henry was glad Sergeant Osborn didn't seem upset that all the men had gotten properly drenched at the party because heaven knew that he couldn't afford another reprimand. (Smith either for that matter.)

Thinking of Smith, Henry glanced over his shoulder again in the waning light of the setting sun, glittering long across the rolling water of the Mississippi below them. He frowned. Smith seemed to have fallen behind. Lagging somewhat, Henry waited, keeping one eye on the squad while waiting for Smith to turn round the big tree. After a minute or two, Henry jiggled one leg, glancing at the retreating backs of his comrades. Smith had told him not to treat him any different. If he'd been Williamson or Webster, he would have gone back for him. Hell, if he'd been Krüger, he would have gone back for him. So after a moment more of pussyfooting, he went back the way they had come.

Around the big oak tree, he heard a retching sound. Peering through the dim light, Henry stepped back into the bramble and nearly fell over Smith hunched over on the ground, puking his guts out. Or her's, as it were.

"Smith?" he said. "Are you alright?"

"Go AWAY!" she bellowed, scrubbing her hands over her sweaty face. "Jesus Christ, why does it always gotta be *you*?"

She sat up on her haunches and promptly lost her balance, tipping back on her rear, her boots splaying out in front of her. She groaned miserably and gave in to gravity, letting her head clunk to the ground. Henry hoped she wasn't going to be sick again. He hated it when people got sick. It made him sick just to think about it.

"The group has gone on," Henry pointed out. Smith didn't respond. "It's getting dark," he added.

"What's it to you if I get lost? Worst case scenario, you get to have the bunk all to yourself."

Henry frowned. What a stubborn ass. He reached out his hand.

"Come on, Smith. You've just had too much to drink is all."

"I did? God, I had no idea."

"Hey, you're still sarcastic, so you must not be that soaked."

Smith groaned again as she pushed herself up on her hands and staggered to her feet, eschewing his proffered hand. "Thanks. 'M fine. You can go catch up to your friends now."

Henry studied her as she stalked back onto the path, trying very hard to appear steady on unsteady feet. Following, he shrugged. "Eh, Elias is just lecturing about his dance partners. I'm not missing much."

Smith snorted. "He would. That man could lecture to a pen of chickens if he thought they'd listen."

Henry nodded sagely. "He has."

Smith started to laugh, then stopped herself and shook her head grimly. Henry couldn't help but be pleased with himself as the two of them fell into step side by side on Fort Road. The trees flapped in a particularly strong breeze as the sun dipped below the treeline, sending the woods into twilight. After a few minutes of walking in thick silence, Smith slowed and groaned.

"Are you going to be sick again?" Henry asked warily, swallowing against his own gorge at the prospect.

"I dunno how I could have anything left to be sick with," Smith replied, her focus inward as she winced. "Uggghh, 'm just spinning."

Henry nodded with understanding. "That's the worst. How much did you drink?"

Smith wrinkled her nose. "I'm just not used to drinking whiskey."

"I'm surprised you're used to drinking anything at all."

Smith's eyebrows tried to join her nose. "What's that s'posed to mean?"

Henry shrugged. "I dunno. You just seem like the type to get on your high horse about drunkenness."

Smith rolled her eyes. "I mighta dabbled in temperance, but I'm no teetotaller."

"How does one dabble in temperance? I should think it's really an all or nothing game."

Smith shrugged. "I used to be a Quaker."

"Used to be?"

"Yeah. In Pennsylvania."

Henry tried to imagine Smith as a straight-laced, devout Quaker girl and utterly failed. Despite that, he nodded, trying to appear amenable. "We stayed with some Friends when I was little, on the way from New York to Ohio. First rate folks."

"They are ... till they're not."

"What happened?"

Smith scuffed her boot into the dirt haphazardly. "Well, you know. I got a big mouth. They have those little meetings every week where everyone sits in silence until the spirit moves you to speak. I was moved a little too often for their tastes."

Henry raised a brow. "That seems kind of counter-intuitive to me. If no one is moved to speak, do they just sit there?"

Smith nodded.

"For the whole meeting?"

She nodded again.

"What is the point of that?"

"Quiet contemplation, I s'pose. Communing with the spirit or something."

"Seems like a monstrous waste of time, if you ask me."

Smith snorted. "It rather was."

Henry studied her face. He could see it now, a bit. He could imagine what Smith's face might look like attached to a female silhouette. In the twilight, her features seemed to soften—or perhaps it was because she was drunk and her face wasn't as pinched as it usually was. She had a strong nose and jaw, her face square and lean, but her lips were full and pink and softly bowed, her dark eyes large and round. They'd be doleful if they weren't always trained into such a hard expression. Under those thick brows and short, shaggy hair, he could imagine there might be a woman under there.

"At the Turner Hall in Cincinnati," Henry recalled, "we had lecturers that came every week. It wasn't always interesting and sometimes it was a big waste of time, but at least we talked about something. We had 'em in New Ulm too, but not as often."

"That'd've suited me better. The silence was s'posed to be time for folks to pray and feel connected to God and such. It wasn't ever meant to be a discussion. But I had a helluva time sitting through that every week. It's hard to be silent when so many people are suffering. It was a waste to sit in silence and just think about it—ugh," Smith tripped over a root erupting from the dirt road. She flailed her arms and caught her balance. "I don't think they were as upset that I had been moved to speak as much as they hated what I had to say. Or maybe that I was the one who said it," Smith added, regaining her footing. Then she paused. Her eyes fluttered. She swallowed hard. Henry winced, half-expecting her to puke again. Instead, she let out a loud belch.

Henry blinked. "Don't mind my saying so, but that was the most impressive belch I have ever heard from a lady."

"Mmh, that feels better," Smith cleared her throat and then glowered at him. "All ladies belch. They just don't do it in mixed company."

Henry regarded her for a long moment. "I suppose..."

Smith rolled her eyes. "'Course, you *would* be skeptical. What do I know? I'm just a lady."

"A lady dressed up like a man and enlisted in the army," Henry pointed out.

"And...?"

"I wouldn't consider you a ... representative sample of the female sex."

Smith lifted a thick brow at him, her expression daring him to challenge her. "You'd be surprised."

Henry tried to imagine Miss Walsh belching. He simply could not manage it. A single glance in Smith's direction told him that she would argue if he pressed further, so he hedged.

"What kinda things did you say that got you thrown out of the Friends?"

Smith pursed her lips. "Oh, y'know. That slavery is evil. That abolition was the only way to save the nation's soul. That we were all wasting our time sitting around praying when we needed to stand up and fight. That it was unfair that women weren't able to speak in front of 'promiscuous audiences' to fight against it, or even vote."

Henry's eyebrows flew up. "...I see."

"That it's outrageous that women lose all their rights, property, even their children to their husbands when they get married. We cease to be people. We cease to exist in the eyes of the law."

"Is that true?"

Smith was taken aback. "Which part?"

"That women give up all those things when they get married?"

Smith blinked. "Yeah, 'course it is. Whaddya think the priest meant today by 'honor and obey'?"

Henry felt patronized, which rankled.

Smith's keen eyes honed in on him, piercing through the haze of alcohol—or perhaps sharpened by it. "You don't like being talked down to, huh?"

Henry lifted his chin. Smith regarded him for a long moment.

"Neither do I," she whispered conspiratorially. She held his eyes with her intense, dark gaze for a long moment. It felt like she could see right inside his mind. Then she turned on her heel, teetering only slightly, and stalked away.

Henry watched her for a moment before trotting after her.

———

Cate could hear Schaefer's footfalls behind her. Why couldn't he just *leave her alone*? She felt like she'd been hit in the head. She was feeling all of the ill effects of the whiskey with none of the benefits. The combination of these—the physical

disorientation, the nausea, the fog in her brain that prevented her from censoring herself, the irritating blockhead trailing
her—made for a nasty mood indeed.

"Is that why you were being such an ass at the reception?" he
asked. "Because you hate marriage?"

Cate let out a frustrated growl as her feet connected with the
ground in different spots than she expected. "No, I don't hate
marriage, don't be stupid. I hate that the law doesn't see married
women as people."

She glanced over her shoulder. Schaefer was closer than she
expected and it made her skin prickle with awareness. He was
studying her under furrowed brow, his mouth tight.

"What would you know about marriage?" he provoked.

If Cate had hackles, they would have raised. "What the Hell
is that supposed to mean?"

"You're not even old enough to get married."

There was a niggling thought somewhere in her mind that
suspected he was provoking her on purpose, but she was too
busy getting angry to pay it much notice. "That so? If that's the
case, we just sent two juveniles to the altar 'cause I'm definitely
older than both Robinson and that Coleman girl."

"And how old is that?"

"Older than you."

"Twenty-two?" he guessed with some skepticism.

She scoffed.

"Twenty-one?" he corrected.

"You're getting colder, soldier."

"Twenty-four??"

"Warmer."

"No way you're twenty-five," he said. He'd fallen in step at
her side. When she tripped on yet another root that seemed to
mock her disorientation, he nudged her with his shoulder to
steady her. She felt herself flush, mostly with embarrassment,
and haphazardly covered it with anger.

"I'm twenty-six, you ignoramus."

Schaefer's eyebrows flew up. "Really?!" He processed this
for a moment. She could feel his eyes studying her, testing her
words against her form. In another world, she would bask in this

sort of attention from him, but as it was, it made her want to shrink into her clothes and disappear before her cheeks began to veritably glow in the twilight. "I don't see it."

"That's nice. Doesn't change the fact that it's true."

"No disrespect, but you don't look a day over sixteen."

Cate rolled her eyes, which made her more nauseous. "That's 'cause 'm dressed like a boy. If I were in a gown, I'd look ancient."

"I'd like to see that," Schaefer scoffed. Cate winced. It was incredible how the application of a sarcastic tone could turn what could otherwise be beguiling words into weapons. She took a deep breath, pressing down both on her nausea and her temper.

"...Would you say that to Robinson? Webster?"

His shoulders shifted uncomfortably. "Well, no..."

"Then *don't* say it to me."

"You were the one who brought it up," he grumbled.

Silence fell like a curtain between them. A dry stick crunched under her boot.

"And it's not as though anyone's around to hear us," he couldn't help but add.

Cate shook her head vehemently, which brought her gorge up worse than the eye-rolling. "You know what? Forget you know. Forget I told you anything. It's safer if you think of me as an obnoxious, irritating little boy. If you start trying to actually know me, you're going to slip up and ruin everything."

"Fine." He shoved his hands in his pockets and glowered at the ground. The shadows were beginning to stretch longer and longer. Twilight was giving way to true darkness and if the river was any indication, they still had at least a half an hour left to walk before they reached the fort.

"Aren't you going to go catch up with your friends?" Cate demanded after several minutes of walking in a petulant silence.

"No."

"Really." She leveled her gaze on him, crossing her arms. "You'd rather pass the time with belligerent old Smith stumbling over my feet and berating you every chance I get?"

"You're not old. Even if you are twenty-six, which I sincerely doubt, but that's still not old."

"It is when you're an unmarried woman," she muttered.

"See? There you go again! How am I supposed to forget about it if *you* keep bringing it up?"

She glared at him sidelong. Schaefer huffed a frustrated sigh. She probably only took five steps before she couldn't help but press. "Well, it's true. A woman beyond the age of twenty-five might as well be dead."

He looked up exasperatedly as though imploring the heavens for help. "Twenty-five *isn't* that old."

"Maybe not for a man. But how many women over twenty-five have *you* ever been in love with?"

Schaefer pressed his lips into a thin, irritated line. "You know, maybe the reason you were unable to attract a partner had more to do with your abrasive attitude than your looks."

"A revelation! If only I had known this earlier in my life! Then I could have taken a different path. Thanks, Henry Schaefer. You freed me. Now that I understand what's at the root of my defects, I can go out and change my personality completely and attract a husband forthwith."

Her chest hurt. Must have been the whiskey.

"You know what? I take it back," he retorted. "Your problem isn't an abrasive personality, it's an overabundance of defensiveness. I wonder what you'd be like if you could just relax and not have to keep everyone at arm's length all the time."

"I guess we'll never find out." Cate focused her eyes on the path in front of her. If she stared at the ground hard enough, perhaps everything—and everyone—else would go away.

A formidable silence dropped between them again. She hated to admit it, but he'd hit closer to home than she'd been ready for. And her chest hurt, like someone was sitting on it.

"At least now," she said, her tongue dry in her mouth, "my body's the only thing I gotta hide. Before, I had to make myself small enough to fit into whatever everyone else wanted me to be. My body, my voice, my money, my passions, my intellect—even my thoughts."

Schaefer looked at his boots scuffing the dirt for a long moment. A moment long enough for Cate's memory to show her a stack of stereoscopes of all the times she'd messed up, been rejected, felt wrong.

"That..." he ventured at length, "that's awful. I think I've felt something like that before. Like no matter what you do, it's never enough for them. But I've never been so trapped. I'm sorry."

"Don't be." She couldn't say anything else. Her throat would catch. Instead, she focused on what was true now. She was in the forest. She was a soldier. She was the master of her own destiny and as long as she just kept her stupid mouth shut for five minutes, she would stay that way, at least as long as she was enlisted. Or alive. Whichever. Hell—time to pull the lifeline. She couldn't bear another moment of this feeling.

"So," she said at length, her voice squeaking from the tight control she'd seized it with. "*Gymnasticks*, huh?"

Schaefer gave a long-suffering sigh. "Don't start."

"What?" she replied, an overly innocent hand on her chest. Their pace slowed as he stared her down under defensive brows. His hair stuck out from his hat and his chin was already stubbly again. His expression was loose with drink. She wondered what he would do if she pulled him near, brought the two of them together. Against a tree. A small smile curled the corner of her mouth. There was no one around. Darkness covered all sorts of sins.

It was one of her more reckless impulses, just the sort she had to stop entertaining. But it was also just the sort of impulse that had the potential to untwist this knot in her chest, help her escape bad memories, help her breathe again.

"Where'd you learn to do all that?"

Henry dithered a bit, his shoulders coming up in embarrassment again. "The Turners work hard to maintain a strong mind and a strong body—"

"No kidding," she replied and ran her hand over his thick upper arm. It was ill-advised, indulgent and stupid—exactly the kind of thing that would surely disgust him coming from a mouthy, mannish woman like her. But she was drunk and stupid and she probably didn't have an ounce of self-preservation in her whole body. She gave the arm a squeeze instead of dropping the touch. He was firm and warm beneath his wool coat.

Henry's blue eyes were engaged. His defensive countenance deepened into confusion as he tried to read her expression. It was hard to tell in the deepening twilight, but she thought she detected a flush in his cheeks.

"Quite impressive," she added, her voice softer. Henry's gaze darted between her eyes and her mouth. She let her lips part. His eyes widened the slightest bit. She could already feel the shame and inadequacy getting trampled by a new tension, and she exhaled with relief. His nostrils flared with his inhale and Cate didn't think she was imagining that their bodies were drawing closer.

"We should..." he breathed, his voice catching in his throat. "We should catch up to the others."

She nodded. The energy in the air between them was exquisite. She breathed it in.

But then he squeezed his eyes tightly shut and winced. "It's getting dark. We—we gotta get back."

The breath squeezed out of her lungs. The coils settled back around her chest. Foolish.

He scrubbed his palm over his forehead and shook his head. "Sergeant Osborn will put us in the guard house again if we lag too far behind."

Cate could imagine the things she might say to argue with him. How she might set his mind at ease, where her words could untangle his confusion. There was something there underneath it. Wasn't there? Or did she just want there to be?

She felt like her feet had landed heavily back on the ground. She was in the forest. She was a soldier. She had no business trying to leverage her feeble wiles against someone this close to her. They shared a bunk, for God's sake. Besides, what made her think that she could attract the attention of someone like Henry? Even in a proper dress, she couldn't garner the notice of any respectable man and it was not for lack of trying. Unless one counted Richard, and by the time she'd realized that his attention was more than passing pity, it had already been too late.

————

XXI

Fort Snelling, Minnesota
Monday, September 2, 1861

WHEN JACOB ROBINSON RETURNED from his honeymoon, he was transformed. Of course, in many ways, he was still the mischievous fellow he'd been, quick to smile and filled with friendly jibes. But there was an air about him when he returned, a confidence that made it clear he had fully come of age, a boy no longer but a young man, with a wife and a duty to his country. He took his drilling more seriously, he quit leering at the laundresses, but best of all, he no longer deferred to Elias Hower.

The first night he was back, Cate was reading some penny dreadful she'd found up on her bunk, high above the action as many of her comrades played cards with the Hastings squad. Jacob was at the center of the conversation, regaling the group with all the lovely things he and Mrs. Robinson had seen while on their honeymoon aboard the Mississippi paddleboat to Dubuque and back.

"The river valley was exquisite," he gushed. "It rained the first day and the mist rising up off the river bluffs—it was picturesque."

Cate looked up from her book and peered passively down at the scene under an arch brow. Jacob seemed to have picked up some turns of phrase from his new bride, no doubt the result of a week spent only in each other's company.

"Truly, it's an experience of a lifetime."

"How many of you were born in Minnesota?" Hower asked with an impish brow. None of the fellows in the room raised his hand. John Williamson carefully put his hand tentatively in the air.

"It was technically still Wisconsin territory when I was born," Williamson offered.

Hower regarded him with a puzzled expression, then turned with a braggadocious swagger on Robinson. "Well, seems like we've all seen that track of river at some point or another. Except for Williamson apparently."

Jacob glared at him. "Well, I highly recommend the journey regardless, if any of you other fellows end up getting *married* before we muster out." His glare turned pointed as he flicked his chin at Hower.

"Those orders are likely to come soon," Webster put in. "Unless any of you already have a bride in mind, you'll be hard pressed to get one pinned down before we go."

"Well, I for one am eager to get to the front," Williamson said. "I'm young—I'll get me a wife when we get back next year. Besides, Maggie said she'd wait for me."

"Yeah," agreed Sam Corbett, the new recruit from Hastings who always seemed to have a secret stash of whiskey on hand. "I hear they don't think the Rebs will last another three months."

"I hope we'll get a chance to fight before it's all over," another added as he anteed up.

"I'm sure there will be girls where we're going," Elias Hower assured, exchanging a card for a fresh one from the deck. "I don't know if you know this, boys, but girls are half of the world's population. They're everywhere."

Krüger boomed a laugh. "Not in this barracks, there's not. It's just a lot of stinky duffers who think they stand a chance." Cate's knees curled up as Krüger showed his hand and the other fellows let out a chorus of grumbles. They'd be surprised just how close, in fact, they were to a girl.

She gave a hard glare to Schaefer, who had glanced up at her at Krüger's comment. He stood behind Robinson, waiting his turn to play at the table.

"Just because they're around doesn't mean they're interested in a lout like you," Webster teased Hower, smiling.

"Yes," Jacob agreed, taking a swig from the flask one of the Hastings boys was passing around the table. "I was shocked how aloof a lady can be, even after she's married you!"

"Oh no," Elias groaned. "Please tell me you consummated the marriage."

"Of course I did, no thanks to you."

"Insolent! My advice comes guaranteed from one of the most delightful girls in Faribault."

"Hate to break it to you, Elias, but your advice was a load of bunkum."

"If it was so bad, how did you end up having such a lovely trip?" Elias replied with a dubious smirk, dealing the cards he had freshly shuffled. "Don't mind me saying, but you've looked like the cat that caught the canary ever since you got back."

"Luckily for me, one of you actually gave some good advice," Jacob said smugly.

Webster preened as Hower demanded, "What, that old married ninny?"

Jacob snorted. "No, it was Smith's."

Cate recoiled as all of the boys craned their necks around to look up at her.

One of the other Hastings fellows whose name escaped Cate bounced his head looking between Jacob and Smith. "Wait, what did *he* tell you?"

Jacob looked as though he might defer to her, so Cate shook her head curtly at him.

"Don't tell me you just asked her like some sort of amateur?" Hower exclaimed.

"Yup, I asked her what she liked. And she told me, and I did it, and it was *marvelous*." Jacob grinned, preening under the fawning attention he was receiving from the Hastings boys. Cate felt her cheeks heat and hid behind her book.

"Really?" exclaimed Sam Corbett, his voice a bit too loud from one too many sips of whiskey. "That little tadpole? He barely looks old enough to be in breeches."

Cate frowned and threw the book at the offending speaker. The corner of the spine hit him square in the head.

"Ow, what the hell?!"

"Don't cross Smith. He's young, but he's got no mercy," Webster pointed out, speaking to Corbett like he might his own children.

"And much more experienced than you might think," Jacob added, then gave Cate a conspiratorial wink. Cate wrinkled her nose and regretted having thrown her book, for now she had nothing to hide behind. What the hell did Jacob think he knew? Cate glared at Schaefer. He was looking at her wide-eyed, a flush in his cheeks as he shook his head and mouthed, *I didn't say anything.*

Cate glowered back at him regardless. She had every reason to believe Schaefer was a terrible liar, though up until now she had been pretty confident that he could keep a secret. How he'd perform under duress, on the other hand ... that was something she had little confidence in.

"Oh come on, Smith, you don't have to be embarrassed!" Jacob assured her, grinning.

"Ah, you got a fancy woman on the side then, Smith?" one of the other Hastings boys said. They were all looking at her now, eager for whatever boast she might offer to the manly pretense game. She shrugged nonchalantly.

"I really can't say," she said cagily. If she was learning anything about lying, letting folks form their own conclusions was far easier than spinning a web of lies she had to remember.

The boys hooted and wolf-whistled.

"Wait, so what do you mean you just 'asked her'?" one of the other Hastings boys asked Jacob. Blessedly, the conversation and the attention of the men in the room shifted back to the card table. Cate let out her breath. She hadn't realized she'd been holding it.

"Hey you," she barked. "Throw me my book back."

Sam Corbett ignored her, but the red-haired fellow next to him bent and tossed up her book. She nodded curtly in thanks and glowered as she tried to find where she had left off. Jacob was waxing poetic about his newly discovered carnal knowledge, and she couldn't bear to listen for wondering if Richard had done the same with his chums at city hall. The idea of him describing anything about their wedding night to those men whom she'd only met on a handful of occasions made her skin crawl. She read the same paragraph three times before she gave up, rolled over, and put an arm over her ear, quietly humming "John Brown's Body" to herself before blessedly surrendering to the sweet blankness of sleep.

When she stirred, it was dark and the symphony of snores played through the tiny, crowded room. Schaefer's back warmed hers, and she was surprised to find that there was a strange comfort to it. A sense of peace, as it were, to be in this space, to have a place among these boys who, for all that they were annoying, were set upon the same purpose as her. A shared purpose towards justice.

It was easy to burrow back into her pillow and let sleep overtake her again.

———

XXII

Thursday, September 26, 1861

By autumn, the companies dispatched to the frontier out-posts were called back to Fort Snelling. Henry didn't much mind; the late September temperature had been so mild it would make for most pleasant tenting weather. Indeed, when the commanding officers broke the news that the entire Second Regiment would be moving out of the barracks, it was most welcome. They were to camp out on the west side of the parade ground beyond the fort walls while a Third Regiment was recruited and set to lodge in the barracks. Even with only a single company being formed in that new regiment, the conditions at the barracks had deteriorated considerably. It had already been a tight squeeze with three companies; a fourth as the weather began to cool resulted in a rash of sickness across the fort. Every soldier Henry saw seemed to be coughing, snorting into a handkerchief, or both.

The worst of it, though, was the bed-bugs. The vermin had spread quickly after the new recruits to the Second Regiment had been crammed into the barracks, and Henry had bites all along the side he always slept on. Moving into the tents would hopefully make the difference, as long as their clothing and bedding were well-boiled by the laundresses.

That Thursday, the first of the companies assigned to the frontier outposts returned, so the commanding officers decided that with such favorable weather, it was high time they cleared the Second Regiment out of the barracks. The sun was shining and perfect puffs of clouds floated across a magnificent stretch of blue sky.

After morning drills, Sergeant Osborn directed the squad to join the line at the quartermaster where they were issued a set of four wedge tents. Each soldier was also issued a gum blanket to lay upon, coated in rubber to keep them dry should it rain. Henry ran his fingers over the sturdy canvas appreciatively, admiring the crisp white fabric folded neatly into a square. It would be so refreshing to have the space to sleep on his back again.

"Peugh, this smells *awful*," Jacob exclaimed, glaring down at the gum blanket like it had threatened him. "How are we expected to sleep on this thing?"

Webster shrugged and sniffed uselessly with his still-congested nose. "I guess there is a bright side to being sick all the time."

"After breathing in Schaefer's stench for a month," Smith drawled, "this thing will be like sleeping in a bed of daisies."

Henry glowered and rolled his eyes. By now, he had settled into his own understanding of Smith's antics. There was the Smith he knew—hard, skeptical, downright mean—who wielded derision like a shield. He had two expressions: concentration and disdain. But every so often, Henry would catch glimpses of what Smith was protecting underneath. A nervous glance, a genuine laugh, a spark of intelligent interest. Because he feared he would be the weak link in Smith's elaborate ruse, he had taken to naming her hidden disposition Charley.

Charley was the person who had been glancing wildly around when the company first assembled, unsure of what to do as the men divided themselves up into squads. It was Charley that he had invited into the squad, not goddamned Smith. It was Charley who had stumbled back to the fort drunkenly, who had drawn him into a moment of shameful weakness with her doleful, dark eyes. It was Charley who snored lightly next to him, fingers tangled up in her short, tousled curls.

It helped to think this way, because in his mind, Smith was "he," while Charley was "she". He hoped the distinction would prevent him from slipping up and using the wrong pronoun aloud. And while Smith was just about the most abrasive and irritating fellow he had ever met, Charley was an enigma that utterly fascinated him.

Charley had become scarce after Jacob's wedding, hidden under Smith's blistering snide comments and short temper. Henry didn't blame her—they had both been too sauced to behave entirely as they ought. The last thing he wanted to do was scare Charley away by showing too much interest. She was wary, and he was certain she'd been made more so by Henry's behavior in the woods, when one sincere compliment from her had set his pulse playing double-time, and his eyes unable to focus on anything but the soft bow of her lips. If there was one thing Henry was sure of, it was that Charley Smith didn't think much of him. She had said so countless times. Furthermore, she had also made it clear that she had no interest in making her precarious existence even more uncertain.

But damn if he wasn't insatiably curious. Not just about that moment they had shared and what might have come of it had he not embarrassedly declared they hustle on, but about who she was. What drove a Quaker girl to become a soldier? What was the silent story she carried?

When the squad arrived on the other side of the parade ground, west of the fort walls, Sergeant Osborn gathered them round while he demonstrated how to erect the tent.

"Gentlemen, this is what is known as a wedge tent," Sergeant Osborn announced to the handful of them gathered around. "See, here now ... what you do is..."

Osborn shook out his folded square of tent and snapped it in the mild breeze.

"There's a seam..." Osborne fumbled with the heavy mass of canvas, "...somewhere..."

"Uh, Sarg, I think it might be here," Elias Hower said and the two of them began to burrow into the tangle of cloth as the rest of the squad awkwardly watched.

Henry glanced around, noticing that they only had half as many tents as they had men. Leave it to the Union army to ask the soldiers to make do. He took stock of who held a tent, like him, and who didn't. It didn't seem to correspond with the previous bunkie pairings. Williamson and Krüger both had one, while Jacob, Webster, and Smith had none.

"Webster, why don't we give this a go over there?" asked Williamson, all artificial innocence as he tried to position himself as far from Krüger as possible. Henry glanced over at Charley, who was looking somewhat pale without a tent issue. He entertained the impulse to assure her that she was far and away the most preferable bunkie. But, no, he couldn't say that. Given what had passed on the road back from St. Paul (and a world of possibility that had not), it would be awkward for him to be so eager. He pressed his lips together and shuffled around, covering his attempt to move nearer to her while pretending to see what the others were doing.

"Back off, Webster is my bunkie," Jacob snapped, sounding surprisingly more defensive than Henry had ever heard him.

Williamson giggled. "Look out, don't tell Mary that Jacob's got someone else to keep his bed warm!"

"Quiet!" Osborn barked, straightening up and letting Elias spread the tent over the ground, still looking for the center seam. "You'll be with your same bunkies as before and there will be no arguing."

"Ah, come on Sarg!" Williamson whined.

"What did I just say?"

"But Sergeant Nelson is letting his men choose," Smith pointed out, voice straining against a strong measure of indignance. Henry glanced sidelong at him. Sharing a bunk in a room filled to the brim with men was one thing. Alone with Smith in the privacy of a tent was another. One corner of Henry's mouth twitched up. With a larger measure of privacy, Charley might be more apt to appear. Perhaps that was what had Smith so wary.

"You're not in Sergeant Nelson's squad, now are you?" Osborn retorted firmly.

"Not for want of trying," Smith muttered under his breath. Luckily, Osborn didn't seem to hear him.

"You all have the same bunkies and that's final," Osborn said exasperatedly. "Krüger, hand your tent to Webster. That's right. Now, what you'll want next is some sturdy branches to use as tent poles."

Elias produced the bundle of sticks he'd toted along when they departed from the fort. It seemed as though he'd had advance notice and did the work of scouting good branches for the whole squad ahead of time. Henry glanced over at Nelson's squad. They were racing another squad to the woods to scout for branches. He threw a thumb after them and leaned in to Smith.

"I mean, Nelson's squad might not be all it's cracked up to be. At least we have a Sarg who's fetched sticks for us already."

Smith leveled a suspicious glare at him.

"Come now, Jacob," Krüger boomed, pronouncing Jacob's name the German way, with a y sound instead of the hard j. "You wound me! I'm an excellent bunkie—just ask Williamson." He also pronounced Williamson's name with a v instead of a w. The man didn't even try not to sound like a greenhorn.

Jacob studied Krüger sidelong, unsure if he was teasing or not. "No offense, Krüger. But you snore something fierce."

The big Bavarian just laughed and then clapped Williamson over the shoulder. "Come now, little friend."

Osborn looked up at them as he and Elias struggled to get the tent to balance on the branches they'd speared into the ground. "Wait, I have it here, hold on. Don't start until you all know what you're doing!"

Webster smiled pityingly at his friend as he walked by with Jacob. "Try staking the opposite corners first."

Osborn glowered at him, but followed his advice. The tent stayed up this time.

The whole company was staking their tents in orderly rows, marked out by twine along the grass. Henry moved to Smith's side quietly, hoping he wouldn't choose this particular order as occasion to lose his temper. Instead, he took the tent from Henry's hands and snapped the canvas into the breeze, chuckling sardonically. "Well, here we are again."

Henry haphazardly tried to grab a corner to spread the tent over the ground. "Seems so."

"Well, I s'pose I'd rather have the evil I know," Smith shrugged, pointedly not looking at him as they tried to figure out which way the entrance flaps of their tent went.

"Hey now," Henry replied, smoothing the sides out as flat as he could manage, considering the shape it was sewn into was three dimensional, "you scarcely know me."

Charley tried to stifle a laugh. Henry's mouth turned up at the corners in a private little smile. Elias chose that moment to intrude, tossing them three sticks-turned-tent poles.

"You might want to take a knife to one end," Elias noted. "Sharpen 'em up and the like. They'll stick in the ground better that way."

Henry's nose wrinkled at the extra step, even as Smith pulled his knife out of his boot and tested the blade's sharpness on his thumbnail.

"Why don't you go grab some stakes," Smith suggested as he took up one stick that bifurcated into two branches at one end. "I'll get these sharp on the ends."

Henry nodded and went out in search of tent stakes. After much aimless inquiry, Elias ended up giving him a few scraps of sticks that he broke up into smaller pieces, preserving bits where a branch or twig extended so that the tent loop would be held fast to the ground.

Charley went round to the rear of the tent while Henry stayed at the front. Together, they each lifted their end of the center pole, drawing the canvas up with it, and dropped it in the cradle formed between the bifurcating branches of their tent poles. The canvas hung limply from the center pole and the edges dragged on the ground.

"I think we're supposed to stake opposite corners," Charley said, her eyes fixed on the canvas with a calculating expression. Henry nodded and countered her as she bent to grab the back-right corner. Together, they pulled the canvas taut and slipped the stakes through the cotton loops. Henry crouched on his haunches and pressed the stick hard into the ground, driving the stake in at an angle so it would not slip out again. He straightened and pressed it down with his boot heel for security. The structure seemed sound so they moved to the other corners and staked them too.

"Voila!" Henry cried triumphantly, standing and dusting off his hands. "Home sweet home!"

Smith looked down at the tent with some skepticism, as though he didn't trust that the thing would stay up. Henry snatched up his gum blanket and threw one of the flaps aside. Crouching in the entry, he spread the blanket out as smoothly as he could, the fresh rubber smell reeking into the small canvas shelter. Shuffling inside, Henry flopped on his back and sighed contentedly.

"It ain't much," he said, "but it's ours."

Smith stared blankly at him, still standing outside the entrance.

"Hm," he said articulately, and then turned off to walk down the row of tents.

Henry sat up and stuck his head out the flap.

"Hey, where you going?"

But Smith didn't respond. Henry laid back again. The prairie grass made for a comfortable cushion over the hard ground. With the sun filtering through the canvas, a fine, fresh breeze tickling his hair, and the warm temperature, Henry felt delighted by the prospect of finally being out of the crowded barracks and in their own tents. Not only was it a relief to have more than a 6 foot by 3 foot rectangle to share as a bed, but being in camp felt that much closer to marching to the front, to face the enemy they had spent all this time preparing to fight. Whatever snit Smith was in about their new living arrangements, he'd get over it when their orders to join the front finally came. It could be any day now. Henry grinned at the canvas gable, plucking a length of sweet grass to chew on.

But then he remembered shipping out would mean he'd finally run out of excuses to not write to his mother.

———

When Cate returned, Schaefer was laid out on his gum blanket, arms behind his head and cap over his eyes, enjoying a piece of prairie grass between his teeth. His shirt stretched over his chest in a way that sharply reminded her that she needed to *stop* being such a shameless lecher. All the more reason to get a blanket to hang from the center pole. There would no longer a group of other men sleeping a foot away from them. She had certainly wished—dreamed, even—of this level of privacy but the fact was, she didn't trust herself in a private tent with Schaefer.

Her own gum blanket was laid out on the other side of the tent and she maneuvered herself inside to sit on it, settling in with the newspaper she had borrowed from one of the St. Cloud boys. She had managed to track down Hower, only to find out that there were no additional army blankets for issue or purchase and that if she wanted one, she would either need to trade for one or buy one from the sutler for a pretty penny. Cate was annoyed but not surprised. All she had to do was find a fellow who had brought his blankets from home and had no use for the additional threadbare army blanket they'd been issued. And then have something he wanted to trade for it. All before winter came and they held on tight to whatever they had to keep warm.

Cate tried to quell her catastrophizing by flicking open the *St. Cloud Democrat* and settled in to read. It was a bit old but she'd take what she could get. It wasn't as though Franklin Steele carried many abolitionist papers at his sutler, though he did have a good number of Democrat titles. Apparently Jane Swisshelm's particular brand of fiery moral superiority and vehement abhorrence of slavery was somewhat of an acquired taste—one that a great many Free Soilers and slavery-complicit Minnesotans found offensive. Precisely why Cate liked her.

"What're you reading?"

Cate looked up over the edge of the paper and peered guardedly at Schaefer. "*St. Cloud Democrat*. One of the St. Cloud boys had it and lent it to me."

Schaefer's eyes lit vehemently. "See, I knew you were a Democrat."

Cate rolled her eyes hard. "I know it breaks your little heart that your theory was completely bunk, but in fact, you are wrong about that too."

"Then why are you reading a Democrat paper?"

"It's not a Democrat paper, it's a democrat paper."

"You hear yourself?"

She'd meant to laugh *at* him, but based on his expression she was afraid she had inadvertently laughed *with* him instead.

"It's Jane Swisshelm's paper." She paused, but no recognition passed his eyes. "She's an abolitionist. She published an exposé on the St. Cloud Democratic mayor for keeping slaves in his house, and he sent a mob to set her printing press on fire or throw it in the river or something. She printed the whole thing with a new press as soon as she could, but then he sued her for libel. Anyway, she just changed the name of her paper so she could stay in business and called it the *St. Cloud Democrat*, just to spite him."

Cate flicked her eyes back to the paper and the reprint of President Lincoln's announcement of a day of Humiliation, Fasting, and Prayer. She let out a murmur of interest as she noticed the intended day was in fact this day. She'd already eaten breakfast. Damn.

"Jane Grey Swisshelm?"

That got her attention. Cate folded the paper down so she could afford Schaefer her entire incredulous focus. He was propped up on his elbows, his cap askew and that stupid prairie grass sticking out the corner of his mouth. His blue eyes were placid, enquiring.

"Yes," Cate replied slowly. "Do you know of her?"

Schaefer nodded, looking up as if trying to recollect. "Yes, actually, I think I saw her speak once."

Cate's eyes widened significantly. "Really? Where?" It was hard to keep the envy from her voice.

"Cincinnati. I can't remember if she was at Turner Hall or somewhere else."

"She spoke at the *gymnasticks* hall?" Cate clarified incredulously.

"No—yes—well, sort of." He squinted one eye as he fumbled for words. "We use the hall for all sorts of things—lectures and dances and *gymnasticks* and community events. The Turners are committed to a sound body *and* a sound mind."

Henry sat up all the way and tipped his head to the side to peer at her newspaper. "I'm trying to remember, but I'm fairly certain she was the fire and brimstone lady my father hated so much."

"Hated? Why?" Cate demanded a little more defensively than she had intended. She loved Jane Swisshelm. If it wasn't abolition, it was women's rights, and she wielded words like deadly weapons in her writing. The woman had left her husband at a train station for God's sake, heading up to St. Cloud with her daughter because the man was such a frightful bore. She was a heroine come to life. Cate had read her a great deal in Pennsylvania and based several of her more controversial speeches during the Philadelphia Friends' meetings on Swisshelm's model. (Not that they had appreciated it.)

"Oh, he just didn't like..." Henry started, but then trailed off, twisting his mouth awkwardly.

"What?"

"Well, my father admires evidence—"

"Swisshelm uses plenty of evidence in her rhetoric!"

Henry shrugged. "I don't doubt it. I—I admittedly don't remember much about her speech. Just that she spent a whole lot of time quoting the Bible and that always gets under my father's skin."

Cate's brow arched. "She uses Bible verse to devastating effect. She drives right to the root of how abominable slavery is by measuring it against the most definitive code of morality there is."

"I suppose, but she's not the only one using the Bible to illustrate her points about slavery. Josiah Priest used the same code to defend the practice in the *The Bible Defense of Slavery*."

Cate faltered; she'd never heard of that. "So?"

Henry sighed, slouching over himself with his legs crossed. "I'm not saying it's inherently bad, it's just really easy for folks to pick and choose the bits that defend their argument and cast out the rest. And that's just sloppy rhetoric."

Cate stared at him with her mouth half open. "Should I take this to mean that you have read more than one book?"

Henry wrinkled his nose in offense. "Ha ha, very funny."

Cate looked down at her paper for a long moment. The dense lines of ink danced in her vision as she tried to parse which thoughts were debate for the sake of winning and which were her actual opinion. Which spurred a curiosity...

"So how many of those arguments that you presented just now," she said slowly. "How much of that was your father's opinion and how much was yours?"

Henry looked up at her, blue eyes deep and limitless and stricken. "Um, all of it, I guess—"

Cate lifted her brow at him.

"I'm certainly pro-abolition, if that's what you're asking."

"I really don't care what your father thinks, Schaefer. You shouldn't either, come to think of it." She folded her paper primly in her lap. "We're our own men now, ready to fight for what we believe in. So, question is—what are you fighting for?"

He stared at her. He looked so young for a moment, guarded yet raw. Then his brows sort of snapped down, like a shield. "I could ask you the same question."

Cate's eyes narrowed. "Only one of us is reading an abolitionist paper. Speaks volumes, I should think."

Henry rolled his eyes and gave an exasperated sigh. "I don't have to prove anything to you."

"I'm not asking you to. I just asked what distinguishes your opinion from your father's. Not my fault you had yet to consider it."

"Of course I have," he insisted as his arms curled defensively around his knees. "I'm ... I want to make something of myself. I want to be the kind of man who stands up and says 'No more.' And I want to prove that Freethinkers can be moral too."

"I'm certain that there are many of us both moral and free-thinking."

"Not just freethinkers. I mean Freethinkers." Henry winced. "All Turners are anti-clerical, but my father and his friends take it a step further. They're Freethinkers."

Cate widened her eyes impatiently.

"You know, Freethinkers? They don't go to church..."

Cate blinked in surprise. "At all?"

"No, uh..." Henry licked his lips awkwardly. Cate became momentarily distracted. "My father was very much against the entire idea of church. So we grew up going to the Turner Hall instead. My father always said it was better to fill our heads with science and history than religion."

Cate licked her own lips. "So you're telling me that there are communities of people who don't worship together or even believe in a God at all?" She blinked slowly. "What do they do instead?"

"Debate, mostly." Henry shrugged. "It's as I described. Speakers and discussion and—"

"But surely the ladies are not included—"

"No, they are," Henry said. "I mean, they certainly aren't turned away, in any case. At least not in New Ulm. Though admittedly there aren't very many about who aren't mothers or grandmothers and choose to spend their time otherwise occupied."

Cate narrowed her eyes in suspicion and grunted.

"I take it you were turned away?" Henry ventured gently.

"Of course I was. Opinionated women always are. We're not even allowed to sit in the main audience at most abolitionist talks. We have to sit behind curtains along the sides, hidden away. What is the point of making women the harbingers of morality when we're constantly being silenced and made invisible? I mean, to what degree do the ladies of New Ulm feel welcome to participate in Freethinking society?"

"I couldn't really say," Henry replied. "As I said, there really weren't enough women among us who were inclined to the Freethinkers. My mother attended occasionally, but come to think of it, only when my father was hosting. But my mother is among the many Turners who are Christian, even if they practice in the privacy of their own homes or in Bible study groups." He paused thoughtfully. "But I can see what you mean. Tolerance is not an invitation."

Cate blinked. "And these Freethinkers. They're atheists?"

"What? No, of course not—"

"Well, they're anti-clerical and they don't go to church. You made a distinction between them and Christian Turners?"

"What?"

"Come now, are you not one of them?"

"No. Well, yes, I mean ... sort of."

"Then that makes you an atheist?"

"No!"

"Then what faith do you adhere to?"

"Uh, Christian, I suppose. Criminy, Smith, if I knew I'd be interrogated, I wouldn't have decided to spend my free time with you."

And he settled back on his gum blanket and pulled his cap back over his eyes, making it very clear he would speak no further on the topic. The infernal prairie grass still jutted out from his freshly-moistened lips. Cate peered at him, trying to determine where Henry's parents ended and Henry began. Why admit to anti-religion in one breath, then claim to be a Christian in the next?

"You don't have to pretend for me," Cate said quietly.

"What?" He nudged his hat up to look at her.

"You don't have to pretend to be religious if you're not just to make me feel more comfortable. And you don't have to be areligious just because your father is either."

Henry stared at her. God, those eyes. Tentative, hopeful even, but also a bit anxious. Then, he looked at the ground and gave a weak laugh.

"What?" She pressed, then clamped her mouth shut. He was right about one thing: he did not deserve to be interrogated.

"It's just..." Henry sighed and pushed a hand through his hair. "I ... God. I wish I could be half as sure of myself as you are."

The words sort of cracked alongside Cate's head like a slap. Which was ridiculous because it was a compliment. A long moment passed, with just the sound of the wind in the trees and the murmur of busy soldier voices humming outside the tent. Cate fumbled with her paper awkwardly, a half-grunt her poor excuse for a response. He sounded like he meant it too. It made her lungs feel like they were curling in on themselves.

She scoffed into the fold of the newspaper. "You really have no idea how wrong you are."

Henry regarded her skeptically. "Oh really?"

"Come now, you're the last person to make a bid for my good character," she snapped, crumpling the paper in her lap. "Until last month, you thought I was an arrogant ass. And you're not wrong. I let my temper and my ego get the better of me. If I was as self assured as you think, I'd be corporal. Or I'd have done some other tangible action to further abolition, instead of stealing and deceiving to enlist. I'd have—" She stopped herself from saying she'd have refused to marry. Or that she'd have taken her ideas elsewhere after getting kicked out of the Friends instead of moping at the backs of other denominations' sanctuaries for years, letting her father convince her of how burdensome she was. She felt her eyes sting and gritted every muscle in her face to push that sensation well away.

"You went to great lengths," he ducked his head to force her to look at him, "to ensure you were able to enlist. Surely that counts for something."

Cate stared at him, fighting the tightness seizing her throat. Tried to focus on his eyes, on his nearness, on the heat that it had conjured in the pit of her belly. All of that was infinitely easier to bear than his unassailable argument to prove her good character. He didn't know her. There was so much he didn't know.

"So," Cate sniffed, glancing up furtively and shifting as she smoothed the paper in her lap. "What else have you read?"

Henry's mouth twitched the prairie grass consideringly before he straightened, pulling his cap back. He regarded her with a frank openness she scarcely deserved after all the hostility she'd heaped on him these past few months. "I quite liked the *Narrative of the Life of Frederick Douglass.*"

Cate stared at him. She had spent the last few months certain that for all his fine looks, this farmhand had no brains. He was a good-looking man with a defective personality, too stupid to know how little he knew. If he were about to prove her otherwise, she would be well and truly done for.

———

XXIII

Cate was well and truly done for. It was after supper and she was dogging Henry Schaefer in the late afternoon glow across the prairie grass, beyond the tents, as he explained his thoughts on Frederick Douglass's escape from slavery.

"I don't really suppose he could have explained what he did to get away, since he didn't want to compromise the people who helped him, but damn if I'm not curious."

"Well, of course you've heard about the Underground Railroad?" Cate said.

"Enough to know it's not an actual railroad. I suppose that's all we need to know. Didn't Douglass call it the 'upperground railroad'?"

Cate smiled. "I believe he did. I admire that he didn't want to divulge his escape methods, though. Folks still use those means to escape, even now." She twisted her fingers in her hands. "Did you ever see slaves? In Cincinnati, I mean?"

Henry frowned. "Yes. We'd see them across the river in Kentucky. Ohio had a law that slaves brought into the state would be automatically free."

Cate scoffed. "We could have used a law like that here."

Henry nodded. "I never knew any personally. We had some free Black folk talk at the Hall. But the Turners are not the easiest people to join if you don't speak German."

Cate nodded wistfully. "We had free Black neighbors in St. Anthony." She could still see Emily Grey's expression of warning, of fear, when the mob had raided her house that night Eliza Winston was freed. "Both of them were born to parents who had been enslaved. But they were free. And I don't understand how that makes a difference."

"What do you mean?" Schaefer glanced up at her as he stooped to pluck another long stalk of prairie grass to chew in his teeth.

Cate's mouth twisted as the sky shot with gradually deepening shades of pink and purple. "This whole defense of slavery seems built on the notion that some people are more human than others. If dark-skinned folks are less human than light-skinned people, then why are free Black people more human than enslaved Black people? What is the difference?"

"I think the real flaw is looking for any semblance of logic in the pro-slavery argument to begin with," Schaefer said, the grass twitching up and down through the air as he spoke.

"But people believe it. And I'd like to believe most people are reasonable. So why would they keep digging in on this issue if it is so obviously wrong?"

"I think they know in their hearts that it's wrong," Schaefer said. "*Damn,* if that don't beat all. That's a beautiful sunset."

He plopped himself down in the grass and laid out his full length, hands behind his head. Cate averted her gaze, looking up at the painted clouds. She'd spent the whole day counting the minutes until she could talk with him again. At first she tried to test him, to see if he'd actually read Douglass' book. Many folks had read excerpts in newspapers but hadn't deigned to read the whole narrative. But he'd easily passed. She suspected he may have actually read it more than once.

After that, she half lost her mind. They'd gushed together about how horrible Edward Covey was over dinner and how satisfying it had been when Douglass finally stood up to him. She looked for Henry in the mess hall and welcomed him with a smile when he returned to their tent after supper. And while she was unsure how accurate her perception was, given her partiality for his finer features, she sensed that he was as eager to discuss it with her as she was with him. It had been such a long time since she'd talked about abolition with someone who didn't think she was a nutter.

Cate sighed and sat down next to him, curling herself in over her knees. "If they knew in their hearts it was wrong, they wouldn't sacrifice themselves on the field of battle for it." She plucked some grass and started weaving it together with her fingers, the absent motions of flower-crown making.

"Denial is powerful," he said. "And when your God lets people run rampant with cruelty, lets people like Edward Covey bruise and abuse with impunity, well, they think He's signed on to their way of doing things."

"Uh oh, should I be guarding my faith against your heathen temptations?"

"Yes, shield yourself. Soon I'll be slinging simple logic and questioning whether we need the threat of a celestial smiting to make sure we're nice to each other."

"I knew you were an atheist."

"And yet, you aren't fainting with shock."

"Even when folks believe God's watching to make sure they're kind, they still treat people like shit on the bottom of their shoe." Cate looked down at the hoop of grass in her hands and tried not to think about Pennsylvania. "Maybe when the Friends forsook me, I started to wonder if He did too."

Henry didn't say anything. Just smiled around that damn overly-long stalk of grass in his perfect white teeth.

"Are you some sort of stock animal, Henry Schaefer? Why are you always eating grass?"

"I resent that remark. I'm a prairie grass connoisseur. It's sweet—here, try it."

He sat up and picked a stalk of grass between his fingers. Twilight played purple shadows across the flat planes of his cheeks. God help her, but she let him set a stalk of grass between her lips.

"Chew."

She wrinkled her nose but obeyed. It was sweet. Damn him. Damn everything. She was doomed.

"Good, right?"

"I don't know what you're talking about. It tastes like grass."

He was two feet away from her, grinning with his hair floating in the breeze. And she couldn't understand why. Not a month ago, he'd hated her. Why did revealing her secret to him turn his regard to such an extreme opposite? Mutual interest in abolition or not, she was no pretty peach to turn his head. It wasn't like they were at the front and she were the only lady for miles. There were pretty girls touring the fort every day, watching drills and bringing tokens of thanks to the soldiers. He could have attracted a wife like Robinson had if he'd given even half an effort. Yet he looked at her with such singular fascination. Why?

A drumbeat rang out from the fort. Henry looked up and Cate took the opportunity to shake her head straight again.

"Taps," he said unnecessarily. "Better get back for roll-call."

Cate stood dumbly and followed. One thing was for sure—no more philosophical heart-to-hearts. She wasn't sure there was anything she could do to resist a man who listened to her opinions with actual interest.

———

Later that night, she lay on her back under their tent watching how the murky shadows blurred the distinctions between the dark center pole and the white canvas. It was long past lights-out, but sleep was elusive through the racket of Henry Schaefer-shaped thoughts bouncing around her head. She couldn't sleep and she stared up at the dark tent gable, listening to the crickets chirp and her comrades snore in adjacent tents as she tried very hard to remember what it was she hated about Schaefer. To think of all the most excellent reasons why she would do well to stay away from him, or anyone else for that matter. To get too close was to compromise her secret.

She rolled onto her side, the hard ground pushing sharply against her hip bone. She looked at his peaceful face and let the insidious thought form. *But he already knows.*

Henry lay inches away, sprawled flat on his gum blanket with his arms curled up over his head. His mouth was soft with sleep, his head tilted towards her, his features obscured by shadows.

Sleep did something to people, relaxed their features to show their faces in their most unadorned form. In the darkness, the shadows carved his face in vague planes, softening any sharp angles or blemishes. His lips, parted slightly, curled around the faintest shadow of his fine teeth and Cate swallowed against a niggling sense of existential dread.

Henry had the sort of face that reminded one of an anvil, but not one made of heavy metals. Perhaps he was more carved from wood, his chin and nose and brow an interplay of finely honed horizontal and vertical lines. Perhaps these features contributed to why he seemed older than the other fellows, even though he was only twenty-one. Cate felt a shroud of guilt come over her. She could ruin this boy. She was old, bitter, not to mention the little inconvenience of being married. All excellent reasons why he shouldn't waste his time.

His sandy-blonde brows cast his eyes in shadow. Cate craned her neck forward, imagining how soft his skin might feel under her fingers. For all the thick toughness of him, his eyelids were as delicate as anyone else's. Some of the hairs of his eyebrows skewed up, out of order. Cate absently lifted her hand and smoothed her finger over them.

Henry stirred at her touch. She flinched to move her hand away, but Henry's arm came down and the smooth callus of his fingers wrapped around her wrist. Cate forgot to exhale as his eyes fluttered open.

Her fingers were frozen upon his brow and she stared at him with wide eyes. His eyelids were heavy with sleep and his lips twitched into a half smile.

"Hi, Charley," he murmured, his voice low and coarse with sleep.

Cate swallowed hard, embarrassed at being caught and utterly taken aback by his serene, unassuming response to her stroking his eyebrow in the dead of night while he was sleeping.

"Hi," she breathed. She surprised herself with the softness of her own usually-harsh voice.

Henry exhaled contentedly and his thumb stroked down her palm. He blinked drowsily at her hand and smiled.

"Laundry."

Cate flinched, but not so much that she snatched her hand away. "What?"

"You were a laundress." Henry looked at her hand, his expression simple and focused. "Your chilblains. When we were inspected, you had chilblains."

He turned her hand over in his. Cate remembered to breathe, but it caught in her throat.

"They've healed up first rate." He stroked a finger up the back of her hand, over her knuckles, down her finger, before he laced his fingers neatly between hers. She swallowed hard. Her skin lit up under his touch. She wasn't sure how much more of it she could bear, knowing it wasn't real. At least not in the way she wanted it to be.

"Well, don't expect me to do your washing." She had intended to snap this at him, but it came out too fluttery to be intimidating.

Henry huffed a chuckle. "I wouldn't dare."

His hand pulled hers in to tuck under his chin. Then, with her hand entwined with his, he gave every indication of falling right back into sleep.

Yes. She was well and truly done for.

———

XXIV

Friday, September 27, 1861

FRIDAY DAWNED BRIGHT AND sunny and warm, another perfect day of late summer. Despite sleeping on the hard ground, Henry felt more refreshed than he had in months. For one thing, there were no bed bugs. But for another, he and Charley had slept facing each other, her hand in his, and he was positively giddy about it.

At least until Smith slammed him back to reality with his biting remarks and cold shoulder. He supposed he should have known better than to expect things to change just because Charley couldn't resist talking to him about Frederick Douglass, but yesterday had inarguably been a wonderful gulp of fresh air.

Drills kept them busy all morning and, after dinner, Henry stood at attention with the rest of Company K, spread in ranks by squad across the parade ground. While Lieutenant Woodbury usually gave musket drills, today Lieutenant Thomas had another sergeant from Company D, just returned from Fort Ridgely, to instruct them.

"Soldiers, this is Sergeant Schmöckel," Thomas said by way of introduction.

Henry regarded the older bearded man. He was short and wiry, his posture rigid, with a sour expression on his face as Thomas introduced him. A Prussian if Henry had ever seen one. "He saw battle in Europe and he'll be working with you all on bayonet drill."

To Henry's surprise, Lieutenant Thomas fell into ranks among them, deferring to Schmöckel's direction.

"Thank you, Lieutenant Thomas." As soon as Schmöckel spoke, Henry's suspicions about his home region were confirmed. "I fought in the Schleswig War against the Danes. Saw many battles, killed many men."

Henry exchanged sideways glances with Jacob, standing on the other side of Smith (who might as well have been a coat rack for all he acknowledged Henry's presence). Schmöckel was little. It was hard to imagine him in the heat of battle mowing down enemy soldiers.

"Many of you think you signed up for a great adventure, but let me assure you, war is no game. It is a loud, inconvenient, messy business, one that will likely claim the lives of a good number of you. Learning how to wield your weapon to the greatest possible advantage is a matter of life or death. Mark me, boys, as I show you how it's done," Schmöckel said, seeming to sense their incredulity with his sharp, creased eyes. He settled his body into the guard position. "Imagine for a moment that I face down a cavalryman."

John Williamson let out a giggle and got himself an elbow from Webster. The Prussian paid him no mind and began a demonstration unlike any Henry had ever seen—and he had seen a fair number of bouts demonstrated at the Turner Halls growing up.

Schmöckel parried imaginary saber-cuts as the phantom cavalryman ran him down, then delivered deadly thrusts with the bayonet in return. His body moved with a dexterity unexpected from a man of his years. He sprang like a panther from side to side, then retired by short, strong leaps to the rear, his face and weapon towards the foe. He used a score of stratagems, a hundred different motions of body and limbs to defend his person, fend off attacks, and to deliver his own—and all as quick as lightning.

At last, Schmöckel rushed forward like a madman, letting out a shrill cry, eyes wide and wild, as he parried with wild cut after wild cut. Then, leaping magnificently, he drove home his final thrust, plunging the bayonet through the body of his imagined adversary, who by this point seemed perfectly real just by virtue of how well, how hard, how vehemently Schmöckel had opposed him. The boys stood for a long moment in quiet awe before letting out a collective cheer of appreciation at the sergeant's triumph over the enemy.

Henry swallowed hard and tried to match the grins Jacob and Elias displayed, their eyes wide and hungry for action. He wanted to want that. He wished he felt excitement, but all he felt were cold chills up and down his back. This was war. Real war, not some demonstration. It was not some game of strategy, of marching or shooting. It was not just a business of keeping himself from being killed. It was a business of killing other men. He knew that—he'd talked about it with Smith just yesterday. But seeing it—even in an imaginary context—was a whole other matter.

He gave a furtive glance around him and caught Smith's dark eyes regarding him behind a mask of impassivity.

"That was really something, wasn't it?" Henry tried, his voice not as smooth and at ease as he would like.

"Indeed. Perhaps he's also a valkyrie," Smith replied, appraising Schmöckel with an arch brow, as he mopped sweat from his forehead and grimly looked down his nose at the boys in ranks as they cheered him on. Henry grinned sheepishly and ducked away as Schmöckel had them pair off, practicing thrusts and parries in slow motion against one another to get the movements into their limbs. Henry found himself facing off with Sergeant Osborn, striking bayonets against one another over and over, per Schmöckel's instruction.

"This must be second nature to you," Schmöckel barked as he strode past the pairs, sharply observant. "In the heat of battle, there is no time to think. Only to act, or die."

Henry didn't want to die. He wanted to act. His brow furrowed and he tried to focus his body into the forms. He carried them through with greater focus than he had ever paid in the gymnasium in New Ulm, or Cincinnati for that matter, striking with incrementally greater urgency, more force. After a few cycles through the form, he struck hard enough that Osborn dropped his bayonet in spite of himself.

"Sorry," Henry mumbled as Osborn stooped to retrieve his weapon. Osborn's eyes were dark for a moment as he looked up and met Henry's. Then, they cleared and he gave an easy shrug.

"No apologies necessary," he replied. "I must press harder next time. Again!"

The mess hall at supper stank something fierce, for all of them were sweat-soaked and weary after pushing hard at hand-to-hand combat for several hours. Smith veritably inhaled his food before slipping away from the heated debate between Jacob and Williamson over which breed of cow produced the most healthful milk (both farmboys, to the marrow). Henry reacted first with suspicion, mostly out of habit, before wondering whether Smith had snuck away for some privacy to wash. He pushed peas around his tin plate with a little secret smile at the corners of his mouth as Williamson conceded that the Holstein cows were admirable for their production, but still he preferred a Milking Shorthorn.

When Henry and the others returned to the tents west of the fort walls, the stakes of the debate had risen. Elias had been dining with other non-commissioned officers, but when he joined their group in their trek across the parade ground, he took umbrage with the fact that Dunlop cows hadn't even borne consideration.

"The Dunlop is a fantastic dairy cow, and far too often overlooked," Elias declared as they ambled as a group into the rows of wedge tents.

Jacob gave a long-suffering sigh. He'd been at this for far too long and was already weary of his apparently considerable dairy knowledge being utterly disregarded as both Williamson, and now Elias, doubled down. "Have you even had a Holstein?"

Elias shrugged. "I haven't deigned, truly. Why bother, when we can have Dunlops?"

"Dunlops are as stupid as they are hard-headed. The Holstein has none of those defects and can produce a Dunlop under the table. It's no contest!"

Henry rolled his eyes, only half listening, when he alighted on his tent. The tent flaps were tied shut and his pulse jumped at the sight. None of the other boys seemed to even notice as he peeled off, stooping before the tent.

"Smith?" He paused but there was no reply. "Are you decent?"

There were some shuffling sounds from within the tent then and it shook for a moment on its makeshift poles. "Gimme a minute," a muffled voice belatedly replied.

Fabric skimmed against fabric, soft shuffles as things moved around. Henry thought back to the guard house, when she had unbuttoned her shirt to display her stays, vaguely compressing and outlining a bosom that had utterly shattered his notions of who Smith was and what he was about. Henry was dismayed to find it was more difficult to imagine what those stays might contain than it had been to imagine the hostile cavalryman Schmöckel had battled that afternoon.

"Alright, come in."

Henry was embarrassed to admit that he felt his heart skip a beat at those words as he released the ties, pulled the flap aside, and made to duck into the tent. But instead of being greeted by a cozy tent space for two, his face was abruptly met by another army blanket hung from the center pole, slicing the space into two small, cramped triangles. Henry flinched back from it and regarded the blanket with disdain as he slipped reluctantly to his side of the tent. Lit only with the orange light of the setting sun, he hadn't managed to even catch a glimpse of Smith on the other side as he'd sidled in. Which, he supposed, was precisely the point.

"What's all this then?" he tried to say mildly, flicking the blanket away from his face as he tried to settle in. "Where did you get the extra blanket?"

"I traded one of Nelson's boys for it," she replied.

"What did you trade him?"

"Money, naturally." He could hear her shrug in the tone of her voice, as well as a heaping dose of defensive disdain.

"That's called buying something, Smith." Henry looked the center blanket up and down skeptically, finding it hard to focus on it at such close proximity. "Are you sure the center is the best place for it? Perhaps we should put it over the back flap and staunch that cold breeze that's come in this afternoon."

"No."

Henry hadn't expected such a clipped, final response. Lacking something tangible to respond to, he was forced to search for his own reasons why he didn't like the blanket. And try as he might, all he could come up with was that it was too close and that it stopped him from seeing her face. From holding her hand. From seeing *Charley's* eyes buried underneath all that wool and sweat and disdain.

"What's got you all ornery?" he asked instead, his voice taking on its own defensive tone.

"Other than the fact that you smell like a pig pen on a hot day?"

Henry glowered in her general direction.

"Here," she said and, from under the blanket, shoved a pitcher of water over to his side, with a wet rag draped over its handle. "Wash up. You smell foul."

And she tugged the blanket back into its place. Henry stared at it for a moment before looking down at the pitcher. Had she just given him her used wash water? He couldn't decide if that was disgusting, insulting, or titillating.

"Oh, and here's the soap."

A bar of soap sailed around the blanket and into his shoulder before bouncing into the grass. It was still wet and the grass stuck to it. Henry glanced from the water to the soap. This was most definitely her wash water. As his eyes took in the soap, the rag, and the implications of where one (or both) of those objects had just been, titillated edged ahead.

"Is this your used wash water?" he exclaimed a little too indignantly. He wanted to hear her say it.

She scoffed. "Don't even try to pretend like you were the first one to use the bathwater in your family. Aren't you the youngest?"

Henry glowered at the blanket again but was already unbuttoning his overshirt. Regardless of whatever the hell was going on with her, he was not in a position to be too upset about who might observe him wash. And she was right about one thing—he did smell terrible.

———

XXV

"Charley? You awake?"

Cate had just been drifting off to sleep, wool blanket pulled tight over her shoulders as the cool breeze blew in through the western facing flap of their tent. She hovered blearily between sleeping and waking, unsure for a moment whether the voice she heard was real or part of a dream.

"Mmm," she replied, turning and packing her pillow into a firmer bundle under her head.

Henry's voice betrayed an alertness she did not presently match. "I can't stop thinking about that demonstration Schmöckel gave this afternoon."

"Mmhm," Cate replied, stifling a yawn even as she was drawn out of her groggy state by the nearness and gravity of Henry's voice. Blanket hanging from the center pole or no, he was scarcely a foot away. She had hoped that being unable to see him would help her stop drawing towards him like a moth with a death wish, but when she'd handed him the wash basin and pitcher, her imagination had filled in all the salacious details she had been trying to avoid by hanging the curtain in the first place. Every swish of a rag in the water, every slip of fabric against skin—it had been such torture that eventually she had just crawled out the west end of their tent and tramped off aimlessly until she trusted herself to return and not rip down the blanket she'd hung to force herself to curb herself in the first place.

"I just ... Charley ... are you afraid?"

Cate tried her best to yank herself back into the tent in the middle of the night rather than dwell upon what the canvas walls had witnessed earlier that evening. She took a moment to settle the question in her mind and evaluate her feelings in response.

"I ... well, not anymore than usual," she settled on.

Henry grunted in response, a low, bass rumble that she had no right to feel reverberating in her bones.

"No," he murmured. Their proximity was such that he needed no more than a soft murmur to be understood. "No, I mean once we're at the front. In the heat of battle. Are you afraid?"

Cate blinked. "No," she replied, surprising herself. "I'm not. I want to fight. Like you said yesterday, we have to become the hand of justice. I suppose if I die, then at least I died fighting for what is right."

He was quiet at that. Cate waited a moment to see if he would respond.

"I suppose I don't know how I might react when face to face with an armed rebel," she continued, "but I am so sick and tired of standing by, trying to reason with unreasonable people. My desire to take action, to make a difference, far outweighs my fear of getting hurt."

Henry hummed in the affirmative. She wondered if his brows were knitted together in thought.

"I wish I could feel that way," Henry sighed. "Truth is, I didn't really comprehend it until today. About fighting a man, fighting to kill. I ... I know Schmöckel was just demonstrating but I felt as though his adversary were real. I could envision him and now I can't shake the image."

Cate noticed the desire to reach out to him in comfort and squashed it like a bug.

"Why are you telling *me* this?" she recoiled, a little too defensively. As soon as she said it, she could feel the stalk of connection he'd offered snap off at the root under the impact of her words.

"Good question," he replied bitterly. She heard his blanket rustle as he turned away.

Cate grimaced.

Good, she tried to tell herself, now he would leave her alone. She closed her eyes and tried to snatch at the threads of sleep that had been so invasive just moments before. But they had slipped away, replaced by this knot in her stomach, a tangle of loneliness and fear and her own shame. While she had been busy batting off her unwanted attraction to him, Henry had been trying to swallow his own mortality. He had reached out. He hadn't treated her differently than he would have any other comrade-in-arms. He'd tried to connect. And she had slammed the proverbial door in his face.

She pushed against her guilt. This was good. He should be kept at arm's length. He already knew more about her than she could afford. One wrong move and he was off to command to tip them off about a woman in their midst. He held this over her whether he meant to or not, and no matter how much she tried to convince herself that she had leverage, she knew she didn't. The closer she became with him, the greater the likelihood that he would hurt her.

Cate sighed. She'd never been very responsive to warnings of caution.

"It's cold," she declared. And then she gave the blanket she had hung in the center of the tent a tug.

It fell all too easily. Swallowing against the thrill of it, Cate propped herself up on one elbow as she pulled the blanket over herself. She was sharing comfort through warmth. Nothing more. "Do you want some blanket?"

Henry looked over his shoulder warily at her and grunted, turning onto his back. Not towards her, but not away any longer either. Cate tossed the far corner of the blanket in his direction and he grabbed it, pulling it over himself and curling his fists around the edge. "So much for the temperate Minnesota climate."

Cate snorted. "Did you see that article in the *Evening Tribune*? Whoever wrote that our 'weather is less susceptible to unpredictable frosts' has *never* wintered here."

Henry huffed a knowing chuckle. She felt terrible. In trying to protect herself, she had pushed away the only chance she'd had in all the months of basic training to connect in a real way, on something that really mattered.

"To be honest," she hazarded, her soft whisper cutting through the dark ambient sounds of the night prairie, "I'm not nearly as afraid of being killed as I am of ... of dying alone."

The words hurt to say, but that's how she knew they were true. True enough to perhaps mend together the remnants of what she'd severed between them. The waning crescent moon cast dim light over their camp, enough to see the shadow cast as Henry squeezed his eyes shut and tucked his chin to his chest, the gesture resolving into a painful nod. When he inhaled, it sounded a little quavery.

"I didn't leave things well with my family," he confessed. His exhale shuddered too. Cate's heart squeezed, perhaps in tandem with his. Her hand twitched to reach out to him.

"Me neither," she murmured. Her fingers found his hand clenched around the edge of the blanket. It was as though her touch had sprung a trap as his fingers needfully twined with hers. Men meaningfully grasped hands. They did it all the time when doing business or making agreements, or even upon greeting one another. Nevermind that she and Henry were in a tent in the middle of the night, facing down the prospect of their own violent deaths. Nevermind that he knew she wasn't a man. Nevermind any of that because after the way his touch cut through her loneliness, there was no way she was letting go.

"My mother didn't want me to go," Henry confessed, turning towards her. She could feel his breath on her cheek as he spoke. "Not any of us, really. But the Turners—well, they're all military precision and dignified courage and there was no way I was going to let my brothers enlist without me. I have two older brothers—twins—and I was always the expendable third. But it was my idea to enlist. They were following *my* lead."

His fingers squeezed tighter around hers. Her eyes strained in the dark, watching his pained expression, suspecting that this story was not one he shared with just anyone.

"When we told our parents we were going, I was too busy trying to show my brothers and my father how brave I was to notice I was breaking my mother's heart."

He swallowed. His voice was softer when he continued. "She lost two babies. One before me and one after. She's borne too much loss already—all she could see when we were leaving was how she would lose three more. I did that to her."

Cate's brow creased. "No. This fight is more than spilling blood and dying. It's to defend our country—to protect the promise our country stands for from those who seek to corrupt it. We fight for the promise that 'all men are created equal and that they're endowed by our Creator with certain unalienable rights. That among these are life, liberty, and the pursuit of happiness.'"

"Are you quoting the Declaration of Independence?" His brow, so tight with fear, pulled back quizzically. She marked this with satisfaction.

"Absolutely I am," she replied in earnest, pulling his hand closer and tighter in her own. "These are the principles that bind a country of strangers together. There is no higher principle worth fighting for. If your mother can't see that, then so be it, but her fears don't land on your doorstep. They're hers to contend with. She could be proud. Proud that her son has the courage to put himself in harm's way for the greater good."

Henry blinked, his lips a flat line across his face. "You give me too much credit. I suspect those reasons are among what drove you to the lengths you took to be here. But they were not mine."

He looked down ashamedly.

"They can be," she pressed. "It doesn't matter how you get there if you end up doing the right thing in the end."

His lips twitched in consideration. In her earnestness, she had pulled herself nearer to him so that they were now nose to nose, scarcely a few inches apart, their hands entwined between them. His eyes regarded her, round as though he did not dare to believe. Believe he could be right, that he could yet be noble or brave.

His chin tilted towards her. Her heart hammered in her chest, threatened to choke her with both eager longing and the frozen terror of rejection. Then, to both her relief and disappointment, he caught his breath and rolled onto his back. Well, not entirely. He still had her hand and pulled it so that their entwined fingers rested on his chest. She fought against a barrage of yearning, frustration, desire, and her old companion, loneliness. Who was she kidding? He could sense her interest. He could sense it and found her lacking. He wanted a friend, a comrade-in-arms. Wasn't that what she wanted too? If she wanted a man in her bed, truly in her bed, she should have stayed in St. Anthony with her husband.

But she couldn't help but notice, with her palm pressed against his chest, that his heart hammered too.

Henry cleared his throat awkwardly. "So, how did you leave things with your family?" He kept his eyes fixed on the center pole of the tent, his quiet voice attempting to sound casual. "If I may ask, that is."

Cate's eyes studied him carefully, calculating risk. She avoided acknowledging how much more discerning she was with information than with physical touch. Instead, she asked herself what Jacob Robinson would do. Would he tell his friend his story, share the same kind of information as was shared with him?

Perhaps Robinson was a poor example.

"I don't know, I never told them anything," she said simply. "I just left."

He turned and looked at her then, his eyes wide with surprise. She shrugged and looked away. She didn't want to see his disappointment.

"I grew up with my grandparents, so I didn't scarcely know my father until after they died ten years ago. He's never thought much of me." She steeled herself, making her heart a hard, empty shell against that heavy truth. "Nor I him to be honest. So when I left, I didn't say a thing."

"Doesn't he wonder where you are, though?"

She shrugged again. "Certainly, I should think, but only as much as it inconveniences him. It's Richard who is surely livid."

She froze as the words spilled from her lips, an errant thought that had absently slipped out her mouth. She managed to at least stop herself from swearing.

He shifted to get a better look at her. "Wait, who's Richard? Your brother?"

Cate, you free-wheeling fool, she berated herself internally. *This is what you get for talking to yourself all the time. You have no capacity to discern between internal and external thoughts.*

He'd given her an out; she had no reason not to take it. No reason except that he'd laid himself pretty bare just now and to return that with a lie—well, that's certainly not what a good comrade would do.

She looked up at him and tried futilely to not show how cornered she felt. He studied her with a soft openness, his lips slightly parted. He squeezed her hand in encouragement, and she realized with sinking finality that he was too earnest, too honor-bound, to allow himself to be tempted by a married woman, much less one as ornery, mannish, and old as her. Richard had marked her as his forever and there was nothing she could do to change that.

"Yes, my brother," she lied before she had even decided to do it. Selfishness won out, as it always did. She shouldn't want, she shouldn't let him close. But she did want. She wanted very badly. And she was letting him close. She should tell him the truth, that's what she should do. Tell him she was married and claimed by another man—wasn't that the only boundary men really respected anyway? It would protect her from herself. As undesirable as she was, she was still a woman. Convenience would wear him down and she would take advantage. That was how basely she wanted him. She should tell the truth to protect herself, her honor, but as she watched Henry accept her lie with a nod, she knew she wouldn't. What kind of honor was chastity anyway?

"So you're not actually the youngest of seven girls in a one-room cabin?" he asked with a sardonic brow.

She smirked in spite of herself. "No … I'm the oldest."

"Now that makes a lot more sense. Any other siblings?"

She pursed her lips at him but her annoyance was all a play. Her guilt about lying had earned him some truths, she decided.

"Just a little half-sister and baby half-brother."

"And a step-mother, I presume?"

"Yes. Contrary to the archetype, she's the best among them."

"Did you tell her you were leaving?"

Cate looked down wistfully. "No. She could never lie to my father. That would be asking too much of her."

"Yet you don't mind lying to your father?"

"I didn't lie to him. I said nothing at all."

Henry shrugged. "Sounds like he was asking for it, if you ask me."

Cate turned into his shoulder with an impish smile. "I stole his hat too."

Henry shook his head and laughed. His fingers squeezed hers.

"You know," he whispered, "I'm glad we were assigned bunkies. I was spitting mad when it happened but turns out, Sergeant Osborn knows what he's doing."

The curve of his shoulder—his delicious, strapping shoulder—fit neatly into the curve of her brow and nose. He smelled perfect, all sweet grass and clean soap.

"Except tents," she replied. "He hasn't the faintest idea how to put up a tent."

Henry snorted and Cate grinned with satisfaction to have caused it. She regarded him calculatingly.

"I suppose ... it does make a kind of sense," she ruminated aloud, watching his face for a response. "It's a lot more material, resources, and I suppose blankets, to have soldiers tent out individually."

She watched his assent carefully. She imagined adding that it's warmer to have two bodies instead of one, strictly from an efficiency perspective. But even with her hand in his, her cheek nestled against his shoulder, even in the dark quiet of the night, when no one could see and no one could hear, she was too scared. Too scared to put him off, to fracture this tranquil, easy moment.

Henry turned towards her, releasing her hand. He watched her carefully as he draped his hand lightly upon her waist.

"And warmer too," he rumbled, his voice tentatively reckless, if that were even possible. Her breath was audible when she remembered to inhale.

He blinked and regarded her more seriously.

"Is this alright?" he whispered. "Strictly to, ah" —he licked his lips— "keep warm, naturally."

No, she thought. *No it is not alright. You are much too close and too warm and too pleasant smelling—why did I make you bathe again?* But her eyes found his and she nodded and pulled his arm more comfortably around herself so that his hand draped over the laces at the small of her back.

"Much warmer," she murmured in reply, eliciting a low, gravelly sound from his throat as she tucked her head under his chin, her breath tickling the hairs that peeked out from under his collar. Her nose nuzzled against his neck, breathing in the scent of him.

"Charley," he whispered, his hand running up the ridges of her laces through her shirt. "You are…"

"Sleepy," she murmured, even as she thrilled at the heat of him against her, the control she possessed. He was her captive audience. Regardless of what tomorrow held, she had his undivided attention now. Liar or not, she was certain of her power. He was tempted.

He exhaled roughly. "Of course," he replied, somewhat sheepishly. "Goodnight, Charley."

"'Night," she breathed, wishing she dared to let her lips brush his neck. He would let her. She was sure of it. But then what? Heaven knew, once he had her and the mystery was gone, he'd find some other temptation. At most it would be until their service was over. Then he'd find some young, dewy-eyed virgin to wed and get with dozens of fat babies. Some German girl, most like. Certainly not a runaway bride, old and used and desperate to be wanted.

No. She would not dwell on that. For now, he was her bunkie. Her confidante. Her ally. Nothing was going to take her out of it now, not when his smell was in her nose and his breath stirred in her hair. She should have realized before she even hung the blanket that it was already too late.

XXVI

Friday, October 4, 1861

SMITH WASN'T IN THEIR tent when Henry arrived, but that was to be expected when they were due for drill in a matter of minutes. He stooped into the tent briskly and stashed his satchel on his side, fetching his musket. Not that they really had sides, per say, not anymore. It had been a week since the whole blanket divider snit and Smith was still as disdainful and prickly as ever by day, but when the night fell and the camp became silent, Charley was the one who warmed his blankets. They would whisper into the night, pile their blankets and huddle together against the increasingly frosty autumn cold. Henry found he could bait Charley out with talk of books—all manner of moral and philosophical works, as well as a few novels (*Uncle Tom's Cabin* had caught her attention quite well). Sometimes she tried to play as though she were sleeping, but one critical observation from him and she couldn't resist sharing her many opinions. And once he got her talking, she would in turn draw him in like a moth to a flame.

Smith was nothing more than an armor Charley wore. Now that he'd learned how to put a chink in it, he was beginning to see the most fascinating person beneath. Fascinating and beguiling. He knew she was a woman—he knew that in an intellectual way. He knew her as "she" in his mind when he thought of her. But she was not like any woman he had ever known or even imagined. She did not align with his oft-visited boyhood fantasy of soft curves and murmuring submission. On the contrary, she was always the one who initiated what had become, in the last week, a much-anticipated inevitability of furtive touches and chaste caresses that came only in the black of night.

She would beg the pretense of being cold—which wasn't such a pretense now that the frost had set in—and curl into Henry's chest. She would run her hands up his ribs, over his chest, as though trying to find a good place to rest them. She would curl her face into his neck and her breath would tickle the hollow at the base of his throat, her lips so close but never touching. Her fingers would play across his arms and shoulders, his neck and back, but she never even ventured towards his waist, much less below it. Charley never kissed. Even as she encouraged his arms to enfold her, she shied away from any touching he attempted to reciprocate. Her firm stays that kept her body secret gave nothing away from the few touches he did manage before she gently but firmly replaced his hands at her waist or her back.

After a week of this, Henry was mad with wanting. He didn't rightly know what it was he even wanted. Nothing he could imagine—not even the most wanton acts he had read in the filthy novels the boys passed around the barracks—felt like enough. His perception of his world, the fort and the soldiers and the endless drilling—all of it felt as though he was viewing it from a slightly different vantage. Because always, whether he was in the mess or bantering with the squad, there was a thread of awareness wherever Smith was and the ever-present anticipation of the night to come. A night with Charley, who only showed her true face to him, held close, her scent filling his lungs and permeating his dreams.

As Henry left the rows of tents, which had rapidly grown since the last of their regiment's companies had returned from post duty, he reminded himself again how ridiculous he had become. Only a month ago, he'd been ready to report Smith to the authorities. He'd hated him. But that was before he knew that Smith was a disguise that Charley wore. It was not her, not entirely. It was the armor that kept her secret safe. She was prickly too, no doubt about that, but it wasn't leveled with the same force. Perhaps his strategy of dividing Charley Smith into two personas was flawed, but the more he came to know her, the more he felt it to be true. And it helped him maintain the pretense because he was at no risk to fumble the pronouns. Everyone else only knew Smith, and Smith was a "he".

Henry found his squad at the head of the field outside the fort walls, waiting along with the rest of the nearly assembled Company K for their first dress parade as a regiment. Smith was standing stoically, musket expertly held with his fingers wrapped around the trigger guard, while Captain Noah led their company onto the field to assume their position.

It took quite some time for all of the companies to assemble and Henry spent most of it sensing viscerally, without needing to look, the presence of Smith at his left shoulder. The presence of Charley. He imagined leaning in, nudging her with his shoulder, a secret reminder of the intimacy they shared. She must know such a thing was not typical. Sure, it was cold and some bunkies were sharing their blankets and their warmth, but not like this. Not with the quiet caresses and the murmured excuses and the breath—the goddamn breath on his neck like a rain-filled cloud that never broke. This was no encounter of convenience. She wanted him—she had to. Why would she spend time she could be sleeping systematically taking the measure of his body if she had no interest in him? She had to want him. And he wanted her back, even if he couldn't quite articulate exactly how.

That was a lie. He could at least imagine how it would sound. Because that night, when he heard her bring herself off as he'd done himself, would not stop replaying in his mind. Elias had been right; a woman could feel pleasure as a man did, and he wanted—desperately wanted—to know more. It was killing him.

Lieutenant Thomas stood at the ready, looking to Captain Noah, who stood at the head of Company K watching for Colonel Van Cleve, who in turn rode a horse at the other end of the line. A shout came from Van Cleve's direction and it echoed down the chain of command until Henry heard Lieutenant Thomas bellow it to them.

They went through the motions of marching, each company parading before Van Cleve in turn, the commissioned officers eager to demonstrate the fruits of their efforts to learn then teach their men the School of the Soldier. The companies generally did well marching as one, as they'd had occasion to practice that already, but they struggled when two companies were moving to occupy the same space. Several collisions occurred, which seemed so absurd to Henry because they did not move fast and there was plenty of time for the groups to stop before collision. But the power of orders they had trained to obey these past four months combined with a confusion about who should make a decision about what and when caused many a squad to march haphazardly into each other.

After about an hour of this, which involved a whole lot more standing and waiting for command to figure out where they had gone wrong than marching, Captain Noah did the mercy of disbanding them for dinner. Henry sat next to Smith on the bench and as he shoveled food into his mouth, he nudged his elbow against hers. She didn't flinch away and in fact applied pressure back. Henry grinned into his tin plate and then looked up to track the conversation.

Krüger was across from him and lifted an eyebrow disdain-fully at him. Henry twitched his arm away and glared back at the nosy bastard. Henry had no intention of letting him pick away at him, making insinuating sarcastic comments about the Turners. But it was a moment that reminded him that he would do well to keep his infatuation with Smith hidden. No one else knew that he was secretly a woman.

"Fellas, I've got exciting news!" Elias exclaimed as he eagerly slammed his plate down and wedged himself in between Krüger and Jacob. "We just got a big load of uniforms from the Feder-als!"

Henry sat up straight in his seat, almost in unison with the rest of the squad.

"Yes!" Williamson exclaimed in a characteristic squeal.

"Did they get the caps too?" Jacob asked. "I want a good CDV of me in the whole get-up for Mary before we leave."

Elias nodded. "Yes, forage caps and everything. Even the knapsacks and water canteens. Bayonet scabbards. The whole kit and caboodle."

The excitement across the table was palpable. Henry shoveled the last of the bland stew into his maw as word spread up and down the tables. As soon as they were through, the squad hustled out to the parade ground, lurking outside the door of the Quartermaster in hopes to be among the first to get their uniform.

Osborn found them there, towards the head of a mob that had turned into a haphazard queue, and regarded Elias with a long-suffering sigh.

"So I take it you told them about the delivery," Osborn said flatly.

Elias grinned.

"Well, I suppose I don't have any orders to give as you're already doing what I was going to tell you to do." And with a shrug, he joined their group.

After a few moments, the Quartermaster opened the door and began shuffling soldiers through, taking a rough measure and distributing blue trousers and sack coats with shiny brass buttons, a heavy wool greatcoat, gaiter shoes, forage caps with a brass pin of two muskets crossing, two shirts, cotton drawers, and knapsacks packed with their kit. With their goods piled into their arms, the entire squad hustled out of the fort and across the parade ground to their tents, eager to put on their new uniforms.

Henry was the first back to his tent, Smith close on his heels. It had begun to rain again—a cold drizzle that cut to the bone. He crawled in first, dumping the pile of brand new clothes onto his gum blanket and seating himself cross-legged to take stock of all he had received. Smith crawled in behind him and began tying the tent flaps together.

Henry eagerly spread the blue wool coat out in front of him. Brass buttons embossed with the seal of the United States marched down the front and a bit of piping lined the collar and cuffs. Blue trousers made of the same fabric were folded neatly beneath it, along with the forage cap. Henry grinned and shrugged his coat and overshirt off, shoving his arms through the sleeves of his new uniform.

When he looked up, he caught a flash of Charley's eyes on him as she hung that blanket from the center pole. He didn't really know what he had expected, but whatever it was, the hanging divider was a disappointment in comparison. There was shuffling as she tried to maneuver in the cramped space she had made for herself.

He thought he might try to convince her that it wasn't necessary, but he hesitated, not wanting her to think him eager to take advantage of the situation. He knew he was trustworthy to not observe too closely (though he would certainly sneak a glance or two—who could blame him after how she'd been touching him this past week?) but she was not privy to his thoughts and might have a number of preconceived notions about what a man might do in a tent with a half-dressed lady. The gray blanket certainly did little to help him forget that that was precisely what was happening. So he did the only thing he could think of to do—he talked about the weather.

"It sure will be nice to have these greatcoats now that the frost has come," he said convivially. "This rain and cold has been awful."

"It'll help to head for the front," Smith responded. "I understand they scarcely ever get snow in Virginia."

"That'll be a relief. These winters here are hell froze over." Henry complained, unbuttoning his suspenders and wiggling out of his wool trousers to swap them for his new blue ones. The air was biting cold, making the hairs on his legs stand up. He kicked the trousers off his ankles urgently so he could pull his new ones on as quick as possible, but trying to get them off over his boots was more trouble than it was worth. Meanwhile, his balls were trying to retreat clear into his body to escape the cold. It was lucky they were headed to the front, because he had not thought to bring his flannel drawers.

"Last winter, I heard there were folks up near St. Cloud who froze to death because they went out in a blizzard to milk the cow and the snow was coming down so thick, they got lost on the way back from the barn," Charley said, slightly muffled. Henry leaned down to pull at his trouser ankles, contorting under the slope of canvas. Now that he was halfway through without removing his boots, there was no reason to double-back and start over. It was just the cuff of the trousers, probably caught on the boot sole.

As he scrabbled, his heel caught the blanket in the middle of the tent and pulled it taut. It held for a breathless moment before the edges tucked around the center pole slid loose and the blanket crumpled with scarcely a rustle to the ground. Henry froze guiltily and stared at what the rough felted wool had been hiding from view.

Charley was buttoning her stays up over a clean white shirt, tightly-woven enough that he couldn't really see the curve of her breast but thin enough that he could see the shadow of her nipples, hard in the cold. And there he was, with his pants caught around his ankles, the drape of his own shirt doing very little to hide his immediate interest. It was cold, but his face was burning with embarrassment. He didn't usually wear drawers but for the first time, he felt strongly that he might start.

Charley hadn't noticed yet. She had her chin tucked to one shoulder, buttoning a shoulder strap in place, her dark curls falling over her brow. Henry thought to reach out and try to replace the blanket but he was terrified that if he moved, she would look up and see that he had a hard one and Smith's disdainful glare would narrow her gaze and he would be humiliated. So he remained frozen, his knees up and his shirt tucked between his bare legs. His mouth was so dry he thought his tongue might get stuck to the roof of his mouth.

She must have sensed something was wrong, because she looked up from her buttoned shoulder strap and regarded him with her wide, dark eyes for a moment that felt like a goddamn eternity. Her expression hardened and she opened her mouth as though to tell him off but right at that moment, they both heard a voice just outside their tent.

"Hello there, Corporal, very fine coat you have there." It was Jacob's laughing tenor.

"Why thank you, I just had it done up," Elias replied, clipping his syllables in an overly elaborate way. Charley shut her mouth, but her eyes were livid as she pulled her stays tight around herself and fumbled with the buttons. Henry winced and mouthed, "Sorry..."

Her eyes darted down at the blanket and then back up at him. Her eyebrows lifted expectantly. Henry reached forward as best he could and snatched one corner of the blanket, dragging it towards him. He tried to tuck it into the center pole, but it pulled itself back down by its own weight. With his ankles hogtied by his trousers and his thighs pressed tight together for modesty's sake, he couldn't manage much more than that.

"What the hell is wrong with you?" Smith hissed.

"I'm *stuck*," Henry hissed back. Smith sneered at him and quickly finished fastening the buttons on the stays, then reached behind and pulled the laces snug. His warm and cozy bed-fellow was nowhere to be found in Smith's flashing eyes. Henry reached down and resolutely tugged on his pant legs, freeing his ankles from the black wool. He quickly shuffled to pull his new blue trousers on, yanking the itchy new wool over his boots and up over his bare knees. Smith, for his part, had slung his new coat over his shoulders and was fastening up the brass buttons with clumsy fingers, trying his best to look everywhere except at Henry. Despite his scowl, his cheeks were pink.

"Really I should get the name of your tailor," Jacob said to Elias, still just outside. The two of them laughed. Smith glowered in their general direction, rolling his eyes. Henry struggled with his trousers, trying to get them up over his hips without compromising his own privacy.

"Could you get that blanket hung again?" Henry murmured absently as he rocked the waistband higher while still trying to keep his knees blocking his more vulnerable places. Smith glared at him and crossed his arms.

"Oh, I'm sorry, did you want privacy?" he said sarcastically and leveled glare at Henry. He felt a strong flush come into his cheeks.

"Come on, it was an accident—"

"Tit for tat, Schaefer. Put your pants on." Charley Smith looked down her nose at him and pursed her lips in a way that seriously reminded him of his primary school teacher in Cincinnati. Unfortunately, it did nothing to toss ice on his erection. Even as his cheeks flamed red with embarrassment, an equal (if not greater) share of blood rushed between his legs to ensure the entire situation became steadily worse. She wanted to watch him. Or mock him. It was unclear whether he was dealing with Charley or Smith. This was indeed less than ideal.

Henry took a shuddering inhale and tried his best to shimmy the waistband of the trousers up over his thighs. Hunching over to hide his tented shirttails, he stuffed the ends of them into his trousers. Shifting from side to side, he tried to get them on the rest of the way but he couldn't get them up over his butt. A glance up at Charley showed her trying hard to hide a smirk. She watched him unabashedly.

Henry shook his head and exhaled defeatedly. Then he tossed himself back and lifted his hips up, shoving his traitor horn into the trousers with one hand as he pulled them up with the other. He fastened the button fly and attached his suspenders, blushing furiously, then glared at Charley.

"Happy now?" he inquired grumpily as he sat up again and made for the front flap.

Charley wasn't even trying to hide her secret little smile anymore. "Mmhm," she murmured, her eyes glittering with amusement as she glanced down at his waist. He waited for her to crawl out of the tent. She regarded him for a moment with that enigmatic smile before she said, "After you."

Henry's brows furrowed. He felt like he was being tricked, but he couldn't put his finger on why. He gave an exasperated sigh and flung the tent flaps aside, crawling out into the freezing drizzle. If that didn't cool him off, nothing would. Luckily, it looked like the rest of their squad had already set off for afternoon drills.

As he stood, he felt a swat on his backside that made him jump a mile high, letting out a startled yelp. Behind him, Smith quit the tent and stood placidly.

"You forgot your cap."

Henry glared and snatched it from him, pulling it down firmly on his head. Smith laughed and loped off ahead for their afternoon drill, Henry jogging half-heartedly behind him, thoroughly confused. He couldn't decide if Smith was laughing *at* him, or if Charley was laughing *with* him.

This two personas business was becoming more effort than it was worth.

———

XXVII

As afternoon wore on to evening, the rain froze to sleet and coated all the tents with a thin layer of ice. When Cate returned to their tent after supper, somewhat reluctantly for a multitude of reasons, she could scarcely get inside it because the ties of the tent flaps were frozen. The severe frost that hit some days ago had sent the trees scrambling to shed their leaves and as the howling winds blew through, soggy brown leaves slipped underfoot, turning to muck underneath so many boots.

Some of the boys had tried to strike up a fire, but most of the men who weren't trying to sleep were back in the barracks, crammed in tight like there was some sort of prize fight to be observed, except there was nothing but over-crowded bunks and tables rotating card players through. As far as Cate was concerned, their departure date couldn't come too soon. She'd had quite enough of Minnesota's weather for the season. The front offered both milder temperatures and an opportunity to fight for something she cared about.

Inside her tent, she huddled under her wool blankets and tried to convince her toes that they weren't freezing. What a bungle of a day it had been. Their first dress parade had been a disaster, Krüger had caught Henry rubbing elbows with her at dinner, and while receiving their uniforms had certainly been a highlight, her first concerted effort of changing her clothes in the tent had come off ... rather awkwardly.

She couldn't decide if she were more embarrassed being caught out by Schaefer in such a state of undress or if she were more delighted by how embarrassed he had been. She wanted to get another glimpse of those thick thighs of his, but she was also a bit apprehensive of lying close to him again. She wasn't an idiot—she'd seen he was aroused, but she didn't know how much or to what end. She wanted to remain in control of their interactions. Thus far he'd let her lead, but after this afternoon's display, she wasn't sure how long that would last. In her experience, men tended to claim what they wanted unless it kneed them in the crotch and ran away. What really worried her was that if he were to try and claim her, she wanted him so much she wasn't sure she'd have it in her to hold back.

Damn. All of this would have been a fair sight easier if she were still a virgin. Then she could at least pretend to herself that sex was something to guard carefully. Even though Richard had been a very rote lover, committed to his routine, the act itself had never been altogether unpleasant, if for no other reason than at least when he was pumping away at her, he was too winded to speak. On top of the fact that she was able to hear herself think, sometimes it had awoken something in her so primal she could hardly name it, something more intense than what she could elicit on her own and so insistent that she would often wait until Richard fell asleep to explore it with her own fingers.

Indeed, not only was she not afraid of sex, she was tempted by it. Women were supposed to be pure, to tolerate the act, but Cate fixated on it as only men were expected to. Having had carnal knowledge didn't demystify the act—it just made it more alluring. Without her virginity, she was struggling to think of any reason to hold herself back, apart from ensuring that she wouldn't become pregnant. And she'd been able to manage *that* right under Richard's nose while he'd been intent on getting her with child, so she was confident that if she maintained control over the proceedings, Schaefer would be easy to manage.

Besides, after all this barracks talk about asking ladies what they like, she had several ideas that did not risk pregnancy that she'd never had a chance to try with her former husband. It seemed likely that a Freethinker would have fewer preconceived expectations about chastity and purity and submissiveness than an Irish Catholic. She turned her face into her knapsack pillow and groaned miserably. What was *wrong* with her?

The canvas cracked as Schaefer made his way through the tent-flap. Cate didn't turn her face away but swiveled her left eye to observe him.

"Hell, it's cold as the devil's tit in here," he grumbled, crawling across the gum blanket and rolling himself up in his own blanket, leaving his new uniform—even the forage cap—on.

Cate pulled her own blanket over her head, trying to find a comfortable position, but no matter how she curled in on herself, whichever part of her that made contact with the ground was immediately chilled through, in spite of the gum blanket, her layers of wool, and her new greatcoat.

After tossing and turning a few times, he gave a long-suffering sigh. "Just get over here, would you? We're probably the only bunkies in this whole camp that aren't sharing a blanket right now. It's too cold not to."

She turned her face towards him and glared. "You're not even going to try and discuss a book with me first?" she complained glibly, but she was already halfway nestled into the curve of his body. The warmth he provided was a comfort and a relief.

"I can if you want me to."

"No, I'm dead tired. Just keep your hands to yourself."

"I should say the same to you."

She swatted at his shoulder as she curled into the warm enclave of his chest. He pulled their blankets together and arranged them over them both. As her nose filled with the scent of him, she struggled to remember why this was such a slippery slope. He was right. She'd be shocked if there were any men across this encampment who were not huddling for warmth inside their tents. Thank heavens they were shipping out—they'd have to build proper barracks if they were to make it through the Minnesota winter.

He settled his arms around her back, his bicep making a comfortable, warm pillow for her to rest her head. She didn't even give a second thought to the way they tangled their legs together beneath the blankets, because it was so much warmer than it had been when she'd been huddled on her own. She slept almost at once.

It was still dark when she woke, though there was a hint of light that suggested dawn was imminent. Her back was tucked tightly against Henry and though her nose was cold, the rest of her was swathed in his ample warmth. She could feel his slow, even breath on her neck, and she couldn't help but smile contentedly at how easily they fit together. She wriggled into him, finding his arm for her pillow and drawing his hands to wrap around her waist.

She was about to doze off again when she felt him. His breath was still coming slow and steady as in sleep, but his body was responding to her and she could feel his prick stiffening against her backside. Her own breath caught in her throat as she realized with a rush of pleasure that he was also drawing her closer into his arms.

If she ended up having to account for herself later, she would go to the grave insisting that she had been too groggy to realize what exactly she was doing. But she knew the truth as she turned in his arms to face him and put one hand on his chest, the other at his waist. She pressed her nose into the hollow of his neck and inhaled as she caressed a path across his chest, shoulders, and stomach, one she had worn well in the previous week. He was so deliciously warm and pliant and his hips tilted up towards her hands, inviting. His breath rasped when her hands traveled down to graze over his arousal. Her palm pressed against the length of him, in hard relief beneath the wool trousers. Biting her lip did nothing to rouse her to rational thought.

"Oh..." he mumbled into her ear, and she was fairly certain he was fully awake now. She pressed her forehead into the place where his shoulders and neck met, unwilling to face him as she rubbed her hands against the straining fabric. He was warm and thick and perfect and she wanted—she didn't know what she wanted. She wanted everything. She wanted to feel his skin, wanted the weight of him pressing on top of her, she wanted his lips and his hands and his warm goddamn skin bare against hers. She wanted to strain beneath him, to fill her lungs with his breath, and to feel sweat not knowing whether it was hers or his. She was an utter hedonist and she just couldn't bring herself to care.

Cate's hips pressed her hands firmly between them. His hands pulled her close by the waist and shoulder, encouraging her. Now it wasn't as much her hands pressing against him as it was her hips, surging against her hands that caressed his erection and providing exquisite friction. Her breath came shallow and she tipped her chin up, her lips skimming against his neck. She could feel caution knocking at her consciousness, trying to tell her that she was being wanton and jeopardizing everything she'd worked for—and for what? Some hanky-panky and a fleeting feeling of being wanted? She locked caution out. She didn't give a damn. Caution wasn't warm and supple and responsive.

Henry tucked his chin, just slightly, to dip down towards her. He wrapped a leg around the back of her knee, rolling his hips to meet hers in a slow rhythm that was—God—exquisite torture. His nose ghosted aside her own, moving slowly but resolutely towards her mouth. Her lips parted in greeting.

His kiss was soft, chaste, tentative—all things his hips most certainly were not. She didn't realize she was holding her breath until she let it out with a shudder, meeting his lips with what she hoped was equal care. His hand moved up her back and his fingers burrowed into her hair as he pulled her closer, kissed her harder. She pulled air in through her nose with the sheer thrill of his touch, and then *reveille* sliced through the cold morning air, its harsh tones greeted with snorts and groans and an oath or two from the tents surrounding them. Cate jerked in surprise. Henry snatched his mouth away, looking at her with wide, blue eyes. The nearness of the sounds of men roused from sleep on all sides of them was like being thrown into a hole in lake ice in January. Could any of them hear anything untoward? Cate's hips and hands shrank reluctantly away from Henry.

She could see desire at battle with caution in his eyes, and she hated that her own reflected that same conflict. She moved her hands up around his waist and winced up at him.

"I am so sorry," she breathed, watching him carefully, anxious that he would be annoyed with her. But she couldn't see a way forward that got either of them the resolution they deserved. At least, not in the next few hours.

Henry took a steadying breath and tried to look nonchalant, though his flushed cheeks and lips betrayed him. He settled his hands on her waist and pressed their hips together one last time, almost unconsciously. He was still enticingly hard.

"Don't worry," he shrugged, sounding more confident than he looked. "Could be worse."

Cate leveled an incredulous brow at him. This was mortifying. "Really? How?"

Henry wrinkled his nose and sighed. "Well, it could have not happened at all."

She hadn't even known how much she wanted to hear those words until he said them. She was filled with a momentary giddiness that filled her chest like a bellows. Cate knew she should nod and leave the warm cocoon of his arms to prepare for the day, but she couldn't quite manage to tear her eyes from his. Her lips twitched into a smile, and her stomach fluttered in a way that would have been more appropriate to a schoolgirl flirtation than this fodder for a yellow-jacket novel. She felt that giddiness bubble up, confident that the pair of them had an understanding. That the attraction was mutual, and she could act on it accordingly. Her eyes narrowed, and she snatched his collar with both hands, yanked him in, and kissed him soundly.

She breathed him in again through her nose, running one hand up over his cheek, rough with the shadow of whiskers, and thrilled when his arm pulled her in tight and his mouth eagerly met hers. He was a sloppy kisser—but for what he lacked in experience, he made up for in enthusiasm.

"God*damn* it's cold," Jacob Robinson exclaimed from the tent next to their's.

"I didn't think it was all that bad," Williamson replied from farther off.

"Easy for you to say," Robinson grumbled. "You have a big German furnace for a bunkie."

Cate pulled back from Henry, looking towards the front flap and then back at him. "You know," she whispered mischievously, "I was honestly amazed when Krüger managed to crawl in and out of his tent without wearing it like a cape."

Henry snorted and sat up, shaking his head and smiling. His eyes seemed stuck on her and it made her feel like she was on top of the world. She was going to need to focus very hard on being her usual ornery Smith today. Honestly, it was going to be difficult to focus on anything except when she could return to this tent and finish what they'd started. Based on how Henry looked at her, she imagined he was in a similar predicament. The hungry gaze in his eyes made her want to damn duty all to hell and crawl into his lap, but there was roll call to get to. If they failed to report, they'd be given double guard duty and that would be a sure-fire way to ensure they were not going to be in their tent together at all today.

There was nothing to change into, since they'd both slept in their new uniforms, so it was simply a matter of folding their blankets away and gathering their kit for musket drill. Cate slung her belt set around her waist and made sure the cartridge box was arranged at easy access to her right hand. As Henry made for the front flap, she stretched out her hand and grabbed him by the shoulder. He was easily persuaded to veer off-course to cup her face with both hands and deliver another searing kiss. When he pulled away, he paused and looked into her eyes for a moment, that crooked grin displaying his most perfect teeth.

"When we're done for the day," she whispered, "I'll meet you right back here."

"Thank God," he murmured, his lips tracing over her cheek and neck, his nose burrowing into the hair behind her ear.

"You know, it's damned difficult to tolerate Smith all day long when I know that you're there, hiding underneath him, and you are *so* much more interesting than him."

She huffed a laugh and spoiled her hands with a nice, slow pass over his shoulders.

A hand smacked their tent's front flap and they both sprang away from one another, staring at the tent exit with trepidation.

"Schaef! Smith! Roll call," Robinson brayed, a courtesy reminder delivered with characteristically loud informality.

Henry tossed back one more lingering look before he crawled out of the tent, the front flap crackling with ice. Cate followed, biting a lip as she tried to train her face into Smith's characteristic glower. It had always come fairly naturally before, but she was having a hard time wiping the stupid smile off her face.

———

XXVIII

THAT AFTERNOON, AS SOON as dinner was finished, Henry tried to slip away as quickly as he could to return to his tent. He knew it was stupid, that Charley was unlikely to even be there since it was Smith's turn for dish duty, and even if she was, there were so many other fellows roaming around that it was sheer idiocy to try and finish what they started this morning. But he couldn't help it. He was a warm-blooded man, inexperienced, and it was about damn time he met someone to indulge with.

He wasn't even halfway to the fort doors when he heard Lieutenant Thomas' dreaded baritone command, "Company K! You're needed for command review! Report to the parade ground."

Which one, Henry thought irately, turning on his heel and rejoining his squad, who had been ambling rather aimlessly behind, deep in debate about whether or not Elias should be permitted to swear since he was a corporal.

"Attention, Squad Seven," Osborn called as he caught up with them. "Our company is demonstrating some maneuvers for command and their guests from St. Anthony. Make sure you're equipped for dress parade. Hower, go fetch Smith from the mess. The others can finish up dish duty. They don't want a gap in the line."

"Sir, I can get him," Henry piped up, trying to sound helpful and not too eager. Elias paused, having already started towards the kitchens and looked at Osborn for further instruction. Osborn raised an eyebrow at Henry and said, "Glad to see you've gotten over whatever squabble you boys had."

Osborn nodded at Henry and he tried to hold back a grin as he made for the kitchens, allowing Elias to hold his rifle for him. As he passed by Krüger, the big Bavarian muttered, *"Tugendlamm."*

Henry glared at him sidelong and hissed back in German, "Mind your own business."

As he crossed the muddy parade ground, he found that it didn't even phase him that Krüger called him a goody two-shoes. He was walking on air this morning. No matter what Krüger thought, no matter how sanctimonious or critical he was, he didn't know about Charley. None of them did. She was his secret to keep, his proverbial dryad hiding in the tree of a soldier, who only showed herself to him.

And she wanted him.

Henry's mouth twitched up in spite of himself at the memory of that morning, one he'd been basking in all morning. He wondered how long she'd wanted him. Maybe even as long ago as that strange night where he'd heard her bring herself off. She must have heard him—there's no way she wouldn't have. Perhaps she had responded to that. The thought made his cheeks heat with pleasure.

He swung into the mess and dashed down the steps. Did she want him when they'd fought over the laundry? The memory of Smith writhing beneath him took on a new color with the knowledge that Charley had been beneath him too. He wondered how interested she was. What she intended for him this evening. All he knew for certain was that his appetite had been most thoroughly whetted.

He turned into the washroom where several fellows were scrubbing big pots and pans.

"Smith," Henry said, consciously reminding himself which name to use. Because the person who turned around and wiped her brow, who regarded him with a quirked brow and a smirk, was not Smith. It was all Charley. In fact, now that he knew her, he realized she'd made the same expression at him from the ferry landing on the day he'd met Mary Coleman and looked down from the Half Moon Battery. Perhaps she had been wanting him for *quite* some time. He grinned.

"Sarg is lining us up for command review and he wants you now," Henry relayed. He did well not to add that he wanted her now too, but not at all in the same way.

The other fellows scrubbing the stew pot glowered at Charley as she happily discarded her scrub brush and hurried to Henry's side. He had to consciously stop himself from touching her.

"Thank God," she said, wiping her wet hands on the front of his jacket in a casual show of impish intimacy that thrilled him. "The water is freezing. My chilblains were bound to flare up if I were at it much longer."

He wanted to snatch her hands up in his and kiss them. If they were alone, he would have.

"Hey, quit it, this is a new coat," he chided, swatting her hands from his chest. She smiled slyly at him. Leave it to Charley to find a way to touch him in the first minute of seeing him without drawing any undue attention. She slipped past him, taking the steps two at a time, and he followed like she was due north.

Outside the mess, she paused to pull her cap off and push her dark curls off her face before fixing it back on. He felt like he should say something clever but he couldn't think of anything. He was filled with this sense of excitement that they had an understanding. He could pull her into a dark corner and steal a kiss. He could brush his fingers over the back of her hand. She would allow him these liberties so long as her secret was safe. All that was required was a little privacy for her to be his. Which, given how the fort veritably burst with people, was a taller order then he would like.

Across the parade ground, near Colonel Van Cleve's residence, Company K was assembling. The Third Regiment was outside the fort practicing large scale maneuvers, but those from other Second Regiment companies were being driven from the parade ground to make way for Company K's lines of 82 men, in ranks two deep.

Henry made his way across the muck, his boots making sucking sounds as he lifted his feet and tried to ignore how cold his toes were.

"This weather is awful," he said aloud. "I can bear the wet, and I can bear the cold, but when it's wet and cold together?" He shook his head and looked over at Charley to gauge her reaction. But she was not there.

Henry stopped and looked back over his shoulder. Charley was standing in the middle of the parade ground, facing away from him. Puzzled, he took a few steps back to where she stood.

"Charley?" he asked, putting his hand on her shoulder as he came around her. Her eyes were wide and her face was tight as she looked past him. Her shoulder felt like a stone. "Charley, what's the matter?"

"Did the Sarg say where those visitors are from?"

Henry looked back at the ranks of Company K lined up in front of the officer's quarters. Captain Noah stood on the boardwalk, talking to a group of men in sober overcoats and top hats. "St. Anthony, I think?"

Charley grimaced and the slant of her eyebrows took on a desperate tilt. Henry's eyes widened in alarm.

"Why, do you know them?" he whispered.

Her breath shuddered, and she scrubbed her hands over her face as she nodded miserably.

Henry's mouth dropped open and he gripped her shoulder tighter. "Which one? Is it your father?"

She shook her head, her fingers pressed between her brows as she squeezed her eyes tightly shut.

"Brother?"

"What? No, it's Richard," she ground through gritted teeth, wincing as she glanced furtively over her shoulder.

Henry's brow furrowed. "Right, your brother."

She growled in frustration, flapping her hand at him. "Of course not, my brother's a baby. Dammit—I gotta get out of here."

Her eyes darted across the fort structures like a cornered animal. But Henry was still processing the first statement.

"Wait—your brother is a baby? Then who the hell is *Richard*?"

She froze.

He felt like time slowed down a bit. Like the noise of all the soldiers milling back from Company K, heading out of the fort walls chatting and laughing, were very far away. Her wide eyes slid over to him and cast that cornered gaze up at him unblinking. Henry's mouth tightened into a thin line.

"Who the hell is Richard?" he repeated tightly. There was some emotion roiling in his chest but he held it back, refusing to acknowledge it. He stared at her, willing her to tell him the truth. He felt like he could guess the answer, but he needed to hear her say it.

Charley inhaled, her eyebrows slanting painfully as she rubbed the back of her neck. "Henry, it's complicated and I—"

"Who. Is. Richard," he bit out.

She looked imploringly into his eyes for a long moment. Everything about her expression read as guilt. Henry could feel all his fluttery excitement fall like butterflies in a frost.

She looked at the ground. "...My husband..." she whispered.

———

XXIX

Of course. Of course there'd be a catch. He clenched his fists and hissed, "Why? Why would you lie about that?"

Charley winced. "I'm sorry, I'm so sorry. I just—"

"Schaefer! Smith! Hurry up!"

Both their heads snapped up towards Elias, who was waving them over. He began to walk towards them, toting both of their muskets on top of his own and looking supremely irritated. Henry shook his head and started off towards him. He couldn't stand to wait for Charley's excuses. He was so angry. And confused. What did this mean? What did she actually want with him? Why was she even here?

"Wait, Henry," she hissed, scrambling after him to grab his arm as she ducked her face beneath the brim of her cap.

He whirled around. "What?" he barked.

She glanced over towards the officers and their guests, then met his eyes resolutely. "Henry, I'm sorry I lied to you, really I am, but you're the only one who can help me. Please. What am I gonna do if he recognizes me?"

The fear, the urgency, that tinged her expression cut through his anger. They both knew what would happen if she was recognized. She'd be gone before nightfall. And he'd be sleeping cold and alone in their tent, wracked with guilt and regret. If she was recognized, he'd never see her again. She'd be sent back to whatever it was that she had run from. And Charley was not the sort of person who backed down from a challenge. No, if she had run, she'd had a good reason.

Henry looked over his shoulder at where Captain Noah stood with the group of men observing the company fall in.

Nevertheless. A man did not need to have a face for Henry to respect his claim.

His claim.

Henry stilled. When they'd walked back from the wedding in St. Paul, she'd told him something of marriage. *Women lose all our rights when we get married. We cease to be people. We cease to exist in the eyes of the law.*

He looked back at Charley. Really looked.

Charley's was not the face of a woman happily married. It was the hard and desperate face of a woman with no other choices. She wasn't Henry's after all. But she certainly wasn't this Richard's possession either.

Henry's mouth twisted and he sighed. "Okay. Just stay behind me. Like you said, people see what they expect to see."

She took in a shuddering breath and glanced towards the officers again. "Right, yes. Alright."

"Just be calm. Don't do anything rash for once." Wary of being overheard on the busy parade ground, he added under his breath, "Your disguise is a good one."

She nodded, her jaw resolute even though her eyes still darted like a cornered animal.

Henry turned and walked towards the company, Smith hovering behind. Elias handed them their rifle muskets as they approached the rear of the company, complaining that a pair of turtles would have assembled faster. Then he pointed them toward the gap in the line waiting for them. Henry stepped into the front line, assuming the Position of the Soldier even as he was flooded with how supremely foolish he felt. Was he a gudgeon to help her after she'd manipulated him so thoroughly? She was right about one thing; he really was a blockhead.

Lieutenant Thomas shouted, "Shoulder ARMS!"

Henry's arms placed the musket on his shoulder and wrapped his fingers around the cold metal trigger guard without any thought at all. He supposed it was a good sign that he could execute his drills while completely preoccupied by his temper. It boded well for battle, in any case.

Henry couldn't help it. He scanned the men gathered with Captain Noah on the boardwalk, wondering which one was the man who'd pushed Charley to assume an entirely new identity. There were six men, young and middle-aged, dressed quite gentlemanly in overcoats and top hats. He wasn't sure what he had expected, but respectable, he realized, wasn't it. Colonel Van Cleve approached from the direction of his residence and joined the group on the boardwalk.

"Sir," Captain Noah greeted with a salute. "We've called Company K for review. I understand you're acquainted with Mayor Orlando Merriman of St. Anthony? Mr. Steele has invited the mayor and a few of the aldermen from that city to review the troops."

Henry tried to keep his expression neutral. Aldermen? Mayor? His eyes studied the faces of the men in question. Bearded, well-dressed, puffed up with importance. The sutler, Franklin Steele, was among them, looking pouchy and whiskered and greasy in the way only a land speculator could. Mayor Merriman stepped forward and shook hands with Colonel Van Cleve.

"Colonel, a pleasure to see you again." The mayor swept his hands towards his companions. "May I introduce Mr. John Pillsbury, alderman of the fourth ward, and Mr. Richard Fewer, alderman of the second ward of St. Anthony."

Henry's eyes narrowed on the alderman's face and felt his resolve falter. The alderman had a full beard, lean cheeks, and kind eyes. For all appearances, he seemed a fine gentleman, with a good position. Certainly a lot better positioned than a private and third son with no position or property to speak of. Henry's toes squirmed in his boots.

"And this is our city clerk," the mayor continued, "Mr. William Wales, and my law clerk, Mr. Richard Ellis."

Henry's eyes darted over the faces of the men, frowning. With only five of them present, what were the odds that two of them would be named Richard? Both of them had to be in their thirties, though the alderman appeared older than the law clerk. The law clerk could only be described as pointy, with a full mustache and slim build. In spite of his slightness, he moved with the showy confidence of a man that had something to prove as he shook Colonel Van Cleve's hand.

"A pleasure to meet you all, gentlemen," the Colonel greeted. "I cannot express the depth of my gratitude to you for coming out here to observe our troops in this cold."

Richard the alderman smiled and when he spoke, he revealed an Irish brogue. "This ain't anythin'. Just wait till December, then we'll all really be shiverin'."

The men all laughed. Henry stood still, waiting with the rest of the company for the important guests to cast a single glance their way, when Mrs. Van Cleve approached. She was dressed finely in a wool gown and paletot, a bonnet bursting with silk flowers at the brim on her head. Her hoop was wide enough to take up over half the breadth of the boardwalk.

"Please excuse my tardiness," Mrs. Van Cleve said, more to the company of men than to the city officials, and held her hand out to Mayor Merriman. "I fear I just missed the introductions, didn't I?"

They did the round of introductions again and Henry twitched, wishing he could see through the back of his head to read Charley's reaction and determine which damn Richard she was married to. His eyes darted from alderman to law clerk and back, searching for some clue, but he couldn't get past the initial shock.

How could she be married? When they'd walked back to the fort from St. Paul, she talked like she was an old maid, unwanted by any man, bullied by her father for not being more marriage-able. The way she described it, how could one assume she was anything but unmarried? He felt like someone had blindsided him with a cudgel.

How long had she been married before she decided she would rather enlist as a man? He had to admit she would make a rather cantankerous wife, bullheaded as she was. But one of these Richards had possessed her, known her in ways he could only dream about, and he hated how jealous that made him feel. The notion that she was his secret shattered and he felt like a fool for reveling in that fantasy. His dryad. His magnetic north. What a load of romantic tripe.

"Captain Noah, if you please," Colonel Van Cleve invited and the Captain nodded, turning and hopping off the boardwalk, then crossing to the lines of men on the parade ground. Lieutenant Thomas deferred to him and stepped aside.

"Present ARMS!" Captain Noah commanded. Henry's arms automatically executed the movement even as his mind continued to spin. Regardless of which Richard it was, both held positions of influence that were not to be scoffed at. Alderman of one of the largest towns in the whole state? Law clerk to the mayor? Given how she'd talked herself down, he was utterly shocked to find her so favorably matched. She had made it sound like she was scraping the bottom of the barrel. Yet, she was clearly well-connected. Why would she run away to enlist? It made no sense.

The city officials watched with delight as Company K drilled through the manual of arms, presenting then shouldering, supporting then shouldering, fixing bayonets then shouldering, as they had for weeks upon weeks. Perhaps Charley was not the victim of circumstance but rather the villain. After all, what did he really even know about her? She only spun webs of lies until she was backed into a corner and had no other choice but to tell the truth. He just couldn't understand why she treated him like he couldn't be trusted, even though he'd been keeping her secret for over a month now. He assumed that once she'd revealed her secret to him, she'd let all her pretenses drop. But now he was questioning everything she'd ever told him.

Henry knew that over eighty men wielding weapons in near perfect unison was indeed a sight to behold and the confirmation of it was evident in the faces of the mayor, clerks, and aldermen.

"Very impressive, Colonel," the other alderman commended as the men all held bayonets in the position to charge.

"Thank you very much, Mr. Pillsbury."

"Say, I wonder which drill manual you are using?" the law clerk Richard asked. It took Van Cleve a moment to register the question as he watched the men drill with an analytic expression.

"Hardee's, naturally," Mrs. Van Cleve supplied as the question hung in the air.

"Yes, quite right," the Colonel murmured absently as he stepped down from the boardwalk, tapping Captain Noah and whispering something in his ear. The captain nodded and carried on shouting his orders.

"Most excellent!" law clerk Richard said. "I found a copy of it recently in Minneapolis and was perusing its contents. Truly a fascinating and efficient resource for this outfit."

"Isn't Hardee a confederate officer, now?" Mr. Wales, the city clerk, clarified.

"Indeed he is," Mrs. Van Cleve replied, holding the conversation steadily in her husband's stead as his attention lay with Captain Noah and the drills. "I understand that the union command has commissioned someone else to write a replacement."

"A keen decision," Alderman Richard put in. "We wouldn't want those Rebs knowin' our entire playbook."

Too late for that, Henry thought sourly, shouldering arms once again. He watched the eyes of Alderman Richard, to see if they lingered upon the faces of the enlisted men for any length of time. He seemed remarkably at ease, but Henry supposed one would be at ease if one made all the decisions but left others to execute them in one's stead. Damn, but he wished Noah would call an about-face so he could check on Charley.

"Order ARMS," Captain Noah commanded and Henry held back a sigh. If he knew the Captain, they were going to do an arms inspection for the sake of the city officials (as though they knew the first thing to look for when inspecting arms for the purpose of battle). Henry grabbed the barrel of his gun with his left hand and let it slip down through his right fingers till the butt was inches from the ground. An inspection of arms would bring the aldermen face to face with the front line. He tightened his fingers around the barrel and let the musket rifle rest gently on the wet gravel as he prayed Charley wouldn't do anything stupid, like punch someone in the face or tackle them from behind.

"Inspection ARMS."

And there it was. Henry placed his piece between his feet and reached for his bayonet at his side, fixed it in place, then pulled the rammer and let it glide to the bottom of the bore before resuming his previous position. As he did this, Colonel Van Cleve stepped back up to the boardwalk and invited the officials to the head of the line, beginning with Sergeant Nelson's squad, and led them through the process of inspecting arms. Henry tried to watch the group sidelong without breaking position, but it was difficult to track them out of the corner of his eye.

"Schaefer." The whisper was Charley. Henry tried very hard not to be annoyed as he held his position firm. Out of the corner of his mouth, hissed, "What?"

"I can't do this," she panted.

"Of course you can," he whispered, aware that Jacob standing to his left and Sergeant Osborn on his right could hear him.

"Private," Osborn hissed warningly, his eyes fixed forward but his mouth frowning.

Henry pressed his lips together and was already glancing over his shoulder before he realized he was breaking form. He caught a glance at Charley's eyes, wide and strained in her drawn face, before Osborn elbowed him and whispered, "Schaefer—*inspection arms.*"

Henry resumed his position as the group of officials worked down the line. Based on what he could tell from the corner of his eye, they were only inspecting the arms of the first row of soldiers, which would help.

As the group approached Jacob, who was the first of their squad on the front line, the alderman Richard said, "My, they are very well-practiced."

Colonel Van Cleve took the compliment with a humble nod. "They have worked very hard in the past few months."

Franklin Steele's mouth sat in a thin line. "They will need a lot more of it to face the well-trained Rebel troops. We lost a good many West Point officers to the other side."

The law clerk Richard's eyes brightened as he said, "While reading the Hardee manual, I saw something about how a good soldier should be able to load his weapon three times in a minute. Are these boys so well-equipped?"

The Colonel made an incredulous expression and said, "Not at this point."

"But are they not readying to go to the front?" the Mayor asked. "I should think they would not make the same mistake of throwing green soldiers up against these trained Rebels after Bull Run."

"I should very much like to see the Load in Nine Times in action," the law clerk said eagerly. Henry peered at him sidelong. The other men generally seemed to ignore him, the St. Anthony officials and the officers alike, yet he seemed eager to demonstrate to whomever was listening his competence in the manual of arms, despite clearly not being an enlisted man. He heard Charley's shallow breaths behind him.

Captain Noah squirmed under the criticism and turned to the Colonel. "Sir—shall we demonstrate the manual of arms?"

The Colonel frowned, but said, "Very well. Carry on, Captain."

The drummer boy began tapping out the pace as Captain Noah turned to face Sergeant Osborn and said, "Squad Seven, attention SQUAD."

Henry straightened with the rest of them and as the focus of the city officials came to bear down upon them, Charley hissed, "He's gonna see me. Henry, do you hear me?!"

"Don't. Panic," Henry hissed back, even as Jacob glanced between the two of them, breaking his position briefly as his eyes filled with the prospect of dramatic gossip.

"Shoulder ARMS."

They all followed without a second thought. The officials flanked their squad, with Captain Noah facing them a few paces off to one side and the city officials standing behind him, eagerly watching. Law clerk Richard sidled to the front, edging a chagrined Franklin Steele to the back. Henry heard Charley's piece clunk to her shoulder.

"Load in nine times. LOAD."

Henry swung the butt of his gun between his feet and held the muzzle with his left hand while floating his right to his cartridge box.

"Handle CARTRIDGE."

They weren't going to load in thirty seconds with Captain Noah commanding each stage, but it was still a thorough demonstration. Henry pulled the cartridge out and placed the twisted end of the paper tube between his teeth. He desperately hoped that Charley wasn't stupid enough to disobey orders or do anything that might bring attention upon her. Not that she wouldn't deserve it if she did, the damn duffer.

"Tear CARTRIDGE."

Henry tore the paper and held the open paper tube of gunpowder near the tip of his muzzle. He suspected the law clerk more at this point, so just to make sure, he watched Alderman Richard with wary eyes, trying to gauge whether there was any spark of recognition in his countenance.

"Charge CARTRIDGE."

He smoothly stuffed the open end into the muzzle and worked the gunpowder out with his fingers. They had no bullets as of yet to practice with, so they made do with blank cartridges. Besides, drilling with live ammunition for a demonstration would be a fool's errand.

"Say, do I know you?"

Henry was startled from the motion. Law clerk Richard was looking at him with an ingratiating grin. Captain Noah looked warily over his shoulder, unaccustomed to men of presumed status interrupting him in the middle of a maneuver involving the handling of live gunpowder.

"I don't think so, sir," Henry said and Osborn shot him a dirty look for talking out of turn.

"No, not you," Law clerk Richard said and Henry felt his stomach drop. "I mean the fellow behind you."

"Draw RAMMER." Captain Noah's voice raised a few decibels, trying to overpower the law clerk's inappropriately-timed comments. Henry swallowed hard, wondering if Charley had run yet but not hearing anything that would indicate she had.

"Mr. Ellis," the Colonel said, "if you could please refrain from interrupting."

"Oh, I'm terribly sorry, Colonel, but I could swear I have met that man somewhere before."

"Ram CARTRIDGE." Henry couldn't help but glance over his shoulder at Charley as he pushed the tulip of his rammer into the muzzle of his gun and packed down the gunpowder.

"Return RAMMER." Charley had frozen with the cartridge paper still between her fingers. She hadn't even bothered with her rammer yet. Her expression was hard and tight, her teeth gritted and her eyes wide under brows at once fierce and terrified.

"PRIME."

Henry rushed to get his rammer back in place before he scrambled for a cap with his right fingers. When he fumbled it to his gun, he realized he hadn't got it half cocked yet, and lost a moment doing that before he slipped the cap onto the nipple.

"Shoulder ARMS."

"Say, boy, what is your name?" Law clerk Richard called out. Henry's throat caught as he pulled the muzzle of his gun towards the air.

"Shit," Charley swore and before she could do anything stupid, Henry's finger fell upon the trigger of his piece and he twitched it. He hadn't intended to, not really, but he acted in panic. His musket kicked back hard into his shoulder and his ear rang with the noise of the charge fired so near. As soon as the gunshot resounded, the whole of the company flinched while several of the city officials tried to fully duck behind one another.

The Colonel's face went flat and he charged forward and stepped in front of Captain Noah. "Hold there," he called with all the force and authority of his rank. "Not a one of you is to move."

Henry froze and the gravity of what he'd done began to settle on his shoulders.

"Private," the Colonel approached and addressed him. "Present ARMS."

Henry shakily handed his piece to the Colonel. Colonel Van Cleve accepted it and then turned to Captain Noah. "Captain, see to it that this soldier understands the consequences of carelessness with live charges."

The Captain looked supremely embarrassed, hiding his flush beneath a firm, angry grimace. The officials looked among themselves with startled expressions. Mayor Merriman had pulled his law clerk away and made his displeasure plain by the set of his jaw and brows.

"Mark this occasion, soldiers," Colonel Van Cleve announced at a volume loud enough for the entire company and any errant soldiers watching could hear. "This is the kind of mistake that can get a man killed by friendly fire. It is precisely mistakes like this that are prevented by continuous drill. I should hope you will all make note of this and remember it next time your mind wanders in musket drill. I expect we will not see any such mistakes again."

The entire company hung in abashed silence, some of the men nearby shooting Henry nasty or mocking looks. Henry wondered if he might just curl up inside his uniform and disappear.

"Captain, have this squad safely discharge their blanks and disband the ranks," the Colonel commanded. "The good mayor, I am sure, has seen enough."

Captain Noah nodded. He bared his teeth somewhat when he shouted, "READY."

The rest of Squad Seven readied their weapons, pointedly not looking at Henry, who could only stand shamefacedly in the position of the soldier, weaponless.

"AIM."

The rest lifted their weapons. Henry's eyes followed the law clerk who was clearly also the man who had bound Charley in marriage. Feeling particularly self-effacing, he wondered if that weasel had deflowered her. Whether she'd sighed for him like she had in the tent that morning. Whether he'd seen her bare.

"FIRE."

A volley rang out almost in unison. It was the best they'd ever done in that regard. The charge fired from Charley's gun rang his other ear unpleasantly. Henry swallowed against the shame of unintentionally cuckolding this poorly-mustachioed stranger and reminded himself precisely who was to blame for that.

"Shoulder ARMS," Captain Noah commanded and the squad complied. "REST."

Law clerk Richard glanced over at the city clerk and shrugged awkwardly before turning and following the rest of the group to Colonel Van Cleve's residence. Mrs. Van Cleve did her best to make light of the situation, but the Colonel's stance indicated that he was very much displeased with how the demonstration had gone off.

Captain Noah ordered the sergeants to report to him and then disbanded the company. Osborn looked over at Henry before he obeyed.

"Don't go anywhere, Schaefer, until you've been dealt with."

Henry swore under his breath.

"What the hell happened, Schaef?" Jacob said as soon as Osborn had gone out of ear shot, his eyes darting to Henry and then over his shoulder, presumably at Charley.

"My finger slipped," Henry mumbled, looking at the ground before he glared up at Charley.

For her part, Charley maintained her hard facade well. Only her shoulders gave away her fear, hitched halfway up to her ears. Jacob followed Henry's gaze.

"Shit, Smith, what were you on about?" Jacob seized, his mouth twitching up in a smile. "Were you afraid ol' Franklin Steele was going to recognize you?"

Smith's eyes tore from Henry's, startled with confusion. "Franklin Steele?"

Jacob leaned in conspiratorially. "Don't worry, Schaefer didn't tell me, I figured it out on my own."

Smith glared at Henry hard. "I'm sorry, *what* exactly didn't he tell you?"

"That you made a cuckold of Franklin Steele," Jacob whispered loudly, giving Smith a slap on the back and a wink. "Schaefer made it out like you were dallying with that laundress, but I think we can all see you set your ambitions quite a lot higher."

"You *what!?*" John Williamson squealed. Webster, Krüger, and Elias also turned their undivided attention to the conversation at hand.

Elias regarded Smith suspiciously. "Really? I didn't think you had it in you."

Smith buried his face in his hands and took a steadying breath in. Henry knew Charley was trying to gather herself, block out their nosey squad-mates, but it fed the lie in the eyes of their comrades.

"Don't worry, Smith, you're safe now," Jacob said, patting her shoulder with performative comfort.

She flinched away from him, glared, and then stalked off toward the fort exit. Jacob shrugged at the rest of the squad.

"Jeez, he sure got lucky. Good thing you shot off that charge, Schaef."

"Wait, he did that on purpose?" Williamson exclaimed.

"No, I didn't..." Henry lied half-heartedly. Of course he had. And for what? To protect some fool woman who would as soon dump him in the river as kiss him if it meant protecting her own secrets?

"Schaefer. Come with me."

It was Osborn. The reckoning had arrived.

———

XXX

Sunday, October 6, 1861

CATE WOKE UP FREEZING when *reveille* sounded the next morning. Henry had been sent to the guardhouse for shooting his musket off and putting the rest of the company in immediate danger of hypothetical friendly fire. Meanwhile, the rest of the men seemed to think he was some sort of hero and that she, or rather Smith, was the hopeless lover of Mrs. Franklin Steele of all people, a matron in her mid-thirties who displayed her husband's wealth in her array of chins. Cate thought she should try to do something to correct their misinformation, or at least lead them down a little less of an outrageous lie, but she had been too overwhelmed with the aftermath of sheer terror as Richard's beady eyes bore down on her, screwing to her face as he tried to figure out where he knew her from. Her entire soldier's life had flashed before her eyes and it had felt like a cruel joke. Why would God permit her to come this far only to be pulled back into the mire? That would have been torture indeed.

Thank heavens for Henry Schaefer and his slippery trigger finger. She felt awful that he'd been packed off to the guard house without so much as a blanket before she'd been able to say two words to him, much less the most important two. Which were of course "thank you". Or perhaps "I'm sorry." Well, there were multiple important words she owed him. The look he'd given her as he'd waited for Osborn ... it had cut right through her, and a deep and abiding guilt had been festering there ever since.

She'd scarcely slept, between the shame and the cloying cold, alone under their blankets as Henry shivered in the guardhouse. She hated what she'd done to him, but she couldn't imagine a course that could repair what she'd broken. If only she'd just left him alone, it would have hurt so much less. If she'd only told him the truth when she had the chance, when it could have served to keep him from her own lack of self control. But she hadn't. She'd chosen indulgence over truth, and now Henry was paying the price.

Cate must have looked like hell when they lined up that morning for roll-call. Osborn distributed duties as usual, but it wasn't until he assigned Williamson to their squad's guard duty that she felt like she actually woke up fully.

She managed to convince Osborn to let her volunteer instead, much to Williamson's relief, and walked as quickly as her legs could carry her to the guardhouse, ignoring the chittering speculation of her squad as she doubled back to the tent for Henry's blanket. If they wanted to spin a salacious story of her recklessness and Henry's undeserved loyalty, they could have at it. It wasn't that far off anyway. When she entered the guardhouse, she realized that of course it wasn't quite the bitter cold she had anticipated, because there was a hearth in the guard room, just outside the prison room.

The fellow who had been on duty before her—from the Third Regiment by the green look of him—tipped his hat to her and ambled off to the barracks rather unceremoniously. She waited for a few minutes to be sure of her privacy before she crossed to the prison room and peeked through the grate in the door.

Henry sat alone in the room, the doors to the two dark cells hanging open and empty, seated on the floor with his legs bent in front of him.

"Schaefer," Cate whispered, and he looked up at her with drawn, contemptuous eyes.

"What are you doing here?"

"I got guard duty this morning," Cate said.

Henry's brow furrowed. "Why? What did you do?"

"It's our turn is all."

He peered at her sidelong for a moment, and then shook his head, looking away like she wasn't there.

"I suppose I deserve that," she said softly, leaning her forehead against the bars in the door.

"You deserve to be in here instead of me."

"I do," she conceded. She twisted her mouth and let out a long sigh. "Look, Henry, I'm really sorry."

"About getting me in trouble or about lying to my face?"

Cate grimaced. "All of it, really."

Henry huffed a poor imitation of a laugh and looked at his hands, draped between his knees. Silence thickened like a miasma in the space between them.

Cate pulled his blanket from around her shoulders. "I brought your blanket," she said, holding the bundle up to the bars in her fist.

Henry looked up from under his brows, his expression flat. "What do you care?"

Cate frowned. "I said I'm sorry. Do you want it or not?"

Henry shook his head and resumed glaring at his hands like she didn't exist. She swallowed against the vice wrapping round her chest as she stuffed the blanket through the bars anyway. It fell to the floor.

"What the hell, Schaefer, come on. It's not like I *made* you shoot your gun or anything. I would have been just fine without you trying to come in and rescue me like some sort of white knight. Don't you think you're overreacting just a bit?"

He turned his glare on her, glanced at the room behind her, and then whispered, "You *lied* to me."

"So?" She tried to sound flippant, but neither her wavering voice or her shame-faced expression could sell it.

"You tricked me. You told me a bold-faced lie to my face—"

"—That's only because I knew you'd make a big deal out of nothing! Because that's what it is. *Nothing.*"

"If it didn't matter, why did you have to lie about it?"

"Because you—" Cate realized she had raised her voice and regulated it down to a hiss. "Because just like everyone else, you care about some man's claim over me more than what I have decided for myself."

"I do not!"

"Don't you? Go on, tell me that it doesn't change anything." She crossed her arms and glared at him.

He looked at her in disbelief. "Of course it does! Don't try to turn this around on me. You're the one who lied to me!"

"Since when do I owe you all the intimate details of my past? Precisely when did you earn enough trust for me to lay my whole life story out for you?"

His mouth dropped open like he couldn't believe what she was saying. He cast his gaze around and his mouth flapped for a moment before he muttered, "I didn't realize you held basic personal information in higher regard than your ... baser ... affections ..."

His cheeks were flushed, whether from frustration or embarrassment or both. Cate squashed down on any part of her that found this endearing.

"Well, you know what they say when you assume," she said, turning away and leaning back on the door to the prisoner room with her arms crossed.

"You know what? Go to hell. After that disaster yesterday, I should think you at least owe me an apology, not some sanctimonious lecture."

"I did apologize! It's not like I told you to shoot the man."

"I didn't *shoot* him! It was a *diversion*!"

Cate let loose a growl of frustration and slid halfway down the door, her hands curling into fists in her hair.

"And it worked, didn't it?" His voice was closer. She looked up and saw he stood at the other side of the door, looking down on her with one hand wrapped around the bars. "He didn't recognize you."

Cate felt the tightness in her chest when she said, "He still might have. He might remember later. He could come back for me."

He glowered at her. "Just because it's possible doesn't make it true."

She sighed and stepped forward, turning with her arms crossed to properly return his glower.

"Come on, Charley, admit it. It worked."

She wrinkled her nose. His blue eyes pinned her down. She refused to give him the satisfaction.

"The least you could do is say thank you," he sighed, stepping back to cross his arms too.

Cate rolled her eyes. "Wait, I thought the least I could do was apologize? Which is it?"

"Both!"

Cate threw up her hands in frustration and retreated to sit on one of the chairs surrounding the table at the center of the room. "Fine! I'm sorry I lied and thank you for your 'diversion'. Are you happy now?"

"Not really."

She groaned again. "What more could you possibly want?"

Her words were met with silence. In the absence of his response, she began to answer the question herself. She thought immediately of the state she'd left him in yesterday morning and blushed hard, disappointed and ashamed that her lack of foresight had utterly bungled what might've shaped up to be a very satisfying arrangement for them both. She could feel him watching her through the bars and she glanced up, holding his eyes for a moment.

"I am sincerely sorry," she murmured, looking back down in her hands. "I didn't mean to be cruel. I would just rather forget everything that happened before I got here."

"Did he ... hurt you?" Henry asked.

The question only amplified her shame.

"No, nothing like that. We were just poorly matched. I..." Cate twisted her thumb between her fingers and tried to release that damned tension in her chest. "I just didn't want to marry him. But my family couldn't understand why, and I couldn't argue against it properly, other than I just didn't like him very much—which, if you weren't aware, doesn't count for much when you're twenty-six and unmarried and your father wants you out of his house."

She chanced a glance up at him. Henry had his hands hung between the bars in the door and regarded her with a quiet gaze. He didn't say anything.

"So I thought maybe I am being too contrary and agreed to marry him. And every minute after that, it became more and more clear that I had made a terrible mistake." She rubbed her forehead. "I mean, you saw him. He has no sense for other people, just carries on like some sort of steam engine without any brakes, assuming that everyone else finds him as fascinating as he does himself. He didn't *see* me." She sighed. "I don't know what I wanted in a husband, really, but I am certainly not cut out for 'Yes dear' and 'Of course darling'. Which was, of course, precisely what he wanted. What you all want, really."

"I don't," Henry murmured.

Cate looked up at him incredulously. "Don't you?"

He regarded her for a moment but didn't respond. She sighed again and sprawled back into her chair, running her fingers over her temple.

"I don't know. I made a huge mistake—he was entirely wrong for me. And by the time I realized there was no way around that, it was several months too late."

"So you put on trousers and ran away?" Henry asked. She could scarcely bear to meet his level gaze and just nodded curtly.

"I hid my body so I could speak my mind."

"You know, the Turners accept both men and women as members."

Cate looked up with one brow lifted. "Do they now?"

"Well, I mean, not all Turners around the world, I suppose, but those of us in New Ulm certainly do."

She blinked. "Are they equal members?"

"I guess I'm not sure," he admitted, "but there were certainly some very vocal ladies in our group in Cincinnati. And we invited Mrs. Swisshelm, and I can't think of any woman more opinionated than her. Except maybe you."

Cate laughed listlessly. "Damn, Henry ... I'm sorry for dragging you into this mess."

"I'm not."

She raised her eyebrow at him again. He shrugged defensively, "What, I'm not. Not really. Well, of course I don't suffer being lied to. But if you hadn't dragged me into this mess, we'd still be at each other's throats, so..."

He shrugged again and tentatively met her gaze. His Adam's apple bobbed in his neck as he swallowed and it drew her attention with such singular focus that she didn't realize she'd stood before she was already moving towards him.

"I really am sorry," she said, searching his face for forgiveness that she certainly didn't deserve but desperately wanted nonetheless. "I ... should have told you the truth."

"You can trust me with the truth," Henry replied. "You've told me secrets. I've kept them. I ... I want to know you. I don't know what else I can do to earn your trust."

Cate sighed. "I know. I just ... I'm not used to people ..." God, this was so pitiful, "... wanting that. To know me. The real me, not the person they would rather have me be."

"Well, other people are fools," he said. "Though I think we've covered that pretty well already."

She looked up into his eyes, blue and tired and ringed with shadows. "I'm a lot, though. Look at what I've put you through already. Henry, not even my own family wants to put up with me."

He frowned. "Stop trying to warn me off you like I'm some kid on the edge of a snake pit. I'm a grown man, I can handle my own decisions, thanks."

She winced and nodded, even though she wasn't convinced he wasn't stepping into a snake pit. She set her hand on the rough wood of the door, eyes fixed on the floor. This felt ... terrifying, if she were being honest. Even if he was confident enough to get entangled with her, she still felt like she was on a cliff trying to convince herself to jump into a pool. She wanted to, so badly, but her fear was in her throat and she knew she shouldn't. It wasn't right, it wasn't what a nice girl would do. Not to mention if she compromised herself, her career as a soldier would be over.

"And another thing," Henry said. His voice was close, his face resting on the bars of the door. "If your family doesn't want you around, that means there's something wrong with *them*. Not you."

Cate pressed her forehead to the door. Damn this door. Damn this man. Damn his stupid compliments and his patient interest and his goddamn casual surety. "Shut up," she said and she looked up at him, his eyes searching hers as her heart roared in her ears.

"You're smart," he said, a smile teasing at the edge of his mouth.

"How dare you compliment me when I'm humbled," she shot back, drawing her body against the door and glancing at the window where the morning was a bustle of drilling and supplies shipments. She looked back at Henry, at his earnest eyes and his trusting mouth and his stupid shoulders. She'd been done in weeks ago. Maybe even months.

"I'm sorry I lied to you about who Richard was," Cate repeated, averting her gaze, "but as far as I'm concerned, he's not my husband. Not anymore. When I left him, I left behind that girl who married him too. I'm Charley Smith now."

"If you say it's over, then I believe you."

She looked up at him and there was something in his eyes, the same thing that had been there yesterday morning, before Richard had arrived to nearly ruin everything she had built here. Something like hope.

Dammit.

Cate glanced around the guard room once more, and out the window to the parade ground bustling with soldiers. The clouds finally having cleared overnight, the bright morning sunshine outside reflected against the windows, making it nigh impossible for those outside to see in. She was closer when she looked back to Henry and she lifted her fingers to the backs of his hands, her touch tentative.

"I'm sorry," she repeated.

"You don't have to keep saying it, I forgive you."

"No, I mean about yesterday morning..."

He looked at her with confusion for a moment, before he realized what she referred to and blushed. "You're ... sorry?"

"Not sorry that it happened," she said quickly. "Just that I didn't, you know, finish. Um. What I started."

"You, uh," he licked his lips and it made her stupid, "you could still finish what you started."

"I would like that," she whispered.

"Me too," he replied, then flushed. "Obviously."

His bashful chuckle was muffled as she raised her lips to his, claiming him through the bars on the door. It was awkward, but his mouth was warm and yielding and he kissed her back, albeit chastely, his hand turning to curl his fingers around hers. She reached through the bars with her other hand and pushed her fingers into his hair, jostling his cap off as she pulled him towards her, pressing her lips harder to his.

"You don't have keys to this door, do you?" he breathed, kissing the corner of her mouth. She groaned. "No."

"Damn." He kissed the other corner of her mouth.

"How long did they say you have to stay in here?" she whispered, tipping her chin down to break their kiss, but only by an inch. His goddamn perfect teeth shone as he smiled impishly, eyelids heavy. "Until dinner. I'm out this afternoon."

"Those are going to be the longest drills of my life," she said and pulled him nearer again, crushing the bars between their cheeks as she pressed another kiss to his lips. He wanted to know her? Fine, let him know her. Perhaps when he finally did, he would no longer want her. But she'd be damned if she wasn't going to ride this wave as far as she could. If he lost interest, so be it. She would be amiable enough. Whoever said ignorance is bliss was a fool. Knowledge was bliss, even if it was also torture.

———

XXXI

EVERY MINUTE HENRY SPENT in the prison room felt like an hour. Jacob Robinson dropped by to chat with Smith and him while Smith was still on guard duty, trying to get details about Franklin Steele and Smith's love affair with his wife, but Smith would have none of it. Jacob ran circles around himself speculating, but Smith just glared at him. Henry did too. If Jacob would just clear off, he and Charley could resume the delightful, albeit awkward, kissing they'd been guiltily startled from when Jacob crashed through the door of the guard house. It was truly a blessing that despite his love of gossip, Jacob (unlike Elias, who could smell a secret from a mile away) was generally oblivious when it came to his powers of observation. If he'd care to look, he would have seen that Smith's lips were flushed and swollen and Henry's face was hot with embarrassment. Good thing he'd had a door between them to conceal his tenting trousers.

So while Jacob was trying his best Elias impression, set upon getting the best gossip first, Smith had wasted the rest of his guard duty with his arms crossed, scarcely suffering Jacob but too afraid of incriminating herself and Henry to try to eject him.

Then Paul Wickman from Company H had come to relieve her and she'd looked regretfully at Henry over her shoulder before heading out to join drills. Paul Wickman wasn't much of a conversationalist, which suited Henry just fine, because he wouldn't have been able to focus on it anyway. Besides, he'd relayed the whole situation to Paul the night before, on his previous duty—well, minus the part where Smith was trying to evade being discovered by her ex-husband. He'd glossed over that completely.

Henry whiled away the hours seated against the limestone wall, watching ranks of men being marched back and forth across the parade ground through the bars and outside the adjacent window, anticipating the moment he could return to his tent with Charley to the point of madness. He played it out a thousand different ways in his mind. He imagined how she would bring him off with her hands, watching with those wide, dark eyes, drinking him in, scattering kisses over his face and neck with her soft, bow lips.

What in Sam Hill was wrong with him? She'd lied to him, deceived him—*seduced* him. And he was happy to merrily skip down that road to perdition? He shouldn't be, but he was. Perhaps it was his anti-clerical upbringing. It was hard to respect a woman's promise to God that she would honor and obey some man she despised when that God did not care one whit if she did, if He existed at all. Henry knew that if her secret were to come to light, she'd be delivered right back into the hands of Law Clerk Richard, but for Henry, when he said he'd accept it if she said it was over—well, he hadn't lied. Marriage was a compact between two people. If the compact was broken by either party, it was null and void.

She'd hid a great deal from him, and he couldn't say he was happy about that, but she was Charley. She was vehement and thoughtful and intent and beautiful. She cared deeply about a lot of things, about people she'd never met and about how well she lived up to her own convictions. So what if they weren't the priorities that everyone else held? Everyone else had let slavery carry on for the past several hundred years so what did they know?

Captain Noah and Sergeant Osborn came at noon and gave him another stern lecture about the importance of exercising care with his weapon. He nodded and agreed to whatever they said, eager to be free and find Charley. They dismissed him to dinner and he nearly ran to the mess hall.

Charley sat with the rest of the squad and when she saw him, she grinned in a way that engaged her entire face, in a way he wasn't sure he'd ever seen before. He took his seat next to her and tried to not grin like a lovesick idiot. He reminded himself extra firmly that he was seated next to Smith—*Smith*—who was an arrogant ass of a boy and whose presence he merely suffered rather than delighted in. He was absolutely terrible at it.

He ended up drawing Krüger's sidelong look as he brought up some newspaper editorial on the fitness of the Union army that he'd glanced upon in Harper's Weekly, and he and Charley discussed it in great excitement despite the topic being objectively dreary. He couldn't help that his body was tuned to her, noticing everything about her in a way he hadn't before. The curve of her fingers around her tin spoon. The press of her lips around the metal as she ate. The darting glances her eyes kept stealing at him. When he held that dark gaze, he forgot what he was saying.

He was only distantly aware that he was ignoring the rest of the squad when he overheard Elias' voice take on that conspiratorial whisper that he always used when about to drop some gossip no one had heard yet.

"I understand we are shipping out next week for the front," Elias shared, his eyes sparkling with excitement. "They'll take us downriver by steamship and we'll be fighting rebels before the harvest's in."

Henry's focus was drawn to Elias only when Charley's eyes left his to look at the Corporal.

"It's about damn time," she said, her voice hard and low with Smith's usual derisive cadence.

"Is it?" Webster replied, looking at her questioningly. "Just yesterday, one of our number—no offense, Schaefer—accidentally fired off a blank in the middle of an arms inspection. We could not perform for an audience of men wishing us to succeed. I shudder to think how we would fare faced with a brigade of charging hostiles."

Henry bit his tongue and avoided making eye contact with any of the other boys. He hated that he'd made himself appear like such a useless dunderhead, but he could not very well reveal that he had done it on purpose. Sure, he'd been flustered and nervous and angry, but he'd be lying if he said it was an accident. He knew his way around his rifle better than that.

"Unfortunate mistakes aside," Elias said, waving away Webster's comments with one hand, "I would say we are more than ready. We can Load in Nine Times nearly to speed, for goodness sake, Schaefer's misfire notwithstanding. Not even the troops at the front now can claim that."

"Where are the troops presently?" Jacob asked. "Mary will want to know where to address her letters."

"Washington DC, I expect," Smith said, reaching for a second bread roll in just such a way that her arm pressed against Henry's. He tried hard not to smirk as he again anticipated their return to their tent. He wondered how long before she would stop worrying about hanging a blanket when she decided to change her clothes. He still struggled to imagine how her body might look under the drape of her uniform, though he remembered the curve of her stays as she pulled them angrily over sheer cotton shirting the day they'd got their Union blues. He glanced up and noticed Krüger regarding him.

"Yes, I had a letter from my brother that the First Minnesota is up on Edward's Ferry, guarding the Upper Potomac." The words spilled out from Henry's mouth. Everyone's attention swung to him and he seized upon it, even though he was loath to think about Franklin or Peter whatsoever, as they had also included in this letter their refusal to continue pretending like he was with them in their correspondence back home. Peter had written to Mutter with the truth, they'd said. And rather than reckon with any of that, Henry had done what he'd been doing for months. Avoided it completely.

"I didn't know you had a brother in the First Minnesota," Williamson said.

"Two actually. They're twins."

Elias then took the liberty to inform everyone of how Henry had tried to enlist in the First Minnesota as well, but they had only taken his brothers and he'd had to wait for the Second Minnesota to be formed before enlisting himself. Henry hardly felt like it was Elias' story to tell, but he supposed it was better than having to tell it again himself. It still stuck in his craw that his brothers already fought the Rebels, and in the first battle of the whole war, no less. Meanwhile, here he was, still stuck in Minnesota shooting off blank cartridges at the mayor of St. Anthony and trying to seduce his bunkie while resolutely avoiding any correspondence with his family.

"Say, did you ever hear from your mother, Schaef?" Jacob interrupted Elias' authoritative account to ask.

Henry blinked for a moment. He was honestly not sure what Jacob was talking about.

"After we all got our CDVs in Faribault, after we enlisted—did you hear from her?"

Henry had forgotten about that. He was fairly certain that CDV was still in the bottom of his satchel, the edges worn and tattered. It only took a matter of weeks for good intentions to feel like a one-way road to Hell.

"Oh, you got your *carte de visite* made? I've always wanted to do that," Williamson said.

"We should all go into St. Paul in our uniforms and get them made," Webster put in, seizing upon the chance to organize an outing.

Anything to move the conversation away from Henry's family.

"I should very much like that," Smith put in. "It's been a long time since I had my picture made."

Henry seized upon her words in respite from his guilt. He should very much like to see a CDV of Charley before her transformation. Although, he supposed the last time she'd had her image made likely was for her wedding and he didn't much enjoy the thought of her sitting under the possessive hands of that spindly law clerk with his outrageous mustache.

He glanced at her sidelong, her dark curls swept over her eyebrows, brown eyes merry as she tracked the banter back and forth across the table. Her hair was somewhere between black and brown, and it occurred to him that in her previous life, it had most likely been long, coiled up in a braid or with pins, to be pulled out and cascaded around her shoulders. The notion felt more incongruent than appealing.

"Well, it's decided," Webster said. "We'll go and get our CDVs taken on Saturday. I'm sure Osborn won't mind getting us a pass."

"I'll bet he'd like to go too," Elias added.

"Wait—will we have time?" Jacob asked. "If we're headed imminently to the front, I don't see why we shouldn't go tomorrow."

Webster frowned. "Good point. Can't hurt to ask."

Men across the mess were breaking up, heading out the door in pairs and groups for an hour's leisure before afternoon drills. Henry nudged Charley's shoulder and looked at her sidelong. She raised an eyebrow at him and he tipped his head in the direction of the tents with a flash of his eyebrows. She huffed a laugh and shook her head.

"Sorry, I have guard duty at 1 o'clock," she said and she sounded like she truly regretted it. Henry frowned. Dammit. He'd forgotten about the two hour guard rotation after he'd been released. She must have seen his disappointment on his face because she patted his shoulder as she rose.

"Don't worry, Schaefer. Good things come to those who wait." She shot him that smirk of hers as she walked away. Henry watched her go. He tried to find some indication of femaleness in her as she went, but from all appearances, she looked like any other soldier. Some outrageous part of his mind briefly entertained the possibility that this was all some sort of elaborate trick, and Smith had always been a boy and he was being made a most ridiculous fool.

"Hmph."

Henry's eyes flicked over to see Krüger still seated across the table, his shrewd, cold eyes regarding him.

"Was guckst du so, Schleicher?" Henry hissed, raising one brow.

Krüger crossed his arms slowly and didn't say anything. He didn't have to. His meaning was clear. Henry rolled his eyes, rose, and stalked out of the mess.

Goddamn sanctimonious bastard. He'd made enough jibes that Henry knew what he was about. He thought Turners were immoral heathens, set upon corrupting others. Well, jokes on

Krüger, because if anyone was doing the corrupting, it was Charley Smith.

"Where you headed?" Jacob popped up at his side.

Henry shrugged noncommittally, even as he cast his gaze somewhat fleetingly at the guardhouse.

"I'm expecting a package from my aunt. Want to come with and see if it's arrived?" Jacob offered.

Henry hesitated.

"Come on, if it's arrived, there's a cookie in it for you."

Henry followed Jacob to the sutler, where the post also came through. The little shop Steele ran was tucked behind the munitions, a stone's throw from the Round Bastion and the guardhouse. When they ducked inside, there was a man behind the counter, but it wasn't Franklin Steele. Henry would be surprised if the man actually ever ran any of his own day-to-day business. He was probably too busy donating land he didn't own to the University of Minnesota board and trying to get a county named after him.

Jacob spoke to the clerk and Henry loitered, running a finger over soaps stocked in a basket to one side of the door as he glanced out the window. Smith was walking out the door of the guardhouse with his arms shouldered, winding round to proceed up the utilitarian wooden stairs to the gatehouse, a narrow covered walkway allowing guards to monitor the main fort entrance from above. Henry's lips parted. The gatehouse was enclosed on three sides, all but the long wall which faced the fort. There wasn't much in the way of privacy up there, unless one considered the small closet on the side opposite the stairs. Henry's eyes narrowed. No one but the person assigned to guard duty had any reason to be up there. The corners of his lips twitched up with renewed anticipation.

"Sorry, Private, doesn't look like it's come in yet," the clerk said.

"Ah, very well," Jacob replied. "Sorry, Schaefer, looks like cookies are a bust."

Henry shrugged. He really couldn't care less. He just needed to find a way to shake off Jacob so he could sneak up to the gatehouse before afternoon drills were called.

"Say, what did you say his name was?" the clerk asked and it took a moment before Henry realized he was referring to him.

"Oh, uh, Henry Schaefer?"

The clerk furrowed his brow. "How do you spell that?"

Henry told him and the clerk began rifling through a pile of letters.

"Oh, I'm not expecting anything," Henry said, but the clerk ignored him.

"Ah, here it is," the clerk said, proffering a fat envelope to Henry. "Looks like it's from New Ulm."

Shit.

Henry reluctantly reached out and took the letter.

"Oh, a letter from back home?" Jacob asked, grinning. "Do you think she fit any cookies in there?"

Henry's lips pressed into a flat line. It was definitely addressed in his mother's hand. "I doubt it."

"Hell, Schaef, you look like you seen a ghost."

Henry looked up guiltily at Jacob. "I ... didn't tell her I didn't make it into the First Regiment."

Jacob's eyebrows flew up and his mouth dropped open. "Oh, Jingo. I don't envy you that letter at all. How did she not know? Did your brothers cover for you?"

"They were for a while, but Peter said he wrote to her with the truth in his last letter." Henry stared down at the letter, afraid to open it. He gave a deep sigh. The clerk busied himself behind the till, pretending he wasn't listening.

Jacob glanced awkwardly past Henry, then back at him. "Well, I hate to leave you to something like that alone, but I'm expecting Mary soon..."

Jacob gave a half-hearted shrug, then skirted around him and out the door, leaving Henry standing there with the fat packet. He looked down at it, trying to gauge if the slant of his mother's letters held any measure of her fury. He glanced up out the door. The gatehouse stood just visible over the roof of the munitions building. He didn't let his thoughts articulate. He just stuffed the envelope in his pocket and strode out the sutler, making a beeline for the gatehouse.

———

XXXII

CATE LEANED AGAINST THE wall, looking down at the men moving in and out of the fort under the gatehouse. The holes set in the limestone were narrow, built to stick the business end of a gun out of. The roof of the gatehouse was constructed of gabled wood, built up from the top of the limestone wall. The passage across was narrow—scarcely five feet wide—and while highly fortified on the outside with both corners solid as a house, towards the fort interior, it was open to the air across the length of the gate with the only barrier a low fence.

When she heard the wooden stairs creak, she turned to the doorway and was completely unsurprised to see Henry peek his head inside.

"What do you think you're doing here?" she said, leaning on propped elbows against the embrasure with her gun at her side.

His face seemed drawn for a moment, but before she could mark it, he tilted his head to one side and smiled that crooked grin at her. He crossed behind her without words, one hand skimming over her hip as he passed. It would have been impossible for her to maintain an air of nonchalance while that touch pulled her towards him like a string. He opened the little door in the far corner of the gatehouse and peered inside.

"What do you suppose this is for?" he mused, nudging a dusty broom with his foot. Cate straightened and craned to see over his shoulder.

"Munitions, maybe, from when the fort was active," she said and sidled over. "Now, it appears to be storage for dust and spiders."

"Hm." He walked inside the closet. It was barely big enough to accommodate his shoulders. "I could think of some other use for it."

Cate raised an incredulous brow, even as her heart lurched eagerly in her chest. If he was angling for what she thought, he was more audacious than she'd given him credit for.

"What're you doing in there?" she asked.

"It's warmer in here."

"Is it?" She entered the dark space and he drew her hands to his waist.

"It is now," he murmured and she felt a thrill run down her spine, settling right in between her legs. She looked over her shoulder, then kicked the closet door shut with her heel, plunging them into darkness. Cate smiled slyly, then murmured with pleasure as she felt Henry's lips ghost over her skin where her jaw met her ear.

"This may be the most reckless location yet," she warned, even as she arched her neck to afford Henry better access.

"I don't give a damn," he replied, his voice rough and somewhat breathless and pushed his fingers into her hair. His other hand pulled her waist nearer, pressing the two of them together from thighs to mouths as he captured her lips with his.

"We should probably have an idea of what we'll say if someone comes up here," she whispered before closing her teeth gently over his lower lip. He murmured his approval and pressed his hips against hers.

"Fighting," he suggested, his tongue tasting her lips.

"Perfect," she replied and she wasn't sure if she was referring to the alibi or to the way his large hands slid down from the small of her waist and grasped urgently at her backside.

This was stupid. It was so stupid. It was worse than what they'd done in the guardhouse this morning. There were dozens of unsuspecting men passing below them every minute and none of them had any idea that she was there, above them, pinning Henry to the wall and taking the liberty to touch him wherever she damn well pleased. She squeezed her thighs together with the thought and reveled in the pulse of pleasure it delivered.

Henry snuck one hand up under her sack coat, his fingers skimming against her laces, then worrying at the knot tied at the bottom. Cate recoiled for a moment, seizing his wrist gently with her hand and placing his palm back on her rear, where it would cause a great deal less trouble. He gripped her, apparently keen to prove her wrong as he rolled his hips into her, his erection pressing between her legs and eliciting a quiet gasp from her. Damn, he was making it difficult for her to keep her head.

She wasn't precisely sure what he was gunning for, but she knew well enough what she was willing to do under the circumstances. She knew she couldn't do anything that might risk revealing any particularly female aspects of her body. She would not be anything less than fully uniformed in such a precarious location—she wasn't even sure the tent was particularly safe, given how flimsy its stick frame was. But Henry? He could reveal whatever he wanted. Whatever she wanted.

She grinned into his mouth as she slipped her fingers under the front of his uniform and worked loose the top button of his trousers. The sound he made in response was quiet enough but it shook her with arousal regardless, and she eagerly released another trouser button, then another. He pressed his hips towards her hands, egging her on.

Cate felt drunk and stupid with want, but what did it matter if she was stupid? So she wanted, so what? She'd wanted for months, and now she had his leave to take and she would, guard duty be damned. Army be damned. Everyone could go to hell as far as she was concerned, as long as she could keep Henry in her hands for the next fifteen minutes.

She slipped her hand inside his trousers, his erection hot to the touch through the thin cotton of his shirt tails. She used her other hand to pull the shirt up, out of the trousers and out of her goddamn way. She wanted skin on skin and she couldn't help the twitch of her hips or the whimper of her voice when her fingers met firm, velvety flesh.

Henry huffed in her ear, his breath short and fast as he clutched her tighter and nipped at her earlobe. She turned her head as she took his prick in hand, seeking his lips and feeling his breath on her cheek as she worked her palm up his length.

"Charley," he gasped, and she seized his mouth under her own to keep him quiet, her hips pushing unconsciously in rhythm with her hand. She could feel how wet he'd made her and imagined what it would feel like if she were at liberty to drop her own trousers and climb his thighs, to let him turn her against the perpendicular wall and fuck her deep and she whimpered in his mouth as his fingers gripped her buttocks through her trousers.

"Tell me…" she started, but then trailed off, losing her nerve.

"I'll tell you anything you want," he panted, "just don't stop."

She slipped her opposite hand up, under his shirt, skimming her fingers over his hard stomach, through the soft hair that led down from his naval, as she continued to work him. She was nervous that the thing she had started to say would put him off, so maybe it was better to say nothing, just in case. She tucked her face into the crook of his neck and tried to focus on how he responded to her movements. She'd only done this a handful of times and never standing up. Besides, it had been with Richard, whose piece was as slender as the rest of him. Henry was thicker, if a little shorter, and the contrast was sort of mesmerizing. She didn't want to muck it up now by saying something stupid.

"Go on," he whispered, his lips against the shell of her ear. "Ask me."

Her face heated red and her stomach coiled, but she had been thinking about this for far too long and the words fell out of her mouth before she had a chance to stop them. "Does this feel as good as when you brought yourself off in the barracks, with me?"

His breath hitched and his hips quivered as one of his arms wrapped up and around her back, his considerable strength holding her tightly as her wrist struggled to keep pace, wedged as it was between them. She wasn't helping it any, either, because as soon as she'd asked, she'd felt a rush of warmth radiate deep in her belly, pulse down between her legs, and she didn't know whether she were more embarrassed or more wanton, but she ground her hips over his thigh just the same. The friction was exquisite torture, at once both more than she could bear and not nearly enough.

"Charley," he gasped, "it's so much better, you're so much better—God—"

He shook and groaned and her hand became slick as he spent, shuddering against her, his guttural growl reverberating on her lips.

He breathed deep as she dropped her face into his shoulder, pushing hard against her own groan. His fingers came to her wrists to still her hand from continuing to work him and she pressed her hips against him again, resisting the urge to whine and whimper for her own release. His breath shook in her ear and he whispered, "So much better."

"Good." Cate swallowed hard. "I ... I haven't been able to stop thinking about what you would look like when you're—you're like this. Not since then. It ..." She felt like her cheeks might burst into flame, she was so embarrassed, but with every word, she felt a transfer of tension, from fear to anticipation, and she wanted the latter a great deal more than the former. "...well, what I imagined of it, it finished me that night."

"I want to do that."

Cate swallowed hard and reminded herself of their circumstances. They were in a communal space, where anyone could enter if they wanted, in a crowded fort. She could hear boys just down below joking to each other about euchre, for Chrissakes. She wanted, so keenly that it almost hurt to say it, but she'd had worse. She was used to ending an encounter still wanting. She could wait until circumstances were safer, until she could take the time to show Henry how she liked it. That would be better than having him fumble around blindly, under pressure to find release quickly before someone came along to see where she was. After months of wanting and waiting and hiding, she could wait a few hours more.

"Not yet," she replied and indulged in a lingering kiss. She slipped her hands out of his trousers and wiped them on her handkerchief. She gave him a cursory swipe and she tucked his shirttails back in, then buttoned him up. She already missed his skin. "I have every intention of holding you to that offer, just not here, not now."

She glanced over her shoulder illustratively at the door. He regarded her with wide, earnest blue eyes and nodded.

"Yes, alright, if that's what you want," he blabbered, his breath still short as he adjusted his trousers with one hand. "I just don't want you to feel like ..."

"...Like what?"

"Like you can't," he finished unartfully. "Because I want you to. I very much want to be the cause of it."

"I would like that." Cate couldn't help a smile play on the corner of her mouth. Who would have thought that, after all that had just transpired, it was those simple words that would make her blush. "I just ... I want to wait, until I don't have quite so many potential interruptions to worry about. I'm not terribly good at doing more than one thing at a time."

He smiled and pulled her near with his other hand, pressing his nose into her hair. Her cap must have fallen off at some point. She leaned into his side as she gave her thighs one last squeeze. Her toes curled with the pulse of her pleasure and she did her best to ignore it. She turned her head and looked up at him.

"Do you feel better now?" she asked huskily.

"Mmmhmm," he murmured, sagging on the wall and holding her by her waist against him. "Though ... I'm not sure how long that'll last knowing you're still waiting."

"Good," she replied and gave a nip to his neck. "I hope, once everyone else is asleep, that we shall each find a good measure of enjoyment in our tent."

She loved how his mouth hung open at her words for a moment.

"I've never met a woman who spoke so clearly about what she wants before," he murmured, trailing his nose over her cheek as his lips sought hers.

"I suspect I could be a good measure clearer, but most men don't like that in a woman."

"Most men are fools," he retorted and smiled into her mouth. She reveled in the warmth of his lips, soft and plush and slick from their efforts. "Probably doesn't help that you've spent the better part of three months cooped up with a bunch of bawdy soldiers."

"Yes, of course, you all have corrupted me, that's it."

She kissed him slow, with a measure of reverence, letting her hands wander over his chest, trying to recall how all the planes of his sinewy torso looked fitted together under pale skin. She needed to stop. The longer they continued to touch, to taste, the more likely it was that they'd be caught out by someone wondering why she wasn't in the guardhouse. Her hands moved down, intending to find the bottom edge of his sack coat again, to feel his warmth, when she noticed something was in his pocket.

"What's this?" she asked, her fingers exploring the shape to determine what it might be.

Henry shifted uncomfortably. "Nothing, it's just a letter."

Cate pulled back and regarded him. "A letter? From the estranged family?"

He pressed his lips together and gave a curt nod.

She was distantly aware of her hands resting on his biceps, his arms easy around her waist. It felt natural, easy. "Surely you've heard from them since you left?"

"Well, no. I ... I told you I had tried to enlist with the First Minnesota and my brothers, they were accepted, but I wasn't."

"Right."

Henry's countenance was a bit cowed, a bit miserable-looking. "I took up the farmhand job in Faribault, waiting to see if they'd call a Second Regiment. And ... in the meantime, I may not have gotten around to contacting my family. At all."

"Perhaps they didn't deserve to hear from you." She tilted her head to one side, to try and catch his eyes. "Did they pressure you to join?"

"No. I suppose my father did want us to fight—there is a great deal to be said of a Turner who defends his people, whether it's a neighborhood or a nation. But my mother was set against it. And I didn't care, I was too busy basking in my father's pride. But then ..." He sighed. "I'd made such a big fuss about it, trying to show off for Vater and my brothers, I just couldn't admit that they'd got in and I didn't."

"So is that letter from your mother, then?"

"I think so. It's addressed in her hand, at least."

"Wait—you haven't opened it yet?"

"No, I … I picked it up at the sutler then came straight here, as soon as I saw you go up to the gatehouse."

Cate couldn't help but smile. "Glad to see you have your priorities straight."

His eyes raked over her form, such as it was, disguised in the unflattering, baggy uniform. He regarded her with a sort of hungry gaze and the implication of his wanting dropped like a stone right in between her thighs. She wished she had met him in some other context, where there was a greater degree of privacy. She wondered if that would be better afforded when they set up camp near the front, but somehow she doubted it. If there was anything that seemed to link her military experience thus far, it was a severe and relentless lack of privacy.

"So what do you suppose she has to say?" Cate asked, hoping her question wasn't too intrusive. She wasn't really sure what could be considered too intrusive after what they'd just done, but the anxiety that he might take offense persisted regardless.

Henry shrugged uncomfortably. "To be perfectly honest, I don't think she can say much that I don't already know." He reached into his pocket and pulled the letter out. It was square and thick with pages. Cate grimaced.

"Whatever it is, she seems to have quite a lot to say about it," she observed.

Henry held the letter in two hands and looked down at it for a moment, his brows creasing together in thought.

"Would you …" he began, then looked up at her. "Would you maybe read it for me?"

Cate stared at him for a moment, stunned to silence. "I, uh … alright. If you think that would help."

His mouth twisted to one side as he handed it to her. "It's not that I'm afraid or anything. I just … I feel awful about not telling them. I didn't mean to keep it a secret but … I thought if I waited until I felt like I had accomplished something, that I had made the best of the situation first, then I could write home without completely embarrassing myself. And I just haven't felt like that yet."

"You don't have to explain it to me," Cate assured, sliding her finger under the flap to break the seal. "Everyone assumes family are the people you should trust the most, maybe because they know you best, but it's been my experience that parents only see what they want to see and no matter what you do, you can't really change their minds."

Henry let out a dry laugh. "You can say that again."

The bugle sounded across the parade ground, calling afternoon drills. Henry looked towards the door and sighed.

"I guess that means me," he said, pushing himself up and off the wall, then opening the door. Cate reached out and caught his arm.

"Hey. I'll see you tonight. Bunkie."

A smile curled back on his lips. "I'm counting the minutes."

Cate followed him out of the closet and watched him walk away with a warm sensation blossoming in her chest. She smiled to herself indulgently as she unfolded the pages of his letter. Looking down, she was confused for a moment as she skimmed lines of utterly incomprehensible script. Blinking, she crossed to the rail to see Henry quitting the steps and striding towards the parade ground below.

"Hey, Schaefer," she shouted. He looked up, startled, and glanced nervously around the many other soldiers answering the call of the bugle. She brandished the pages in one hand as she called, "You know this is in German, right?"

Henry scrubbed his face with his hands and shook his head, grimacing.

"Would you consider me a complete blockhead if I told you I forgot you don't know German?" he replied, loudly enough so that she could hear him over the din.

Perhaps it was some sort of strange and ignorant compliment, that he not only trusted her to read this truly vulnerable letter, but also that he assumed of her the same understanding as he. Or perhaps he was just so used to moving between two languages that he forgot other people don't have to do that.

"Yes!" she answered and she laughed at the absurdity of it, folding the letter back into its envelope and sticking it in her pocket.

—

XXXIII

HENRY WASN'T SURE IF it was his mother's letter hanging over him, or the prospect of encountering Charley in the tent later that had him more nervous, but whatever it was, it set him on edge enough that he made multiple stupid mistakes during company drill. Captain Noah was clearly still annoyed with him, and the mistakes only managed to further embarrass him after the misfire episode the previous day. His comrades didn't make it any easier and spent the hour before supper giving him grief about it. He tried his best to bear it good-naturedly, and he did for a while, but it got under his skin rather quickly, so he slipped away to do his warm-up routine by the river and get his head on straight.

He'd never done anything with a woman before. He knew what all to do—his father had clinically educated he and his brothers in gleeful defiance of Christian purity. Elias had also lent him a sordid yellow-jacket novel as an "illustrative example" back when they were working on the farm in Faribault that, to his great discomfort, served to both horrify and arouse him. His imagination had trod scenario after scenario to a well-worn path, his right fist there to make the sensation at least a partial reality. But to have Charley's hand do the job ... that had felt so singularly wonderful. The pressure to do the same for her, knowing he was not her first, made him supremely nervous. Especially since he wasn't entirely sure what Charley did to bring herself to such a state, not for want of trying to imagine. His father's very thorough lecture had visited strongly on male self-control and conception prevention, but had only touched vaguely on female pleasure. And from what he'd gleaned from novels and conversations with other men, it seemed to be some-what of a challenge. He was also concerned about the potential intersection between female pleasure and conception, but he figured if she could bring herself off, he could likely do the same without any danger of putting her in the family way.

There was a substantial part of his ego that desperately wished that he could simply sweep in and do everything just as she liked it, but he knew better. She had told him—all of the boys—that one needed only ask a woman what she would enjoy and trust her to guide him. He had every intention of doing just that, but it made it quite difficult to anticipate what might happen. He could only hope he would do her justice.

Charley had spent afternoon drills catching up on sleep in the guardhouse after her shift was done. In the cold and the rain, the large board where those who were off-duty could catch a few hours of sleep probably seemed much more appealing than it ever had when there was an actual bunk to nip off to. At 6 o'clock, just before supper, she went back on duty. Henry spent supper moving peas around on his tin plate, listening to Williamson and Krüger complain, justifiably in Henry's opin-ion, about the mundane and flavorless menu, and Webster re-laying his plan for an afternoon of furlough to get their *carte de visites* made in St. Paul. It seemed Osborn had agreed to ask the Lieutenant on their behalf.

Henry made a point to bring Charley some food when he finished with supper. Elias seemed more than happy to let him take on the task, as no one else seemed to remember Smith was not among them and Elias only because it was his duty as corporal to look out for such things. Charley gave him a smile and gratefully accepted the meal, but Henry didn't stay as the other two fellows from the other companies on the guard duty rotation were sleeping in the pallet, and Charley seemed reluctant to have him stick around and wake them with idle chatter. She did hand him his mother's letter back with a shrug, which he shoved deep in his pocket with every intention to continue avoiding it. He couldn't believe he'd asked her to read it. Why on earth would he assume she read German? She was right, he was a dunderhead.

By then it was after seven and the sun had set—as much as one could tell, at any rate, through the persistent cold and cloudy weather. Charley was on duty until 8 o'clock, and would then rejoin the rest of the squad until roll call and lights out at 9. After that, it was the long wait until everyone else fell asleep, then they only had a couple hours before she'd be off again for the midnight to 2 am guard duty. He would not blame her at all if she ended up sleeping the rest of the night off in the guardhouse and rejoining the squad at morning roll call. The thought, though, of being left alone after ... intimacy ... it annoyed him. Or perhaps he was annoyed that he was annoyed. Regardless, he was a bit surly as he joined his squad, along with the Hastings boys and Nelson's squad around a campfire centrally located at an intersection of two perpendicular rows of tents.

"So, what did your mother have to say, Schaef?" Jacob asked, looking up from a button he was attempting to sew back on his coat while still wearing it. Henry nearly turned on his heel to stalk right back down the row to his tent. But he settled on leveling a glare at Jacob and said nothing.

"Ah, that bad, eh?" Jacob replied with a sympathetic grimace. "No cookies then?"

"Definitely not," Henry said. He knew at least that much was true.

"Ah yes, how are all your tumbling buddies getting on?" Elias asked with a grin. The calming effects of Henry's warm up routine cracked, and he felt his temper darken.

"Now, now, leave him alone," Webster cut in, as if *he* were the corporal watching out for the interest of the squad.

Henry pretended he hadn't heard Elias and skirted the fire to get nearer to the Hastings boys. They were often passing around a flask, and if there was one on hand, he wanted a draught from it. Sam Corbett and his friends were off to one side, playing poker on someone's gum blanket with an oil lamp for light.

"Oh hi, Schaefer, wanna join?" Corbett asked and Henry, at a loss of what else to do and not terribly interested in talking to his own squadmates, agreed. He had time to kill. He was two swigs of whiskey and three hands down when he saw a shadowed figure walking towards the fire. The flickering light shadowed her brows and nose and Henry was reminded uncomfortably how well she passed for a boy. Or perhaps he was uncomfortable with the knowledge that even when she was passing, he still thought she was beautiful. Perhaps part of his hatred for Smith had been the discomfort of knowing he'd felt an attraction before he'd ever known she was a woman. That maybe Krüger was right about Turners, or at least about him. But then Charley joined the circle and her face was lit and his gaze was drawn to her deep eyes and the hunger they regarded him with as she caught sight of him in return.

"I fold," Henry said absently and set his cards down, standing.

"Where's he...?"

"Who cares? My turn! Royal flush, boys. Read 'em and weep."

The group groaned as Corbett cackled in triumph.

Henry picked his way back to the campfire as Jacob said, "Hi, Smith, how's the guard—OUCH!"

Jacob shook his hand out, having pricked his finger on his needle. Smith frowned at him and squinted at his mending.

"What are you doing to your coat?" Smith asked, his voice thick with judgment.

Jacob regarded him defensively and said, "Mending the button. We're going to get our CDVs made tomorrow."

"Oh, is that tomorrow?" Smith asked.

"Yeah, Osborn got it all fixed," Elias replied. "We'll still do morning drills, but we have the afternoon to go and have them made. Though heaven knows how, after the poor showing we've made the last few days." Henry met Elias' snotty glance with a glare of his own.

Smith blinked slowly at Jacob. "If you want to look your best, you may want to let me do that for you."

Jacob looked up at Smith for a moment then shrugged his coat off and handed it over to him. "*Hell* it's cold. Be quick about it, won't you?"

"Don't look a gift horse in the mouth." Smith took a seat on the ground next to Jacob near the fire, pulling the coat into his lap and taking up the needle and thread. Henry sidled along the edge of the fire, taking up the pretense of looking for a place to sit so as to move nearer to him. Her. It didn't help his unease how smoothly Charley moved in his mind between female and male.

"Jacob, where's your greatcoat?" Webster asked, his fatherly eyebrow quirked at Jacob shivering in his suspenders.

"In the tent. It'll only take a minute, right Smith?"

"Jesus," Smith swore, holding the needle out and trying to discern the tangle of threads around the button. "What did you do? Did your mother never teach you to sew a button?"

"His mother's dead," Elias said.

Smith raised a brow at Elias, then glanced at Jacob briefly before informing the corporal, "Well, that excuse never worked for me."

Jacob stared at her for a moment. The rest of the boys hesitated, the tension building before Williamson let out an awkward guffaw that sounded more like a bird squawk than a human laugh. It was enough to set the rest of the boys laughing. Henry shook his head. Smith was effective armor much of the time but it was a thin line between prickly and downright mean. Webster raised his eyebrows and quickly changed the subject to the photographer who had come highly recommended.

Jacob ignored them. After the group had sufficiently started in on CDV excitement, Jacob leaned over to Smith and said, "How'd yours go?"

Charley's nimble fingers stilled over the threads. Her hands were callused, strong, but elegant somehow. She had long fingers and she kept her nails clean, which was saying a lot considering the amount of mud and dust they tramped through at the fort. She blinked at Jacob for a moment and said, "Putting me into the world."

Henry's chest squeezed. He felt like an intruder, a cheap and lascivious observer to someone else's heartfelt moment. He envied Jacob, jealous that this coveted piece of Charley's past was being given to him. That shamed him, but not as much as his mother's unread letter weighing in his pocket.

"Mine was typhoid. When I was eight."

Charley regarded him for another moment. "Be glad you knew her."

"Every day," was his reply. Charley nodded, then returned her focus to the task at hand as Jacob shivered uncomfortably.

"Ugh," she grumbled as she picked a knot out of the thread.

"You don't have to," Jacob said sulkily.

"I'm not marching next to a soldier missing a button when I can do something about it." Smith got the thread free and deftly began anchoring the button shank to the fabric. "Really, Robinson, it's lucky you're married because apparently you can't handle even the simplest of mending."

This was loud enough that all the boys all laughed and Jacob smiled, though it didn't quite reach his eyes. Webster reached over and patted his knee. Their impending departure had Mary visiting nearly every day, and after she left, Jacob's countenance grew darker and darker. Henry was fairly sure that if his friend had the opportunity to stay at the Fort, or unenlist altogether, he would, but the army wasn't terribly amenable to that sort of change of heart.

Smith knotted the thread tight and broke it with his teeth. Then he handed the coat back to Jacob. He pulled it back on eagerly, shuddering in the cold.

"Thanks," he said begrudgingly.

"Say, Smith, while you're at it—" Elias started but Smith stood abruptly, dusted his hands on his trousers, and cut him off.

"Before you begin, Corporal, I'll have you all know that I am not about to be responsible for the squad's mending. If you want buttons sewn again, ask a laundress you can fairly compensate for it." Smith caught Henry's eye for a moment, his expression void of any feeling before he leveled his gaze back on their comrades. "Or—heaven forbid—learn to use a needle and thread yourselves. Goodnight, fellows."

Charley turned on her heel, and looked once more at Henry with great intention and significance, and walked off towards their tent. Henry couldn't help but watch her go.

"Isn't it a little early to be going to bed?" Williamson commented. "We haven't even heard Tattoo yet. He knows he's going to have to get back up for roll call, right?"

Henry shrugged, trying to simultaneously focus on the conversation around the fire and find an excuse to follow Charley back to the tent. With all the boys gathered by the fire, their tent would be relatively isolated—and private. Surely she didn't mean for him to come to her now, while everyone was still awake?

But she had given him a glance such that he thought that must have been what she intended.

"Hey, every minute of beauty sleep counts," he blathered, glancing back at the squad and giving a little belated shrug. "Especially when you look like him."

The boys laughed, and Henry smiled along with them, trying his best to fight the urge to follow her like a dog to his master. He hoped the jab might do well to cover his eagerness as he stood. "After all that bayonet drill, I'm beat, though. I think I might take a bit of a lay-down before roll call, too."

"Oh Schaefer, you know that won't work," Elias said. Henry looked up at him, perhaps a bit too sharply. "There's no amount of rest that will help you with—" he gestured around his face with his hand "—all this."

The boys all laughed. Henry smiled, rolling his eyes, and strode off, trying to get his heart to beat at a normal pace. Between Elias' comment, which had him fearful for a split second that Elias might suspect, and the anticipation that multiplied with every step, he couldn't manage it. Thank heavens that Krüger was in the barracks or something and wasn't around to glower at him suspiciously.

The tent flap had thawed during the day and smelled of damp canvas as he pulled it aside and climbed through. It was dark, the moon scarcely waxing and covered by a bank of low-lying clouds, so her face was shadowed when he entered. She'd removed her cap and had her blanket draped over her shoulders. She simply looked up at him and cleared her throat.

Henry tried to situate himself somewhat elegantly on his gum blanket but felt like he was all legs and muddy boots.

Everything inside the tent was as cold and damp as it was outside. He looked up at her, his arms draped over his knees, and tried to think of something dashing to say.

"Um," he managed.

"Everyone's by the fire," Charley whispered, and he felt more than saw her eyes regarding him intently. "This might be our best chance for at least some semblance of privacy."

Henry swallowed hard. This was it. This was when he was going to finally ... something. His mind reeled with possibilities and, he shifted his knees up in front of him to conceal his overly-eager response.

"Will we have time?" he croaked.

She regarded him plainly for a moment, her fingers gripping the blanket more tightly around her shoulders. He shifted forward onto one knee, doing his best to duck beneath the center pole of the tent as he leaned towards her. Her expression was inscrutable as she raised one hand to his chest.

"Before anything else happens, I need to tell you two things," she said quietly. Henry flinched back with surprise. His chest suddenly felt tight. What could she need to tell him now? Did she have a second husband? Or a child? Was she not even a woman after all? After the last few days, anything felt possible.

"Of course," he managed, sitting back.

"First," she whispered and took a deep breath, as though bracing herself, "I'm not taking my clothes off."

"I supposed as much," Henry agreed, trying to appear calm and casual, even as his heart hammered against his ribs.

"Second, you will not fuck me."

"Oh!" The exclamation had come out of him unbidden, such was his surprise. She peered at him sidelong.

"Is that a problem?"

"No, no, not at all, I just ..." he stammered, pushing his hand nervously through his hair and knocking his cap off. He fumbled for it but it dropped into the murky darkness somewhere on his gum blanket. "I'm sorry, I just didn't expect you to be so..."

"Clear?" she asked, her voice soft but somewhat confrontational. "I thought you said you liked a woman who says what she wants."

"I do, I do." He rubbed his face with a hand, cursing his foolish, tangled tongue. "I just ... well, I ..."

He looked up at her. The light was dim, but his vision had adjusted, and he could see her eyes more clearly now. They were wide, and her chin revealed an anxiety her voice had not betrayed.

"I don't have any assumptions about what might happen," he said quietly. "I mean, I know how these things may go, but I haven't ever ... that is ... I would appreciate some, uh, guidance."

She'd made him feel so unspeakably good this afternoon. He wanted to see her similarly undone, but he wasn't confident he could do that without her direction, especially if she didn't want to have him, well ... as she had said. What foolishness—he couldn't even think the words, and she'd had the confidence to say it aloud.

Charley's fingers were on the back of his hand, and he looked up at her, trying fiercely to hide how nervous and unmanned he felt.

"I know," she smiled, her other hand cupping the side of his face.

"You do?"

She shrugged. "What I hope you will do is something I've only ever done by myself, too."

It took him a moment to process what she was saying. He wanted to ask her to clarify, to explain what it was that she intended, that she had never done with anyone else, but that would have led to an inquiry, whether explicit or implicit, of what she had done with her husband, and he very much didn't want to know about that.

Her hand snaked behind his neck, and she delivered a soft kiss to his lips. He found he didn't hardly care about his lack of experience. She had made clear what she didn't intend, none of which honestly surprised him (the only surprising thing was that she had said it aloud instead of patiently guiding him away from what she did not want). The fact that she desired from him something she'd never known with her husband made him hard on its own, without knowing what the hell it even was. All he knew was the shuddering gasps he'd heard that night in the barracks, sounds that had taken on an entirely new color when she'd told him her secret, and he wanted to know precisely how to make her do that again.

His hands seized around her waist and pulled her close. Her waist was hidden in the unflattering drape of her sack coat, but when he placed his hands upon it, she felt so slight. Soft at the hip, curved, delicate in a way that made his hands feel large and powerful. She cupped his face with both hands, pulling him towards her as she parted her lips and tasted his. God, but she moved with such certainty that he found himself relaxing under her touch, trusting her intention. Her directness had been startling, but it also took the edge off. He'd always assumed when he ended up in a compromising position with a woman that he would be expected to lead, to determine his partner's desires through audacious trial and error, and the fact that she had no intention of even allowing him that, much less expecting it from him, was liberating.

He wasn't sure who initiated it, but in the next moment she was on his lap, her hips pressing indulgently into his groin. He let out a soft groan and smiled into her lips.

"Oh—" She abruptly pulled back from his kiss, and he blinked. "One more thing. We must both be silent."

He didn't hide the hunger in his gaze as he quietly replied, "I'll do my best."

She didn't breathe for a moment as she studied him. "You damn well better."

He kissed her hard this time, one hand grasping at her hair while the other seized her hip and pulled her into him. He was hard, and she could feel it, and judging by how she was rocking against him, she loved it. She sucked breath in through her nose and pressed her tongue into his mouth. It was a cold night, but he quickly forgot about it as her fingers traced hot urgency across his skin.

He let both of his hands travel up her sides, fingers finding the upper edge of her stays through her coat, and he turned his head to the side, kissing her jaw as he murmured, "Can I touch you?"

Her breath shuddered, and she nodded. His hands slid to the front of her chest, curving over the mound of her compressed breasts.

"Fuck, Henry, you make me want to throw all my contingencies out the window," she breathed in his ear, nipping at the lobe.

"I want to see you bare," he whispered back, "but it's not urgent. I can wait."

Her breath hitched, like she was suppressing an involuntary sound, and she seized his wrist and shoved his hand down between her legs, wedging his fingers between the two of them as she pressed her apex against them. The wool of their trousers was an unwelcome barrier, but he hesitated to breach them, not wanting to press his advantage in an unwelcome way. Her hand slid down his wrist so her fingers pressed against the back of his. Her fingertips moved as though she were operating a telegraph, rubbing out a code he did not understand but also did not question, and he followed her movements. His fingers pressed into the vague, wool-shrouded softness between her thighs and she sighed, tipping her head back.

Her knees squeezed around him, and he pulled his face back an inch to enjoy how her eyes squeezed shut and her breath panted through her lips. He wondered at her, not sure exactly what it was he was doing but delighted by the result, his cock straining against his trousers with increasing interest. She pulled at his hand, adjusting the placement of his fingers slightly and encouraged the movement anew, her other hand gripping his shoulder tightly, hard enough that her nails might have left a mark were it not for his wool coat.

"Goddamn mother fucker," she enumerated on a breath and sidled back, robbing him of the delicious heat and pressure of her on top of him. He nearly tried to stop her before she grabbed his lapels and pulled him after her. "You're incorrigible."

"How am I—" he began but choked on his words as she lifted her hips and unbuttoned her trousers, pulling her shirttails up and out of the way. It was too dark to discern much of anything, but he didn't need to, because she pulled him over her with such force that he came down hard on his elbow to catch himself from crushing her. She didn't seem to notice or care and pulled his hand back down between her legs, only this time, she pushed his fingers inside her trousers. Henry swallowed hard as his fingers pushed through coarse curls and then between, where her skin was hot and slick.

"See what you do to me?" she whispered. He shuddered and involuntarily bucked his erection against her hip. He curled his fingers farther, expecting to explore deeper, but she pulled him back up and prompted him once again to twitch his fingers, to circle and rub. As he did as he was bid, she pressed her mouth into his shoulder and softly moaned, leaving his hand to his work and pulling hard at both his shoulders.

He wondered at her, watching her expression strain, her hips rising to meet his fingers as she fluttered her eyes open and met his gaze. Her eyes were deep, clouded, animal-like, and if he could have fallen into them, he'd have drowned. As it was, he rutted against her hip, their heated breath mingling as he kissed her. He wanted her so bad, to push his cock into her, to feel her surrounding him as she shook and strained and curled up around him, breaking his kiss and panting into his ear.

She sounded like she was lifting something incredibly heavy and her skin was like fire against his fingers, slick even as her thighs pulsed, crushing his hand. She gripped his shoulders as she shook, straining in midair, her feet dug in as her hips arched off the ground. He watched her in wonder. The pains she took to try and stay quiet shot straight to his prick, and he hoped to fucking God she would work him over again when she was done, because if she didn't, he'd have to take matters into his own hands and they paled in comparison to hers.

"Ahh, too much, too much," she hissed and pulled at his wrist, where his fingers continued to work with singular focus, like they were made for nothing else. He stilled but did not remove his hand from her trousers. He could not see her, but he could feel her and she felt incredible. If his cock couldn't be between her legs, his fingers damn well would be. Her other hand skimmed up his neck and pulled him in by his hair for another kiss. He wasn't sure if she initiated or if he did, but his fingers slid down deeper into her folds, meeting searing wetness, and pushed inside of her so that soft, slick walls enveloped his first two fingers up to his knuckles.

She gasped into his lips and used her hold on his wrist to push his fingers deeper. He pulled his head back to watch her again with wonder. One second she was telling him too much, the next she was fucking herself on his fingers and ... and ... he couldn't even complete a thought he wanted her so damn much.

She looked wild, her hair tousled and her mouth gasping, heavy eyebrows slanted in ecstasy as her hips moved to meet his fingers. She bit her lip hard and her eyes squeezed shut as she shuddered again. Henry gaped at her as he felt her seize and strain around his fingers until he couldn't stand it anymore.

"Touch me, please," he begged, his words on a breath into her ear.

"Mmm." She reached for his trouser buttons with both hands even as she continued to rock herself on his fingers.

She wrestled his shirttails impatiently and seized his cock in both hands, one wrapped around and the other cupping over the head. It was the work of a few moments to get him to his peak. He shuddered with the rush and release and was extremely proud of the fact that he spent with no more sound than a huff of breath and a strained grunt.

Henry let himself hang off his forearm, his face pressed into her shoulder as he fought to catch his breath.

"Well..." she breathed. He lifted his chin and peered at her expression. Her eyelids were heavy and the corners of her mouth curled as she regarded him. "I'm gonna sleep well tonight."

He snorted in amusement and shifted his fingers out of her, snaking his hand over her hip and pulling her closer. He was sticky and he had every intention of changing his shirt before sleeping, but all that could wait. She was so warm and obliging, tucking her face into his chest, and it didn't even matter that they were tangled together across their gum blankets at a diagonal and his had shifted through the course of their efforts such that their thighs laid across a cold patch of trampled prairie grass.

"That was..." he trailed off, his nose in her hair reveling in her earthy scent.

"So good you can't think of a word for it?" she offered. He squeezed her tight and agreed with a rumbling murmur. She tipped her head up towards him, searching for his mouth, and he tilted his chin down to provide her ample access. They kissed, slowly, languidly, for a few moments, until the rhythm of the Tattoo tapped out, calling the men to the final roll call.

"No..." Charley grumbled unhappily, stealing a few more kisses before drawing away. After a few moments, footsteps padded past their tent and they heard the friendly banter of their comrades as they assembled at the head of their tent row.

With the imminent presence of their squad upon them, Charley pulled quickly away and stuffed her shirttails back into her trousers, buttoning urgently. Henry scrambled away from her, trying to restore his gum blanket to rights while on top of it (futile, he soon realized). He was uncomfortably damp and he pulled his handkerchief out of his pocket and tried to resolve the mess he'd made of his shirttails before he gave up and stuffed the damp cotton back into his trousers. He'd change it later and send a bundle to the laundresses in the morning. He supposed it was futile to hope they would not notice the cause of its soil.

"Wake up, beauty queens," Jacob exclaimed as he thwapped at their tent. Charley startled hard and the branch frame shook precariously. The center pole must have slipped out of the bifurcated branches of the front pole, because canvas came collapsing down over their heads.

Henry suffered very brief disorientation before he swore loudly, which elicited a raucous guffaw from outside. Charley grappled with the canvas for a moment before throwing it off them both.

The boys veritably pointed and laughed as Henry and Charley glared at them, their disheveled appearance made more so by the collapsed canvas.

"Goddammit Jacob, what the hell?" Henry exclaimed, supremely annoyed that not only did he now have to get up for roll call, but he also had to reset their tent in the dark.

"Robinson, I'm going to murder you," Smith shouted and sprang up, taking only a few long strides toward Jacob before the other boy bounded away, slamming right into Osborn.

"Wha—Robinson, get off! What's all this now?"

Henry dashed after Smith and grabbed her round the chest to stop her from trying to punch Robinson in the balls. Jacob stumbled back from Osborn and grinned sheepishly.

Osborn took in the collapsed canvas, the circle of laughing men, and looked for a moment like he might send them all to the guardhouse before he sighed and commanded, "Squad ROLL CALL."

———

XXXIV

St. Paul, Minnesota
Monday, Oct. 7, 1861

THE PHOTOGRAPHER FIXED THE plate into the camera box and disappeared under the drape hung over the back. Cate shifted nervously on the chair, straightening her sack coat and feeling hyper aware of her hands.

"Stay very still, sir," the photographer said, his voice muffled by the cloth. "I shall prompt you when you may change your pose."

"That won't be necessary," Cate replied. "We will each get one image on the paper and share it between us."

"Up to you," the photographer said, suggesting he disagreed with this strategy but didn't particularly care one way or the other. The drape shrugged with his shoulders.

How the hell did Cate get wrangled into being the first photographed? She would have expected the others to be eager, but they had tried to provoke each other to go first until finally she'd had enough of their petty posturing and volunteered. Cate squared her shoulders and tried to look seriously into the lens, though there were four fixed into the camera box in a square, and she wasn't too certain which she should look at in particular. She supposed the upper left, but perhaps the photographer would begin with his upper left, which would be her upper right—it was too much to determine, so she just sighed inwardly and fixed her eyes upon the spot at the center of the lenses.

"Very good, sir," the photographer said. "Hold that there..."

He reached around the camera box and pulled the cap from the front of the first lens, his upper right and her upper left. Cate resisted the temptation to flick her eyes at the selected lens and concentrated on staying completely still. After what felt like an eternity, but was likely more like thirty seconds, the photographer replaced the cap rather anticlimactically and popped his mustachioed face out from under the drape. "Well done. Are you sure you wouldn't like another pose?"

"Yes," Cate said, perhaps a little too tersely, as she rose and thumbed Robinson to the wooden chair. It was staged at an angle next to a round side table covered with an embroidered tablecloth. Behind it all was a long drape hung from a rod near the tin ceiling, light blue and setting off the shade of their uniform trousers.

Cate breathed for what felt like the first time in a whole minute and gratefully retreated to the back of the room where the others stood in a circle, watching the process and fussing with their hair. Jacob leapt double quicktime and settled himself on the chair, crossing and uncrossing his legs in indecision. Cate shook her head.

"How was it?" Williamson asked.

Cate shrugged. "I sat still for a minute. Nothing special, really."

"Have you never had your photograph made?" Webster asked Williamson. The boy grinned sheepishly.

"No, we always lived so far out of town. It would have been a real fancy treat."

"Well, I'm sure your mother will be delighted to receive this one."

"I wish I could get a whole set."

"Too bad *Vater* Lincoln can't be bothered to pay us all on time," Krüger grumbled. "If we had our wages, we could all get a set each instead of having to pool together."

The rest of the men grumbled in agreement. Wages were late, but of course they were. There was a war on, etcetera.

"Alright, Jacob's next," Hower directed. "Schaef, you're on deck. Fellow says he needs to get the plate to his assistant in five minutes or it'll get all dried out."

The photo studio was a lovely room on the third floor of a brick building on Wabasha and Third Street in Saint Paul, with tall panels of windows in the southerly-facing wall, bathing the room in ample sunshine. The photographer also had a large mirror set up to reflect even more light onto his subject. His assistant, a boy no more than fourteen, waited at his side for the plate to be completed. The *carte de visites* were made in a small postcard size, and while the photographer did his damndest to get each of them to purchase a set of four, as his camera had four lenses to do the work quickly, they had opted to try and save a penny and split each set among themselves. This seemed to irritate the photographer, and when Jacob was through, he shouted rather impatiently, "Come now, next!"

Henry hustled to the chair and sat gingerly, arranging his trousers. Cate watched as he patted his thick hair down and fixed his kind, open eyes on the lenses. She refused to acknowledge anything resembling a feeling squeezing in her chest.

"Stay very still, sir," the photographer intoned and removed the lens cap. Henry looked like he desperately wanted to blink, but he managed for the obligatory thirty seconds before the lens cap was replaced, when he squeezed his eyes shut and swore in German.

"Next, next!" the photographer called more urgently. "We only have a minute before we need to get this plate into the developer."

Osborn shoved Williamson forward, and the boy stumbled once over his overly large feet but sat with a fair amount of dignity for someone with such big ears.

At the back of the studio, there was a sofa, wood with red velveteen upholstery, and Cate wandered over and sat gingerly, looking out the window. The walk to Saint Paul had been tiring after a morning of drills, but having now made the trip, she was looking forward to having the rest of the afternoon free. It sounded like it wouldn't take very long for their plates to develop and be printed onto cardstock for their *carte de visites*, so they had spent the walk here chatting amiably about what they might do before heading back to the fort for Tattoo. Regardless of the many conflicting ideas that had been pitched, they were all in agreement that they would find someplace to get a good, hot meal. The fare at the fort was dreary indeed, and growing drearier the more they complained.

She was roused from her thoughts as Henry flopped onto the other side of the sofa, obscuring her view out the window with his angular profile. She unconsciously scooted away to ensure there was space between them, glancing at the other fellows to make sure they didn't appear too suspicious.

"Did you keep your cap on?" he asked conversationally.

"No, I took it off," she replied quietly, trying not to meet his eye. She was reminded of the previous night, when he'd gotten flustered and fumbled his cap into the dark of their tent. And there she went again. Thinking about it when she'd told herself she wouldn't. Because every time she did, she could feel her body heat up. She couldn't blush every time Henry Schaefer said anything to her. Someone would eventually notice and suspect.

They had been damn lucky it had been dark out when Robinson had toppled their tent. Lucky they'd had their more vulnerable parts concealed by that point. She had been utterly terrified and ready to murder Jacob Robinson. By the time she and Henry had gotten the tent poles back up in the pitch dark, the rest of the bastards were asleep—because heaven forbid any of them volunteer to help.

It had been such a satisfying encounter up to the point of the tent collapsing, so why did she feel so embarrassed now? Henry sought her company at breakfast, at dinner, and on the walk to Saint Paul, but she had been so awkward and tongue-tied, she had no idea what to say to him. All she could think of was how good he'd made her feel, how responsive he'd been to even the most minute of directives, and she couldn't stop thinking about that every time she looked at him. She had known from the start that it'd been a stupid, reckless risk, and now that the tension had broken, that they'd had their pleasure at the other's hand, the fog of need had cleared somewhat and she was left feeling rather ... exposed.

Certainly, she would like to do it again. But where? When? They were surrounded by men every minute of every day, waking and sleeping, and they were about to ship out any day now. What they'd done in both the guard house and the tent had been careless to the point of idiocy. Robinson had made that abundantly clear. She fully blamed Henry's goddamn thighs for it, because if he'd been anything less than a perfect ham hock of man-flesh, she would have been able to resist. At least, that was what she'd been telling herself all day.

If it had been different circumstances, if she'd been dressed as a woman, if there had been privacy even, or a spare room she could have hosted him in, then it wouldn't be so bad. As tempting as he was, as much as she wanted him, she could *not* risk another incident like last night. If Robinson had come by just five minutes earlier, he would have heard them. He would have suspected. If he'd knocked their tent down, she'd have been caught with her pants around her knees. She would already be back at Richard's house by now, chastened and scrubbing his fucking dinner dishes.

Henry raised an eyebrow at her. "Penny for your thoughts?"

Cate grimaced at him. "No. Certainly not right now."

"I was, uh, thinking," he mumbled under his breath, slouching down to watch Webster try a pose with his head resting smartly on his fist, "maybe, after this, we could—"

"I'm gonna stop you right there, Schaefer—"

"But we're shipping out soon—"

"No, there's no way. Nobody books a hotel room in the middle of the day with no intention to keep it overnight without being the *embodiment* of suspicion."

"Hotel room? What kind of money do you have floating around in those pockets of yours?"

She glowered at him.

"What are you guys talking about?" Williamson chirped, stepping over to stand before them. Cate's heart leapt into her throat, and she almost made a gasp of surprise.

"Jesus, nothing, go away." Cate pressed her fingers to the bridge of her nose. Williamson continued to stare at her expectantly. She rolled her eyes and added, "Just how stupid Schaefer is."

Williamson barked a laugh, then bounded to Hower and Robinson next to join their conversation.

"Are you, uh, having second thoughts?" Henry whispered, leaning forward on his knees and not looking at her.

Cate wanted to snap that yes, she was having second thoughts and please leave her the hell alone, but when she glanced at his face, she could perceive how brittle his casual countenance was. And if she said she wanted him to leave her alone, it would have been a lie. She wanted the opposite, and that was precisely the problem, but given the conditions, her ambitions of fighting in the war and having Schaefer between her legs were not compatible. And it was obvious to her which was more important.

Cate let out a sigh and stood. "We can talk about it later."

She walked over to the others, standing just outside their circle and very concertedly not looking at the angry and hurt expressions battling for control over Henry's eyebrows.

———

XXXV

Cate held the cardstock photo in her hands. It was about 4 inches by 6, a quarter of the wet plate the photographer had made, and she thought she looked quite dashing in it. Her brows shadowed her eyes, her mouth was pressed grim and determined, and she looked a right soldier in her uniform.

"Let's see yours then," Jacob exclaimed, snatching her CDV from her and shoving his into her hands to admire. "Ah, very Smithy."

"Thank you," she deadpanned. "It's too bad you look like such a ignoramus in yours."

"Did you really smile for a whole half minute?" Hower asked. Jacob narrowed his eyes and snatched his card away from her.

"Look, I'm in the army and I'm happy about it, alright?"

"You are not. You're just putting on a brave face for the missus."

"Fine. I'm *married* and I'm happy about it. Are you satisfied?"

Hower shrugged. His CDV featured him looking sidelong at the camera with an imperial expression, as though he were looking down his nose at the viewer. He'd turned three-quarters to ensure that his corporal stripe was on full display. His essence perfectly captured, in Cate's opinion.

"Shall we find some supper then?" Webster asked. They were standing out on the street at the corner of Wabasha and Third Streets, trading CDVs and shuffling around each other on the corner outside the photographer's building.

"It's only 3 o'clock," Osborn said with a raised brow.

"Lord knows you're an old man, Webster, but surely you'll be able to make it until 5?" Hower teased.

Cate glanced over at Henry, who was looking down at his CDV and then off over his shoulder at the river bluff. He'd been petulant ever since she'd put him off. Cate pressed her lips together to hold back any guilt that tried to surface and redoubled her efforts to focus on what the other boys were saying.

"In the meantime, I saw a saloon with billiards just there," Krüger offered with a conspiratorial grin, pointing across Wabasha Street at the tall, four-story stone building. Jacob looked intrigued but ultimately shook his head.

"That sounds fun, but I'm meeting Mary for the rest of the afternoon. I'll meet up with you all at 6 o'clock, at Seven Corners?"

Osborn nodded and waved as Robinson trotted off up Wabasha Street. Then the Sergeant turned back to the group and shrugged. "I'd rather take a walk around Rice Park and enjoy this break in the foul weather."

"I'll join you," Webster said. "I want to see the new opera house."

John Williamson looked over at Krüger and Hower as the older men walked off.

"Well, I guess we're the only ones young enough to have a good time," Hower exclaimed and started off toward the saloon, Krüger and Williamson close behind. Cate started after them, but halfway across Wabasha Street, she realized Henry was not following. Glancing over her shoulder, she saw him ranging off toward the river bluff with his hands in his pockets. She looked back at the other boys for a moment.

"Hey, get out of the road!"

She startled and dashed to the nearest side of the street, towards Henry. A matron passing on the sidewalk frowned at the teamster in the road, then said kindly to Cate, "Please beg your pardon, sir. Thank you for your service."

Cate couldn't manage much more than a startled nod before she dashed off after Henry. She looked over both of her shoulders, even as she knew it would make her look supremely suspicious, and then followed him around the side of the building where the photographer had his studio.

She caught up with him as he slipped behind the building. There were a few warehouses at the top of the bluff, just east of the Wabasha Street bridge. The bridge spanned the wide river from a great height, connecting the bluffs on either side. It was the only bridge that crossed the Mississippi this far north, apart from the one that connected Minneapolis and St. Anthony. The other nearest bridge was all the way down in Illinois.

"Hey, where are you going?" she asked and was surprised when Henry startled.

"Oh, uh," he regarded her with a mixture of surprise and wariness. "I was just going to read my mother's letter."

"You *still* haven't read it?"

Henry scratched the back of his neck guiltily and shrugged. Cate dithered for a moment.

"Oh. Well. I suppose you'd like some privacy. I'll just—"

"—No, don't," he said, grabbing her wrist before she could retreat back to the saloon. "That is, I'd rather—"

He dropped her wrist and his mouth twisted up in frustration and confusion. Cate felt a pang of guilt as she simultaneously tried to force herself to double-down on distancing herself from him while wanting to kiss his mouth until it relaxed.

She gave out an irritated sigh and pushed his shoulder, urging him on ahead behind the building to where they would presumably find more privacy than bustling Third Street. They walked between the building and a tall bridge-house, behind which were worn footpaths snaking through prairie grass that lead to several warehouses perched on the edge of a steep, tall bluff. The view was spectacular. Cate rounded the south side of the first warehouse and sat on the grass, leaning her back against the clapboard and wrapping her arms around her knees. The rain had cleared and the sun shone bright, scarcely a cloud in the sky, warming the sodden river valley pleasantly as golden leaves fluttered on the breeze.

Schaefer rounded the corner of the warehouse and stood beside her, looking down at her as he made to tuck his CDV into his pocket.

"Wait, can I see it?" Cate asked, looking up and holding her hand out. Henry shrugged and handed his photograph to her. He looked so smart in his uniform, his cheeks freshly shaven and his stiff, straight hair combed back. His pale eyes looked into the camera with a pleasant sense of curiosity.

Cate's eyes flicked up at him. "Very handsome," she remarked in a tone that she hoped would be mistaken for sarcasm but wasn't.

"Thanks," he replied and looked down at the CDV, leaning against the warehouse with a sigh. "I thought I would bite the bullet and send it to my mother."

"That would be very appropriate," she said.

"Unless ... unless you want it?"

Cate looked up at him in genuine surprise. "Me? No. Why would I—"

Henry shook his head. "Never mind, it's stupid. I just thought, most fellows, you know, if they have a girl—"

This was when Cate was supposed to tell him she wasn't his girl. Set a firm boundary, let him know where he stood. But she was too busy trying to put out the friendly little fire his words had lit in her heart.

When she spoke, her voice was surprisingly gentle. "I—I'm flattered. But ... I'll still get to see you everyday. Send it to your mother. She needs it more than I do."

Henry's eyes were drawn, almost sad, as he looked at her. Then he nodded and put the CDV in his pocket.

A silence grew thick between them. After a minute, when it became clear neither of them had anything to add, Henry pulled his mother's letter out of his pocket and unfolded it. Cate looked at her hands and tried to order her thoughts.

How could she tell him that she just couldn't risk being caught again? After she had done just that yesterday? Happily, in fact. Twice. How could she make him understand that it was just too close for comfort, that the tents weren't safe for her to do anything with him even if they were technically alone. If she told him this, would he not want her anymore? Would he stop speaking to her or treat her differently? She supposed if that were the case, she had better know now. Before that fire in her heart grew any larger. She turned and gathered her courage to lay the line.

But as soon as her eyes turned onto Henry's, the words rather died on her lips.

"Are you alright?" she asked, pushing herself to her feet upon seeing his expression. Henry let out a long, low breath.

"She says to come home," he said roughly, and then cleared his throat. His eyebrows twitched in an effort to maintain composure. "It sounds like my father is becoming more and more eager to enlist himself, and she's afraid he'll leave her to fend for herself."

Henry's mouth was pressed in a thin line.

"Many women are being left in similar conditions," Cate couldn't help but point out as she looked in futility over his shoulder at the foreign script. "Surely your Turner society will provide support."

Henry's exhale shook slightly. "Yes, they will. That's true."

His eyes skimmed over the first page, then the second, and he swallowed hard. Cate regarded him with concern. "What else?"

He groaned and shook his head. "She's laying it on thick. Who will run the farm, who will protect them from Indians, who will escort them to *Turn Halle* and on and on. And of course, it's my duty to return and support them, since it's my fault my brothers enlisted and I lied about joining the First, so I owe it to her to return." He let out a disgusted grunt of frustration and scrubbed his face with one hand.

"Did she say it was your brothers who tipped her off?" Cate couldn't help but ask.

"They did. Peter said he wasn't going to keep lying to her in his last letter. But she's gone for the omnipotent, 'I'm your mother, I know everything' tack."

Cate shook her head and sighed. "Why do parents seem to feel the need to simultaneously complain that their children need them and then also get angry when their children do not need them?"

Henry let out a humorless chuckle and sagged against the wall, pushing his hair up with his hand in frustration. "I don't even see why I should bother. I kept waiting to write to her until I had some sort of tangible success to share. But I should know by now that nothing I do will ever be enough."

"Amen," Cate agreed, leaning against the wall next to him and nudging him with her shoulder. Her touch earned a side-long glance from him.

"I suspect your father is the same way, then?"

Cate gave a hollow laugh. "Most definitely. Except it's not that he's angry that I don't need him. It's that he doesn't trust me to do what he wants once independent. As if that matters to him one jot."

"What happened to your mother," Henry asked, then quickly amended, "if I may ask, that is."

Cate glanced up at him and considered him for a moment. His blue eyes regarded her with curiosity and a bit of shame, as though he thought he shouldn't ask, but he didn't care enough to stop himself. Cate shook her head and looked at the ground, "She died. Not much to tell."

"When you were born?" he ventured.

Cate's mouth twisted. "Yes, I was just a baby. It broke my father's heart. He loved her. He didn't even know me. He couldn't help but blame me. He left me with my grandparents—her parents."

"I think you said they passed away, right?"

Cate nodded her head and tried to push away at the tightness that strapped around her chest, concentrating on taking a deeper breath.

"Mmhm. Cholera. When I was twelve." Cate picked at her fingernail until it broke. She ripped it off, leaving a jagged edge. "I nursed them, then buried them, before my father ever showed up."

Pale blue lips dry-heaving over a chamber pot. Shaking hands, wasting skin and bone. Dark putrid smells and the hopelessness in the eyes of the doctor. She gritted her teeth and pushed that life away, hard. Her chest and shoulders clenched with the effort. "The only way I could bear it was because I was certain it would take me too. I never expected to have to remember that."

"Charley."

Cate's head snapped up, and she could have sworn for a split second, his lips were blue too. She stumbled back into the clapboard wall and shook her head hard.

"Are you alright?" He set his hand on her forearm, his brows furrowing with concern.

"Yes, I'm fine," She shook his hand off. "Christ, it was almost fifteen years ago. Of course I'm alright."

"Let's sit down," he said and he held her hands as she slid to the grass. He leaned in and gripped one of her shoulders. "Breathe."

Cate laughed somewhat hysterically. "What are you talking about? I'm fine. I'm just..."

She looked up into his eyes just then and the words fell away. There was no hiding from his keen gaze. His thumb grazed over cheek and she realized with horror that he had swept a tear away. When had she started crying?

"You don't have to be fine," he said.

She swallowed hard. "I would much rather be fine, if it's all the same to you."

He laughed. "Wouldn't we all?"

She scrubbed her face with her hands. "Dammit, anyone on the bridge can easily see us."

Henry looked up at the bridge, then craned his neck as though to see around the side of the wall they sat against. "Maybe this warehouse is open..."

He stood and rounded the corner. She turned, watching the corner he'd disappeared around. Heard the door creak open through the rushing sounds of her breath in her ears. Henry appeared again and grinned, a perfect slice of teeth, an unguarded expression that sliced through the straps that had tightened around her chest. She let him take her hand as he pulled her to her feet.

Inside, barrels, pots, and bags of brewer's barley and malt lined the walls, stacked haphazardly towards the front and more orderly toward the back of the building, perhaps only fifteen feet deep. It reminded Cate sharply, both in smell and atmosphere, of the shed she'd used in Minneapolis to change into her male clothing for the first time. As her eyes blinked to adjust to the dim light inside the little wooden building, she saw Henry a few paces away regarding her carefully.

"Here, sit down." He gestured to a short barrel stowed near the door. She sat on it gingerly.

"Henry, I'm fine. It was a long time ago. I don't want to talk about it."

"Alright." He pulled another barrel over and sat on it next to her. He sat there in silence, looking around for a moment. "Shall I distract you?"

Cate felt the heat rush into her cheeks as much more welcome memories from last night washed away the other ones. "Yes, please."

He looked at her quite startled and said, "I thought you were having second thoughts."

"I said nothing of the sort." God, her stupid mouth.

His brow furrowed and he said, "No, I asked you if you were having second thoughts and you said—"

"—I said we should talk about it later."

He blinked. "Well, is it later yet?"

She sighed. "Is there any chance we can just … kiss … and not talk about it?"

"No. I think we have to talk about it first."

"Because if you really want to help me feel better—"

"—Charley," he said warningly. "I'm not going to take advantage of you after you cried about your dead grandparents."

"What if I want you to?" She tried to smile winningly. He just shook his head at her.

She sighed. "It's just—Robinson really startled me last night. If he'd come round five minutes earlier—Christ, I shudder to think."

Henry nodded. Cate looked down at her hands. "I just don't know how we can do it. There's nowhere to be alone together. I keep thinking it might be different when we ship out. Picket duty and such. But it's so fraught. We're always going to be outside, where anyone can come along. I just don't see how we can manage it."

"By it you mean…"

"The, uh, canoodling, yes."

"You know that's not the only thing I want with you, right?"

Cate blinked. "I mean, I—well, no. What is it that you want from me?"

Henry paused for a moment. "I'm not sure. I never really imagined I'd fall for someone I was enlisted with. I'm not sure how these things go."

"I'm not sure they do. I imagine our situation is rather singular."

"I just..." he considered her for a long moment, his eyes searching hers. "Who knows what we'll find at the front. I don't want to regret anything."

She managed a small smile. "I think in that, our desires align." He returned it, an expression soft and tender and that little flame she'd felt heating in her chest flared like he'd tossed a handful of dry kindling on it. She really hoped she wouldn't regret this.

Cate stood up and made a point to thoughtfully consider the dim warehouse around them. "Do you suppose we might... *regret* it if we don't take advantage of the privacy of this place just now?"

She suppressed a smile and tried her best not to look too eager.

"Insatiable!" Henry chided, but he was grinning. Cate's smile escaped, and she reached out, snatching the collar of his uniform and pulling him towards her. The momentum she'd set off caught her by surprise with its force and she stepped back so that he had her pinned against the door. He didn't hesitate to dip his chin and claim her mouth with his. She met his lips eagerly, drinking in his warmth and pressure. She kissed her way over his jaw, scratchy with stubble a mere handful of hours after his morning shave and snaked one hand around to seize a handful of his firm backside.

"God, you're greedy," he said, his hands raking up her sides and catching the wool of her uniform with them. She captured his mouth again with hers and surrendered herself to the oblivion of sensation, arching her back into his hands as he explored over the upper edge of her stays, his fingers catching on the buttons as though asking for permission.

"Ah," she gasped, lifting her chin slightly to part their lips. "Do it."

He grinned, lopsided mouth and straight teeth and the hungriest hooded eyes lighting a goddamn fire in her belly. His fingers, up inside her coat, fumbled with the top button of her stays. She let out a frustrated sigh and pushed his hands away, unbuttoning her sack coat and waistcoat with swift fingers. The sides fell away to show her stays in the filtered light. She slipped the buttons of the stays next, then the smaller buttons of the shirt that she wore underneath.

"That's a lot of buttons," Henry stated dumbly, his eyes fixated as she worked, revealing a widening V of skin down her neck. She glanced up, suddenly taken with a wave of self-consciousness, and pulled his hands back up, slipping them beneath the neckline of the shirt. His hands pressed in eagerly, skimming over the firm buds of her nipples and cupping her breasts, fully claiming them in his palms. Her breath shuddered as he kissed her and she could feel his aroused response press into her belly as he passed his thumbs back over her nipples again.

"I want to see you," he murmured into her mouth, and she couldn't help but wrinkle her nose with how much that mortified and appealed to her simultaneously. She dipped her head and squeezed her eyes shut, but she nodded as he stepped back. He pulled the edges of her shirt aside, exposing her.

"Yes," he exhaled heavily, "you are most definitely the fairer sex."

Cate opened her eyes to look up incredulously at him. "I'm sorry, was that in *question* after last night?"

He shook his head, his eyes drinking her in and his lips quirked in amusement. "Certainly not."

He looked back up at her and he grinned mischievously. "It's just such a pleasant reminder every time, especially after having to spend the day with Smith."

She huffed in amusement, which turned into a sharp intake when his thumbs returned to circle her nipples again. "You keep talking about me like I'm someone else when we're not alone."

"You are," he murmured, bending to kiss her neck. "When you're Smith, you're in your disguise. I thought it would be helpful to think of you as 'him' when you're Smith."

"That is helpful, I suppose," she managed, her eyelids fluttering as his lips made their way down over her collar bone and she intensely anticipated where he intended to take this trail of kisses.

"But every time I realize I'm speaking to Smith, I just wish I were with you," he continued. "He's a bastard, but you..."

Henry tasted one nipple with his tongue and her toes curled in her boots. She bit her lip, the sensation and the exposure and the newness of the touch colliding in a sweet thrill that raced through her blood and dropped heavily between her legs. A quiet whimper escaped her throat.

"...You are just so..." he continued and his teeth scraped gently and she wanted to punch him in the gut for how he was torturing her.

"Yes, yes, I am many things," she gasped, her hands fumbling blindly at her trouser buttons. "Chief among them, needing your hands here."

And she pulled his left hand down and shoved his fingers between her thighs. His voice rumbled with pleasure.

"I was going to say decisive," he pointed out, and she shook her head.

Cate didn't need to show him what to do this time. As soon as she got his hand in the right spot, he played his fingers between her thighs in ways that made her legs feel like aspic, that made her sag against the door of the warehouse. She pressed her chest to his mouth and her hips to his hands such that she was suspended between her shoulders on the door and her toes on the earthen floor.

"Yes, Henry," she moaned without thinking, clutching his hair in her hand. His tongue drew circles around her nipple and it shook her with sensation, like there was some sort of conduit directly linked between her chest and her thighs. She wanted everything. She wanted his fingers and his mouth and his cock in her hand, inside her, she wanted all of it. At the same time, impossibly, but it wasn't rational, this wanting. It was urgent and animal and compounding, and she could scarcely breathe, much less form a coherent thought as she scrabbled haphazardly at his trousers. His right hand met her fingers and unfastened the buttons for her. She wormed her hand inside and grasped hard, velvety flesh and wished—*wished*—he could just fuck her and she could just enjoy riding him without having to worry about becoming fucking pregnant.

His breath was hot and fast on her breast now, and she pulled his hair insistently with one hand as she worked him with the other. He pressed his fingers into her, his thumb riding on the spot that sent quakes reverberating through her limbs as his other two fingers pumped inside of her, mirroring the rhythm she set with her hand around his cock. She distantly, quietly reflected that this was exactly what she had previously determined was not worth the risk and could only judge herself completely deluded because this was *everything*. Her hips moved to meet his fingers. She shuddered as her pleasure pulsed with increasing intensity, and she was distantly aware that she was moaning, and not quietly, so she pressed her lips into his hair.

Her crest was like a loud crack snapping through her body, a delicious, rolling reverberation that seized every muscle in her body as it passed. He tipped his chin so that his stubble scraped between her breasts. She gripped him tighter, pulling at the length of him frenetically.

"God, Henry, I wish you could fuck me," she mumbled, not entirely meaning to say it aloud, but there it was, the sounds falling off her lips.

"Oh, Charley, oh," he groaned and shuddered, his hand tangling up in the hair at the back of her neck and gripping as he spent on the dirt floor. Cate watched him hungrily, watched his cheeks flush and his mouth gape and she couldn't remember why the army had seemed so important after all, if it meant to come between her and *this*.

They leaned upon each other for a moment, panting.

"So...about those regrets," Cate murmured after a minute or two, and grinned as Henry's face snapped up to look at her with some alarm.

Henry regarded her seriously. "I've got none whatsoever. Do...do you?"

She smiled. "None whatsoever. I think we've applied ourselves quite courageously."

He smiled incredulously and laughed into her shoulder, a laugh that quickly turned into a rather helpless moan.

"God, Charley, look at you," he said, straightening to admire her in all her disheveled glory, her uniform haphazardly unfastened like some sort of ridiculous classical painting with conveniently revealing togas. "You're magnificent."

Cate grimaced even as she felt herself blush. "You're just saying that because mine are the only breasts you've actually seen in real life."

"True, but irrelevant," he countered and gave the said breasts an appreciative squeeze that made Cate squirm with sensitivity. "I've seen plenty of pictures and these far exceed any I've encountered."

"That is patently ridiculous," Cate replied, trying to hide that his blatant flattery was actually working by batting his hands away and ducking her chin to button her layers back up. "Of course they're better than a photograph. For one thing, they're bigger than anything you'll find on a postcard."

"Decidedly," he agreed with a grin, as he tucked himself back into his trousers and shuffled his shirt beneath his waistband. "And much softer and warmer than albumen paper."

Cate squeezed her eyes together and shook her head, trying to hide the fact that he was making her blush. Which was stupid, because judging her breasts finer than egg white emulsion on photographic paper was hardly a compliment.

"But in all seriousness," he went on, pausing and tilting his head, "you are beautiful."

Cate's lip curled and she looked away. "You *really* don't have to say that."

"But it's true," He reached out to tip her chin up to him with his knuckles. He smiled with one quirked eyebrow. "I don't need to see a world's worth of naked women to call a spade a spade."

She was mortified to feel her eyes prick and her stomach flip. Her face must have looked like she was trying to hold back a wave of nausea, and yet, he still looked at her like he believed what he was saying. She couldn't bear it. Her fingers fumbled with the button of her trousers.

"I'm sure the others are wondering where we are," she said a little too loudly, just as he said, "You *are* beautiful, you know."

She wrinkled her nose like he'd just said something disgusting and turned to the warehouse door. "Stop it, just let that go, would you? You're being ridiculous."

Henry grinned and snaked his arms around her waist. "I'm not, it's true, and I won't have any *regrets* about not convincing you of it."

She made a show of swatting his familiar hands away even as she tilted her head to the side to provide access for the kiss he placed on her neck. "Quit it, you're incorrigible."

His hand pressed against her hip in a way that made her feel claimed. Goddamn Henry Schaefer, if he broke her heart she would regret it. But how could she ask him for promises when they were facing down the front lines of a war? How could one live with no regrets *and* no guarantees?

"You like it," he teased back.

She did, she really really did, but that was neither here nor there. If she let him carry on, she might end up in an even more compromising position and that was not something they had the time nor the capacity for at present. So she pushed the door open and strode out, a show of impartiality that she hardly felt.

"Don't forget you have to write a letter to your mother," she reminded, scrabbling for the least flirtatious words she could find as she led the way out into the sunlight.

"Now who's incorrigible?"

———

XXXVI

Fort Snelling, Minnesota
Monday, Oct. 14, 1861

HENRY DUG THROUGH HIS knapsack again, his brow furrowed in frustration as he pushed his things from one side to the other one more time. Spare shirt, pencil, hussif, socks, more socks, letter from his mother, a folded back-issue of *Blätter für freies religiöses Leben*. He could have sworn he'd tucked it into the folds of the *Blätter,* but he shook out the whole paper and it was nowhere to be found.

"Hurry up," Charley barked from outside the tent. She was already rolling up her gum blanket with her wool one, strapping it to the top of her knapsack. The regiment was packing up and heading out to the front. Orders had arrived calling them to Washington D.C. and everyone was at once anxious and eager to get out of Fort Snelling.

The fort had been teeming with civilians for the past two weeks, but the place was absolutely crawling with them today, as mothers, fathers, wives, and children bid their boys farewell. And what was Henry doing on this most auspicious day? Trying to find his French letter, of course. What else?

Even as he felt like an utter imbecile for wasting time on such a stupid and completely inappropriate task (not to mention unimportant—there was a war on, for God's sake), he couldn't help but check his haversack one more time to make sure. Ever since the encounter he'd had with Charley in the St. Paul warehouse, he'd heard her words echo in his mind whenever he had a free moment. *I wish you could fuck me.* Oh, he wished too. He wished so very much. And the most frustrating part was that he *had* the means to make it possible, if he could only find the goddamn French letter his father had given him, along with his brothers, when they'd left to enlist in the First.

Henry sat back on his heels and sighed, the haversack only containing his tin cutlery and a number of greasy crumbs. He could have *sworn* he'd tucked it into the *Blätter* for safe-keeping. He'd scarcely thought of it since, to be honest. It hadn't really been relevant (and the mere suggestion of the memory of receiving it was mortifying enough to avoid any potential reminder). But now it was *immediately* relevant.

"Schaefer," came the low tones of Smith, and Henry's shoulders slouched. "I'm taking the tent down so it might behoove you to get out of the way before I let it come crashing down on your dithering head."

It was no use. It was gone. Gone or stolen by one of his bastard brothers. He wouldn't put it past them. It was a damn shame too, because his father had got them through one of his Freethinker friends, and he couldn't even begin to imagine where to find another one. Damn it all.

Henry shook his head and slung his knapsack over his shoulder, crawling out of the tent as Charley wrapped her fist around the front pole in a threatening way (though given the gutter his thoughts had been in for the past week, it elicited an entirely different feeling). They hadn't had much opportunity to take advantage of the tent's relatively little privacy in the past week, given how worn out they were at the end of each day rushing to get everything ready to depart, but it had been a lovely refuge and he was sad to see the little canvas shelter go. Regardless of anything else, they'd spent many cozy nights curled into each other, his nose filled with the scent of her, and he wasn't sure if or when they'd be able to be bunkies again, just the two of them.

"What are you so mopey about?" she inquired with one impatient eyebrow raised. "Cheer up. We're headed to the front. *Finally.*"

"Oh, it's not that, I just lost something," he said absently as he crawled out of the tent and turned to pull up his gum blanket.

Charley released the stakes as soon as Henry had the last of his things out from under the canvas, tossing the water-logged sticks aside. "What is it? Maybe I've seen it."

Henry flushed bright red. "Uh, it's nothing I can't live with-out—"

"Regardless, I shared the tent with you. If it was in there, I might have seen it." She yanked the front pole out from under the tent and the whole thing collapsed in a puff of mud-trimmed canvas.

She was right. Although Henry suspected if she had found this particular item, he would know about it, as she would have been either delighted or furious upon its discovery.

"It's, uh, just a little paper packet," he ventured, looking at her face to read a spark of understanding as he picked up the tent corners and commenced with snapping the canvas in the wind. She stared at him blankly.

"Of what?" she asked, gesturing impatiently.

"Oh, well, uh, German spices from my father," he lied, his eyes fixing widely on the canvas that refused to fold nicely. "Just a taste of ... home. Like I said, nothing too serious."

"German spices?" she asked incredulously. "Aren't you the people who boil everything with a little salt and call it a cui-sine?"

"No, that's the English," he quipped.

"Hey, Schaefer!" Williamson came jogging up, all kitted out with his haversack, equipment belt, cartridge box, bayonet scabbard, and knapsack bouncing off him at all angles. He was winded as he approached. "By Jingo ... this stuff ... is heavy ..."

The boy was huffing and puffing such that he couldn't even get three words out.

"Can we help you?" Smith snapped unhelpfully.

"There's a letter for you, Schaefer," he managed.

Henry blinked with confusion. "Letter? From who?"

"Dunno, Robinson gave it to me to give to you," Williamson shrugged, handing Henry the thin envelope. "Sheesh, I'm al-ready sweating!"

Charley rolled her eyes at him and cast a wary glance at Henry, whose stomach was veritably dropping out of his body and trying to crawl away on the ground. He hadn't answered any letters yet, not from his brothers nor his mother. He was still too much of a coward. But he couldn't imagine who would send him a letter, except his parents. Or perhaps one of his brothers, if something had happened to the other of them.

"Hell," he swore aloud as he looked at the envelope in his hand. Charley took up the forgotten tent and edged closer with some concern.

"Do you think it's your mother?" Charley whispered as Williamson trundled over to Elias and Webster to complain about how heavy his kit was.

"I can't think of who else it would be." Henry scrubbed his hand through his hair, then replaced his cap. He could feel his stomach flopping over with fear.

"Do you think she'll try to..." Charley began, not willing to voice what they both knew was most likely based on his mother's previous letter.

Henry winced. "I hope not. If she does try to make me come home, I'm sure Captain Noah and the Colonel will have something to say about that."

Charley stared at him with wide eyes, holding the tent canvas to her chest. He regarded her for a moment, distracted by another line of thought that had returned to him again and again this past week. Her dark brows framing those round, owlish eyes, the curved lips, the angular face, the tousled curls. He didn't know who had convinced her that she was plain, but for the past week, he couldn't stop noticing how beautiful she was. Dark, secretive, brooding—and truly beautiful. He could spend the rest of his life trying to make those scowling lips smile. Or sigh ... God dammit all, where the *hell* was his French letter?

"Henry."

He shook his head. "Hm?"

"Aren't you going to go read it then?"

He looked at the letter and broke the seal, unfolding a single piece of folded paper. He felt his heart thump in his chest as he looked down at the short message, scrawled in German.

Heinrich,

We understand you're shipping out, so I hope you get this before you go. Franklin's been promoted to Orderly Sergeant. Peter is coming home on sick furlough, so your mother is busy getting ready for his care. He has pneumonia, but he's on the mend now. Don't forget to write to your mother, every day if you can. You were always a good fighter when you weren't too busy thinking. Give those rebs hell.

Father

Henry blinked, staring at the letters. His mouth hung open, and he shut it with the click of his teeth. Charley approached and looked over at the paper, but of course, she couldn't read it.

"Henry—what's going on? What did she say?"

Henry looked up at her and took a shallow breath. "It's ... from my father. He said to give those rebs hell."

Charley's eyebrows furrowed. "What?"

He was horrified to discover his eyes were prickling, and he bore down to stop whatever emotion that was brewing from bubbling over. He pressed his lips tight together and frowned, staring at the words.

You were always a good fighter when you weren't too busy thinking.

He blinked.

"Henry." Charley stepped to his side and placed her hand on his arm. "Henry, what is it?"

Henry twisted his mouth up, trying to staunch the emotion from displaying on his face.

You were always a good fighter.

He couldn't remember the last time his father had praised him. He quickly flipped through memories to confirm. It wasn't even a real compliment, sort of a backwards way of reminding him that he got caught up in his head too much. But it was a vote of confidence, an expression of faith in his ability to fight, to do his duty. He shakily folded the paper back up, hiding the words while he struggled to clamp down on how foolishly moved he was by such a short and simple letter.

"Henry, hey," Charley said again, her voice soft and her hands on both of his biceps as she tried to catch his eyes with hers. "Are you alright?"

A traitor tear slipped down his cheek, and he was horrified, which just made everything feel more precarious, more distressing. This was so stupid. Why should one off-hand compliment undo him so utterly? He thought distantly that perhaps this was how Charley felt when he had told her she was beautiful.

Henry took a deep breath through his nose and let it out. "I'm fine, everyone's fine. I'm just … it's foolish, really … I'm just not," he cleared his throat, "used to hearing my father express encouragement."

Charley's face broke into a smile and the expression yanked back his whole attention, drawing him out of the trap he'd made of his body to contain his sensibilities. Her eyes were warm, glittering, her brows slanted in a way that drew him in, and he hadn't ever noticed it before, but she had a slight gap between her two front teeth that for some stupid reason he found overwhelmingly endearing. For a split second, he thought she might kiss him, right there in the middle of breaking camp.

"Well," she said, giving his arms a squeeze, "you deserve it."

This time it was Henry scrunching up his nose and turning away.

"Alright, fine, I get why you don't like being showered with compliments now."

"It's terrible, isn't it?"

"The worst."

"You know you are very skilled, right?"

"Stop it." He shoved his father's letter in his pocket and started toward the fort, trying to hide his smile.

"And you're the only person I've ever met who can do a flip."

He rolled his eyes and kept walking. She dogged after him.

"And your teeth are just perfect. Very straight, very clean."

He cocked his head and peered back at her incredulously over his shoulder. As a group of soldiers passed, Jacob wove out between them to approach Henry, also kitted out in his gear.

"What's wrong with you?" he asked Henry, turning to join him as he made a show of trying to lose Charley in the crowd.

"Charley is torturing me," Henry replied.

"With compliments!" Charley chirped from behind them. She was damned fast for someone with short legs. Jacob glanced between the two of them, at once both puzzled and amused.

"Well, I'll be damned. If I'd known compliments were the best way to give you guff, I would have started months ago."

———

St. Paul, Minnesota

The kit was heavy. But the way it bore down on Cate's shoulders made her feel grounded somehow. Solid. Formidable. Her boots seemed to connect with the packed dirt of Third Street more firmly, precise and purposeful with the weight not just of her kit, but of her mission.

The Second Regiment had boarded the steamboat and sailed down the river to the upper landing of St. Paul. There, the soldiers had disembarked to march down Third Street, a final farewell to their home before heading to the front.

Cate looked up around her at the crowds thronging either side of Third Street. People waved handkerchiefs and flags and shouted encouragement as the regiment marched past, company by company, arms shouldered and cheering along with the crowd in defiance of military form. Cate absorbed the spectacle, reveling in the power of her musket rifle's weight in her hand. The buildings were bedecked with bunting and folks hung out of windows to hear the band and wave farewell. A loud group of young men led three cheers for the Union, and stood waving their hats until the regiment had marched well around the bend. It seemed all work had been given up for the day in favor of celebrating the Second Minnesota Volunteer Infantry's departure.

Cate drank it all in.

She had never felt so part of something in her life. Not in any church, not in any dance hall, not in any house or home. Big or small, she had never felt so important. She had always been the girl that made other girls go silent when she entered a room, because they didn't want to do anything to encourage her to join them. She was the child who made her father sigh every time she said, "Did you read...?" She was the woman that was so arduous, so tedious, so unwelcome, that George Jacobs felt it necessary to make a public display of her rejection from the Philadelphia Society of Friends.

Shame had been wielded as a weapon to silence her for so much of her life. But she hadn't given up. She couldn't have stopped caring if she tried—about justice, about the promise of liberty, about the abolishment of an institution that made human beings into chattel, about the equal participation of women in the things that mattered most in society. She couldn't stop caring about those things, and now she was going to fight for them. She would prove how much a woman could accomplish. Perhaps, when all was said and done, if she managed to maintain her artifice throughout her enlistment, she could write a memoir. Show the world what a woman could do.

When she marched by, people saw her. They looked at her with admiration and cheered. The boys wearing red, white, and blue neckties or fatigue caps; the girls who carried flags or threw flowers out into their paths; the women waving their handkerchiefs, teary with emotion; the old men waving their walking sticks and shouting, "Union forever!" She made eye contact with them all as she marched by, smiling and filled to the brim with their energy and excitement.

She was important. She was fighting for something righteous, something that mattered, and she was going to make a difference. Save the union, fulfill its promise. The experience was ... moving.

What was difficult to ignore as they traversed past the Wabasha Street bridge towards the Lower Landing was that joy was not the only emotion being expressed with abandon. Here and there as they passed along, at windows and doorways, were faces red with weeping. There was no escaping the fact that Johnny was off to the war and mother, sisters, and sweethearts would never see him again.

When they approached the Lower Landing, there was a great crowd lined up on both sides of the road, reaching out to shake the hands of the soldiers as they passed to the gangway and back into the steamboat that had proceeded to meet them from the Upper Landing. Cate grinned and tried to lose herself in the encouragement, averting her eyes from the sorrowful, grief-filled farewells.

Jacob Robinson was right ahead of her in ranks, however, and it was impossible to miss Mary Robinson when she burst from the crowd and into his arms, openly weeping. Jacob squeezed her tight, buried his drawn, tight face in her neck, and held her.

Cate wondered if she should walk around them to board the steamboat. Their attempts at marching in ranks had rather disintegrated as they approached the gangway, so she didn't have to expressly wait for Robinson. She didn't want to embarrass them, but there was something about the display of grief and passion that compelled her, that demanded she bear witness, that sliced through her heart in a way that made her feel at once sympathetic and desperately lonely.

"I wish you wouldn't go," Mary Robinson whimpered into Jacob's shoulder.

"It'll be over before you know it," he assured, though his words carried a despair that contradicted their meaning. "This fight is important."

"More important than what we've found here together?" Mary pulled back and looked up into Jacob's face, her cheeks streaked with tears and her eyes red and swollen. Jacob pressed his lips into a line, then gripped her neck beneath her bonnet curtain and pressed those lips to her forehead. Cate suspected he'd wished to kiss her lips but did not for propriety's sake. To hell with propriety, she thought. They were headed to war. There was no space for social niceties when any number of men among them were being sent to their deaths on the battlefield.

"Go, then," Mary whispered. "Go, if you think it your duty."

Oof. Cate grimaced and pretended she wasn't listening as she skirted around them, following Henry towards the gangway. It didn't escape Cate's notice that many others in their regiment had family members seeing them off. Loved ones, parents, siblings, friends, lovers—embracing them and wishing them well, not because they were Johnny Soldier, but because they were people they loved. Even Henry had received an encouraging letter from his far-flung family earlier, one that had made him choke up with sentimentality.

Webster was embracing two small children who had traveled with their mother and grandparents all the way up from Faribault to see him off. He threw them up in the air, smiling with forlorn eyes as his wife silently wept. Osborn shook hands with an aging father, who gripped his arm with his other hand and gazed at him with deep and abiding pride. Krüger embraced three loud and exuberant German fellows who eyed his uniform and musket rifle covetously in such a way that Cate thought they were likely to enlist in the Third in the coming days.

She couldn't help but imagine what it would be like to bid her family farewell, if there were some alternative universe where she could openly muster out as a soldier. Margaret would probably cry—she had at the wedding. Etta would have loved all the flags, the excitement and the shouting, and would have waved her handkerchief long after the regiment passed by. Baby Joseph probably would cry, too, but mostly at the loud crowds than for missing his older sister. Her father would begrudgingly nod, his respect and pride finally earned.

"Charley?" came Henry's voice from the head of the gangway.

Cate looked up and realized she had stopped in the middle of the gangway, staring down at the dark, churning river water beneath. She shook her head and hurried to join him at the steamboat rail.

"It'll be some time until we see old St. Paul again," Henry said. Cate regarded the brick buildings, the spires from the churches, and the yellow, red, and orange leaves fluttering through the packed dirt streets. Then, she turned her head downriver, where the bluffs stood tall along the east side of the river, prairie grass waving on the top, glinting gold in the sun.

"I have no great affection for St. Paul," Cate shrugged. "I don't suppose I'll miss it much."

Henry nodded, his mouth turned down in consideration. "True. I shall greatly miss that brewer's warehouse, I'll say that much. I have a particular nostalgia for that humble building."

Cate shook her head and exhaled as though she were exasperated, in spite of a marked heat rising in her cheeks.

"Very well. Although, I'm sure there will be more brewer's warehouses and wedge tents and other nooks and crannies ahead of us to soothe your loss of this one."

Henry gave her a small, secret smile. Below the rail, where no one could see, he found her fingers with his own and squeezed. Cate looked away, downriver again, and made a very particular effort to not name any of the feelings that warmed her against the chill breeze just then. Her eyes surveyed the crowd below, the excitement, the pride, and the grief displayed among the teeming faces. She couldn't help but count her lucky stars. Unlike all the poor girls like Mary Robinson, she was going with her

Johnny Soldier. Right to the front. They'd fight, they'd win, and they'd do it together.

Henry and Charley's story continues in Volume 2: *A Right Honorable Soldier*.

Coming to *Hadley's Romance Book* 2025.
Subscribe at janehadleywrites.com.

FOOTNOTES

I have so much to say about the historical research that went into this book. Maybe too much? Since this was my first novel, I did a lot of procrasti-research, as evidenced in the works cited that follow. I wanted to write historical fiction that was deeply grounded in evidence, to the point that the plot was sacrificed on the altar of historical accuracy. Since the 2nd Minnesota Regiment is very well-documented, I ended up with a lot more than I bargained for (hence the story splitting into two volumes).

If you subscribed to *Hadley's Romance Book* and read this story issue by issue, you will have had line footnotes, but in an effort to be less distracting, I have excerpted my favorite footnotes here. I love learning what elements of historical fiction is grounded in what really happened, so I hope to provide you with much of that context here.

Women soldiers

<u>They Fought Like Demons</u> by DeAnne Blanton and Lauren M. Cook was a key source of inspiration for this novel. They documented over 300 assigned female at birth (AFAB) soldiers who fought in the Civil War, and more are being discovered as newspapers continue to be digitized and keyword searchable. There are some amazing details in that book, including documentation of six women who served while pregnant (none of whom were discovered until their babies were born), and the fact that none of the people documented were discovered

because they could not physically perform the work of soldiering. Albert Cashier, Sara Emma Edmonds, and Frances Clayton (who enlisted in St. Paul, MN) are just some of the many documented cases of women and AFAB people joining the fight. Albert Cashier, for instance, lived the rest of his life identifying as a man. Upon his death, he was outed as AFAB and many of his comrades from the war spoke up publicly, defending his service and advocating for his widow to receive his pension just as any other soldier's widow would have.

Menstruation

One key principle I was interested in exploring was how a menstruating person would navigate enlistment without being discovered. Generally, between child-bearing and nursing, menstruation was an infrequent experience for most fertile women in the nineteenth century. Women of means used a t-bandage sanitary belt, usually homemade before the war, with a dozen interchangeable napkins or guards to stem their flow. They also had tampons, made from linen, cotton, or sponge rolled into a ball. Female soldiers also may have experienced amenorrhea, or the cessation of menstruation caused by intense athletic training, substantive weight loss, poor nutrition, or severe psychological distress—all of which quite common in a war zone. I really appreciated Tess Frydman's Master thesis on the topic, titled "America's Bloody History: Menstruation Management in the Mid-19th Century," as well as Blanton and Cook's interpretation on this topic.

Fort Snelling presented quite a challenge from a privy perspective, with the soldier sinks scaffolded over the river. Blanton and Cook supposed that menstruating soldiers would have not attracted too much attention in their quest for privacy, given how disgusting soldier sinks tended to be. However, the fort walls made this much more of a challenge for Charley than it would have had she been in the field. Nonetheless, there is a documented case of a woman enlisting at Fort Snelling. Mary McDonald of Sibley County signed up for a regiment of mounted rangers at Fort Snelling in 1862. She was an excellent horse-rider and she experienced a meteoric rise in rank before her father came, quietly revealed her, and took her back home. Meanwhile, Mary W. Dennis of Stillwater joined the Second Minnesota Volunteer Infantry Regiment in 1863. So the idea of Charley operating clandestinely at the Fort is not a stretch according to the historical record, nor is the presence of an AFAB soldier in the Second Regiment.

I'm grateful to Stephen Osman's <u>Fort Snelling and the Civil War</u> for detailed description of soldier's daily lives at the Fort. I am compelled to inform you that the wedge tents Cate and Henry are issued are not accurate. According to Osman and the fellows in the First Minnesota reenactors group, Sibley tents would have been used at that time, which housed 10-15 men per tent. This was not conducive to Only One Tent vibes, so I (gasp!) took Liberties.

Bed-sharing

Bed-sharing was extremely common in the nineteenth century, particularly among people of the same gender. Children often grew up sharing a bed with their siblings. It was common to share beds with strangers too, at roadside inns and boarding houses to save a few pennies. Bed-sharing and emotional intimacy were also understood to be connected, with sisters sharing secrets after lights out and young men admitting their darkest fears to their best friends. None of this behavior was viewed as socially unusual and in fact, romantic friendship was common and accepted behavior for young men and women of any age. The army benefitted from bunk-sharing as both a means to save space and resources and to build comradery. Anthony Rotundo's "Romantic Friendship: Male Intimacy and Middle-Class Youth in the Northern United States 1800-1900" was a key source (and my gratitude goes out to author Aster Glenn Gray, without whom I never would have discovered this article, had she not referenced it in her author's note for *The Sleeping Soldier*.)

Turners, Freethinkers, & Gymnasticks

When I decided Henry Schaefer would be from New Ulm, I did not know it had been founded by anti-clerical gymnasts. Sometimes history comes up with plot twists much more random and bananas than any this humble author could come up with, and I welcomed these wild coincidences throughout the book with open arms (with the noted exception of that damned Sibley tent...).

The founders of New Ulm hailed largely from a community of German immigrants by way of the Cincinnati Turnverein. They had immigrated from Germany in large numbers after the failed rebellions of the liberal German Revolution of 1848 and founded the Over-The-Rhine neighborhood in Cincinnati. In 1855, the Know-Nothing party, convinced that the Germans had fixed a local election, wheeled a canon across town to lay siege to Over-the-Rhine. The German Turners organized quickly and staved off the attack to the extreme embarrassment of the Know-Nothings.

New Ulm was founded as a utopian-style community for German Turners and Free-Thinkers. Free-Thinkers were anti-clerical like the other Turners, but they took it a step further and were entirely non-religious. I am grateful to Alice F. Tyler's article "William Pfaender and the Founding of New Ulm" and Bernice Cooper's "*Die freie Gemeinde,* freethinkers on the frontier" from Minnesota History Magazine for this context.

Turner gymnasticks was drawn largely from <u>A Treatise on Gymnasticks</u> by Friederich Jahn, which outlined the exercises as well as the operating of a gymnasium to conduct them in. I strongly encourage you to check this volume out on the Internet Archive or similar, because it has some excellent Regency-era illustrations.

Feminism and abolition

Cate was brought up in the context of a Quaker community in Pennsylvania. I was inspired by Carol Berkin's <u>Civil War Wives</u> book and the profile she did on Angelina Grimke (who deserves her own rivals-to-lovers romance novel). When we think of the mid-nineteenth century, we often think of conservative Victorians and traditional female roles, but the early American feminists of the woman suffrage movement were nothing of the sort. Like Angelina, there were many women fervently against the institution of slavery and disregarded their social roles to protest it. Along the way, they determined that women would be much more effective in their efforts if they could vote, so in 1848, the Woman Suffrage movement was born in Seneca Falls, New York, where a convention was held to organize in support of women's rights. Lucretia Mott, Elizabeth Cady Stanton, and Frederick Douglass were all there. Their treatise, the Declaration of Sentiments, was modeled after the Declaration of Independence and is a founding document in United States history (although the original was not preserved because of course it wasn't).

Jane Grey Swisshelm was another such woman who published her own abolitionist newspaper in Pittsburgh before moving to St. Cloud, Minnesota and founding the *St. Cloud Visiter* newspaper there. According to her autobiography, <u>Half a Century</u>, she left her husband at a train station and departed for Minnesota with their child in epically dramatic fashion. (This is sort of her brand.) She got into trouble in St. Cloud when she accused Sylvanus Lowry, leader of the local Democratic party, of illegally holding slaves in his household. Mysteriously, her printing press was shortly demolished and tossed into the Mississippi River. She got another one and renamed her paper the *St. Cloud Democrat*, just to piss him off.

Jane Grey Swisshelm is not all bad-assery and girl power, however, because after the US-Dakota War of 1862, she left Minnesota for Washington DC for the sole purpose of advocating for the mass genocide of Dakota people. Which will forever make her ick.

The Second Minnesota Regiment

One of the exciting things about writing in this period is that it is so extremely well-documented. I pulled multiple accounts of the Second Regiment's exploits from the primary source record, from the official account by Captain Judson Bishop, the memoir by drummer boy William Birch, or letters from David Griffin to his wife and the diary of Thomas Fitch (which provided reliable weather reports in addition to day-by-day goings-on).

When I set upon this project, I wanted to sacrifice plot on the altar of historical accuracy because the stories that happened in real life are often so much more outrageous than anything I could dream up on my own. I'm not sure to what degree this effort was successful. I invite you to weigh in on Good Reads or Storygraph, and to catch up with our heroes in my next round of serialized issues in the style of the mid-nineteenth century literary and ladies journals.

janehadleywrites.com/hadleys-romance-book

———

Abbott, Karen. *Liar, Temptress, Soldier, Spy*. Harper Collins: New York, 2014.

Blanton, DeAnne and Lauren M. Cook. *They Fought Like Demons: Women Soldiers in the Civil War*. Louisiana State University Press: Baton Rouge, 2002.

Bircher, William. *A Drummer-boy's Diary: Comprising Four Years of Service with the Second Regiment Minnesota Veteran Volunteers, 1861 to 1865*. United States, St. Paul Book and Stationery Company, 1889.

Bishop, Judson Wade. *The Story of a Regiment: Being a Narrative of the Service of the Second Regiment, Minnesota Veteran Volunteer Infantry, in the Civil War of 1861-1865*. United States, Published for the Surviving Members of the Regiment, 1890.

Bishop, Judson Wade and Family Papers. Minnesota Historical Society, Manuscripts P1922 Box 1 vol. 1-2.

Cooper, Bernice. "Die freie Gemeinde, freethinkers on the frontier." *Minnesota History*, vol. 41, issue 2, 1970, pp. 53-60.

Edmonds, S. Emma E. *Nurse and Spy in the Union Army.* 1864, republished 2019 by Lakeside Press.

Thomas Fitch Diary. Minnesota Historical Society, Manuscripts, P961.

Giesberg, Judith. *Sex and the Civil War.* The University of North Carolina Press: Chapel Hill, 2017.

Goodman, Ruth. *How to Be a Victorian.* Liveright; Reprint edition. September 21, 2015.

Green, William D. "Eliza Winston and the politics of freedom in Minnesota, 1854-60." *Minnesota History*, Vol. 57, issue 3, 2000, p. 106-122.

Green, William D. "The Summer Christmas Came to Minnesota: The Case of Eliza Winston, a Slave." *Law and Inequality*, vol. 8, no. 1, 1990, pp. 151-177.

Griffin, David Brainerd. *Letters Home to Minnesota: Second Minnesota Volunteers.* Minnesota Historical Society, Stacks E515.5 2nd.G75 1992.

Lehman, Christopher. *Slavery's Reach: Southern Slaveholders in the North Star State.* Minnesota Historical Society Press: St. Paul, 2019.

Lowry, Thomas P. *The Story the Soldiers Wouldn't Tell: Sex in the Civil War.* Stackpole Books: Mechanicsburg, 1994.

Olmanson, Bernt. *Letters of Bernt Olmanson, A Union Soldier in the Civil War 1861-1865.* Compiled and Translated from the Norwegian Language by his Son, Albert Olmanson.

Osman, Stephen E. *Fort Snelling and the Civil War.* Ramsey County Historical Society: St. Paul, 2017.

Schmid, Bendict. *The Bendict Schmid Civil War Diary, Company G Second Minnesota Regiment.* Minnesota Historical Society Stacks E601.S35 A313 1976.

Swisshelm, Jane G. *Half a Century.* Jansen, McClurg, & Company, 1880. *Google Books.*

Tyler, Alice F. "William Pfaender and the Founding of New Ulm." *Minnesota History*, vol. 30, no. 1, 1949, pp. 24-35.

Acknowledgements

A big heaping thank you to my daughter, for being born and providing me with the time to start this novel while on parental leave (sleep when they sleep ... more like *write* when they sleep!). Also, strangely, thanks to the pandemic for completely sabotaging any other potential distractions. My deepest gratitude to my beta readers Louise, Katie, Catie, and Katy (did not mean to name the main character after any of you, but also maybe subconsciously I did???)—your feedback and encouragement on my very first novel meant *the world* to me. Special shout-out to Catie for German-picking, checking my laundry facts, and interfacing with the guys in the First Minnesota reenactment group to help me get Essential Tent Information. May the gatehouse at Historic Fort Snelling forevermore be deliciously tainted.

Deep and abiding thanks to my spouse for being my first and favorite reader and putting up with my endless developmental edits. Finally, thank you so very much to all the *Hadley's Romance Book* readers who followed this story in 16 parts and put up with my absolutely shameless cliff-hangers. There shall be much more where that came from in the new year!

A Right Honorable Soldier

Secret Soldier Vol. 2

Pittsburgh, Pennsylvania
Friday, October 18, 1861

Henry regarded the food before him with eyes as wide as saucers. A large vase of flowers adorned long tables arranged in rows in the Duquesne Grays' Hall. Throughout the room, the Minnesota Second Infantry Regiment was being served by young, patriotic ladies of Pittsburgh in their finest dresses. Between the tables buckling under the weight of sweetbreads and roast goose and aspics of all varieties and the lovely ladies sweetly offering refreshment, the men were beside themselves with delight. Except for Charley Smith, of course. Charley sat beside him and only managed to look extremely sullen.

To be fair to her, she'd been through somewhat of an ordeal since their departure for the front. Every step of the way, from the boat to the train to the Wigwam to the train again, had been utterly devoid of privacy. She took it in irate stride, and luckily the others didn't seem to assume anything amiss other than that Smith was rather overly modest for someone who swore so much.

Henry was feeling the pressure too, but for entirely different and admittedly selfish reasons. He'd also become accustomed to privacy, and with loutish comrades trundling around everywhere he looked, he'd scarcely had a chance to exchange significant glances with Charley, much less anything close to physical touch. And he missed it. He missed her.

Because, with the constant barrage of people all the time, Charley had veritably locked herself up inside of her prickly Smith persona and become utterly insufferable.

"Smith, are you gonna eat that?" Williamson asked, his eyes covetously on the flank of roast goose left on Smith's plate.

"Yes," Smith retorted from under his brow. Henry tried to hold back a sigh of annoyance as he tried to get a piece of aspic to stay on his fork. The flavor of the peas and gravy suspended in gelatin was surprisingly rich and delightful, although the texture was still very much an aspic.

"Excuse me, miss," Elias said ingratiatingly over his shoulder. The young woman in question slowed and smiled widely at them all in turn. Her hair was dark and sleek, parted at the center and wound demurely at the nape of her neck. He wondered if Charley had set her hair in such a way before cutting it, although with her curls it certainly would not have laid so straight. "Could I trouble you for some more roast goose?"

The girl looked at Elias with doe eyes, like one might regard a stray dog or some other pitiful creature that one longed to care for.

"I'll see what I can do," she replied, her voice light and airy and wonderfully effeminate. It reminded Henry of how Charley had sounded in the brewer's warehouse last week, voice light and airy and gasping for more. He squirmed in his seat, trying to hide his little secret smile as he nudged Charley's knee with his own under the table. To his chagrin, she flinched away from him. It was woefully unfair that after a week of consistent carnal satisfaction, Henry should be left in the same condition he'd been in for years prior but somehow markedly less apt to bear it. He supposed it was more difficult when he knew what he was missing.

"I wonder if there will be dancing after dinner," Robinson asked with a grin, watching the girl depart with an appreciative gaze.

"I should think you were too busy missing your wife to worry about that," Smith said snidely.

Robinson glared at him and rolled his eyes. "I'm married, I'm not a priest. Besides, after that dreary night in Chicago, we deserve a little bit of fun."

Henry added his voice to the murmur of agreement before they fell into a companionable silence, each too focused on shoveling the excellent fare into his mouth to say much more.

A few moments later, the girl returned. "Here we are, fellows," she said, brandishing a plate of cut slices of roast goose. In a conspiratorial tone, she added, "It's the last, so shh—don't tell."

Elias slid a slice onto his own plate and then gestured for Williamson to take some as well. "Our deepest gratitude, Miss ... um ... ?"

The girl smiled. "Miss Loy, at your service. And you all are?"

"A pleasure to meet you, Miss Loy. I'm Corporal Hower," Elias said with a grin. Henry tried not to raise an eyebrow. He sure was laying it on thick. "And this is my squad. Privates Williamson, Webster, Robinson, Krüger, Smith, and Schaefer. And Sergeant Osborn."

"How do you do," Miss Loy said, nodding at each one in turn.

"Say, Miss Loy, are you aware if there are any further festivities after the meal?"

"Oh, yes," Miss Loy replied eagerly. "They will clear the tables and there's a small quartet that will play and we'll have a lovely set of dances before you all march back to your quarters."

This news brought a murmur of excitement around the table.

"I'm so happy to hear that," Elias replied with a grin. "May I save a place on your dance card, Miss Loy?"

The girl flushed attractively. "I should be delighted, Corporal."

Henry felt uncomfortable. Miss Loy was charming, and he wasn't the only one in the squad who'd noticed. But there was something missing in her sweet, smooth countenance. Perhaps she lacked the dark smolder that Charley wielded without even thinking. But Henry couldn't save a place on his card to dance with Charley, because if she even bothered to dance (the numbers were such that she wouldn't have a problem sitting out if she so desired), she'd be competing with him for the hands of the lovely loyal ladies of Pittsburgh.

Henry snuck a glance at Smith beside him. The soldier had her hand in her dark curls, hunched over her plate seemingly under some duress. Henry leaned over and hissed, "Anything wrong?"

Henry almost missed her response under the clatter of cutlery and the din of affable conversation. "I don't know how to lead."

Lead? Henry was puzzled a moment before he realized she was referring to dancing.

"Well, I could show you how," Henry offered quietly, his eyes darting around the far corners of the room wondering what other chambers might lead off from the main hall. He could show her how to lead and pull her close and perhaps, if they could find enough privacy for a dance lesson, they might find enough for...

"Don't be absurd," she hissed. "I'd rather pretend to be too fatigued for the entire evening than have everyone see you teach me how to waltz."

"Well, what about the set dances?" Henry suggested. "Those don't require a lead, per say. You just have to make sure you put out the correct hand."

Smith glowered but didn't reply.

"Say," Henry said louder, addressing Miss Loy. "What sort of dances might we expect this evening?"

———

The dancing was lovely. Cate knew this intellectually as she watched from the benches lining the walls. All the boys cut a smart figure in their uniforms while the loyal ladies of Pittsburgh were resplendent in their best wool and silk, their hoops flouncing about like puffs of dandelion fluff in a late summer wind. There were many lovely young girls and Henry was eager, doing his best to engage a partner for every single dance.

Cate had spent much of the evening sullenly watching him dance with other girls and stewing indulgently in a miserable brew of frustration and jealousy. He led his partner with as much grace as possible given that they were dancing a polka and it was basically just turning and hopping. She spent the duration of the dance watching him while she scrolled self-pityingly through memories in her mind; of him squatting during drill to pick up a charge he'd dropped; of his thighs bare while shuffling into his new uniform; of his lips ghosting against her skin; of him straining against her as she pulled him off. She should have taken him up on his "dance lesson." Surely there must be some private place somewhere in this enormous market house. She missed his touch. And she hated that he was passing it out liberally to every little chit who batted her eyelashes at him.

When the polka concluded, Cate sighed and tried to look as unapproachable as possible. Her strategy thus far had been inexcusable rudeness, but her capacity for it was wearing thin. She had no idea what it was—she was doing everything she could to look sullen and surly, but it seemed the younger girls of the group didn't find that very off-putting. She kept getting giggling teenage girls trying to get her to strike up a conversation with them.

This break in the music was no different, it appeared. Miss Loy, escorted by Hower off the dance floor, met another girl with fine, white-blonde hair in a blue print wool, and walked straight towards her.

"Good evening, Private Smith was it?" Miss Loy said. Cate nodded churlishly as she begrudgingly stood. She wasn't a complete boor to remain seated when approached by a lady. "I'd like to introduce you to my friend and neighbor, Miss Kincaid."

"How do you do," Cate said, taking the girl's hand and receiving a charming giggle. Miss Kincaid was short, a full half foot shorter than Cate, and she wouldn't put her any older than sixteen. Behind her, Cate caught a glimpse of Henry returning from the dance floor with his partner, a round-featured brunette whose silhouette bore more impressive proportions. Cate decided much of it was hip and bust padding in spite of the lively bouncing polka having previously suggested otherwise.

"Miss Loy," Henry greeted with a smile after leaving his previous partner with her companions. "I believe I have you for the next dance?"

"Oh, yes, La Tempête!" Miss Loy replied with a grin. She had lovely teeth. She and Henry would make a whole family of children with perfectly straight, clean teeth. Cate took a perverse pleasure in the proportion of misery that thought delivered.

"I love La Tempête!" Miss Kincaid pouted, her eyes darting sidelong at Cate. "But I sadly am not engaged for this one."

Miss Loy, Miss Kincaid, and Henry all looked at Cate. Cate blinked. "I, uh, I don't think I've ever danced this one before. What is it?"

Miss Loy's eyes narrowed slightly, but her smile stayed strong. "It's a wonderful set dance! It couldn't be simpler, it's really only two figures repeated with different couples. It's such a delight. Oh, Adaline, we must find you a partner so we can be in a set together."

Cate's ears perked at that. Set dances were social dances, where partners danced in groups of four or even eight people. Partners were exchanged and returned in simple steps, the idea being to get folks interacting with as many others as possible. It was an excellent way to get all the town gossip efficiently. If this were a multi-couple set dance, Cate would dance largely with Miss Kincaid, but she would also dance with Miss Loy and, depending on the set dance, the other gentleman too.

As the two girls made a show of looking around the room for a partner for Miss Kincaid, Cate caught Henry's eye and held it.

"Say, Miss Kincaid," she said, only tearing her eyes away from Henry to look at the girl after she'd turned. "Would you be so kind as to allow me to have this dance?"

Miss Kincaid grinned and Miss Loy smiled with great satisfaction.

"Why, yes, Private Smith, I would be delighted," Miss Kincaid said, setting her gloved hand in Cate's. Cate gave Miss Kincaid a small half-smile and then glanced up at Henry again. He was watching her carefully, his eyes slightly narrowed, but she couldn't tell quite what he was thinking. It thrilled her.

On the dance floor, they arranged themselves across from one another, one couple facing the other. Two other couples joined them—one was an officer and a matron, the other pair led by Jacob Robinson, grinning and looking flushed enough that Cate suspected some spirits were being passed around under the table.

"Sidle down, Schaef," Robinson insisted, taking up the place across from Miss Kincaid and shoving Henry and Miss Loy down such that Cate was now catercorner from him. Apparently Robinson had little interest in being across from the matron, which really shouldn't have gotten under Cate's skin, but it did. As she glared at him, Miss Loy took the liberty of explaining the dance to the group.

"Each figure will start with greeting your opposite," she said, gesturing between the couples facing each other. "Then we'll *chassez* and exchange places with the couple to our right or left."

Just then, the quartet of instrumentalists struck up the beginning bars of the dance. Miss Loy opened her mouth wordlessly for a moment and then flapped her left hand. "Don't worry, you'll pick it up easily."

Cate grimaced and took Miss Kincaid's gloved hand in hers.

"Leave everything to me, Private Smith," her dance partner said assuringly. "I'll guide you."

Miss Kincaid's eyelashes fluttered, doing nothing for the state of Cate's grimace. Henry snorted back a laugh and did his best to smooth it over with a gentlemanly nod to Miss Loy as they stepped forward and back with the rhythm of the music, honoring the person opposite them with a nod. The matron to Cate's left was older, her braided and looped hair streaked with gray, but her smile was demure and her silk plaid dress fine. It took Cate a moment to realize that her partner was none other than Captain Noah. Cate blinked and tried to focus on what was to be done.

"We pass in front," Miss Kincaid murmured, and she and Cate *chassezed* to the left in front of Captain Noah and his partner. "Then return behind."

Cate did so. Then they greeted their opposite again. Cate's opposite was Robinson's partner, a young woman with a mouth that curled either in pleasure or disdain—she wasn't quite sure which.

"Right-hand star," Henry directed then and the music moved so fast, Cate would have missed it if Henry hadn't reached out and snatched her hand in his. The ladies grasped hands over top of Henry and Cate's, and they circled.

She wished it was just that she'd been surprised, but the feel of his hand in hers after the better part of the last week spent without a chance to touch one another, even in the most trivial of ways, sent a tingle of sensation up her arm. Neither of them wore gloves and his calluses were warm and smooth and dry on her palm. Cate couldn't help but lock eyes with him.

"Now left," he said and turned abruptly, offering her his left hand this time. Cate scrambled to turn and offer him her left hand, quite off beat by this point. She glanced over at Miss Kincaid, who was turning demure circles with Robinson. Apparently this dance was one that ensured one danced scarcely *at all* with one's partner.

"Circle four," Henry instructed and the four in the center grasped hands and spun like a wheel. Cate held his gaze opposite her—she was dependent on his instructions was all—and a small smile quirked at the corners of his mouth. When they returned to their places, Miss Kincaid's hand was there for Cate's, and she said, "Now greet your opposite and pass through. There now, see, couldn't be easier!"

Cate's feet were already carrying her through the steps as she acknowledged an annoying desire to stay in this set, so that she might grasp hands with Henry once again. She looked at him over her shoulder as she fell into the figure from the top (greeting her opposite rather poorly, as she was looking away from her). Henry was looking back at her too; when he caught her eye, he grinned. Cate swallowed hard. What the hell was she doing? She wrestled her mind to focus on the dance.

The sets proceeded down the line, the couples who made it to the end of their line waiting when needed and then retreating back up to the head of the line to continue the form. It was such a simple dance that after a few rounds, it scarcely took any concentration to repeat the movements.

Cate made a point to grip the hands of the other soldiers in each set firmly, setting her opposite hand at her back in a most gentlemanly fashion. Several of the girls she greeted as her opposite delivered her coy smiles to her utter bamboozlement. While as a woman, she largely passed unnoticed, she seemed to make not only a passable young man, but an appealing one. It was entirely baffling.

Once the initial discomfiture of the realization had settled, Cate began to wonder what would happen if she engaged with this female notice. In the next set, she caught the eye of her opposite, a girl scarcely twenty, with chestnut brown curls rolled and pinned behind her ears. She held the girl's gaze from under her brows and the girl responded with a slow smile. This was outrageous. Surely, Cate did not make an attractive boy. How could feminine plainness translate to male allure?

The song went on, repeating through the figure set after set, until she and Miss Kincaid ended up at one end of the line and began to proceed back down it in the opposite direction. Cate grew increasingly bold with her newfound boyish charm, adding a sly grin to her expression and even took the liberty of glancing one girl up and down, which earned her a soft *oh* of parted lips. While not precisely her taste, she did find herself enjoying the attention.

Such was her line of thought when she reached out cater-corner for the right-hand star and looked up to find she grasped Henry's hand again. His head was tilted to the side, and he looked at her with incredulous amusement. Cate regarded him with wide eyes and lips pressed together, trying hard not to laugh. His hand was warm and solid in hers and this time, she was right on time with the music as they turned and grasped left hands, spinning opposite. She'd been so caught up playing with flirtatious glances that she found herself applying the expression on Henry without thinking. She could see his Adam's apple bob in his throat as he swallowed. Her smile grew positively impish.

The figure went all too fast and before she knew it, they had passed through again, on to the next set of couples. It wasn't long after that—perhaps a figure or two more—when the quartet concluded the song with a tag ending and Cate bowed to Miss Kincaid.

Her dance partner regarded Cate with a self-satisfied grin. "See, didn't I tell you? So easy, and so much fun!"

Cate looked at the floor sheepishly. "I suppose."

"Now, there's still at least three dances left before we must see you off. Please don't disappoint the ladies by sitting the rest of the night out." Miss Kincaid's blue eyes lingered on Cate's for a moment longer than seemed polite. Cate blushed—not because she resented the attention, but because she realized she had absolutely no idea what to do with it now that the dance music had ended and she was forced to make polite conversation. Luckily, Henry approached just then with Miss Loy.

"Private Smith, I had no idea you were such an accomplished dancer," Miss Loy gushed.

"Indeed, Smith," Henry added, his scarcely contained amusement a little too thick to be entirely sincere. "Where have you been hiding those tapping toes?"

Cate shook her head and rolled her eyes, hiding behind her usual mask of disdain. "Don't be absurd—Miss Loy said it herself, La Tempête couldn't be easier."

"And yet I just had my friend Lottie asking me to make an introduction to you," Miss Loy replied with a significant expression. "She's looking for a partner for the Scot's Reel and you apparently caught her eye."

Cate blanched. The Scot's Reel was markedly more difficult and she hadn't been at a dance where it had been done since the last time she'd been in Pennsylvania nearly a decade ago.

"I'm terribly sorry to your friend, Miss Loy, but I'm afraid I don't know that one either," Cate demurred, glancing reproachfully at Henry, who was being entirely useless, chortling away under his breath.

"Well, I'm quite sure Lottie—or Miss Price, as you will soon know her—would be more than happy to teach you the steps," Miss Loy replied and then exchanged glances with Miss Kincaid. They both giggled, and Cate was forcibly reminded how simultaneously endearing and terrifying a group of giggling girls could be. The two of them tugged Cate's hand off toward the center of the ballroom. Cate looked imploring over her shoulder at Henry, but he just doubled over laughing.

Miss Price, as it turned out, was the young lady Cate had delivered an appraising and (she hoped) appreciative once-over during La Tempête. This would teach her to play games with the hearts of girls. If she could have got away with it, she would have hid her face in her hands, but as it were, she was forced to face Miss Price, deliver a gracious introduction with flaming cheeks, and accept that to all appearances, she seemed nothing more than bashful boy with great interest in this particular girl. It didn't help that Henry had seemingly rounded up Robinson and Hower to observe and snicker as Cate led Miss Price onto the dance floor, trying desperately to remember the steps well enough to execute them to speed.

She joined a circle of four couples and put her hand out to Miss Price absently. Miss Price laughed, smiling through puzzled brows as she sweetly turned Cate's hand over, setting her fingertips on Cate's palm. Cate flushed again, mortified that she'd offered her hand in the lady's position as a matter of habit. Just then, the fiddle struck up a lively tune and the group of them were all bouncing on tip-toe, their feet shuffling sevens-and-threes in a circle. Cate could scarcely keep her feet under her as they moved back and forth and then turned straight into a ladies right-hand star, the gents on the outside in open position. Cate knew only as much about this dance to make it mortifyingly confusing to dance the male position. The couples turned as one, bringing the gents in to circle a left-hand star. Cate had hardly taken her opposite's hand before the group broke into a grand chain. She felt rather strongly a visceral understanding of why it was called a reel.

Cate was winded at the end of the dance, escorting Miss Price back to where they had met, handing her to her next partner and glaring daggers at Henry, Robinson, and Hower, who stood a little ways off snickering like they were barely out of primary school.

"I didn't see any of *you* attempting the Scot's Reel so don't even start," Cate snapped at them as she approached. They only busted out in full guffaws. She held herself back from flashing a rude gesture at them.

"Smith—that was—" Hower gasped, unable to form two words together for laughing.

"Masterful, truly!" Robinson exclaimed, his full grin displaying all of his teeth. "Did you see him, Elias? Two left feet the whole way through, but Miss Price was still batting her eyelashes at him all the way off the dance floor."

Henry snorted loudly. Cate tipped her head back, imploring the ceiling to grant her patience.

"What's so funny?" Williamson said, popping into their conversation circle. The other fellows ignored him.

"Well, this was truly first rate," Hower said, wiping tears from his eyes, "but I have a lady to lead in our final song of the evening."

"Oh, which is it again?" Williamson asked, and Henry snatched his dance card from his pocket to check.

"Soldier's Joy," he confirmed.

"A fitting tribute, and I haven't even got a partner for it!" Robinson exclaimed woefully.

Couples made their way to the dance floor as the opening melody rang out from the fiddle. There were at least twice as many gents as ladies and given that the dance was titled Soldier's Joy, it seemed evident that Robinson wasn't the only one who felt left out. From the opposite side of the dance floor, some of the Hastings boys leapt out partnered with one another, to the great amusement of the dancers on the floor. They joined the line, making over-gesticulated gestures of honoring their opposite and their partner, kicking up their heels in exaggerated steps.

Williamson laughed aloud and Robinson grinned.

"I'm not missing my soldier's joy just because there aren't any ladies left to dance with!" he exclaimed and snatched Williamson's hand, dragging him out to the dance floor laughing and protesting.

Cate's eyes flicked over to Henry and his mischievous grin provoked her head to follow warily.

"Don't you dare—" she began, but he'd already snatched her hand, hauling her to the dance floor and assuming the other side of Williamson and Robinson's set.

The music was quick and lively, reminiscent of "The Sailor's Hornpipe" or other such tunes celebrating the jolly life of a man in service to his country. Henry kicked his heels high and let out a shout, leaping about as he dashed headlong into the ladies chain, taking the role of the lady as Cate tried her damndest not to fall over laughing. Their hands fell naturally together and despite being in the man's position in the set, Cate's fingers rested upon his palm like they belonged there.

When they passed through, he made a show of swinging his elbows in a dreadful imitation of a jig and they weren't even through the figure twice before Cate fell into the steps with him, grinning in spite of herself and stomping her feet in time.

———

Serializing in <u>Hadley's Romance Book</u> 2025,
free to newsletter subscribers.
Sign up at janehadleywrites.com.

ALSO BY JANE HADLEY

Mrs. Milner Gets a Kitchen

St. Paul, Minnesota
1955

Marion Milner is the only divorcee she knows (other than her ex-husband, of course) and she's sick and tired of being the target of all the neighborhood gossip. So how better to silence the whispers than to use her divorce settlement to upgrade to the latest in electric kitchens, just in time to host the annual Sokol Ladies' Auxiliary Christmas party?

Harry O'Conner has been laying low since he got back from Korea, installing new kitchens for the spoiled housewives of Summit Hill. But when he meets his newest client, he finds a kindred spirit in the lady of the house. Mrs. Milner talks a mile a minute, but unlike most people, she she can't help but be anyone except herself. (Doesn't hurt that she's a knock-out in that green sweater.)

But even as Marion and Harry find their connection growing much stronger than any contractor-client relationship really should be, the risk of neighborhood gossip and its impact on Marion's children forces them to contend with what they really want from one another. Can their fragile new romance stand up under the pressure of a community that values conformity above all?

They only have until the kitchen is done to find out.

ABOUT THE AUTHOR

Jane Hadley writes historical romance teeming with footnotes and feels. She lives under seven layers of blankets where she can comfortably survey the cold tundra of Minnesota through wavy glass windows which she refuses to replace because old things are inherently valuable.

jane@janehadleywrites.com
On Instagram @janehadleywrites